Enjoy a trip to the South Pacific in

Célestine Vaite's

Breadfruit

A wise and enchanting new novel of romance,
matrimony, and family life, Tahitian-style

... and in

Frangipani

Vaite's internationally celebrated novel about big dreams
on a small island. *Frangipani* introduced Materena Mahi,
the best listener in Tahiti, whose cleverness, generosity,
and appreciation of Tahitian tradition make her
one of the most appealing heroines in contemporary fiction.

"Would a few hours in Tahiti lift the spirits? In *Frangipani,* Célestine
Vaite has created the perfect guide: Materena Mahi, professional
housecleaner and mother of three. . . . Materena's journey from
cleaner to Tahiti's answer to Oprah makes for the most memorable
debut for a character since *The No. 1 Ladies' Detective Agency* introduced Precious Ramotswe to the world. . . . Generous and funny,
Frangipani offers all the warmth and delight of a tropical vacation,
without the jet lag. Best of all, there are two sequels to come."

— Yvonne Zipp, *Christian Science Monitor*

"*Frangipani* is a feast. It is bursting with vitality and charm."
— Michael McGirr, *Sydney Morning Herald*

"Vaite takes us beyond the resort compounds into the rhythms and rivalries of a tropical culture. A novel about two strong women, *Frangipani* testifies to the necessity of upholding traditions and defying them too."
— Carrington Alvarez, *Elle*

"A warm and lyrical look at the fabric of family life in Tahiti. Vaite uses words to paint a vivid Tahitian landscape worthy of a Gauguin painting and delivers a memorable story about big dreams on a small island. Vaite has crafted an unforgettable heroine: Materena is passionate, clever, and never without words of wisdom or a bit of folklore to share with a troubled soul. By the end, the reader is left wanting more, more, more. The good news: there are two more installments to come."
— *Kirkus Reviews*

"*Frangipani* celebrates women of all generations, affectionately portraying their strength, resilience, and humor. The tale is told in enchanting episodes that give a glimpse into Tahitian life and a loving insight into the hopes and dreams that shape the relationships between mothers and daughters. . . . Bubbling with humor, gossip, and worldly advice, *Frangipani* is a delight."
— Jody Lee, *Good Reading*

"A story told in charming episodes, brimming with the wisdom of a strong Tahitian cultural history. . . . It is a style that transports the reader to a land rich in breadfruit and traditional stories."
— *Australian Bookseller & Publisher*

Breadfruit

Also by
Célestine Vaite

Frangipani

Breadfruit

a novel

Célestine Vaite

BACK BAY BOOKS
Little, Brown and Company
New York   Boston   London

Back Bay Books / Little, Brown and Company
Hachette Book Group USA
1271 Avenue of the Americas
New York, NY 10020
Visit our Web site at www.HachetteBookGroupUSA.com

First United States Edition: September 2006

Originally published in Australia in 2000 by the
Text Publishing Company

Cover illustration and interior art by Philippe Lardy.

The characters and events in this book are fictitious. Any
similarity to real persons, living or dead, is coincidental
and not intended by the author.

Library of Congress Cataloging-in-Publication Data
Vaite, Célestine Hitiura.
Breadfruit : a novel / Célestine Vaite. — 1st U.S. ed.
p. cm.
ISBN-10: 0-316-01658-6
ISBN-13: 978-0-316-01658-2
1. Tahiti — Fiction.   2. Women domestics — Fiction.
3. Weddings — Fiction.   4. Domestic fiction.   I. Title.
PR9619.4.V35B74   2006
823'.92 — dc22   2006003953

10   9   8   7   6   5   4   3   2   1

Q-FF

Printed in the United States of America

*For my mother, Viola Vaite, who taught me
that love is the greatest motive of all*

*And in the loving memory of my godmother,
Henriette Estall, who taught me to believe in
willpower and to get up after each fall*

Breadfruit

A Love Movie

Materena likes movies about love.

When there's a love movie on the television, Materena sits on the sofa, her hands crossed, and her eyes focused on the TV screen. She doesn't broom or cut her toenails, she doesn't iron, or fold clothes. She doesn't do anything except concentrate on the movie.

Movies about love move Materena and sometimes it happens that she imagines she's the heroine.

The love movie tonight is about a woman who loves a man with a passion, but, unfortunately, she has to marry another man — it's the plan of her parents. Her future husband is not bad-looking or mean. It's just that she feels nothing for that man. When she looks at him, it's like she's looking at a tree — whereas when she looks at the man she loves, her heart goes *boom, boom,* she wants to kiss him, and she wants to hold him tight.

The woman in the movie meets the man she loves one last time — it is a day before her grandiose wedding, and he's leaving for a faraway country, never to return, because it's too much for him to bear to stay in the neighborhood. It's easier for him to just disappear.

The lovers meet behind a thick hedge. They kiss, they embrace, then he falls to his knees and declares: "I will love you till I die, till I die, I swear to God, you are the center of my universe, my guiding light, the only one."

The heroine hides her face in her gloved hands and bursts into tears. There's violin music, and a tear escapes from the corner of Materena's eye. She's sad for the woman. She can feel the pain.

"Poor her," Materena sighs.

"Zero movie! What a load of crap!" This is Pito's comment.

In his opinion, there is too much crying in that movie, too much carrying-on, no action. And the man, what a *bébé la la* — wake up to yourself.

"Well, go read your Akim comic in the kitchen." Materena wipes her eyes with her pareu.

But Pito is too comfortable on the sofa, and he wants to watch the end of that silly movie. Materena wishes she could transport Pito somewhere else. He's been annoying her ever since the movie started with his comments and sighs.

Pito doesn't like movies about love. He prefers cowboy movies, movies with action and as little talking as possible.

The movie is near the end and Materena hopes Pito is not going to spoil it with a stupid remark. Materena needs complete silence. The end of a love movie is very crucial. There's a lot of tension. In Materena's mind, the heroine will be reunited with the man she loves, but love movies don't always end the way Materena would like them to end.

There's the grandiose wedding and it is clear to Materena that the bride's thoughts are not in the church. She keeps looking back, waiting for the man she loves to appear and rescue her. Materena can guess it. Materena expects the man to barge into the church at any second too, but he's far away, riding on his horse. Materena says in her head, Eh, go get the woman you love, you idiot. But he keeps on riding that horse.

And meanwhile, to Materena's sadness, the heroine becomes the wife of the man she doesn't love.

Confetti greets the newlyweds outside the church and doves are set free. The heroine watches the doves fly toward the gray sky.

It is the end of the movie and Materena is really annoyed, she prefers happy endings. She listens to the soft melody of the piano during the credits and reads the names of the principal actors. It reminds her that the sad story is only a movie and not the reality.

After the final credits have finished, she switches the TV off.

"Zero movie!" Pito gets off the sofa like he weighs over two hundred pounds.

Materena tidies up the living room.

"Zero movie!" Pito is now making himself comfortable in the bed.

Materena pulls the bedcover her way and rolls to the far side of the bed.

"I tell you, Materena, if I was the man in the movie, I tell you, if it was I, the man . . ." Pito says he would have snatched the woman and escaped with her on the horse.

"Yes, okay. Good night." Materena is not listening to Pito anymore.

She closes her eyes and drifts off to sleep. And she dreams she has to marry the man in the movie, but the man she loves is Pito. She's in the church, about to pronounce "I do," when the door of the church swings open. It is Pito.

He is on a horse and he's wearing cowboy clothes and a cowboy hat.

People stare as Pito makes his way to the altar, they also stare at the horse.

Pito grabs Materena by the waist and he says to the man she's supposed to marry, "Listen, that woman, she's for me — you go look for another woman, okay?" Pito has a fierce look on his face.

Pito and Materena ride out of the church, they ride far away, far away, to the desert.

When Materena wakes up, she's laughing.

The Proposal

By eleven o'clock that night, Materena, scrubbing her oven, is still laughing about her dream — the part when Pito barges into the church on a horse, wearing a Stetson! Can you imagine?

Well, Materena might as well laugh now, because once Pito is home from the bar, she won't be laughing at all. He'll be drunk, talk a lot of nothing, as usual, and get on her nerves. Last time he was drunk, he went on about how he had to push women away — they were all over him and all he wanted to do was drink his beer at the bar and talk with his colleagues about fishing.

Here he comes now, Materena can hear him fumbling with the door.

"*Materena!*" Pito bursts out as he lurches through the doorway. "Ahhh, Materena," he slurs, red-eyed, swaying on his feet. "Marry me, Materena."

Materena just smiles at him, all the while scrubbing her oven.

"Are you going to marry me or what?" Pito looks like he's going to fall on her.

"All right, okay." Materena drops the scrubbing brush as he pins her in his arms. She's got to get Pito into bed before he wakes up the kids.

Five minutes later, Pito is in bed, unconscious and snoring. And Materena is glad. She isn't going to take his marriage proposal seriously. Ah no. A ring on her finger, it's not an obsession. In her opinion, they're like a married couple, anyway — they share a bed and they share the kitchen table. He's her man, she's his woman, and it's no different from being husband and wife. She doesn't need a ring on her finger and a framed marriage certificate displayed on the wall. Materena goes back to her oven. She scrubs, and thinks back to the day she met Pito.

When she was sixteen years old, Materena worked at the local snack during the school holidays. Pito came to the snack one afternoon with a friend, Ati.

Aue, when Materena first laid her eyes on Pito, she liked the look of him instantly. It's not that he was the most handsome man her eyes had ever seen, but there was something about him.

Pito wanted a ham sandwich, so Materena made him a ham sandwich. Pito took it and gave Materena his money. He looked at her, but it was like she didn't exist. The other fellow gave her the interested look, but she wasn't interested in him. She served him and went on serving the other customers, but every now and then her interested eyes would drift to the sexy man wearing the ripped T-shirt.

When Pito left, Materena wanted to follow him. His friend winked at her, but she gave him a dirty look. She didn't want him to think that she was interested in him, because then he would tell Pito.

The next day, Materena agonized in front of the mirror, trying to do a complicated style with her hair instead of the usual chignon. But it was hopeless. She'd never bothered with a complicated hairstyle before, it had always been the same chignon, since the age of eight years old. She got so frustrated she felt like ripping her hair out. In the end, she decorated her chignon with tiare Tahiti flowers, and Loana, Materena's mother, got mad because the flowers were reserved for the Virgin Mary, Understanding Woman. Materena had to take every single flower out of her chignon and put it back in the bowl next to the statue of the Virgin Mary.

Pito didn't come to the snack that day. In fact, a whole week passed before he made another appearance. When he did, Materena was very nervous.

"Ham sandwich?" she asked, wanting to show Pito that she remembered him.

He gave her a smile.

It was impossible for Materena to do her job after that. The afternoon was a total disaster, and the boss yelled at her quite a few times.

But Pito came to the snack the following day.

And the next.

A little laughter, a little giggle, eyes meeting eyes, and all kinds of ideas coming into their heads. The boss was forced to remind Materena that her job wasn't to giggle but to make sandwiches. The boss gave Pito a dirty look, but she couldn't tell him to stop coming to her snack just because he was making Materena soft in the head. He also ate a lot of sandwiches. He was a very good customer.

Pito finally arranged a rendezvous with Materena for nine o'-clock at the frangipani tree behind the bank. As soon as Materena got home from work, she went into the bathroom to scrub her hands to get rid of the onion smell.

At eight thirty, she was in bed.

By quarter to nine, she was sneaking out the window and over the side fence.

And there was Pito, waiting for her under the frangipani tree — with a rolled quilt in his arms.

They talked for about two seconds.

Then his mouth touched her mouth . . . and that was the end of Materena the good Catholic girl.

She had discovered sexy loving.

Loana had warned Materena that if she ever found out about a boyfriend from the coconut radio and not from Materena herself, there would be syrup — meaning that Materena would get a couple of slaps across the face.

Materena didn't pay attention to her mother's threat. She was too hooked on Pito to care about slaps and other punishments. As far as Materena was concerned, she was going to keep on meeting Pito at the frangipani tree until . . . well, until he decided to get serious.

Three weeks after their secret meetings began, Pito announced to Materena that he was leaving Tahiti for France to do military service and that he'd be gone for two years.

Materena was devastated with the news. "When are you leaving?"

"Tomorrow," Pito replied.

"Tomorrow!" Materena was even more devastated.

She held on to Pito and promised she would be at the airport to bid him farewell. But Pito told Materena not to worry about going because there were too many of his relatives going to the airport already.

Materena didn't insist. It was clear to her that Pito didn't want her at the airport meeting all his relatives and, above all, his mama. It was much too soon for a formal introduction to his mama.

"At what time is your plane leaving?" Materena asked.

Pito's plane was leaving at two in the morning.

"And are you going to write to me?" Materena was hoping that Pito would say, "Of course I'm going to write to you!"

"We'll see," Pito said.

Materena started to cry.

"I've got to go home and pack." Pito rolled the quilt.

He kissed Materena and Materena kissed him back with all her heart and soul.

"Take care," Pito said.

"I'm going to wait for you." Materena couldn't stop the tears.

When she got home, Loana was still watching the TV. Materena wanted to ask her about going to the airport to bid Pito farewell, but she sneaked into her bedroom instead and snuggled up to the pillows. She couldn't ask her mother for advice about Pito, since Loana didn't even know there was a Pito.

By midnight Materena's mind was made up. She took a shell necklace off the nail in the living room and ran to the airport.

There was a crowd: sleeping babies in their mothers' arms, children running around playing ticktack, and, most of all, crying mamas holding on to smiling young men with too many shell necklaces hanging around their neck.

And there was Pito.

A big mama was crying her heart out as she held on to him, and every now and then a relative would try to drape a shell necklace on Pito, but the big mama wouldn't let go of him.

Pito looked so handsome, dressed in navy blue pants and a white shirt. Materena wanted so much to go over to him, but she just stayed half-hidden behind a pillar and watched him. It was enough that Pito had to deal with his crying mother.

Materena stayed at the airport until Pito's plane took off, and as she ran back to her house still clutching her shell necklace, she thought about how two years were like an eternity.

Two years passed, two long years thinking about Pito non-stop, and Materena finished school and started her career as a professional cleaner. She was waiting for a truck home from the market one day when Pito walked straight past her. He was thinner and paler.

"Pito!" Materena was ecstatic. She couldn't believe her eyes.

Pito stopped walking and turned around. Materena was about to go and jump on him, but a voice in her head told her that she best not make a fool of herself in front of all those people waiting for a truck, because it looked like Pito wasn't going to open his arms to her. He expressed no emotion at all when he saw her. Materena thought perhaps he didn't recognize her.

"It's me, Materena." Materena was all smiles.

"I know it's you," Pito said. "And are you fine?"

"Yes, I'm fine," Materena replied. "And you? Are you fine?"

"Yes, I'm fine."

"So, you're back from France?" Materena asked, all the while telling herself that she was so stupid, asking this question. She could see Pito with her own two eyes. Of course he was back from France.

"I came back two days ago," Pito said, then excused himself. He had to rush off somewhere.

"Okay," Materena said, as if she didn't care that Pito couldn't spare five minutes to talk to her. "I'm in a hurry too."

Materena jumped into the first available truck and thought about the two years she'd wasted longing for Pito, that *fa'aoru,* that snob! Two years of waiting for a letter from him, a package, a telegram, and not looking once at another man! She had been faithful to Pito.

Materena's mind was made up about Pito. He belonged to the past and she was going to start looking for someone for the future.

But how could Materena forget Pito when she kept bumping

into him? It was as if God was putting Pito in her path. She'd be at the market waiting for a truck and Pito would walk straight past her or she'd see him standing on the other side of the street. She'd be in a shop and Pito would walk into the same shop. She'd be eating at a snack and two seconds later Pito would appear. Pito would always raise his eyebrows to her — meaning, hello. And Materena would smile at Pito. But there was no conversation.

One night, Materena asked God if it was his plan to always put Pito in her path. And if it was, could God give her a little sign? And the very next day Materena literally bumped into Pito as she stepped off the truck. This was a good enough sign for her. Their faces just inches away from each other, she asked, "Are you doing anything tonight?"

That's how Materena and Pito began to meet again at the frangipani tree behind the bank in the middle of the night.

These secret rendezvous went on for weeks. Materena told Pito all about her family: her hardworking mother, her brother, who was working on a pearl farm in Manihi, the French father she'd never met. And Pito told Materena about his three brothers, his father, who had died, and his mother, who liked to pick up leaves with a leaf pick. Pito and Materena talked about all sorts of other things too, from the weather to fishing.

After a while it seemed to Materena that Pito was getting serious about her. One night she mentioned to Pito the possibility of him meeting her mother, as Materena was a bit *fiu* of having to sneak out of her bedroom and only meeting her boyfriend in the dark. Materena felt it was time for her mother to know about Pito, since Materena was past eighteen years old now and very serious about him.

"I'm not ready," Pito said.

"Mamie isn't going to eat you, she's really nice."

"It's not that, Materena. I'm just not ready."

"Ready for what? All you have to do is say *iaorana* to my mother."

"Eh." Pito was in a bad mood now. "I don't want to meet your mother, okay? When you meet the mother, that's it, you have to get serious."

"Okay then," Materena said. "Don't meet my mother. I'm not going to force you."

"Well, you can't force me anyway. I don't like to be bossed around."

"Yes, that's what I said. I'm not going to force you." Materena got up to go home. She was cranky, but not for too long. She understood that Pito just needed time to get used to the idea of meeting her mother.

Several weeks later, Materena was suspecting a pregnancy. She bought a pregnancy kit and locked herself in the bathroom. She sat on the toilet and read the instructions, which took her almost an hour, since she had never used a pregnancy kit before. Then Materena got a sample of her urine into the jar and put the tester in it. She counted up to sixty, retrieved the tester, and carefully laid it on the floor.

Then she started to pray. But she wasn't quite sure what prayer she was supposed to pray. She wanted to be pregnant, as she loved Pito, and at the same time she didn't want to be pregnant.

The pregnancy test was positive, and Materena cried her eyes out because she was happy but at the same time she wasn't happy.

Loana didn't react well to the news of her daughter being pregnant. She had said to Materena, and many times too, "Don't make me a grandmother before I'm at least past fifty years old." And here she was, about to become a grandmother before the age of forty, when she thought Materena was still a virgin.

Loana made Materena tell her who had got her pregnant, and two hours later, Materena, Loana, and Pito's mother, Mama Roti, were in a meeting.

"Pito didn't tell me about a girl he got pregnant." Mama Roti looked at Materena in the eye and Materena felt like crawling under the couch.

Loana looked at Mama Roti in the eye to show her that she wasn't intimidated at all. "He doesn't know about the baby yet."

"What are you expecting from my son?" Mama Roti asked.

"We're not expecting anything. We're just here to talk," Loana replied calmly.

So the two mothers talked, getting more and more annoyed with each other, until Mama Roti said, "Well, maybe you should tie your girl to a tree at night."

That was the end of the meeting. Loana got to her feet and commanded Materena to do the same.

At that precise moment, Pito appeared. He looked at Materena, he looked at Loana, and then he looked at his mother. She explained the situation, and Pito didn't shout with joy, like they do in the movies.

"Ah, it's you, Pito." Loana looked at him up and down like she didn't think much of him. "Well, now you know that you got my girl pregnant, and good day to you two people."

Materena didn't go to the frangipani tree that night or the following night, or the next, but she waited for Pito to come and see her. And every single day, Loana said, "Girl, waiting for a man is like waiting for a chicken to have teeth."

When Pito came over a week later to ask Materena to move in with him, Loana informed him that her daughter was going nowhere. She was staying right where she was.

"With respect," Pito said, "I'm talking to Materena, not you."

"Do I look like a mother who doesn't care about her daughter?" Loana snapped.

Pito and Loana then both stared at Materena for a comment, and Materena felt like the tomato between the lettuce and the cucumber.

"You two talk," Loana said to Materena. "I'm going out the back. But if you decide to leave this house, don't expect me to help you pack."

Pito sat next to Materena on the sofa. Materena longed for him to take her in his arms, but she could see that he was *chamboulé* by the situation. So they talked about their living arrangement, with Materena saying that she couldn't leave her mother and Pito saying that he couldn't leave his mother.

After a while, Pito stood up to leave, saying, "I'll just come to visit you."

Pito was there when Materena got her first contractions, at nine thirty in the morning. He ran to catch the truck home to get his mama and they both came back with a cousin, who drove Materena and Loana to the hospital.

When they got to the hospital, a nurse led Materena to the delivery room for an examination. Pito, his mama, and Loana sat on the bench in the corridor. Hours later, after Loana had inquired several times about her daughter, a nurse finally came to inform them that the baby was definitely coming today.

"You better go to Materena," Loana said to Pito.

"No, it's okay, she'll be fine," he replied.

Mama Roti decided to agree with her son. "In my day, men just stayed outside."

"Yes," Loana snapped. "In your day . . . but we're not in your day now."

Loana commanded Pito to go to Materena, because a man should see these things.

"It's fine," Pito insisted.

But a nurse came to get Pito because Materena wanted him to see the baby come out.

So Pito saw his son being born, turning green every time the midwife yelled, "Push, girl. Push like you're doing a big caca. Push!" And when Materena moaned, "*Ah hia hia,* it's hurting," he didn't know what he was supposed to do.

Tamatoa was born at eighteen past two in the afternoon and when Pito held his son in his arms, he cried his eyes out and said to Materena, "You're my woman."

One week later, Pito got a job at a timber yard, packed his bags, and moved in with Materena.

All was well the first few days, but it soon became apparent to Materena that Pito and Loana would never get along, because both wanted to be the boss of the baby.

Pito would rock Tamatoa to sleep his way and Loana would say to him, "You don't rock a baby that way. Heavens, boy, I can see you've never rocked a baby before. Don't you know that your rocking could cause damage to my grandson?"

Loana would pick up Tamatoa every time he cried and Pito would say to her, "Let that baby cry a little, eh? That's his only exercise. You're going to turn my son into a fairy."

On and on and on.

Every single day.

For months.

Pito kept telling Materena that her mother was a bossy colonel. And Loana kept telling Materena that Pito was just a typical man.

Materena finishes scrubbing the oven. Pito and Materena have been together for nearly thirteen years. She is still a professional cleaner and she likes her job. Pito, he still works at the timber yard and he doesn't like his job, though he's happy to have a job. They have their own house now.

Pito and Materena, they get along well, but there are days when Pito gives Materena ideas of murder. She can hear him snoring now.

She tidies up, checks that the gas is off, and goes to kiss her children good night.

She always does this before she goes to bed.

She kisses her daughter, Leilani, on the forehead very lightly, as Leilani wakes up easily.

"What's the time, Mamie?" Leilani asks.

"Go back to sleep, girl." Leilani lives in fear of missing the truck to school. She checks her alarm clock every night before going to bed. She's ten years old.

And now Materena is in her boys' room. The boys sleep on mattresses because they want to. Materena bends down and kisses the eldest child of the family, Tamatoa. He doesn't even stir. He'll be twelve in three months, and some days he thinks he's the boss of the house.

Materena's youngest child, eight-year-old Moana, is on the floor. Materena picks him up and puts him back on his mattress. He's very light — or perhaps she's just got strong arms. She thought she was having a girl when she was pregnant with him.

She did the needle test, like with all her children. You put a thread through a needle and hold the needle above the belly button. If the needle swings from left to right, the baby is a boy. If the needle swings around, the baby is a girl. And the needle swung around, so Materena named her unborn baby girl Loana, after her mother. But then a boy was born instead and Materena substituted an *M* for the *L* and the name became Moana — "ocean."

And now Materena is going to bed.

The lights go out in the little plywood house — behind the petrol station, close to the airport, the church, the cemetery, and the Chinese shop.

Pito is still snoring and Materena gives him a gentle shove. Pito stirs and mutters. Usually she pinches him on the nose or smacks him on the head. Not all the time, but usually. Materena cuddles up to Pito. She can't believe that marriage proposal. In all the years they've been together, they've never discussed marriage. Tonight's marriage proposal is certainly a big surprise, but Materena reminds herself that Pito was drunk, which means that the proposal was only a whole lot of wind. Which is fine with her. The children don't hassle them to get married. Materena is Mamie and Pito is Papi, and that's enough. Pito's mother, Mama Roti, doesn't mind her son not being Materena's husband. And Materena's mother, Loana, doesn't put pressure on Materena to regularize her situation with Pito.

Everybody is quite content with the situation.

But Materena gets thinking about being married. Thinking it would be nice.

She feels her naked hands and pictures a gold band on her finger. She sees that framed wedding certificate displayed on the wall in the living room. She hears herself tell people, "It's me, Madame Tehana."

Being a madame, eh yes, Materena wouldn't mind. She's been called madame many times, but only by the *popa'a,* and it embarrasses her a little, since she's not a madame. It's like falsifying her identity. The Polynesian people, they call her mama or *vahine.* Her cousins call her Materena or Cousin.

Materena starts thinking about a wedding ceremony. Pito could wear his navy wedding-and-funeral suit. Materena knows him — he'll want to take it off as soon as they get back from the church for something more comfortable, like his ripped T-shirt.

Materena isn't fussy about her wedding dress, as long as it's new.

Materena is getting excited. . . .

The Man Loana Was Supposed to Marry

So excited she can't sleep. She knows it's a bit silly to get excited about Pito's drunken marriage proposal, but she's thinking that perhaps he really meant it, because some people need beer in them to dare talk about serious matters. What about that dream she had yesterday? Materena is now trying to analyze it. She was getting married to the man in the movie and Pito barged into the church on a horse and rescued her!

Materena kisses Pito on the neck and presses her body against his. Usually when she does this and he's asleep, he wakes up and jumps on her. But he's drunk, so he just stays still like a statue.

Materena thinks about what her mother would say if she announced that she was getting married.

Loana might say, "About time that Pito decided to marry you, after all you've done for him."

Or, "Are you sure you want to marry Pito now? You don't want to wait until you two are older?"

Or, "*Oish,* what is a marriage worth?"

Or even, "I've never told you that the day of your marriage would be the happiest day of your life!"

Loana has told Materena often about a marriage proposal she received when she was seventeen years old. The young man's name was Auguste.

It was only a few months ago that Loana told Materena how she had seen Auguste for the very first time since she refused his marriage proposal. Loana instantly recognized him. He was tall and lean, but the hair was gray.

He was walking past the post office and Loana said she was about to call out, "Eh, Auguste, are you fine?" but she changed her mind at the last second.

What do you say to a man who tried to commit suicide for you thirty-five years ago?

So, Loana said, she just watched Auguste walk on, a well-dressed man carrying a briefcase — a man of business, or a professor, perhaps. And Loana felt strange. This is the story of the marriage proposal Loana got from Auguste.

After her mother died, Loana went to live with a distant auntie and her Irish husband. The auntie and her husband were devoted churchgoers. Well, Auntie was the devoted churchgoer and her husband had to follow her or Auntie would get into a bad mood with him.

They went to Mass at Sainte Thérèse, and Auntie made Loana join the church choir because in her opinion Loana had a magnificent voice and a girl who sings for God is bound to catch a good husband — at the church. Auntie hadn't met her husband at the church, but he was a good catch anyhow. She was fortunate.

So Loana sang in the church choir every Sunday morning.

One Sunday, Auguste and his family began to attend the Mass at Sainte Thérèse — they'd previously gone to the cathedral.

Auguste fell in love with Loana at first sight. Every Sunday he would sit in the front row of the church and just admire her. Loana didn't notice him, being too busy concentrating on the songs.

One day, right after Mass, Auguste's mother approached Loana's auntie. She wanted a bit of information about Loana, and Auntie said, "Ah, my niece, she's a very good girl. She goes to Mass every Sunday — she's not the fooling-around kind of girl." The two women spoke for a while and embraced each other good-bye like they knew each other well.

The following Sunday, Auguste and Loana were formally introduced to each other.

And for five Sundays, they did chitchat after the Mass.

One day on the way home from church, Auntie, winking and giggling, said to Loana, "You caught a very good fish, girl."

Soon there was a marriage proposal, and the answer the auntie expected was, of course, a yes, because Auguste was from a very respectable family, with a great future ahead of him as a schoolteacher. He was also a devoted churchgoer, and, what's more, he had a good-looking face and irreproachable manners. Irreproachable.

Auntie said to Loana, "Think about that marriage proposal, girl. Think about it seriously."

In the meantime, it was organized that the young man could come to visit. Auntie set the time and date.

Auguste arrived at six o'clock precisely, as commanded by Auntie — he came with a potted plant for Auntie. Auntie was greatly surprised by the gift.

They sat at the kitchen table: Auguste and Auntie on one side and Loana on the other. The Irish uncle was very busy with a bottle of whisky out the back.

Auguste came again the following day, and the following, and the day after that. Two weeks passed in this way. Then he demanded an answer. Auntie confessed to Loana that the marriage would give her peace of mind.

"I'm not young, girl," she said. "I could die any day."

Auntie wanted to die knowing Loana would be well looked after, with a roof over her head, food on the table, and a good, hardworking husband.

Loana accepted the marriage proposal.

Auguste fell to his knees and said to Loana, "I swear to you that I will make you a happy woman."

But one night as Loana sat thinking on the verandah, she realized that she didn't want to be Auguste's wife. She felt nothing for him and she knew that you were supposed to feel something for the man you were going to marry. Loana knew, for instance, that when Auntie met Gordon for the first time, she said to herself, "That man, he's for me. I want that man!"

Loana told Auntie of her decision not to marry Auguste.

"I can't force you, girl, but you're making a great mistake," Auntie said, disappointed. "One day you're going to regret it. Well, you tell Auguste. I wash my hands."

Auguste cried when Loana told him, he fell on his knees, he begged, he threatened to kill himself.

The next morning, Auguste tried to hang himself. Luckily, the neighbor who was outside feeding his dog saw him. He jumped over the fence, but by the time he got to the breadfruit tree, Auguste was on the ground — alive. The branch had broken. He wasn't meant to die that day.

Auguste's mother was so devastated that she sent her son away to France.

Loana and Auntie and her husband had to change churches. It was too much to bear to be sitting in the same church as the mother of that poor seventeen-year-old boy who'd tried to commit suicide for Loana.

Auntie didn't make Loana join the choir at the new church.

Aue . . . Loana told Materena how she felt bad about it for months. Then she fell in love and she was glad that she didn't marry that Auguste. Then her heart got broken and she wished she had married that Auguste. Then she fell in love again.

Loana loved many times, and two of her lovers gave her chil-

dren. One was a French *militaire* who went back to his country
and the other a Tahitian who went back to his wife.

Loana says she's through with men now and content with her
life. She goes wherever she wants to, no need for authorization,
a leave pass, nobody pestering her, asking where are you going,
how long are you going to be, who are you going with *patati
patata* . . .

Not that she goes anywhere. She likes to stay home.

But when she feels like sleeping on the mat in the living
room, well, she sleeps on the mat in the living room, and when
she wants to stay awake, well, she watches the TV or she listens
to the music on the radio.

She's alone but free.

Aue, life, it's simple.

But there are days when she thinks it would be nice to have
somebody.

Materena rolls to the other side of the bed. It's too hot to be
hugging Pito. And, plus, the alcohol smell on Pito is a bit too
strong. Materena tells herself that she should get some sleep,
even if she's not going to work tomorrow, Saturday. But the
marriage proposal is in her head. She keeps hearing Pito say,
"Marry me."

Marry me.

Go to sleep, Materena, she tells herself.

Who Is Going to Walk
Materena down the Aisle?

B ut she can't.

Materena knows that there will be a crowd at her wedding, because she's got hundreds of cousins — and her cousins, they like to go to baptisms, Communions, confirmations, weddings, birthdays, even if they're not invited.

And when an uninvited guest comes to your party, you can't say, "And what are you doing here? I didn't invite you. Go back to your house." That is not the proper thing to do. One day, you might need that particular cousin. Uninvited cousins always come with food and drinks, though, and that is a good thing, so it is fine with Materena if they come to her wedding.

But the guests, they will get an invitation — like pregnant Cousin Giselle, Cousin Mori, Cousin Tepua, Auntie Stella — and Rita will be matron of honor, because she's Materena's favorite cousin.

Then Mama Teta will drive Materena to the church and around Papeete, Cousin Moeata will make the wedding cake, which will be chocolate, of course, and Cousin Georgette, professional DJ, will ensure that there will be dancing songs for everyone from the young to the old.

Materena thinks how it's a shame a mother can't walk her daughter down the aisle. For the hundredth time in her life, she wonders what would have happened if her father hadn't gone back to his country.

His name was Tom Delors. He came to Tahiti to do military service. He was eighteen years old when he met Loana, who was also eighteen. Tom and Loana met at the Zizou Bar, in Papeete, the bar where the French military men and the local women make contact.

Loana was chatting away with her girlfriend at the bar when Tom invited her for a dance. She accepted the invitation because she was in the mood for a dance and Tom had a good-looking face. She certainly wasn't going to spend the whole night chatting away with her girlfriend!

Loana and Tom danced all night long, with brief moments of rest in between when they would have a little chat and a whisky Coca. At the end of the night, they arranged a rendezvous for the following Saturday because they really liked each other. Loana thought Tom was a great dancer as well as being funny. Tom was captivated by Loana's exotic beauty — the long black hair and the short thin-strapped local pareu dress.

Within three months of their first meeting, Loana and Tom were living together in a bungalow at Arue with three other couples — military men and Tahitian women.

Loana's elder sister was ashamed that Loana was messing around with a *popa'a* — worse, a *militaire*. In those days, local women who messed around with *militaire popa'a* had a bad reputation. They were called easy women, sluts — desperate for a ticket to France. But Loana wasn't desperate for a ticket to France — she just loved her Tom.

When Tom was away on a mission at an outer island, Loana would go out dancing with her woman friends for something to do, but it was rare. Tom didn't appreciate it. He was the jealous type, Materena's father.

"Tom, eh," Loana would say to him, "it's you I love."

Eh yes, she loved him real bad. And he was good to her.

They were together for six months before they separated.

It was quite silly, their separation.

That day, they were having guests to dinner and Loana had made a special effort to cook chicken — chicken split peas.

When the chicken was served, Tom said, "You don't cook chicken like this." A few of the guests went on about how Loana's chicken split peas were delicious. But Tom insisted that the chicken was really awful. Humiliated by Tom's rudeness, Loana threw a plate at him. He ducked and laughed. But before he could make it up to her, Loana packed her bags and one of the guests drove her to her sister's house on his Vespa.

Now, there was a possibility the chicken *was* awful, as Loana wasn't the good cook she is today. But, still, as far as Materena is concerned, when you love somebody, you don't criticize their cooking and you don't criticize the person you love in front of a whole bunch of people.

Loana waited for Tom to come say pardon to her and she was going to say pardon to him. And then they would get together again.

But he never came.

Loana was devastated. And three weeks pregnant, though she didn't know it.

When Loana realized that there was a seed in her belly, she cried her eyes out. Her sister said, "I warned you against those people. Now look at you. What name are you going to put on that child's birth certificate, eh? It's going to be a bastard. Give it up for adoption. You've got no money, you've got no job, you've got no papers — you've got nothing. I told you. But you had to go shame yourself with a *popa'a* like there's not enough local men for you to choose from."

Every time Loana cooks chicken split peas she thinks about Tom and their silly separation.

Materena too — every time she cooks chicken split peas, she thinks about Tom and Loana and their silly separation.

Materena was eight years old when she first saw her birth certificate and, on it, Father Unknown. She asked her mother, "You don't know who my father is?"

Loana got cranky. "What," she said, "do you think I would open my legs for a man I don't know? Of course I know the man who planted you."

Materena wanted a bit more information, but all Loana was prepared to reveal then was the man's nationality. "He's a *popa'a* — final point."

Materena was fifteen years old when she got to hear the whole story, and she cried because it felt strange for her to know about her father.

She doesn't have a photograph of him. There used to be a photograph of him in a swimming costume at the beach, but one of Loana's lovers tore it to pieces because he was jealous. Loana must have told him how she'd loved Tom real bad.

According to Loana, Materena has Tom's almond-shaped brown eyes, and the dimple on her left cheek belongs to him too.

Materena closes her eyes, and when she opens them, it is Saturday morning.

The first thought that springs to her mind is about her wedding and how she will keep it quiet for a while. Materena doesn't want her wedding to turn into a family circus, with relatives stressing her out regarding seating arrangements, etc. A wedding shouldn't be about giving the bride stress, it should be a celebration. A new beginning.

Kika

Keeping a wedding a secret is like keeping any kind of secret. It's not complicated. Basically, when you bump into a relative, you bite your tongue for a few seconds and hurry to make small conversation. So far, in the space of half a day, Materena has bumped into six relatives and told them nothing of her secret plan. When they asked her, "So, what's the news?" she replied — with her normal voice — "There's no news, Cousin. It's still the same, and how's everything with you?"

Now, however, with her mother visiting, Materena is very tempted to exclaim, "Eh, Mamie! You're never going to guess! Pito asked for my hand!" But Materena bites her tongue instead.

Loana only meant to drop in at Materena's house for five minutes (she was on her way home from a prayer meeting), but she ends up cuddling with her grandchildren on the sofa, and they watch *Inspector Gadget* on the TV. After the movie the children go to bed, and, since Pito has gone walkabout with his friend Ati, Loana decides to stay longer and keep her daughter company.

"Pito and Ati, they're like a married couple," says Loana. Materena chuckles as she gets her mother a glass of red wine.

They talk about plants, the funny weather, the traffic jam, menopause, and Loana drinks her glass of wine.

And now Loana is going to talk about her mother, Kika, because she feels like talking about her mother, and Materena is going to listen.

Tonight isn't the first time that Loana has felt like talking about her mother, but tonight is the first time that Loana feels like recording herself talking about her mother. Materena takes down the radio from the top of the fridge and goes into her bedroom for batteries and a blank tape. Now the radio is on the kitchen table and Materena is waiting for her mother's signal to press the record button.

But first Loana wants a bit more wine. Materena gets the small flagon of red wine from the fridge and refills her mother's glass. Loana drinks. There are tears rolling down her cheeks already. Just thinking about her mother makes Loana cry.

Loana loved her mama — Materena knows this.

It's not unusual for Loana to go to the cemetery for a little talk with her mother any time of the day, even in the middle of the night. "I'm going to see Mama," Loana will say, and off she'll go and come back hours later. Some nights, Loana sleeps on her mother's grave.

There's no more wine in the glass.

"Ready?" Materena's finger is on the button. Loana nods and Materena presses record.

After a few minutes, Loana finally begins.

"We are at the church and it's the Communion. I can't go and eat the body of Christ because I'm only five and I haven't done my Communion yet. I stay seated and I look at the people lining up for the body of Christ. Mama too stays seated. She can't eat the body of Christ because she's living with a man who's not her husband. Her husband, my father, he ran away to Tahiti with another woman, and Mama had to get another man to help her in the copra plantation. Mama isn't looking at the people lining up for the body of Christ, she's looking at her hands. Then she looks over to my stepfather, who's sitting on the other aisle. Men and women sat in different aisles in the church those days. My stepfather seems to be looking at his hands too, but his eyes are closed, he's tired.

"I want to go to the toilet and it is night. The bathroom is far away from the house, past the pigsty, in the coconut plantation. I tell myself, Wait for the day, wait for the day, but I can't wait for the day. Mama is sleeping and I wake her up.

"I say, 'Mama, my belly is hurting.' She says, '*Ah hia,*' and I think that Mama isn't going to get out of bed, but she does. She holds my hand as we walk to the toilet, and I'm not afraid. I feel protected.

"Another time we are at Otepipi Isle, picking limes, but I get bored of picking the limes, I want to wander around. I wander around, then I step on something. I look down and I see three skulls. They are a bit covered by the grass, but I can see the skulls. I scream. Next second, my mama is by my side. There are scratches on her arms because she ran through the lime plantation. Mama hits me. Then she hugs me. I tell her about the skulls. She says, 'Be more afraid of the living.'"

Loana wants a refill. She drinks it in one gulp and continues.

"It's a while later and I'm coming up for my confirmation. We are sitting under the *tau* tree. Mama is looking for lice in my hair. There are no lice in my hair but Mama just has to keep her hands busy. She asks me questions and I answer. When the answer is correct, she says nothing. When the answer is wrong, she thumps me on the head or pulls a hair. It's a great shame to fail the confirmation test and Kika doesn't want any more shame than what her husband gave her when he ran off with another woman. I pass the confirmation test and Mama kisses me on the forehead. She says, 'You made me very proud today.'"

Loana wants another refill, but she doesn't drink it. She just holds the glass.

"Mama is leaving for Tahiti to go visit my older sister, and my stepfather is going back to his island to visit his relatives. Mama's very good friend, Teva's grandmother, is going to look after me. Mama is very happy. She hums. She counts the coins in the milk container she's saved, money from working the copra plantation. Mama is going to buy my sister new dresses and I get jealous because I only have two dresses and they're old. I'm also jealous because Mama doesn't want to take me with her to Tahiti.

"I cry when she gets on the schooner, and she turns her back to me. And Teva's grandmother scolds me. She says, 'Stop your crying.' She tells me it's safer for me to stay here because Kika will surely die if that *titoi* ever used the law to steal me like he stole my sister. I miss my mama. I think, What if she doesn't come back? Teva's grandmother is a really nice woman, but she's not Mama.

"When Mama comes back I run to her. She doesn't hold me and she kisses my forehead like it's an obligation. It's like she's not happy to see me. So I go hide in the bush. I hide there for a long time. Mama calls me and I don't answer. She calls me again and I answer, 'Yeah!' She comes after me with the broom and beats me. Teva's grandmother runs to save me. Mama tells her good friend to mind her own business. And the good friend shouts, 'It's not Loana's fault that *titoi* Tahitian husband of yours wants to divorce you!'"

Loana drinks her wine and tears well in her eyes.

"I'm fourteen years old when Mama leaves me." Loana's voice is trembling. "We're both in Tahiti this time, staying at a relative's house in Faa'a — Rita's grandmother. We are in Tahiti to pay a visit to my stepfather, who's sick at the Mamao Hospital.

"I'm asleep when Rita's grandmother comes to wake me up. It's about twenty past six. I open my eyes. She whispers, 'Loana, come to the kitchen.' I go to the kitchen and I see my mama lying on the kitchen table, her hands clutched in prayer, with coins pressed on her eyelids. I don't understand. Rita's grandmother says, 'Loana, say adieu to your mama, she's dead.'

"I open my mouth to shout, but the relative puts her hand on my mouth. She says, 'Don't cry now, your mother's soul is still in the kitchen, hold your tears for another hour.' She goes on about how it's good Mama died in Tahiti and not in Rangiroa. Yes, it's good she died here alone, without her second man. That way, her dead body will be allowed into the church. Here, she's Madame Mahi, whereas there — she's 'Mito's woman.' The relative says, 'We're going to give your mama a grand funeral, the choir is going to sing for her, and we'll play the accordions. Don't be too sad.'"

The tears are now streaming down Loana's face and Materena hugs her mother.

"I miss my mama," Loana cries. "She's been dead for over thirty-eight years but I still miss my mama."

Materena doesn't say anything. She just hugs her mother real tight.

Loana gently pulls away and wipes her eyes with the back of her hands. "Fill my glass, girl."

Materena doesn't really want to give her mother more wine, because in her opinion wine and sadness don't go together. "Mamie," she says softly, "maybe you've had enough to drink, eh? You want me to make you some coffee?"

"You want me to stay up all night?" Loana grabs the flagon of wine and fills her glass. She savors the wine and sighs. "You know, my parents' separation traumatized me." She looks up. "Yes, that's the word. Traumatized."

"*Ah oui,*" Materena agrees. "It's hard on the children, but sometimes separation is for the best."

"It's not the separation that traumatized me the most. It's my . . . it's my mama." Loana bites her quivering lips. "It's my mama not wanting to be a divorcée. Today, there are so many people who are divorced that to be a divorcée is normal. Nobody cares."

Materena slowly nods.

"But in my mama's days," Loana continues, "nobody divorced. You were supposed to stay married for life. It was expected. You know, when my father left my mama for another woman, my mama's confirmation wreath was taken down from the wall of the church. It was like a condemnation."

"But it wasn't Grandmother who left her husband," Materena says.

"That didn't matter." Loana shakes her head. "My mama died with her wedding ring on her finger. Her wedding photograph was glued in her suitcase and I caught her looking at it so many times . . . so many times. She was obsessed."

"With her husband?"

Loana looks at Materena in the eyes. "With being married." She sighs a long sigh filled with sadness. "Marriage," she says. "It's . . ." But Loana doesn't continue. She gets up.

She's going to the cemetery to talk to her mama. Materena proposes to go with her but Loana doesn't want any other company except the company of her mama.

"We'll continue taping another night," she says. "I'll see you at the cemetery on Saturday morning."

"Sure, Mamie." Materena hugs her mother one more time.

In two days it will be Kika's birthday. She would have been eighty-one years.

Materena labels the tape Kika, My Grandmother. Then she puts the tape in her box of things that are very important — like her children's birth certificates.

The Peg

Kika is eighty-one years old today.

"Eh, eh," Materena whispers, making her grandmother a bouquet, "if only Grandmère was alive today. That would have been so nice for Mamie." Materena steps back to take a good look at the bouquet, asking herself if she should move the red *opuhi* a bit more to the left and, perhaps, add a few more white *pitate* flowers. She squints.

Something is missing in this bouquet. It's a beautiful bouquet, made with love and affection, a bouquet consisting of flowers growing in Materena's garden, but the bouquet is not yet finished. There's a missing ingredient. So Materena continues to study the bouquet until she notices her eldest son waving a hand in front of her face.

"You're dreaming or what, Mamie?" he asks.

"*Non,* I was —"

Tamatoa interrupts his mother to deliver the strange news. "Leilani has a peg on her nose. She's in her bedroom. I saw the peg on her nose with my eyes." Tamatoa shows his mother his eyes to show her that he's speaking the truth here.

What is that girl doing with a peg on her nose? Materena is concerned. The idea that comes into her mind is that Leilani is playing a game that has to do with respiration.

Materena goes to investigate the situation. The door is half-open and Materena barges into the bedroom. Leilani is lying on her bed — a pink peg on her nose. She sees her mother and automatically takes the peg off.

"What is this peg-on-the-nose story?" Materena asks.

"Nothing." Leilani gives Tamatoa the *tiho-tiho parau* look.

"Ah, so you just felt like pinching your nose with a peg today, eh?" Materena knows Leilani's answer is going to be a yes because a yes will mean the end of this interrogation.

Leilani's answer is a murmur. "Yes."

Now, Materena accepts the fact that her kids don't want to explain every single thing to their mamie, because some things are secret. But that peg on the nose, it is really intriguing her.

"Just tell me about that peg, I'm not going to get cranky at you."

Silence. Leilani stares at the ceiling.

Materena insists on knowing if the peg on the nose has something to do with respiration.

"A game that has something to do with respiration?" Leilani is almost laughing.

"So, is it or not?" Materena asks.

"*Non!*"

"Okay. What is the story, then?" Materena sits on the bed.

Tamatoa, standing at the door, briefs his mamie on the situation. The peg has something to do with Leilani wanting her nose to be pointed.

"Shut it!" Leilani looks like she's going to stab her brother with her eyes.

Materena commands Tamatoa to disappear and to close the door. She also warns him in advance that if she ever catches him listening in to a private conversation again . . .

The door is closed.

Materena looks at Leilani, who's now hiding her nose behind her hands.

Materena takes Leilani's hands away. "Come on now, girl. There's nothing wrong with your nose."

But, in Leilani's opinion, her nose is too flat, like the nose of a boxer.

Materena wants to laugh, but this is a serious situation. She knows lots of cousins who are sensitive about their nose. You can tell these cousins anything you want, but mention their flat nose and they're going to give *you* a flat nose. Loma, for instance, once told Tapeta during Mass, "I can't believe how flat your nose is!" Tapeta kept on singing and waited until after Mass to punch Loma on the nose.

"How come the size of your nose is bothering you now, Leilani?" Materena sounds and looks serious. "You never complained about your nose before."

Leilani admits that she looked at her nose for a long time in the mirror this morning and realized that her nose was flat.

"How come you decided to look at your nose for a long time in the mirror this morning?"

Leilani doesn't know why she felt like looking at her nose for a long time in the mirror this morning. She just felt like looking at her nose for a long time in the mirror.

Ah hia hia . . .

"Your nose, it's nice to look at," Materena says.

"You're not lying, Mamie?"

"*Ah non,* I'm not lying. Do I look like I'm lying?"

Leilani caresses her nose.

"If you want to see a big nose, just look at my nose." Materena points to her nose. Leilani is feeling much better about her nose now.

And Materena can get back to her bouquet, but she's got a

question for her daughter, and she's only being curious. "Tell me, girl, that trick with the peg, does it really work? Is it something you learned at school? If you put a peg on your nose — the nose is going to get pointed?"

Leilani isn't 100 percent sure. She's only testing her invention at this stage.

Materena goes back to her bouquet. But first, she goes to look at her nose in the mirror. She always looks at her nose when she's in front of the mirror, because it is in the middle of her face, but right now, she's more than looking at her nose. She's studying it.

"My nose is flat." Well, Materena has always known her nose to be flat.

She was born with a flat nose.

Her auntie Stella delivered her, and apparently she said to Loana, "That's a flat nose. Quick, girl, massage your baby girl's nose before the bones harden." But Loana told Stella to worry about her own nose.

Loana was proud her baby girl had a flat nose just like hers. In her opinion, a flat nose was a sign of character. And she made sure to repeat this to Materena over the years, so by the time Materena was a teenager, she was very proud that her nose was flat.

Once Loma said to Materena, "I can't believe how wide your nostrils are!" And Materena said, "Loma, that's because I've got character, and not everybody is born with it. I love my flat nose."

But when Materena gave birth to Leilani and saw the flat nose, she decided to massage it before the bones hardened — as by then Materena was beginning to be a bit *fiu* of her flat nose — but Loana slapped Materena's hand. She said, "I know a woman whose mother massaged her on the nose as soon as she was born, and you know what? That woman's nose is crooked now. It's so crooked, she's got trouble breathing."

Materena lifts her nose up so that it is pointed. "Ah, now I look ridiculous!" Well, anyway, there's more to life than worrying about the size of your nose.

Chuckling, Materena hurries to finish her grandmother's bouquet. Okay now, what is missing here? Tapping a finger on her nose to help her think, Materena stares at the bouquet until, at last, she has a revelation.

All the bouquet needs is a bit of yellow!

Eternal Sleep

Sitting under the frangipani tree beside the white-washed, white sand–covered grave where Kika is buried, Loana and Materena are admiring each other's bouquets, both made with love and a dash of yellow.

"Your bouquet is beautiful, Mamie," Materena says.

"Yours too, girl." Loana takes her daughter's hand in hers and gives it a little squeeze, meaning, *mauruuru,* thank you so much for making this beautiful bouquet for my mama's birthday. My sister forgot, as usual.

Leilani and Moana are playing ticktack along the paths, sometimes they stop playing to read the name of a deceased engraved on a white concrete cross. When there's a photo, they look, and say, "Poor her — she's dead."

Materena calls out, "You two, don't step on the graves!"

The kids call back, *"Oui,* Mamie!"

It's nice to sit under the frangipani tree. There's shade and it smells sweet.

Loana and Materena have cleaned Kika's grave and they're going to rest under the frangipani tree until Loana decides it's time to get a move on.

"I wanted to get sand from Rangiroa for my mama," Loana says.

"Ah — and did you get it?" Materena asks.

"*Non.* I rang Poiro to see if he could send me a bag of sand," says Loana. "I was going to pay him for the sand and for the time it took him to shove the sand into the bag and put it on the boat, but he's too busy with his bungalows."

Materena doesn't know Poiro, but he must be a relative.

"I tell you," Loana goes on, "his bungalows are not going to do well this year. Is it so difficult to shove sand into a flour bag, write my name on it, and chuck that bag on the boat? When I think of all the things my mama did for his mama, and now here's the gratitude.

"We'll see who's going to cry when nobody is going to rent those bungalows. I wanted so much for my mama to have sand from her island to make her feel a bit more at home. One of these days, I'm going to go get the sand myself." Loana sighs. "One day — when? Every year I say I'm going home for a visit, but something else always comes up. Something to pay. Your brother rang me last night."

"Everything's fine?" asks Materena. "Kids are good?"

"*Ah oui,*" Loana replies. "Kids are good, but . . . money is tight."

Materena knows her brother rang to ask Loana for money. In fact, Tinirau only calls his mother when he's got a money situation.

"Eh," Loana says. "I would have gone home a long time ago if my mama was buried there."

"*Ah oui,* Mamie. I can't imagine you not visiting Grandmother at least three times a year."

"*Ah oui.* I wouldn't let my mama alone like that, with weeds growing all over her grave. It's good my mama is buried in Tahiti."

"*Ah oui,*" Materena says.

"That way I can be buried next to my mama."

"*Oui.*"

"I know I've told you before, but I'll tell you again, you kids better bury me next to my mama."

"*Oui.*"

"Don't you lot bury me next to my father. You bury me next to my mama."

"Okay, Mamie."

It's quiet at the cemetery. Leilani and Moana know that when you play ticktack at the cemetery, you don't yell and you don't laugh. You play quietly.

There's a woman crying silent tears on a baby's tomb. There's an old man smoking by a grave, his head down.

And there's Materena and Loana, sitting under the frangipani tree.

"I pray I'm going to die old," Loana says. "Not so old that I can't go to the toilet by myself and one of you kids has to feed me pureed food with the spoon. *Non,* not so old that you kids can't wait for me to die because I'm such a nuisance."

"Mamie! We're never going to think, 'Hurry up, you, and die.'"

"Don't take me to the Capa."

"*Ah non,* we're not going to take you to the Capa."

"When you go to the Capa — it's the end of you. After the Capa, it's the cemetery. At the Capa, you just sit and wait for your family to remember to come visit you. You sit and you think and you get sad. That's what happens when you think too much — you get all sad. It's best to have something to do, to occupy the hands. I've wiped your bottoms a thousand times — don't you lot take me to the Capa. I swear, if I die in that place, I'm not going to be happy. I want to die in my house. In my garden with my plants would be better, but I can't demand too much of God. But I don't want to die at the Capa."

Tears well in Materena's eyes. Why is her mother talking

about death? Is she sick and not telling? "Mamie, you're not dying?"

Loana laughs. "But *non!*" She straightens up her legs. "The old legs are a bit stiff when I get up in the morning, but apart from that I'm in good health. What is this question you're asking me?"

"We were talking about the sand, then we were talking about my brother, and now you're talking about death."

Loana shrugs. "We're at the cemetery, so why not talk about death?"

"Ah." Yes, Materena understands. You don't talk about death at the beach, you don't talk about death in the kitchen. You talk about death at the cemetery. It makes sense.

"It's not like we're never going to die," Loana says. "It's good to talk about your death. Like, when I die, I want to be buried the next day. Don't put me into the freezer, I don't want to be in the freezer. It's horrible to be in the freezer."

"What if Tinirau is still living in France when you die? Then you'll have to go in the freezer."

"*Ah non,* don't you lot put me in the freezer. Bury me, don't wait."

It is very difficult for Materena to talk about her mother's funeral, but this story about the freezer must be resolved. "You don't want all your kids to be at your funeral?" she asks.

"I don't want to be in the freezer — full stop. When I die, give me a wake and then bury me. And don't cry over my dead body. Leave my soul free to leave this world. Don't you lot disturb my soul with your loud crying. Cry over me when I'm alive, not when I'm dead."

Loana holds her daughter's hand. "Eh, girl, it's sad, death. But it's not the end. We get reunited. There's that place. And you're going to be buried here too, girl — next to your mamie and your grandmother."

Materena looks at the sky but says nothing.

"Eh, girl? You're going to be buried next to me?"

Materena hesitates. "Okay."

"What, you don't want to be buried next to me?"

"Yes, yes, it's fine."

Yes, it's fine for Materena to be buried next to her mother and grandmother, but what about Pito?

At the Day of the Dead celebration, Materena prays at the cemetery of Faa'a and Pito prays at the cemetery of Punaauia, where his family is buried. And the kids take turns: one year in Faa'a — one year in Punaauia. It'll be much easier for the kids if Pito and Materena are in the same cemetery — and the same grave, if possible.

So Materena asks Loana if it's all right with her if Pito gets buried here.

There's a silence, and Materena immediately regrets the question. Pito is not part of the family, she realizes. He's only part of her life. Materena wonders if her mother would be more willing to have Pito buried here if he were her husband.

"You don't think Pito wants to be buried with his family in Punaauia?" Loana asks.

Materena confesses that they have never talked about their funeral arrangements.

"People should talk about their funeral arrangements," Loana explains. "There's an old woman, she died without a burial arrangement. Well, there was a lot of arguing at her wake between the children she had from her first man and the children she had from her second man. Words flew above the dead body, with one clan believing their mother belonged there and one clan believing their mother belonged somewhere else. The poor woman, she had to go in the freezer and it was a whole month before her body was finally laid to rest."

"Where did the woman get buried in the end?"

"Next to her first man."

In Loana's opinion, the old woman had wanted to be buried next to her mother, but she had never thought of mentioning this to her kids.

"It's nice to be buried next to your mother. Everybody wants to be buried next to their mother," Loana says.

"And if Pito wants me to be buried next to him in Punaauia?"

Loana snaps her answer, and she's not holding her daughter's hand anymore. "Do what you want, it's your dead body."

Materena feels like the tomato between the lettuce and the cucumber. She always feels like the tomato between the lettuce and the cucumber when there's Loana and Pito in the story.

"Eh, Mamie. Don't be angry with me." Materena is pleading.

"I'm not angry. If you want to be buried next to Pito, go get buried next to Pito. I'm not going to say you can't be buried next to him."

"Pito comes here, then. I'm going to tell him."

Loana takes a deep breath. "All right. But you two better sort out your funeral arrangements. Eh, Pito might have other plans."

Materena and Pito are in bed that night and Materena knows Pito is not sleeping. When he's sleeping, he snores, and at the moment he's not snoring.

"Pito, you're sleeping?"

There's no answer from Pito.

Maybe he's sleeping and not snoring. Materena closes her eyes, but she really wants to talk about their funeral arrangements, and right this moment is a good time to talk about that kind of subject. The kids can't come interrupt the conversation.

"Pito?"

There's no answer from Pito.

"Pito, I know you're not sleeping, because when you're sleeping, you snore. Pito?"

Pito reluctantly opens his eyes. "Okay, what?"

"Ah, you're awake. I knew you weren't sleeping. When I die . . ." Materena pauses. It's difficult for her to talk about her death in the bedroom and in the dark, but she must. She continues. "I don't know where I'm supposed to be buried."

"I'm going to bury you in Faa'a," Pito says.

"You don't want me to be buried in Punaauia?" Materena can't believe how well Pito is accepting the subject of conversation.

"Your family is not in Punaauia," Pito says. "Why am I going to bury you there? Loana, she's going to be buried in Faa'a, *non?*"

"*Oui,* next to her mama."

"Well, you can be buried next to them two."

Materena has to ask the next question, but she hesitates. Pito always says that they should move to his part of the island (if he had land they would have moved there from the day they became a couple), that he sees Loana a bit too much, that there are just too many of Materena's relatives here. Pito's relatives from both his parents' sides are from Punaauia, about fifteen minutes away by truck. Pito is not going to accept being buried in Faa'a, and Materena doesn't want to be separated.

"What if you die before me, what am I supposed to do with you?" Then, speaking quickly, Materena adds, "It's fine with Mamie for you to be buried in Faa'a. She said to me, 'Ah, it's okay if Pito is buried next to us, no problem.'" Materena is now caressing Pito's hand.

Yes, but Pito doesn't want to be buried next to Loana, so he tells Materena. In fact, Pito doesn't want to be buried, full stop. He doesn't want to be put into a hole and to be eaten up by the worms. He doesn't want to be buried.

Materena is shocked. What is this story? What is she going to do with him if she can't bury him?

"Don't bury you?" she asks, as if she didn't hear properly.

"Don't bury me," Pito repeats. "Cremate me and throw my ashes into the sea."

Cremate? Materena has never heard of anyone getting cremated in her family. And it's the same situation in Pito's family. Everyone gets buried. It's the tradition. There's the wake and then there's the burial and then the name is written, the date of the birth, the date of the death, the little message of love, on the white cross. Cremate? What is this nonsense?

"How are the kids and I going to pray on you if you're not in the grave? I can't cremate you, Pito. *Think* a bit!"

"Materena, I tell you, don't you bury me. If you bury me I'm not going to be happy. You cremate me and then you put a bit of my ashes in a box for you and the kids."

Materena is sad now. In her opinion, when you get cremated it's like you've never existed. Whereas with the grave, your kids can come visit you, and your grandkids, their kids, and on and on. There's proof that you were born and died.

She visits her great-great-grandmother sometimes. She sits on her grave and says *iaorana.*

Well, you can talk to the ashes, but it's not the same as talking on the grave, all the while weeding and clearing up the sand.

Maybe it is, Materena doesn't know. She's never talked to ashes before. And, the box, it can be dropped, broken, lost. And who is going to keep the box of Pito's ashes after she dies? There are three kids.

She's not going to cremate Pito — *ah non.* She's going to bury him, and she's going to bury him in Faa'a. That's her final decision. She best write the funeral arrangements and put them in her special box for the kids to act upon.

And now that the matter is resolved, Materena is going to sleep.

"Materena," Pito says.

She doesn't answer.

"Swear to me that you're going to cremate me."

She's not hearing anything — she's asleep. But Pito is not having that comedy. He gets out of bed and switches the light on, and Materena covers her face with the pillow.

Pito snatches the pillow away. "You're going to swear to me that when I die, you're going to cremate me like I said. I never thought about all of this, eh? You got me thinking. And I'm telling you again. I don't want to be buried, okay?"

Pito looks so serious about his cremation. Materena nods slowly. "Okay, Pito. I'm going to cremate you — don't you worry."

Frying Pan

I t is Mama Roti's birthday tomorrow, three days before Pito's birthday, and she wants a present.

She's been hinting about it for the past week — in fact, the past month.

"Twenty-nine days until the day I was born."

"Twenty days until the day I was born."

"Five days until the day I was born."

She has to get a present on her birthday, otherwise she won't speak to you for days. She'll sulk. Mama Roti likes it when her kids remember the day she was born. She often says, "All those years I wiped your bottom — you better give me a present on my birthday."

She's not fussy about the present as long as there's something for her to unwrap and there's a card with *Happy birthday, Mama* written on it. She's got boxes full of birthday cards.

Usually, Materena chooses the present and she wraps it in nice colorful birthday paper. But this year, for no particular reason, Pito wants to be involved. He wants to do more than write *Happy birthday, Mama, from your son Pito, Materena, and the kids.* So Pito and Materena are going to Euromarché to buy Mama Roti her present. And Materena has a few ideas.

She suggests a hand-printed pareu for Mama Roti to wear on special occasions. But Pito doesn't approve, because, according to him, his mama has got enough pareus — hundreds, as a matter of fact.

"Ah, you counted?"

"There's pareus all over the house," Pito says.

And apparently Mama Roti sometimes even uses a pareu for mopping. So Materena proposes a coupon for a manicure, with a couple of nail polish bottles.

Pito gives Materena a funny look. "Mama? A manicure?"

"Or a brooch, a brooch is nice. Not a big one, a small one, like a bird or a flower."

Pito grimaces, and Materena realizes that the search for Mama Roti's present isn't going to be an easy task with Pito involved.

It is never an easy task, searching for Mama Roti's present. Mama Roti may say that she doesn't care about the present as long as there's something for her to unwrap, but, deep down, Mama Roti does care about her present — Materena knows this.

Materena always starts looking for Mama Roti's present a few weeks before her birthday, which is why she has so many ideas today. But since Pito wants to be in charge of Mama Roti's present this year . . .

"What do you want to give to your mama?" Materena asks Pito.

Pito wants to give his mama something useful, something practical. He doesn't know what that useful-and-practical something is yet, but he trusts his instinct. His instinct will tell him: This is for Mama.

Pito heads to the cleaning department, and Materena follows him. She's dragging her feet because, in her opinion, you don't get someone a present from the cleaning department, especially when that someone is a woman.

And especially when that someone is Mama Roti!

Mama Roti hates cleaning. Her house is always a mess, and Mama Roti likes to say, "*Ah hia,* if only I had a magic wand to clean the house for me."

Last year, Materena got Mama Roti a coupon to the hairdresser for the value of five thousand francs. Mama Roti got herself a perm, she was very happy. She thanked her son over and over, knowing full well that the coupon to the hairdresser wasn't Pito's idea.

Last year, Materena was really pleased that Pito had remembered the day she was born. Pito gave her a box wrapped in newspaper and said, "Here."

Materena delicately tore the newspaper and slowly opened the box (it was a plain box — no relation to the gift). Then she saw the frying pan and said, smiling, "Ah, a frying pan."

Mama Roti, who was present at the time, caught her disappointed look. She shook her head and mumbled, "What does a man have to do these days to make his woman happy?" She rolled her eyes and went on and on about how her son's gift was well chosen — how a woman could always do with a frying pan. Mama Roti inspected the frying pan, nodding several times. She tapped her fingers on it and declared, "This is no cheap frying pan, this is a good-quality frying pan. Not too big, not too small, medium-size."

Materena was disappointed with the frying pan because she had expected to see a new pair of shoes — a few days prior to her birthday, she'd complained to Pito about her shoes getting a bit worn-out and how they were hurting her feet.

This year was worse because Pito forgot her birthday completely.

In the cleaning department, Pito's first choice for his mother's present is those perfumed mushrooms you put around the house to make it smell good.

"Pito. Are you serious or are you fooling around?" Materena doesn't know if she should be annoyed or laugh.

Pito is serious, and why wouldn't he be serious? Perfumed mushrooms are nice.

Materena tells him (speaking in a low voice because of the other customers) that his mother sprays her deodorant around her house when she wants it to smell nice, and she's very content with that technique, plus, the smell of the mushrooms is horrible.

"How about this?" Pito says.

Materena tells him that his mother will definitely not appreciate a family-size packet of washing powder.

Pito moves to the gardening department and picks up a rake. Materena reminds him (speaking in a low voice again because of the other customers) of his mother's relationship with her leaf pick. She loves her leaf pick, she gets a lot of satisfaction stabbing the leaves one by one, and very slowly, for hours.

Materena decides to take charge now. She's seen enough of Pito's nonsense. She barges toward the perfume department. A whole hour they spend at the perfume department. They smell fifteen bottles of eau de cologne, and Pito complains about the smell every single time. Either it is too sweet, too spicy, too strong, or rotten.

"Since when did you become a professional smeller?" Materena isn't speaking in a low voice anymore.

"Give your own mother eau de cologne," Pito snaps back. "Mama, she's not getting eau de cologne."

Materena comes up with the idea of a jar filled with mints for Mama Roti to munch on when she reads the Bible, watches the TV, or rests on the mat. She can also use the jar to store something else. But, in Pito's opinion, his mother much prefers to munch on Chinese lollies, and, anyway, she's got jars galore as it is, and another jar she really doesn't need.

"How about that crystal wineglass?" Materena is losing hope.

"That wineglass is only going to last one day in Mama's hands. Mama, she breaks everything."

Fed up, Materena suggests a frying pan — as a joke.

Pito's eyes light up. "Now you're talking, woman."

He did notice that the last time he was at his mother's house, her frying pan didn't have a handle. In fact, she burned her hand with that frying pan — she showed him the scar. Mama Roti had also showed Materena the scar on her hand, but she'd said it happened when she took the baking dish out of the oven.

Pito grabs a frying pan. It is a 100 percent stainless-steel frying pan, like Materena's, except that it is smaller. Materena advises him to get a bigger size.

"Mama only needs a small size. She doesn't use the frying pan heaps," Pito says.

Materena insists on the family-size frying pan and Pito wants to know why she's insisting on a family-size when he told her his mama doesn't use the frying pan heaps. But Materena isn't going to tell Pito that he cannot give his mama a frying pan that is smaller than Materena's frying pan, because Mama Roti would sulk and go on and on and on about how she'd suffered for two whole days pushing Pito into this world.

Pito wouldn't understand this delicate situation. He'd most likely say, "Ah, you women. You're so complicated."

Materena grabs the small-size frying pan out of Pito's hands and puts it back on the shelf. Then she gets the family-size frying pan and gives it to Pito.

"When the kids go visit your mama," Materena says, "and they feel like an omelette, Mama Roti can make a big omelette. It'll be easier for her. Plus, the price difference isn't great."

Pito shakes his head like Materena's explanation is too much to comprehend. "My mama, she gets a bigger frying pan than my wife. I thought it was supposed to be the contrary."

Materena grins. "Eh? I'm your wife these days? It's not 'woman' anymore?"

But Pito is already heading toward the cash register. He's never ever called Materena "wife." He calls her Materena or "woman." Pito sometimes calls Materena Mama, but she always tells him to keep that name for his own mama.

"Wife"! Not once!

It's been two weeks since Pito has proposed, and, in Materena's opinion, Pito is trying to get used to the idea of being married, for a man simply doesn't call his woman "wife" unless he secretly wishes that she *were* his wife.

Materena is still grinning when they get outside the shopping center.

"Why are you grinning?" asks Pito.

"I'm just happy about Mama Roti's birthday present," Materena replies.

"*Ah oui,*" Pito says. "Mama, she's not going to believe her eyes."

"Happy birthday, Mama."

Pito gives his mama her present. He's wrapped it in newspaper. Mama Roti presses both hands on her chest and acts surprised. She rips the newspaper, she rips the box (it's just a box, no relation to the gift), all the while smiling and looking at her son like he tricked her.

She sees the frying pan and for a moment it is not clear what her reaction is going to be. She seems to be searching for the right words to say.

Finally. "A frying pan! How did you know I needed a frying pan! Now I can throw the old one in the garbage!"

Mama Roti inspects her frying pan. She taps her fingers on it. "This is no cheap frying pan, this is a good-quality frying pan."

Then, later on . . .

Thinking no one is watching her . . .

Mama Roti, in the kitchen, compares her frying pan with Materena's frying pan. "Eh-eh, my frying pan, it's bigger." She chuckles to herself.

The Colorful Shirt

With Mama Roti's birthday out of the way, Materena can now concentrate on Pito's birthday present. But the problem is that Pito specifically asked her not to get him anything this year.

Last year Materena bought Pito a love-song tape and he didn't appreciate it. He said, "Why are you giving me this love-song tape? You know I don't like love songs." True, Pito doesn't like love songs — love songs irritate him or they make him laugh. Materena listens to that love-song tape — she likes love songs.

Pito told Materena that what she buys and what he wants are always two different things, so it's best she doesn't get him a birthday gift at all.

So Materena is not going to bother buying Pito a birthday gift this year. She feels a bit sad, because she likes to give birthday presents, but it's like that.

But, here, she's walking past a clothing store and a shirt hanging on the rack at the entry to the store captivates her. She stops walking to inspect that shirt.

It's a beautiful shirt — yellow and green, with splashes of red petals. Materena goes inside the store and feels the fabric. It is soft and silky and feels wonderful on the skin.

"*Iaorana,*" the salesperson says.

"*Iaorana,* I'm just looking, girlfriend."

"Okay, girlfriend, it's fine for you to look."

Materena gets out of the store. She stands outside to admire the colorful shirt. The salesperson is rearranging the rack, she glances at Materena and smiles. Materena smiles back and she wishes that the salesperson would go rearrange some other clothes. She's a bit in the way.

"It's reduced by fifty percent," the salesperson says.

"Ah, okay."

"Normally, that shirt costs three thousand francs, but now it's only one thousand five hundred francs," continues the salesperson.

"Eh — *oui,* thank you."

"It's the last shirt in stock. It's from Hawaii, girlfriend. It's very popular, the whole stock sold in a week."

"*Ah oui?*" Materena is interested now.

But she doesn't have any money on her, and it really bothers her. She wants to buy that shirt — for Pito's birthday. It doesn't matter that he ordered her never to buy him a birthday gift ever again. She wants to give him a gift. She wants to give him that shirt. You can't go wrong with a shirt. Pito can wear it on special occasions, like when there's a function at his work. He can't wear that shirt at the bar, though. She won't permit it. Women are sure going to admire that shirt and then they're going to admire the man who's wearing the shirt — even if he's married. They're not going to care about any wedding band on Pito's finger, because he'll be so handsome with that shirt on. She's got to have that shirt. If she doesn't grab it now, another woman will grab it for her husband.

"Eh, girlfriend, you accept a deposit?" says Materena, and goes on about how she usually has a couple of banknotes in her wallet. Today is an exception.

The salesperson is willing to accept a deposit. Materena goes back into the store and takes the shirt off the rack.

Materena rubs the fabric on her cheek. It is *so* soft. It is like a caress. She follows the salesperson to the counter. The salesperson opens a black book. She asks for the name and the deposit amount.

"Materena Mahi, and it's two hundred francs."

"Eh, girlfriend, you can't give me a little bit more? Two hundred francs is not enough to hold the shirt."

"Three hundred francs."

"A little more, can you?"

"Five hundred francs."

The salesperson writes *Materena Mahi* and *Five hundred francs* in the black book. "When are you coming to get the shirt and pay the rest?"

"Tomorrow, girlfriend, after I get paid." Materena counts her coins and gives them to the salesperson.

The salesperson counts the coins and puts them in the cash register.

Materena asks if she needs to sign the book.

"*Non,* you don't need to sign. Why do you want to sign?" asks the salesperson.

Materena doesn't particularly want to sign, unless her signature is required. No, her signature is not required.

"That shirt is for my husband," Materena says. Materena just can't stop herself from thinking of Pito as her husband. They're not married yet, but in her head and in her heart they are. "It's his birthday in three days."

"Ah, it's good. Lots of women bought that shirt for their husband."

Materena is pleased with the information. That shirt *is* popular.

Materena goes and picks up the shirt the very next day. She wraps it in silver gift paper and ties a red ribbon around it. She hides Pito's beautiful present under the mattress and pats the mattress. She's happy. Pito thinks she's not going to get him a birthday gift this year. He's sure going to be surprised.

Two more days and it's Pito's birthday.

But she's going to give him his birthday gift right now. Two days, it's too long to wait. Materena is impatient to see Pito with that shirt on. And what if the shirt doesn't fit him? It's better that she finds out about it now rather than in two days in case she has to take the shirt back to the store and exchange it for another shirt. She hopes the shirt is going to fit Pito. That shirt will really suit him. She can picture him wearing it.

So here she is, standing behind the sofa, hiding the silver specially wrapped gift behind her back. Pito's watching the TV.

"Pito," Materena says.

"I'll take out the garbage tomorrow morning," Pito says before she can continue.

"*Ah oui,* it's fine."

He turns his head to look at her, and she gives him a look of tenderness. She knows that he thought she was going to annoy him about the garbage.

Usually she pesters Pito to take the garbage out at night, because when you take the garbage out in the morning, you can miss the garbage truck. The garbage truck doesn't always come through at the same time. Sometimes it comes late and sometimes it comes very early. And when it comes very early, Materena is stuck with a full garbage can and she has to jump on the plastic bags to fit more plastic bags of trash in the can.

And usually there's a little argument — which Pito always wins because nothing can make him take the garbage out at night, because he prefers to take the garbage out in the morning. When you take out the garbage at night, the dogs knock the garbage cans over and there's a mess and you have to clean up the mess *illico presto* because everybody in the neighborhood knows which garbage can belongs to whom.

Materena chuckles.

"What's with you?" Pito asks.

Ah, it's so nice when you've got a gift for someone and that someone isn't expecting it. She hands Pito his birthday gift.

"What's this?" he asks.

"It's your birthday gift."

"Eh, didn't I already tell you —"

She doesn't let him finish his protestation. "Just open that present, you're going to like it." Materena's heart is beating with excitement. She can't wait to see the look of joy in Pito's eyes.

He prods the package. "Is it a towel?"

She wonders why he would think she'd get him a towel for his birthday. "Why, do you want a towel?"

No, he doesn't particularly want a towel. He was only guessing.

"It's not a towel. Open the present and you're going to see." Materena's eyes are sparkling.

Pito rips the silver gift paper. He scratches his head and grimaces. There's no look of joy in his eyes.

"What? You don't like the shirt?" Materena's eyes are furious now.

"Materena, *this* . . . it's not my style," Pito starts.

In Pito's opinion, the colors scream out, *Admire me! I'm beautiful! I'm a flower!*

In Pito's opinion, *raeraes* wear that kind of shirt, and, actually, Pito saw a *raerae* in town yesterday and that *raerae* was wearing the exact same shirt. And Pito doesn't want to be mistaken for a *raerae* and he doesn't want to be mistaken for someone who likes *raeraes*.

He's never going to wear that shirt, not even for *cent mille* francs.

Materena snatches the shirt away. "Eh, you don't need to say you're never going to wear that shirt, not even for *cent mille* francs, you know well nobody is going to pay you *cent mille* francs to wear that shirt."

Materena's disappointed, she's angry. She scrunches the shirt and gives Pito a dirty look.

"Did I ever ask you to buy me a shirt?" Pito asks. "No, I never asked you to buy me a shirt, because what I like and what you like, it's not the same."

Pito likes to buy his own shirts. He knows best what suits him.

"It's like that love-song tape you got me last year," he says.

"You already told me about that love-song tape," Materena snaps.

"And that straw hat you bought me the year before. I never wear it. It's you who always wears that hat. You know I prefer caps, so why did you give me a straw hat — plus, a woman's straw hat?"

"You already told me about that hat."

"Take that shirt back to the store and give me the money for a case of Hinano." Pito goes on watching the TV.

Materena drags the ironing board into the bedroom to iron the shirt, as you can't take a scrunched shirt back to the shop. It must be crisply ironed.

She was going to get Pito to show off that beautiful shirt on Saturday at the birthday party at Mama Roti's place, but it's not going to happen, since he thinks only the *raeraes* wear that kind of shirt.

Materena plugs the iron in, berating herself — and Pito. It's the last time I'm buying that Pito a birthday gift! You *andouille*, Materena. She knows what Pito really wants for his birthday. He wants a speedboat. Eh, as if we have the money for a speedboat. It costs a lot of money to buy a speedboat. Plus, there's the repairs and the petrol, and the motor. And what are we going to do with a speedboat?

Materena takes the shirt back to the store the following morning on her way to work. She smiles a big smile to the sales-person. "Eh, *iaorana,* girlfriend, it's a beautiful day today, eh? I thought it was going to rain, but it doesn't look like it's going to rain. And are you fine?"

The salesperson just glances at the shirt.

"Girlfriend, I have to give you that shirt back. It doesn't fit my husband. It's too small."

The salesperson gives Materena the *do I know you?* look.

"I was here yesterday," Materena says. "Check in your black book."

Ah yes, the salesperson remembers. But she can't take the shirt back — it is the store's policy.

Ah, now Materena is annoyed. "I can't exchange the shirt for a dress?"

The salesperson gives Materena the *I'm sorry* look.

Materena wants to say that it is the last time she buys some-thing from that store, but it's not the fault of the salesperson that there's a store policy. The salesperson is just an employee — she doesn't own the store.

Materena leaves the store.

She could give that shirt to her cousin Mori. It's not money lost. But first, she's going to try it on. She tries it on as soon as she gets to her work. The fabric feels really nice.

She inspects herself in the mirror in the room of her boss. Eh, the colors suit her. The shirt is a bit big but it still suits her fine. Materena lifts her arms. It looks a bit like a blouse on her. That can be my uniform, she thinks. A blouse and a pareu — it matches.

She leaves the blouse on. It's nice working with that blouse on. You don't sweat as much. She checks herself in the mirror again before leaving the house of her boss. Ah yes, it's her style.

And now, she's noticing how people are looking at her as

she's waiting for the truck at the market. People — men especially. She knows it is because of the colorful shirt. Nobody looks at her when she's wearing her clean, ironed oversize T-shirt.

A tall, lean woman walks past Materena and smiles a big bright smile at her. Materena smiles back. They're wearing the same shirt. The tall, lean woman is wearing it with bright red tights, though — she's got nice legs. Nobody is looking at Materena anymore. The tall, lean, muscular woman is more interesting because she's wriggling her bottom and swinging her bright orange handbag.

Then the suspicion that the woman is a man comes into Materena's mind.

It's not always obvious — a *raerae*. Some of them are hopeless at disguising themselves as a woman. One look at the face and you know it's a man — there's the spiky hair.

But some of them are experts, and the only thing that gives the truth away is the deep man voice.

There's a street in Papeete for the *raeraes* to wait for their clients. Materena had been past that street one night. Her cousin Mori was driving the car. And Mori yelled out from the window, "And it's how much?" And the *raerae* called back, "Come see me, my little cabbage, and I'll show you what love is all about."

They're quite flamboyant, the *raeraes*. They like to show off. They like colors.

Was that woman a *raerae?*

Materena looks down at her chest. You can't see the form of her breasts with that shirt.

Eh — people, they're thinking she's a *raerae?*

Materena chuckles and gets into a truck.

Mori and Teva, another cousin of Materena, are drinking

under the mango tree at the petrol station when Materena gets off the truck. Mori is playing "Silent Night" on his accordion and Teva is humming, but they stop to call out, "*Iaorana,* Cousin," to Materena.

"*Iaorana,*" says Materena. She wants to add, "Are you still waiting for a job to fall out of the sky?" But they are nice cousins. They just like the drink a bit too much. There are quite a few empty bottles of Hinano in the beer case.

"Eh, Materena, you're flamboyant today," Mori says.

Teva laughs.

Materena stops walking. She demands to know what Mori means by *flamboyant.*

"Well, you're colorful. I can see you really well," Mori says. "You're like, how can I say this, you're like —" Finally, Mori finds the word. "Like a peacock, Materena, Cousin."

Mori is now laughing his head off. He's laughing so much that his dreadlocks are trembling. Materena looks at him, then she looks at Teva, and she can see by the redness of their eyes that they've been smoking marijuana on top of drinking Hinano.

Materena puts her hands on her hips. "Well, you two, I prefer to look like a peacock than to look like a good-for-nothing. Are you two still waiting for a job to fall out of the sky?"

She marches away and hears her cousins say, "What's wrong with Materena today?"

"Ah, she's just in a bad mood. Some days it's best not to say *iaorana.* Some days, it's best just to drink your beer and say nothing."

Materena marches back to the mango tree and asks her cousins if the shirt makes her look like . . . like a *raerae.*

The cousins are perplexed by the question. Mori says, "Well, we know you're a woman . . . so . . ."

Teva says, "We know you're not a *raerae* . . . so . . ."

Materena waves a hand. "Ah — who cares about what you two say?" Then she stomps off again.

Marching home, Materena thinks about how difficult gift giving is. There's no guarantee. It seems that what people give and what people expect to receive are often two different things.

Materena knows this will happen with her wedding gifts, but she will accept them gratefully because that is what you should do when somebody remembers to give you a gift. In Materena's opinion, Pito should have accepted the colorful shirt that she bought him with such good intentions. He could just wear it at home if he's so concerned about his image.

Now, standing in front of the mirror, Materena asks herself if that colorful shirt is making her look like a *raerae*. No woman wants to be mistaken for a man.

"*Alors?*" she says out loud. "You look like a woman or a man?"

Later, Cousin Rita, visiting, reassures Materena. "Cousin, you have nothing to worry about. You look like a woman because you *are* a woman, and you are beautiful in that shirt, like in anything else you wear."

New Bed — New Beginning

Materena is making the bed. It's an old bed and it came along with Pito because Materena's bed was single-size, meant for one body. Materena had never felt the desire to know the history of Pito's bed, but Rita came to visit today and told Materena that she'd bought a new mattress.

Well, it's not really a *new* mattress Rita bought. It didn't come from the mattress store. Rita bought it at the secondhand store. But even if it's not brand-new, Rita said it looks brand-new. According to Rita, the person who owned the mattress before must have only used it for a week.

In fact, it's not really a *mattress* Rita bought. It's more a Japanese-style bed. It's low and a bit hard to sleep on, but Coco will get used to it. Coco says he misses sleeping in his old bed, but Rita likes the new bed better than she liked the old bed.

Here's the story.

Rita knew Coco had had lots of women before she caught his heart, and these women had never really bothered Rita until Coco's mama said to her last week, "Ah, my son, he had lots of women. They used to sneak into my son's bedroom, those women." Apparently Coco's mama had heard the *clap-clap* noise of the high-heel shoes. These women didn't come barefoot.

Coco's mama cackled and Rita cackled along. Rita's cackle

was louder. And she said to Coco's mama, "Eh, I know all about sneaking into a man's bedroom. I've done lots of sneaking myself. Ah, all that sneaking us women do."

Coco's mama looked at Rita and Rita could tell that she didn't believe her story about sneaking into men's bedrooms. Everybody in Coco's family knew Rita was a virgin when she met Coco. Coco had told his mama about Rita being a virgin and his mama had made sure to pass this information on to the coconut radio. Coco's mama was very proud her son caught a virgin.

She's always talking about Rita's virginity. One day Rita asked her, "Why are you always talking about my virginity?" And Coco's mama replied, "It's so rare, that's why I'm always talking about your virginity."

Rita wishes she hadn't been a virgin when she met Coco.

Anyway, back to the mattress story.

Within two days of Rita finding out about all those women sneaking into Coco's bedroom, she developed an allergy to the mattress Coco got from his mother for his seventeenth birthday.

Rita tried to fight her allergy. It's a bit silly to be allergic to a mattress just because other women used it before you, it's only a mattress and there's a sheet on it. Rita tried to be sensible about that mattress, but it was no use. There were just too many women linked to that mattress.

Rita revealed her allergy to Coco and he roared with laughter. In his opinion, it was months since another woman had slept on that mattress, so it was clean now. Rita's sweat and Rita's perfume had cleaned it.

Yes, true, but still Rita's allergy got worse.

In the beginning, Rita's allergy was a general physical discomfort like you get when the mattress is too hard or too soft, but within days Rita's allergy transformed into a rash all over her body.

Rita rubbed cream on her skin to no effect. She slept on the mat for one night (Coco commanded her to stop being ridiculous) and the rash went away. She slept on the mattress again and the rash came back.

Then Rita suggested to Coco that they get a new mattress and he got cranky. He said, "Rita, there are days when you tire me with your nonsense." He told Rita her allergy was in her imagination. So Rita showed Coco the rash and said, "And these red spots — it's my imagination?"

One morning, Rita carried the mattress out to the backyard and hosed it good, then she scrubbed it with lavender fabric softener, then perfumed it with lavender oil. She did all this while Coco was out, and when he came home and saw the mattress drying outside, he said, "And where am I going to sleep now?" He was really baffled.

Rita and Coco slept on the mat, and all night long Coco complained about the hard floor. The next morning it rained. And the day after, and the day after. Every morning, Rita would look at the gray sky and smile. It suited her that the mattress was getting ruined outside. But Coco was very fond of that mattress, and he didn't appreciate sleeping on the floor. He cursed Rita every single day it rained. It rained for a whole week.

So one afternoon Cousin Rita decided to buy a brand-new mattress.

In Rita's opinion, when a man and a woman get together, they should buy a new mattress, because a mattress is very important. A mattress is for sexy loving, a mattress is for words of love — a mattress is for intimacy.

So she went hunting for a new mattress, but then she spotted that Japanese-style bed in a secondhand store. She lay on it for about one hour and realized that she not only wanted a new mattress but a whole new bed. So she bought that Japanese-style bed.

A new bed — a new beginning.

Cousin Mori organized the delivery of the bed to Rita's house, and when Coco saw the Japanese-style bed, he said, "And where's my bed?" Well, Rita gently informed Coco that her cousin Mori took the old bed, along with the wet, ruined mattress, to give it to a friend who didn't have a bed, only a very old torn mat. "What!" Coco was out of his mind, and it took Rita a while to calm him.

Now everything is fine with Rita.

She sometimes thinks about how someone may have died in her bed, but she much prefers her bed to be the souvenir of a dead person than the souvenir of thousands of sweating women.

That is the story of Rita's new bed, and so Materena is checking Pito's bed, sniffing the mattress and looking for marks, when Pito comes into the bedroom to get an Akim comic.

"What are you doing sniffing the mattress?" he asks.

"Did Mama Roti buy you this bed for your birthday?" Materena looks into Pito's eyes.

"What! What is this story?"

"You bought the bed, then?"

"You want to know how I got the bed?" Pito challenges Materena.

"*Oui,*" Materena replies, although she's not so sure anymore that she really wants to know how Pito got that bed, when he got it, and how many women have slept in it.

Pito tells Materena that the bed belonged to an uncle who died. The uncle died in his bed (Pito is pointing to it), but it was days before he was found dead in his bed, as he lived alone. There was vomit and caca in the bed and the family wanted nothing to do with that bed, so Pito took it and washed it clean. He needed a new bed and free beds don't come to you every day.

Materena's eyes are popping out of her head by this time, but suddenly Pito bursts out laughing.

"You silly woman, my auntie Agathe gave me her bed when she moved to France."

Pito grabs a comic and Materena is about to inquire further about the bed but on second thought decides she doesn't want to know anything more about it.

Nobody died on Pito's bed and, as far as Materena is concerned, that is the most important thing.

But here she is now, at Conforama shop, where they sell really nice beds and you can take one home today and only start paying the installments in three months' time. Materena only wants to have a quick look on her way home from work. There is a young couple in search of a very hard bed. They sit on a bed, hop up and down with their bottoms, giggling at the same time, and at each bed one of them says, *"Non,* it's too soft." Materena thinks the couple is so cute.

But the salesperson doesn't think so. "Eh, you two," she calls out from the office. "How about you buy a bed and try it for real in your own house!"

The couple burst into laughter as they get out of the shop.

Then the salesperson spots Materena and she forgets all about the young couple. Materena is lost in admiration in front of a wooden queen-size bed that has a carved-wood headboard. She's never seen such a beautiful bed. She can visualize herself sleeping a beautiful sleep on that bed, and she'd like to sit on it, but after the salesperson's comment to the young couple, she just runs a hand over it.

"Good afternoon." The salesperson is now standing beside Materena.

Materena smiles at the salesperson. "I'm just looking," she says politely. Materena is always polite to salespeople, but even more so when the salesperson is older than she is, and she guesses that the salesperson is over fifty years old.

"Instead of just looking," the salesperson says, "why don't you make yourself comfortable on the bed? Come on."

"You're sure?"

"Of course. That's what the showroom is for. Our top-quality beds aren't just for looking at."

Materena takes her thongs off, rubs her feet clean with her hands, and hops onto the bed. Ah, she's in heaven.

"It's so comfortable," she says. "Ah, it feels so nice on the back."

"After a hard day at work, let me tell you, a woman can always do with a comfortable bed."

"*Ah oui,* that's for sure." Materena has to drag herself away from the bed.

"Stay a bit longer," the salesperson says. "It's okay."

Materena falls back onto the bed.

"Beds aren't just for reproducing," the salesperson says. "Beds are for recharging the batteries, especially when you're a woman, with all the things we do. You've got kids?"

"*Oui,* three."

"You must be busy."

"*Ah oui,* there's always something to do."

"I've got five kids," the salesperson says. "They're grown up now, but when they were little, I was always running from one kid to the other. You know what I'm saying?"

Materena nods.

"I tell you," the salesperson continues, "if it wasn't for my bed, I wouldn't be able to get up in the morning to start another day. I didn't have much money, but I've never cut costs with my beds. For me, my bed was and still is today an investment. When you have a good night's sleep, the next day is not so bad. And you cannot have a good night's sleep, I mean a *good* night's sleep, when you've got a cheap bed."

"True."

"Your bed at the moment, is it comfortable? You sleep well?"

"Ah, it's okay."

"How long have you had your bed for?"

"I've been sleeping on that bed for over twelve years," Materena says.

The salesperson does a horrified look. "Twelve years!" She shakes her head. "You should get a new bed at least every five years, because your body changes. Is it a single bed or a double bed?" The salesperson is now speaking softly, and Materena guesses that the salesperson doesn't want to offend her. The size of a bed can say a lot about a woman's situation.

"It's a queen-size," Materena says. "It came with my man, but . . ." Materena hesitates. She doesn't want to tell the salesperson the whole story about new bed, new beginning. The salesperson is waiting for Materena to continue. "Well," Materena begins, "my man and I, we're getting married this year, and —"

"Congratulations!"

"Thank you," Materena says shyly. "We've been together for over twelve years, it's about time, eh?"

"Better late than never." The salesperson sits on the bed. "I totally understand why you'd want a new bed, because it's a new beginning for you and your man. Well, why don't you put that beautiful top-quality bed on your wedding-gift list?" She pats the bed several times.

"A wedding-gift list?" Materena has never heard of such a list. All she knows is that you accept what you get. You accept the salad bowls, the pillow quilts, the sheets, the dishes . . . a gift is a gift.

"Haven't you heard of wedding-gift lists?" asks the salesperson.

"*Non.*"

"Ah, the Chinese and the *popa'a* have them, and I think it's a wonderful idea, that way the married couple gets what they want."

Materena wonders who could afford to buy her that bed. It looks like an expensive one. She can't think of anyone except, perhaps, her mother. "It might be a bit too expensive for my guests," she says.

"You can have more than one person paying for it," the salesperson says. "But it'd have to be cash on delivery, because we can only do installments with one bank account."

"So how do I go about it?" Materena is certainly very interested.

"I explain." The salesperson clears her throat. "You give us a deposit and we'll hold that bed for you, because if not, I can't guarantee that by the time you get married, that bed will still be in the shop. But, your marriage, is it for this year? We can't hold the bed for an eternity."

"It's for this year," Materena confirms.

"Okay," the salesperson continues. "You give me a deposit and I give you a receipt and make copies of it, and you just give them out to the people you want to contribute to your new beginning. They will feel very special that you've chosen them."

Mosquito Coil

After that nice saleswoman's passionate speech on wedding gifts — the kinds you want to receive — Materena signed her name in a blue book, giving Conforama the authorization to withdraw the deposit for the new bed: five thousand francs per month for the next three months, starting next month. And now, half-comfortable in the old bed, next to Pito complaining about mosquitoes, Materena is thinking of relatives who will feel honored to contribute to her new beginning. Who will she ask?

Pito kicks the quilt, but Materena is just going to ignore him.

She forgot to buy a new packet of mosquito coils. There was only one mosquito coil left in the packet, so she put it in the boys' room and Leilani dragged her mattress in there for the night.

But Materena doesn't tell Pito about that last mosquito coil, because if Pito knows there's a mosquito coil smoking away in the house, he's going to make sure that it is smoking away for him. All he knows is that there are no mosquito coils left in the packet and Materena forgot to buy a new packet.

Materena wraps herself with the quilt from head to toe, except for her mouth and nose. She doesn't like to breathe in the quilt. It makes her claustrophobic.

She can hear the irritating flying of the mosquitoes and she stays still like a coconut tree. She thinks, Soon, these mosquitoes, they're going to realize they can't get through the quilt. Now, back to the relatives and the new bed.

"*Eh hia* — these mosquitoes!" Pito growls. He hides his head under the pillow. "These mosquitoes!"

"Eh, Pito," Materena says. "The more you think about the mosquitoes, the more they're going to annoy you."

Pito slaps the pillow and kicks the quilt again. "How can anyone forget to buy a new packet of mosquito coils?"

"Do you think complaining is going to scare the mosquitoes away?" Materena asks.

"Damn mosquitoes," Pito replies.

"Go drink a beer," Materena says.

"What beer? There's no beer." Pito sits and rips the quilt off Materena to shake it.

"Pito, you're really starting to annoy me now." Materena rips the quilt back off Pito. Pito gets out of bed and switches the light on.

"Now what?" Materena sighs. Pito grabs the quilt off Materena again and starts to wave it around toward the open shutter. "What is this?" Materena asks. Well, Pito informs Materena that he's chasing the mosquitoes out of the bedroom. He waves the quilt around for a while, then he closes the shutter and switches the light off.

"Okay," Pito says as he gets back into bed. "Now try to get into the bedroom, you bloody mosquitoes."

But it is so hot now with the shutter closed, and Materena can't breathe. She's suffocating. She needs air. She gets up and opens the shutter, she's not paying attention to Pito's complaining.

She goes back to bed and wraps herself in the quilt.

And the mosquitoes fly back into the room.

Pito slaps his cheeks. "These mosquitoes! *Merde!*"

All right, that's enough now. Materena is not staying in that room one more second. She refuses to accept Pito's comedy any longer. She gets out of bed. "If a mosquito, a tiny, miserable mosquito, is too much to bear . . . imagine, a little, the contractions when us women give birth!"

"Eh-oh," Pito protests. He goes on about how he's had a mosquito coil by his side ever since he was a baby. You can't go from thirty-five years' sleeping with a mosquito coil by your side to sleeping without one. If he'd been on the booze, maybe he could, but he's sober. And he can feel these bloody mosquitoes biting into his flesh.

Materena storms out of the room and sneaks into the boys' room. She lies beside Leilani and closes her eyes, enjoying the beautiful smell of the mosquito coil.

"Did you have a fight?" Leilani asks.

Materena tells Leilani that Pito can't sleep without a mosquito coil and she can't sleep with his complaining.

"Ah . . . but can't Papi smell the mosquito coil?"

"Just go to sleep, girl," Materena says. "You've got school tomorrow."

The next morning Pito's face is sparkling with mosquito bites.

He looks very funny and everybody at the table wants to laugh, but Pito also looks very grumpy, so everybody makes sure not to look at him. But Materena has to look at Pito and she eventually bursts into laughter. The kids leave the table in a hurry to laugh in peace in the living room.

Pito gives Materena a dirty look.

"*Aue,* my husband, eh," Materena says amid her laughter. "You look so funny."

"Eh," he snaps. "I'm not your husband. I don't see a wedding band on my finger."

Materena keeps on laughing. She doesn't pay attention to Pito's remark. She knows well that when someone hasn't had a good night's sleep, there's grumpiness the next morning.

As for Materena, she had a very pleasant evening. The mosquitoes didn't bother her at all, and she was able to think in peace before falling asleep. She now has a list of possible contributors for her new bed.

The Birth of Isidore Louis Junior

Cousin Giselle is one of the possible contributors to Materena's new bed, and what luck for Materena to bump into her now! But for the moment, Materena (with daughter, Leilani, on her way home from the Chinese store) is more interested in Giselle's newborn baby boy.

She puts the shopping bags on the ground and opens her arms, meaning: let me hold that baby right now. Giselle passes Materena the baby. She's going to have a smoke.

"And how are you, girl?" Giselle asks Leilani.

"I'm fine, Auntie Giselle." Leilani is not even looking at the baby.

Giselle is all dressed up and she looks good for a woman who gave birth only a week ago. It's a bit like that with the first baby, Materena thinks, you lose the stomach quick. But past baby number three, and you still look pregnant two months after the birth.

He's so beautiful, Giselle's baby, with his brown skin and flat nose. He's all dressed up too, in a blue jumpsuit and a matching blue beanie. The beanie looks nice but it's a bit hot to be wearing a beanie. Materena lifts up the beanie a bit — that poor baby is sweating. She should tell Giselle that it's not a good day today for the baby to wear a beanie. But only Giselle's mama can tell her this and even then there's no guarantee Giselle is going to listen.

Materena rubs her nose against the baby's nose. The baby smells of talcum powder. Materena remembers when she used to put talcum powder on her babies. *Aue* — it's so long ago. Materena is feeling all bizarre inside — she's got ideas of breast-feeding that baby. It happens every time she holds a newborn baby, and she holds newborn babies on a regular basis. There's always a cousin with a newborn baby.

"You want to kiss the baby?" Materena asks Leilani.

Leilani lightly kisses the baby on the forehead.

"And where are you two going?" Materena asks Giselle.

"To town. Get a couple of things. I've just got my maternity allowance, so I'm going to spend it."

"I'll wait with you until you get the truck," says Materena, and looks down at the baby again. He's so beautiful. All babies are beautiful. Materena's babies were very beautiful. There was always a nurse to say, "Such a beautiful baby."

"And what is this beautiful baby's name?" Materena asks.

Giselle smiles a beaming smile. "Ah, Materena. I can always count on you to say nice things about my baby. You know, that good-for-nothing James, he dared tell me that my baby looked a bit like a chimpanzee. I'm never ever going to speak to him again. He was drunk, but that's no excuse — he's barred for all eternity."

"Ah, *oui alors!*" Materena can't believe that cousin. You don't tell a mother that her baby looks like a chimpanzee! What an idiot!

"And what is the name of this beautiful baby?" Materena asks again.

"Isidore Louis junior," says Giselle, looking into Materena's eyes as if she's waiting for a comment.

And for a second Materena thinks, Isidore Louis junior! What kind of name is this? What on earth made Giselle give that name to her baby?

But, then, we call our babies what we want.

"It's a nice name," Materena says.

Giselle puffs smoke. "A good name, you say? Eh, I don't really like that name."

"So why did you call him Isidore Louis junior, then?"

"I had no choice."

Materena knows she's in for a wait to find out because Giselle always has to start at the beginning of a story.

"You're not in a hurry?" Giselle asks.

"No. I'm just on my way home from the shop," Materena replies.

"There's nothing in those bags that's going to melt?"

"Ah, you're not going to talk for hours."

"Mamie, I can take the shopping home," says Leilani.

Materena discreetly widens her eyes at Leilani, meaning — *I can't believe you!*

Materena is quite annoyed with Leilani because you just don't walk away when a mother is showing off her baby to you. You're supposed to admire the baby for at least fifteen minutes.

But Leilani isn't into babies and stories about births yet, and she's bound to get bored. And, also, the butter is going to melt. "All right, then, girl," Materena says. "You go home, I see you later. And put the butter in the fridge."

After more light kisses on the baby's forehead, Leilani escapes with the shopping bags.

"Okay, Cousin," Giselle begins. "Now, here it is . . . I had my contractions at about eight o'clock."

"Eight o'clock at night or eight o'clock in the morning?" Materena is asking this question because there aren't many trucks during the night and if your car breaks down or if the person who was supposed to drive you drank too much, there can be some serious problems.

"Eight o'clock at night," Giselle replies. "I was scrubbing the kitchen."

Materena nods knowingly. "When you get into the scrubbing, it means the baby is coming."

"Well, yes, but I didn't think my contractions were the real contractions, because Isidore Louis junior wasn't due for another week. According to my doctor, he was supposed to be born today."

Materena smiles at the sleeping baby. "You're an early baby, eh?"

"When I got the contractions," Giselle goes on, "I didn't panic. I thought these contractions were only the contractions you get before the real contractions come along. Eh, how was I to know they were the real contractions? It's my first baby."

"*Ah oui,*" Materena says. "It's hard to know with the first baby. You don't have the experience with the contractions."

"Right. So I went to bed. I didn't want these contractions to turn into real ones on me, because I was alone in the house."

"And, Ramona, where was he?" Materena is asking, but she already knows the answer.

"Drinking with his mates."

"And your brother?" Materena knows the answer to this too.

"Drinking with Ramona."

"And Mama?"

"Praying at someone's house."

"You were all alone, then, eh-eh?"

Giselle nods. "If there was somebody at the house, I would have scrubbed the kitchen floor harder and with joy to get that baby out. I was a bit sick of being pregnant."

"*Ah oui,* it's like that the last month. You just want to go have that baby."

"You just want to see your feet again." Giselle looks down at her thongs.

"You want to feel light," says Materena.

"You just want to sleep on your belly."

"So you went to bed," prompts Materena.

"Yes, and I closed my eyes to sleep," Giselle says. "I thought, If I sleep, the contractions are going to go away. But I couldn't sleep."

"The contractions were hurting too much." Materena grimaces. Even though it has been years since she last had contractions, she still remembers them. Not the actual pain but the fact that she was moaning, and she was moaning because the contractions were hurting.

"*Ah oui,* they were hurting," Giselle says. "But that wasn't the reason I couldn't sleep. I couldn't sleep because I got thinking about the baby's name."

"Ah, you didn't have a name for the baby organized?" This is a shock for Materena. In Tahiti, you've got to have a name for your baby organized before the birth. There are many women giving birth at the Mamao Hospital at the same time as you — ten, sometimes fifteen. You're in this big room and the only thing that separates the women giving birth is a curtain. It can get confusing. Once, Materena was on the delivery bed with her legs apart, waiting for the doctor, and a strange man came into her room. She shrieked, and he quickly retreated. He got confused because Materena was wearing the same color socks as his woman.

It's the same confusion with the newborns. They are put into this room to get washed and if there's no name on your baby's tag, you can get another woman's baby by mistake. With Materena, as soon as she gave birth, Loana followed the nurse holding her baby.

You've got to have a name organized.

Well, Giselle had a name organized — sort of. Her mama wanted to call the baby this. Ramona wanted to call the baby that. And then there was the *maman* of Ramona, who wanted the baby to be named after one of her ancestors.

"And you — what did you want to call the baby?" Materena asks.

Giselle lovingly looks down at her beautiful baby. "I wanted to call my baby Michel."

Materena thinks how the name Michel is so much nicer than the name Isidore Louis junior, but there are circumstances when you've got to give your baby a name you don't like.

"So, you were in the bed trying to sleep," Materena says.

"Yes, and the contractions got stronger and stronger. I turned this way, and I turned that way. Then there was a popping noise."

"Your waters broke." Materena remembers the popping noise.

"*Ah oui,* the bed was all wet," says Giselle. "I cursed Ramona because he was drinking with his mates. I cursed my brother because he was drinking with Ramona, and I cursed Mama too because she was praying at someone's house."

Giselle was in a lot of pain by then, and when you are in pain like this, curses just fly out of the mouth.

"I got out of bed to call somebody," Giselle goes on. "But then I remembered that the phone was disconnected because my brother spoke to a mate who's doing military service in France, and, that brother of mine, he spoke on the phone for two hours and seventeen minutes! The telephone is still disconnected. He wanted me to pay the telephone with my maternity allowance and I told him to go to France to see if I'm there."

"Ah, *oui alors,*" Materena says. "The maternity allowance, it's not to pay telephone bills."

"*Ah non,* it's to buy yourself a couple of nice things, like a new dress . . . So here I was, I couldn't telephone anyone, and I was panicking, so I went into the kitchen to look for that coconut Mama bought for me a few days before."

"To drink the juice to make the baby come out easily," Materena says.

"*Oui*. Did you drink the coconut juice with your births?"

"*Oui*."

"And it helped you with the pushing?"

Materena thinks about this for a moment. She's not sure that drinking the coconut juice actually made her babies slide out easily, because it never seemed to her that any of her babies slid out easily when she was pushing them out. But you're expected to believe in the powers of the coconut juice because thousands of women before you have.

"Yes, it helped a bit," Materena says. "And with you, it helped?"

"I couldn't find the coconut. I looked in the fridge, I looked in the pantry, I looked everywhere, but I couldn't find it. I didn't know Mama had put the coconut in the baby's suitcase."

So in desperation Giselle drank half a bottle of cooking oil because, in her opinion, oil makes things slide.

Materena laughs, but she can't laugh her hysterical laughter because of the baby sleeping in her arms. Her laughter is more a snort.

"Eh, Cousin," Giselle says, "I was desperate . . . I drank my oil, then I went outside. I looked at the sky and I cried, 'God, Virgin Mary, Jesus Christ — please help me. I don't want to give birth all by myself. I'm afraid. Please send someone my way. Send me an auntie who's an expert at giving birth to help me.'"

Materena stops snorting. It's not good to give birth by yourself — especially when it's your first time.

"And an auntie arrived?" she asks, hoping for Giselle that it was their auntie Stella who arrived, she being an expert midwife. Stella delivered Materena, and Loana was so pleased with Stella that she requested her to deliver Materena's brother. Loana didn't want the doctor.

"No. It's Cousin Mori who arrived," replies Giselle.

"Cousin Mori!" Materena exclaims, and thinks, What help would that cousin be to a woman in labor? But Cousin Mori is better than nobody.

"Mori arrived in his rusty clunker Peugeot," Giselle says. "He was looking for François — to go out drinking, of course. And I said to Mori, 'Mori, it's a good thing you're here. You can drive me to the hospital.' But first I had to ask him if he still had his driver's license. I just wanted to make sure that his driver's license hadn't been canceled. When the gendarmes pull you over and there's no license, they give you all sorts of troubles, you have to get into their car and go to the gendarmerie for hours of questions."

"Ah, they would have seen you with your big belly and driven you to the hospital — pronto," Materena says.

"It's not for sure," replies Giselle. "There's a story about how a gendarme stopped a car and the driver didn't have a license, so he got his woman, who was pregnant, to act like she was about to have the baby. And the woman went on moaning and complaining about the pain. So the gendarme put his flashing red light on the roof of his car and escorted the other car to the hospital. But the gendarme decided to escort the pregnant woman right to the delivery room. A nurse examined the pregnant woman with the monitor, then she told the gendarme that there was no way the pregnant woman was in labor. All the gendarmes in Tahiti know that story. And now when they see a pregnant woman acting like she's about to have a baby, they get suspicious."

"Ah," Materena says. "But they would have known you

weren't acting when you started pushing that baby out at the gendarmerie."

Giselle gives her a horrified look. "I don't want to push no baby out at the gendarmerie. Think about it — you're born and the first person you see in your life — it's a gendarme." Giselle shakes her head. *"Ah non."*

"So Mori had his driver's license?" Materena asks.

"Yes, he showed it to me, and I checked the date. Then I asked him if he'd been on the booze. I didn't want a drunk driving me to the hospital."

"Ah, true, it's not sure you're going to get to the hospital," says Materena.

"Yes, it's more guaranteed that you're going to be dead. Like with Ramona, he was going to stop his drinking one week before the birth, I made him swear on his grandmother's head. That's why that night he was out drinking big-time — to make up for a whole week of abstinence."

"And, Mori, he wasn't drunk?"

"*Non,* Mori said he'd only drunk a miserable half glass of beer. I got him to breathe on my face and I smelled his breath. His breath smelled more of onions than beer. I was satisfied. Then I asked him if he was sure that his car was going to get me to the Mamao Hospital in one go."

"How many questions did you ask Mori?" Materena is beginning to wonder if Giselle was truly in labor, because, to her recollection, a woman in labor doesn't think about asking questions.

Giselle only asked Mori three questions. One question about the driver's license, one about the booze, then one about the car.

"And what did Mori say about his car?" asks Materena.

"He said, 'Eh, Cousin, maybe my car looks like it's a pile of shit, but, I tell you, it's a good car, the engine is in perfect condition.' Then Mori went on and on about how his car just got a complete tune-up and how he much prefers a car that can drive around the island over one hundred times without stopping to a car that only appears to be in good condition. So I went to get the baby's suitcase, then I wrote a note for Mama to say that I was at the hospital — then I got into the car. It's okay with you to hold the baby?"

"Of course," Materena says. He's sound asleep, baby Isidore Louis junior.

Giselle rolls another cigarette. "Mori's pile of shit broke down at Tipareui. First there was a clunking noise, and soon after that there was another clunking noise, louder, then a bang, then nothing. And it was a good thing Mori got the car to stop on the side of the road and not in the middle. I don't like it when the car breaks down in the middle of the road. A car can come flying into you."

Materena shivers, then nods in agreement.

"I didn't panic," Giselle says. "It's no use to panic."

"*Ah oui,* it's best to stay calm and breathe slowly," says Materena.

"Yes, I breathed slowly. And Mori said, 'Ah, don't worry, Cousin.' He grabbed the flashlight from the glove box and the tool kit from the trunk and he got into fixing his car. And I spoke to the baby. I said, 'Don't you come now, it's not a good time.' But one minute I was fine and the next minute I got this contraction and it was hurting so much, I cried out loud. Then I yelled, 'Mori, what's with your bomb?' And Mori announced to me that his car was now a wrecked and smoking pile of shit."

"*Ah hia hia,*" Materena says. "And after? What?"

"Eh, what was I supposed to do? Here I was, contracting, and Mori's car was smoking, and Mori was moaning about all the money he paid for the complete tune-up."

"Some complete tune-up."

"He got done real bad. He went to the wrong mechanic."

"He got a cheap job."

"That's what happens when you pay shit — you get shit."

"True, Cousin. And what did you do? Did you walk to the hospital?"

"Walk, Materena?" Giselle looks at Materena like she can't believe what she's hearing. "You're crazy! With me contracting? *Non,* I decided to stop a car."

"Ah, that's good thinking."

"Yes. A car passed us and I waved and put my hands on my belly to make the person in the car know that, my waving, it had something to do with me being pregnant. But the car didn't stop."

"The car didn't stop!" Materena exclaims. "There are some people in this world!"

"Another car passed — same thing. Then I realized that perhaps people didn't stop because of Mori."

"Ah." Materena understands. Mori is over six feet tall, he's a big man with a beard down his chest, and a Rastafarian hairstyle. He is also covered in homemade tattoos. If you didn't know Mori, you might get scared of him. He looks . . . well, he looks a bit like a thug, and he is, but he's no mean person. In fact, he's quite gentle.

"What did you do with Mori?" Materena asks.

"I got him to hide behind his wrecked car. Another car passed me and I waved and pointed to my belly and the car stopped. It was a brand-new Mercedes-Benz. A young man — a *popa'a* — got out of the car. I told him about my contractions and he said to get in the car, so I got in the car."

"What about Mori?"

"Ah, Mori got into the car too," Giselle says. "I'd completely forgotten about him when the back door opened and Mori appeared with the baby's suitcase. Mori said to the driver, 'Don't worry, mate, she's my cousin.' So, here we were, speeding away to the hospital, and seconds later, I got this urge to push. I tried to hold myself from pushing, I didn't want to mess up the man's brand-new car, but, Cousin, I could feel the baby's head. I wanted to scream because it was like my arse was getting ripped, but I controlled myself. You don't scream out in front of people you don't know. Eh, I was a bit embarrassed. If the driver was old — okay, but he was young and so handsome, Cousin. He looked like an actor."

"You, eh," Materena chuckles.

"It's not every day we see a handsome man." Giselle winks and laughs. "Anyway, we got to Papeete, and I said to myself, Baby is coming — baby is coming. So I asked the young man, 'Is it okay with you for me to have the baby in your car? Because my baby is coming.' The young man just looked at me for one second and then he pulled over to the side of the road. And I said to him, 'My cousin Mori, he's going to clean up the mess.' And I said to Mori, 'Eh, Mori, you're going to clean up the mess?' And Mori said, 'You can count on me.' I took my undies off, I put my feet on the dashboard, and I pushed."

And Isidore Louis junior was born.

Materena's eyes are teary. Birth stories always make Materena's eyes teary.

"The young man — his name was Isidore Louis junior?" she asks.

"*Non,* just Isidore Louis. It's me who added *junior.*"

"Ah, and, Mori, he cleaned up the car?"

"*Non,* because when Isidore Louis junior was born, Isidore Louis drove us to the emergency room at the hospital and then he just took off."

"Maybe he wanted a professional cleaner to clean his car."

"Eh, he'd need a professional cleaner, with all the blood and the shit."

Materena looks down at Isidore Louis junior. "You sure have a story to tell your kids."

Giselle smiles. "*Ah oui*. It's not every day a baby gets born in a brand-new Mercedes."

Here's a truck coming, and Giselle waves a little wave, meaning, please stop right in front of me. Then she flicks her cigarette away and, smiling, takes her precious son back.

"Have fun shopping," Materena says after one more kiss on her nephew's forehead.

"Oh" — Giselle shrugs — "I wish." She adds that she'll probably end up paying for the phone bill because she wants the telephone connected in case there's an emergency with her baby, like she needs to call an ambulance. One thing is for sure, though, the telephone will have a padlock on it and the key will be with Giselle twenty-four hours a day. She's not paying for long-distance calls. She has enough bills coming out her ears.

And, having given this insight into her poor financial situation, Giselle walks to the truck while Materena mentally erases her cousin from the list for the bed.

Sexy Loving

What about Rita? thinks Materena as she's walking home. For sure, she'd love to be part of the contribution team, being Materena's favorite cousin and everything. If she's not chosen, she might actually be very offended. But, first of all, it might be a good idea to see what Rita thinks about wedding-gift lists.

Some people prefer to surprise the bride. Now is a good time for Materena to inquire, since Rita is coming around for a while.

Presently, the two cousins are soaking themselves in tubs filled with cool water, legs and arms dangling and bedsheets hanging on the line for privacy.

"Rita," Materena begins, "what —"

But Rita has her own ideas for the topic of conversation. "Cousin," she blurts out, interrupting, "I wanted caresses two nights ago."

Ah, okay. That kind of conversation. "With Coco?" Materena asks.

Rita raises her penciled eyebrows. "Of course with Coco. What do you think?"

Materena was just being curious. Sometimes it happens that a woman wants caresses from a man other than her man.

"I decorated the bed with frangipani flowers," Rita goes on.

Materena chuckles. "*Ah oui?*"

"I massaged my body with coconut oil. I combed my hair wild-style, put a bit of rouge on my cheeks, and sprayed eau de cologne behind my ears and on the pillows. Coco was watching the soccer match on the TV."

"Pito watched that soccer match too."

"Well, Cousin, it would have suited me more if there was a documentary on the TV instead of that soccer match. I waited for Coco to come to bed, I kept calling out, '*Ouh-hou,* Coco, I'm waiting for you, darling.' But Coco was too hypnotized by the soccer match to hear my calling. After a while I got out of bed and marched to the living room. I paraded gracefully in front of the TV, and then I accidentally let my pareu slip away — to show off my oiled body. Coco didn't even blink. So I said — with my sexy voice — 'Coco, my Coco.' But he just waved for me to get out of the way."

"*Ah non!*" says Materena.

"*Ah oui!* So I turned the TV off, and Coco ran to the TV and turned it back on. Then he said to me, 'Are you going to let me watch my soccer match or what?' Oh-la-la, I was so cranky, I tell you, Cousin. You know when you're in the mood, you've got to be satisfied, eh?"

"*Ah oui,* Cousin. You've got to have satisfaction."

"I went back to bed," Rita continues, "and I waited for my Coco to come give me satisfaction. He cheered, and I cheered too. I wanted Faa'a to win, that way Coco would feel like celebrating."

There and then, Materena knows Rita didn't get her satisfaction. Faa'a lost to Pirae by two scores. She knows this because Pito was in a bad mood all through the second half. He kept on swearing birds' names, and at one point he got so angry with the players, he swore at Materena because her ironing was disturbing his concentration. She had to resume her ironing in the kitchen.

Eh, but maybe Coco decided to forget the loss in the arms of Rita.

"He came to bed in a bad mood," Rita says. "I knew Coco was in a bad mood — all the swearing he did, all the thumping, and I thought, Ah, I'm going to give him a little head scratch and then he's going to relax on me."

"That's a good idea."

"I scratched Coco's head for about five minutes." Rita glances at Materena and smiles. "Sexy scratching, of course."

"Yes, of course." Materena smiles back at Rita.

"I waited for Coco to attack me," Rita goes on, "but there was no attacking and I was getting *fiu* of scratching Coco's head, so I attacked Coco with kisses. I attacked for about two minutes, then I got *fiu* of kissing, so I got on top of Coco. And his *moa,* it was soft. He said to me, 'I'm too sad about the match, Rita.' And I said to him, 'Okay, but tomorrow you better give it to me . . .' But he didn't give it to me last night."

"Eh, he was probably just tired, Cousin."

"I can't believe Coco refused to give me satisfaction last night. He's never refused to give me satisfaction in all the six months we've been together. I tell you, Cousin, there's another woman feeding my Coco. My problem, Cousin, is that Coco is handsome. So many women look at him. They walk past and they turn around. They can't help themselves, because, my Coco, he's got beautiful eyes. So many women want my Coco. Sometimes I think I should have got myself a bald man."

"It's hot, eh?" says Materena, trying to change the subject.

But Rita doesn't want to talk about the weather, she wants to talk about her Coco and how he didn't give it to her last night. "I'm going to do some investigation, Cousin. That Coco better watch out, because if I find out that there is another woman, I'm going to give Coco the potion — there will be no hesitation."

"What potion are you talking about?" Materena is worried now.

"The potion that makes the *moa* soft," Rita says.

"There's such a potion?" asks Materena.

"*Ah oui.* An old woman who lives in Taravao makes that potion. Lily told me about that old woman."

"Our cousin Lily?" Materena wants to make sure Rita is talking about their cousin Lily and not another Lily, because it seems so unlike their cousin Lily to use a potion that makes a *moa* soft. Lily is much more likely to be interested in a potion that makes the *moa* hard.

"Yes, our cousin Lily," says Rita. "Anyway, that old woman, she told me how when she was young she got hurt so bad by a man that she decided to dedicate her life to helping other women who get hurt by a man. That woman, she was in love with that man and he promised to marry her, but he married another woman instead. Her potions are cheap, and any woman can afford to buy them. You buy the potion in a bottle of whisky. You put two teaspoons of that potion in the beer for ten days and then the *moa* becomes soft . . . and it stays soft forever."

"The *moa* stays soft *forever?*"

"*Ah oui,* for eternity, Cousin." Rita nods several times to confirm this. "That Coco, he's going to regret the day he decided to get himself another woman. What, I don't feed him enough?"

"Cousin, you feed Coco plenty," Materena says, and she should know, since they talk about it often.

"I tell you, Cousin, he better give it to me tonight . . . It's his last chance." Now Rita has a mean look on her face. "No sexy loving tonight, and I'm going to get that potion, give it to Coco for ten days, and then I'm going to burn all his clothes and get myself another man."

"You're not going to do the investigation first?"

"*Ah non*. It's too hard to do the investigation. No sexy loving for me tonight equals soft *moa* for Coco for the rest of his life."

When Rita leaves, Materena is tempted to run to the telephone booth to contact Coco at his work and tell him that he better give Rita some sexy loving tonight, but . . . women's talk is secret.

On her way to the Cash & Carry store the next day, Materena can't get Rita's threat off her mind. Materena isn't comfortable about Rita giving that potion to Coco. What if the potion made Coco have a heart attack? Rita might be charged with murder, and Materena with conspiracy. She has to ring Rita.

Rita works at a shop where they sell fabric, and the person who owns the shop always answers the telephone because Rita is supposed to be selling the fabric to the customers. And when you call Rita at her work, you have to tell the boss of the shop that you're family and that your call is about something important regarding the family.

"Hello, it's Rita's cousin here, and I have to talk to Rita now — it's about the family."

"Don't you two speak for too long." The shop owner is quite abrupt.

"*Ah non*, I only need to talk to Rita for one second."

"This is a business."

"Yes, okay."

Materena hears the shop owner yell at Rita to come to the phone, it's her cousin and it's about the family. Rita comes to the phone.

"Rita, it's me." Materena knows the shop owner is looking at Rita. "Just say yes or no. Coco, did he give it to you last night?"

"*Ah oui*, ten out of ten." Rita sounds so happy today. "And tell Grandma I'm going to take her to the hospital for her checkup, okay? I go now, there's customers."

Materena is relieved. Then she starts to laugh.

That Rita, thinking her Coco has a mistress. Materena can't imagine Coco doing the sexy loving with another woman. In fact, she can't imagine Coco doing the sexy loving, full stop. The thing with Coco is that he's quite large. Not just large — he's massive. He must weigh over 280 pounds. His nickname, it's Sumo. When Rita introduced Coco for the first time, Materena said to Rita, "Have you got eyes?" But it is Rita's affair if she wants a sumo. Plus, Rita is quite large herself. She and Coco go well together. But it's really funny to think about two sumos doing the sexy loving.

And that Rita, she's always on heat.

Eh, that's because she was thirty-two years old when she discovered the sexy loving — with Coco. Now she's catching up for all those years when she was a virgin and her cousins were having babies.

Tapeta

Materena bumps into her cousin Tapeta outside the Cash & Carry just as they are getting their shopping carts to go inside. They give each other two kisses on the cheeks.

"It's hot, eh?" Tapeta says.

"*Ah oui,* Cousin," Materena agrees. "It's hot."

"And you're going to do some shopping?"

"*Oui,* just a couple of things."

"Ah, me too. A few corned beef cans, toilet paper, soap."

"And how are the kids?" Materena asks.

"My Rose, she wanted to play the piano," Tapeta says.

The piano! Materena thinks, but she best not sound too surprised about it. Tapeta might snap, "What is so surprising about my Rose wanting to play the piano?"

"The piano?" Materena sounds interested.

"Eh, it was a shock for me when Rose told me she wanted to play the piano. Well, Rose didn't actually say to me, 'Mama, I want to play the piano.' She more said, 'Eh, Mama, if I played the piano . . . eh, I like the music.'"

This is strange, Materena thinks. We don't listen to that kind of music and there are certainly no piano people in the family, and that's going back one hundred years. We sing; we play the guitar and the ukulele.

Well, Cousin Mori plays the accordion. He "found" an accordion in a truck when he was about twelve years old and took it home and taught himself to play. He's very good at it.

But nobody plays the piano. There must be some piano-music tapes at Tapeta's house. In Materena's opinion, you can't want to play the piano if you've never heard the music or if you don't have the musical instrument to play it with. Materena knows there's no piano at Tapeta's house, so since when do they listen to the piano music?

"You listen to the piano music at your house?" Materena asks.

Tapeta gives her cousin a funny look. "Us? Listen to the piano music? You're laughing!"

"How come Rose wanted to play the piano, then, if she's never heard the music?"

"Eh, you don't need to hear the music to want to play. Like me, when I was little I wanted to play the violin and I've never heard the violin music."

"You wanted to play the violin!" This time, Materena shows her surprise.

"Well *oui*." Tapeta giggles. "But don't tell anyone, eh? I'm embarrassed."

"Ah, okay. So Rose wanted to play the piano."

"Yes, my Rose, she wanted to play the piano. They have a piano at the school."

Ah, well, now Materena understands.

Apparently, every lunchtime Rose would sit next to the piano-lesson room and listen to the enchanting music of the piano. They have piano lessons at that school if you've got money to pay for them. So Tapeta decided that her daughter was going to play the piano too.

"You know I'm the kind of mother who'd do everything for my kids."

"*Ah oui,* I'm the same too," Materena says.

She could go on about all the things she does for her kids, but the story isn't about her kids. It's about Rose and that piano.

"You know I don't have much money." Tapeta does her air of pity.

"Yes, it's the same for me too." Materena also does her air of pity.

"But when your kid wants — you try your best to give," Tapeta says.

"True, you're a good mother, Tapeta."

"Thank you, Cousin. You too, you're a good mother. We all know what you do for your kids."

Materena wants to ask for some examples, but it's up to Tapeta to list the examples. You don't just ask . . . But Tapeta isn't going to list examples — she's got her story to tell.

"I got all dressed up and I went to the school office to get a bit of information about the piano lessons. I wore my matching blue long skirt and blouse. They're my best clothes."

"I wear my best clothes too when I go to the school office to pay the school fees," Materena says.

"You should always wear your best clothes when you go to the school office."

"Ah, true. It's all about presentation." Materena checks on her chignon.

"It's fine to wear your pareu when you go to the school office to pay the school fees," continues Tapeta. "But when you go to the school office to get a bit of information about the piano lessons, you have to look really presentable. Because, the piano lessons, they're not for us people, they're for the rich, so you have to look a bit rich."

Materena wants to say that it's no use pretending you're rich to the school office people, because they have information about everyone in their filing system. They know Tapeta is a cleaner at the hospital and that her man is a good-for-nothing. But Materena keeps her mouth shut because her cousin doesn't like to be reminded that her man is a good-for-nothing, and she doesn't like to be reminded that she's a cleaner at the hospital. As far as Tapeta is concerned, she's a nurse.

"So, you told the school office people Rose wanted to play the piano?" asks Materena.

"*Non,* I just asked for the price."

"And it was how much?"

"Ten thousand francs — for the month."

"It's not bad."

"It's still a lot of money. I can feed my family for a whole week with ten thousand francs. That ten thousand francs missing, I felt it, let me tell you. We ate a lot of breadfruit."

"Breadfruit is nice," says Materena.

"*Ah oui,* I could eat breadfruit every day."

"Me too."

"It's good to have a breadfruit tree."

"*Ah oui,* you can always rely on the breadfruit tree when money is a bit low." Materena knows what she's talking about.

"I always tell the kids that when they buy a house, to check that there's a breadfruit tree in the garden first. And even if the kids are just going to rent — they should check that there's a breadfruit tree in the garden first."

"Rita and Coco did this when they were looking for a house to rent," says Materena. "They checked the garden for a breadfruit tree first before checking the house. There are three breadfruit trees where they live now."

"Rita and Coco don't need a breadfruit tree," says Tapeta. "They've got money and no kids."

"Eh, Cousin" — now Materena is on the defensive — "just because you've got money and no kids, doesn't mean you can't eat breadfruit anymore. Rita, she loves breadfruit."

"I like breadfruit in the stew." Tapeta is back to her bread-fruit recipes.

"Me too. I prefer breadfruit in the stew to potatoes."

"And barbecued breadfruit — it's nice, eh, when the butter melts on the breadfruit."

"Fried breadfruit too, it's nice." Materena hopes this talk about breadfruit isn't going to go on for hours. She's getting hungry.

"Baked breadfruit. I like breadfruit. It tastes nice and it fills the stomach quick. We ate a lot of breadfruit for Rose to play the piano." Tapeta smiles for a while.

"*Aue,*" she goes on. "My Rose, she didn't believe me when I told her that she was going to learn to play the piano. I had to show her the official receipt for her to believe that her piano lessons weren't an invention."

"She was happy, eh?"

"*Ah oui* — she said to me, 'Thank you, Mama,' and when she said this to me, eh, I didn't regret the ten thousand francs anymore — because when I found out about the price, I told myself, 'Ten thousand francs!' But then I told myself, 'Eh, you're going to be really proud when your daughter plays the piano. And what's ten thousand francs? Money is just money — you spend. When you die, you can't take money with you.' And, Robert, he had the nerve to go cranky at me about that ten thousand francs, and you know what I said to him?"

What could Tapeta have told Robert? Materena thinks for a few seconds. "Pack your bags and move back to your mama?"

"But *non,* I didn't say that! I just said, 'Shut it.'"

"Ah."

"It's not his affair what I do with my ten thousand francs," says Tapeta.

"*Ah oui,* you work hard."

But what happened with the piano lessons? Something did

happen, because otherwise Tapeta would have said, and right from the beginning, "You know what? Rose, she can play the piano!" Materena waits for her cousin to carry on with her story.

But first Tapeta has to fan her face with her hands, and after several long, annoyed sighs, she continues. "I asked Rose after the third lesson what song she could play and she told me that she had to do a bit of study about the notes of music first. And I said to her, 'You tell me when you can play a song, and I'm going to come to the school to listen to you.' And Rose said, 'Okay, Mama.' I paid another month. And there was still no okay. So one day, I decided to go to school on my way to work to listen to Rose play the piano. I stayed outside the piano-music-lesson room and opened my ears and what I heard . . . *Ah hia hia,* let me just tell you that it wasn't a melody. And I said to myself, 'Twenty thousand francs for that horrible noise!' Eh, I wanted an explanation. I waited for the lesson to finish. When Rose got out of the piano-lesson room, I hid behind the wall. Then I went to see the music teacher."

Materena listens intently.

"I asked that woman how come, my daughter, she's not playing good. And the woman said, 'Your daughter must practice every day, she must dedicate herself to the piano . . . playing the piano must become an obsession.' And I said, 'My daughter, she must practice every day?' 'Absolutely,' the piano teacher said. And I said, 'Practice on what?' And the piano teacher said, 'On her piano, of course!' I was getting more and more confused by the second. 'What piano are we talking about here?' I asked."

Tapeta looks into Materena's eyes. "You know what that Rose did?"

Materena guesses that Rose lied to her music teacher that she had a piano to practice on, but it's best to act like you don't know the rest of the story. "*Non.*"

"That coconut head lied to the piano-music teacher that her

grandmother bought her a piano! Ah, I tell you, I was so cranky with Rose. When I got home from work, I went straight to her and said, 'And how are your piano lessons?' Rose said, 'Everything's going well, Mama.' And I said, 'So, you're practicing every day on the piano your grandmother bought you?' Rose, she looked at me and then she started to cry on me. You know how kids cry on you when there's trouble coming their way. You haven't even done anything yet and they're bawling. Eh, I slapped Rose full on the face . . . It's okay now. Rose gave me some explanations. She realized from the third lesson that you're supposed to have a piano when you're learning to play the piano, and she was going to tell me that she didn't want those piano lessons anymore, but I'd already paid for another month.

"And when the piano teacher asked Rose if she had a piano, Rose thought she better lie. She thought if she told the truth, the music teacher was going to stop the music lessons and then my hard-earned money would be gone in the wind."

"Kids, eh." Materena smiles, thinking how nice Rose is, inventing that story about her having a piano so that her mother's hard-earned money wouldn't be wasted.

Tapeta must get on with her shopping now. So the cousins wheel their carts into the Cash & Carry store.

But Tapeta has one more thing to add. "You can draw a piano on a piece of cardboard and practice on that . . . but you need to hear the sound."

"Ah, true, Cousin," says Materena. "With music you need to hear the sound."

Inside the Cash & Carry, Materena thinks about how, Tapeta, she's by far the greatest singer at St. Joseph Church. There's always a bit of showing-off at Mass, with one cousin trying to sing higher and better than another one. But when Tapeta decides to go to Mass, no one dares try to surpass her, not even their cousin Loma, who has quite a beautiful voice herself.

Tapeta's voice is deep, powerful, and very moving. It comes from her soul and it is impossible to compare. When Tapeta sings "Ave Maria," mamas cry, papas cry, the priest cries, everybody gets goose bumps. As she pushes her cart, Materena hopes that Tapeta won't mind singing "Ave Maria" for her as she enters the church to get married. That would be a wonderful wedding present and an honor for Materena.

And Tapeta won't have to spend money she doesn't have.

Imelda

Later, waiting for the truck to get moving, with her Cash & Carry bags at her feet, Materena realizes that all of her relatives (well, 99 percent of them, anyway) are, like herself, struggling with their finances. It's not like they have money to spare for a bed they'll never sleep in.

There's no way Materena can ask her relatives to contribute to her bed now. She can't believe she ever thought of asking them in the first place! How insensitive of her! It's best she forgets about that bed completely. Or pays for it herself, though she'll have to ask for an extension with the payments.

In fact, Materena thinks sadly, it's best she forgets about the whole marriage story too. No wonder only a few Tahitian people get married. Between the gifts, the food, the drinks . . . forget it. Might as well keep living in sin.

Sighing, Materena looks out the window and recognizes her godmother, Imelda. Yes, that's Imelda's bleached pandanus hat and her missionary dress. Materena hops off the truck with all her stuff clattering and bumping around her and starts chasing her godmother. But another woman beats her to it. Imelda and the woman are now hugging and talking. Imelda sees Materena and waves, and now Materena has to wait for her to be free.

Materena wants to talk to her godmother. She hasn't seen her for almost a year because Imelda is always overseas now with her husband, Hotu, Materena's godfather, visiting their children.

Imelda looked after Materena and her little brother for a while when they were kids and she made them feel very welcome in her life. Imelda, she's got a gift for making people feel welcome in her life. Materena remembers the story of the Australian surfer.

Imelda immediately liked the look of the tourist her man brought home. The tourist was from Australia, Imelda had never heard of that country before then. The Australian had two surfboards and a backpack, a good-looking face, and good manners, and his handshake was strong and honest.

That day, Imelda was going to cook lentils, but since there was a tourist, she changed the menu to barbecued fish and rice, raw fish, and taro.

She forced the tourist to eat. He was shy, embarrassed to help himself a second time. There was a lot of giggling at the table, Imelda had to tell her daughters to quiet down or they were going to scare the tourist away.

The tourist got up to clear the table. Hotu, using sign language, told him to sit down, digest well, the girls here do the clearing. But the Australian went on with the clearing-up, smiling and nodding all the while. The girls hurried to beat him to the clearing-up. It was the same with the washing-up.

The word around the neighborhood was: *Leave that tourist alone or you're going to regret it. Steal his surfboards and no more teeth left in your mouth.*

The tourist was protected and he didn't even know it.

Imelda took her looking after that tourist kid seriously. When he wasn't home by dark, she would worry herself sick. She imagined a shark having attacked him or him having drowned. By the third day of his stay, she was giving him long hugs like he was her son.

One Saturday morning, the whole family caught the truck to Papara with him. Mats, *glacière,* ten bread sticks, bits and pieces . . . they settled on the black sand. They watched him surf. "Good wave!" they cheered. When he fell off, they sighed. Then Imelda's daughters went for a swim in their shorts and shirts, and her son walked around the beach showing off Andrew's surfboard, pretending that he was a surfer.

That morning, Imelda thought how nice it would be if the Australian surfer stayed with one of her daughters. Good-looking grandchildren with blond hair and green eyes would result, for certain.

As to her daughters, the three of them had an interest in the Australian, no denying it. They'd had an argument at the beach and Imelda knew it was about him. If she were their age, she'd be fighting over him too. But he must have had a woman waiting for him back in his country, because all he did to Imelda's daughters was smile. Or perhaps the daughters weren't his style.

Imelda really wanted the Australian tourist to be part of her family, but you can't force these things.

The tourist stayed twenty-three days at Imelda's house, a long time, more than enough for Imelda to grow very attached.

The day Andrew left was a sad day. Everyone in the family cried at the airport as they farewelled him with shell wreaths, and they watched the sky until they couldn't see his plane anymore.

Aue . . . they missed eating with him at their table. The girls had trouble eating for a whole week.

Imelda never heard from her adopted Australian son again. No letters, no visits, nothing. It's been six years now. Everyone else who had ever stayed at her house sent Imelda photos and letters written in another language. And four of those tourists came back for her daughters and her son.

But all Imelda got from Andrew McMahon was dead silence.

"He must have died in the surf," Loana reassured her cousin.

"You just don't eat at someone's table for twenty-three days and give nothing in return. The poor kid must be dead — bless his soul."

Every now and then, Imelda goes to the church to say a little prayer for Andrew McMahon. That is how nice she is.

Imelda is still listening to the woman talk, but her eyes are on Materena. She finally excuses herself and hurries to greet Materena, her arms open wide.

"Materena, girl!" Imelda grabs Materena's face and kisses her on the cheeks, the forehead, the eyes, the nose, and the mouth. "How are you?"

"I'm fine, Godmother," Materena replies as she hugs her godmother real tight. The two women go on with their hugging for several minutes.

"How's Mamie?" The women are no longer hugging, but Imelda is holding Materena's hands.

"She's good, Godmother. The legs are a bit stiff when she wakes up in the morning, but otherwise her health is good."

"Eh," Imelda says. "It's from all the dancing your mamie did when she was young, but better the legs being a bit stiff in the morning than something more serious."

"*Ah oui,* Godmother."

"I'm going to see Mamie, if not tomorrow, the day after," Imelda says.

"*Ah oui,* Mamie will be very happy to see you."

Imelda looks at Materena and there are tears in her eyes. She hugs Materena again. "My girl, eh," she says. "But you're not a little girl anymore."

"*Eh oui,* Godmother," Materena says. "I've got gray hair now." The hug tightens before Imelda gently pulls away.

"And you? You're fine?" Materena asks.

"*Oui,* girl, health is good, but I'm a bit tired. Godfather and I have just come home from Australia yesterday. You know it was our twenty-ninth wedding anniversary last week. Chantal, she took us to that restaurant on top of a tower. We could see the city of Sydney."

"*Ah hia!*" Materena has no idea what the city of Sydney looks like, but it must be impressive to see it from the top of a tower.

"And you, girl" — Imelda rubs Materena's hands — "any marriage plans?"

Materena frowns. "Marriage plans?"

"Don't forget: when you get married, Godfather and I, we will be paying for the wedding."

"Really?" Materena beams. "You're serious?"

"Of course I'm serious. That's what godmothers are for."

Materena squeezes her godmother's hands. "Thank you, Godmother!" But she can't resist asking, "Ah . . . and how do you know I'm going to get married one day?"

Imelda smiles and wags her little finger. She always does this when she means to say, "My little finger told me." And when Imelda's little finger tells her, she's never wrong.

New Carpet

Since Imelda's generous proposition to pay for the wedding, Materena has been very conscious about her house. Well, she's always been conscious about her house, but more so since she's decided that's where her wedding reception will be. People might say, "We're not here to look at the house," but people always snoop around for things to notice. Materena certainly intends to have the bathroom tiled before her wedding. She's got a few hundred tiles her cousin Lily gave away, but there's not enough to tile the bathroom.

But today Lily is giving away some carpet to the first person who comes and gets it from her house. Materena can hide the old linoleum underneath the carpet that Lily doesn't want anymore, and that's a start. So Materena gets the wheelbarrow — Lily's house is only about two hundred yards away.

It's a good thing Pito and the kids are out visiting Mama Roti.

Materena looks strange pushing the wheelbarrow on the side of the road, and people look at her. Materena doesn't care — all she's thinking about is her brand-new carpet. That carpet falling from the sky is a chance and she's grabbing it.

Someone toots the horn and Materena waves without paying attention to the driver of the car — it must be a relative. She doesn't recognize the white Fiat, though — it must be a relative who has a driver's license but doesn't have a car, and that relative must have borrowed the car from a mate. It's not important to Materena who tooted the horn.

But, here, the car stops, right in the middle of the road, and a voice yells out, "Materena!"

Materena looks at the person who's driving the car. It is Mama Teta. Mama Teta toots the horn again and she's all smiles.

"*Iaorana,* Mama Teta!" Materena waves at Mama Teta and glances at the two cars stuck behind the Fiat.

"I just bought this car for my business," Mama Teta says. "It's beautiful, *oui?*"

"Ah, it is, it is." Materena mentally counts the cars now stuck behind Mama Teta's Fiat. There are seven.

"And where are you off to with that wheelbarrow?" Mama Teta asks.

But the angry drivers are now tooting their horns and a few of them are yelling obscenities. And so Mama Teta waves to Materena and speeds away.

Materena goes back to pushing the wheelbarrow as fast as she can.

When Materena arrives at her cousin's house, she's sweating already. When there's something free, you can be sure lots of cousins are going to want it, and the news about that free carpet must already be on the coconut radio. Materena stops at the grapefruit tree — about five yards away from the house — and calls out, "Cousin!"

It's not recommended to stand at the front door and call out — you should always stand away from the house. Cousin Lily might be doing something of a private nature — something only *she* needs to know about — and Lily might get real cranky at Materena for finding out about her private business. And the last thing Materena wants is her cousin to get cranky at her and decide that she's not really giving her carpet away.

Materena waits for Lily to call back to her. Perhaps Lily is putting a pareu on. Every two seconds, Materena turns around to see if someone else is arriving.

Lily is not at the house, she must have gone to the carpet factory to buy her new carpet, but Materena is not sure. Before, it was easy to know when Lily was home, because her old Citroën would be parked outside. But recently Lily sold her car and bought a Vespa. And Lily keeps her Vespa in the house. She keeps her Vespa in the house because she's afraid it's going to get stolen if she keeps it outside. She also keeps her Vespa in the house because she doesn't want people to know when she's home. She might be very busy with one of her many secret admirers.

Materena slowly walks toward the house, all the while calling out, "Cousin, are you in the house?"

There is a note taped on the door. *Carpet out the back.*

Materena runs to the wheelbarrow and then runs to the back of the house. The carpet is neatly stacked on some old tin roofing. Materena grimaces. The carpet is bright green.

Green carpet? she thinks. I thought the carpet was brown. That carpet looks to me like the grass a bit, *non?* Eh, but we don't care about the color!

The carpet is cut into squares, and Materena is happy. It's easier to load squares of carpet into the wheelbarrow than a roll of carpet. She takes a square and puts it under her feet to test.

Ah, it's so soft. It feels really nice on her feet.

So Materena loads as many squares of carpet into the wheelbarrow as she can. Still, she will need to do quite a few more trips. There's no time to waste. She pushes the wheelbarrow along the side of the house and stops at the front door to rip the note off.

Materena is about one hundred yards away from her house when she hears a cousin calling out to her. It sounds like Loma. Materena walks faster because she doesn't want to stop and have a little chitchat, and especially not with her cousin Loma.

"Eh, Cousin! Cousin! Cousin!"

Loma's high-pitched voice is getting on Materena's system and she could just keep on going and ignore it. But the thing with cousins is that once they've decided to talk to you — you can't escape. And the thing with Loma is that once she's decided to talk to you, she'll follow you right to your house. Materena has to stop for a little talk, here, on the side of the road. She doesn't want Loma to follow her home. It's easier to cut a little talk short when you're talking on the side of the road than it is in the house. She puts the wheelbarrow down and turns around.

Loma's face is all red from the running she's had to do to catch up with Materena, which was difficult with the bags of groceries she's carrying with both hands. Loma's face is also all red from the blush she's smeared on her face. Loma plonks the bags of groceries on the footpath and bends down. She's got a stitch.

Materena wonders why Loma wants to talk to her now instead of going straight home with her shopping. Her butter will melt.

"Cousin — I can't believe you didn't hear me!" Loma puffs.

"I was thinking about something," Materena says.

"It's hot, eh?" Loma is lifting her T-shirt up and down to let some air get in.

"And, Mama, she's fine?" Materena asks.

"*Ah oui* — Mama is fine. Last night she wasn't fine. Last night, she was a bit sick. But she's fine now." Loma is eyeing the carpet.

"Ah, that's good your mama is fine," Materena says, all the

while thinking, What is it Loma wants to tell me? What's the gossip?

"Is this the carpet from Lily?" Loma asks.

"*Oui.*"

"Lily is getting herself new carpet?"

"I don't know," Materena replies.

Loma feels the carpet. "That carpet is like new, why does Lily want to get new carpet?"

"Who said Lily's getting new carpet? Eh, what if it's new linoleum she's getting? And that carpet is not really like new. It's an old carpet. Some of the squares are ripped — there, at the bottom of the pile."

"*Ah oui,*" Loma says.

Materena doesn't want Loma to think that the carpet Lily is giving away is of good value, because Loma will put the news on the coconut radio and then cousins from everywhere will start invading Lily's property for that carpet. At the moment, the cousins might be thinking that the carpet Lily is giving away is old and ripped. Usually when you give something away, that something is not top quality.

"The color is a bit bizarre," Materena says. "I mean — for a carpet."

"Ah yes, now that I'm looking. The carpet looks like grass, eh?"

"But when you get something for free, you don't complain about the color."

"Ah, true. You just accept the color."

Well, now Materena is going to get rid of Loma. It's enough talk for today.

"Okay, Loma, I'll see you another day."

"Okay. But, Cousin, can I ask you something? Can I put my plastic bags on top of the carpet? I push the wheelbarrow."

Loma is already picking up her plastic bags off the ground.

Ah, now it's too much. What is it with cousins that they

always ask you for a favor when you're not in the mood to grant it? And how can you refuse a cousin? A cousin who's going to tell everybody about how she was really tired that day and then she saw Materena with the wheelbarrow and then she asked Materena if she could put her bags of groceries in the wheelbarrow and then Materena said, "*Ah non!*"

So Materena is pushing the wheelbarrow to Loma's house and Loma is holding on to her bags of groceries so that they won't fall off the wheelbarrow.

It's a good thing for Materena that it is Loma who's asking her the favor and not a cousin who lives past Materena's house.

Materena can't push the wheelbarrow as fast now — the groceries are heavy.

"What's in the bags?" she asks. "Rocks?"

"No — cans of pineapple juice," Loma replies. "It was on special. It's for the punch."

"Ah well."

So Materena is pushing and Loma is babbling away about how Lily always makes her boyfriends jealous and she should be careful because one of these days a boyfriend is going to go mad on her. Already, the last boyfriend burned all Lily's clothes. And the boyfriend before that one smashed all Lily's expensive china bowls. What is Lily's new boyfriend going to do?

"I can't believe Lily's choice of boyfriends!" Loma is rolling her eyes.

Materena wants to tell Loma to shut it. She's not particularly interested in backstabbing Lily, considering the carpet. But Loma is only trying to make compensation — the babbling is to entertain Materena. That way Materena won't think too much about the extra load, and before she knows it she'll be at Loma's house. Also, Loma always finds something bad to say about people, she just can't help herself.

They're at Loma's house.

Materena unloads the bags real fast. The last thing she needs is for Auntie to decide to have a little talk with her about how her mama and the rest of the family are doing. Loma thanks Materena, but Materena is already pushing her wheelbarrow away.

Then Loma runs after Materena. "Cousin, can I ask you something? Can I have some pieces of carpet, not many? Ten is plenty."

Ah, now she wants Materena's carpet! It's too much!

"It's to put in the bathroom." Loma does her air of pity.

And before Materena has the chance to tell Loma that you don't put carpet in the bathroom, Loma is explaining that when she gets out of the shower and her feet touch the concrete floor, she gets cold and she'd much prefer her feet to touch the carpet.

Materena gives Loma ten pieces of carpet and she's off, pushing that wheelbarrow as fast as she can.

Materena is at her house — finally. She unloads the carpet onto the terrace.

Back for another load.

The living room is fully carpeted now, and Materena is resting on her new floor, arms and legs stretched out. She's tired. All that pushing, all that moving things from the living room to the terrace — from the terrace back to the living room.

Pouf.

But it's all done now — everything is super. When you lie on the linoleum, you can feel the hard concrete. But you can't feel the hard concrete when you lie on the carpet, which is on top of the linoleum. All you feel is the softness of the carpet.

Materena is still enjoying her brand-new floor when Pito and the kids come home. They see the green carpet and they look like they can't believe their eyes, because when they left the house this morning, there was linoleum in the living room, and now, this afternoon, there's carpet.

Ah yes, they're surprised.

"What is this?" Pito points to the green carpet.

"My new floor," Materena replies as she gets up.

"Where did you get the carpet?"

"From my cousin Lily."

"And where did you put the linoleum?"

"It's underneath the carpet."

Pito shakes his head. "You're not supposed to put carpet over linoleum. You're supposed to take the linoleum out and then put the carpet over the concrete."

"Eh, you know how hard it is to take the linoleum out! And we don't care if the carpet is on top of the linoleum. I prefer the carpet on top of the linoleum."

"Okay," Pito says. "But don't come telling me later on that there's a problem with the linoleum."

Materena frowns. There's a problem when you put the carpet over the linoleum? "What problems are you talking about?" she asks.

"Eh, the linoleum can rot," Pito says. "I don't know. All I know is, you don't put carpet over the linoleum."

Materena shrugs. "It's done — it's done."

"It looks like grass." Tamatoa is laughing.

"When you get a job," Materena says to Tamatoa, "you can buy your hardworking mother a carpet of another color."

"The living room looks like a soccer field." Now Pito is laughing too.

"I prefer a soccer field to old, ripped linoleum," Materena snaps.

"Me too." Moana and Leilani are relaxing on the soft carpet, and soon Tamatoa joins them.

"Ah well, one less room for you to mop, then, eh?" Pito goes on.

"I didn't think about that, but, yes, no need to mop the living room anymore — it's good for me."

It has always been a nuisance for Materena to mop the living room. When she mops the living room, she has to guard it to make sure no one is walking on the linoleum until it's completely dried, and it is a nuisance to guard the living room, because she has to stay in it. Most of the time, though, she waits until everyone is in bed to mop the living room.

"No need to sweep either." Pito is grinning.

And Materena knows he's really happy about her not sweeping the living room anymore. She knows very well that Pito thinks she's a pain with her broom because he'll be reading his Akim comic on the sofa and she'll start sweeping all over the place and wanting him outside.

But how will she clean the living room now? She didn't think about that matter when she hurried to get that free carpet. She'll need to buy a vacuum cleaner.

"I'm buying a vacuum cleaner," Materena says.

When she sees Pito's expression, she goes on about how she'll go to that place where you can take things today and pay later on — little by little. A vacuum cleaner can't be that expensive. But Pito hurries to warn her that vacuum cleaners are the worst equipment, vacuum cleaners break down easily in Tahiti because of the humidity, and it's very difficult to get the parts — you can wait up to one year for the store to get the parts from America.

Materena is startled by that revelation. She's thinking, and then an idea comes into her mind.

"I can use the straw broom," she says.

Pito hurries to agree with her. Apparently, one of his aunties' friends who's got carpet in her house uses the straw broom too.

Let's do a test.

Materena gets her straw broom, which she uses to sweep the terrace and the bathroom. She also gets a bit of soil from outside. She spreads the soil on the carpet and vigorously sweeps.

The straw broom works fine and Materena knows that Pito is very happy about that because, if she drives him mad with the broom, she'd drive him even madder with a vacuum cleaner.

And now Materena is taking a lemon tart to Lily to thank her for the carpet. Materena would have got her a chocolate cake from Chocolate My Love, but Lily doesn't like chocolate cakes. She only likes cakes with fruit in them.

Materena knows that a lemon tart is a small thing compared to yards of carpet, but when you give a small thing the right way, it becomes a big thing. And Materena intends to give the lemon tart the right way — the only way that shows deep appreciation.

First she's going to give Lily a big hug, and then she's going to say, "Ah, thank you so much for your carpet, it's so much better than my old, ripped linoleum." And then she's going to give her the lemon tart and say, "I made it especially for you — my cousin."

Materena doesn't want to hear on the coconut radio that Materena got all the carpet from Lily (and isn't it a miracle how she managed to get all the carpet before we got a chance) — and what did she give Lily in return? Eh — the wind!

There's a BMW parked in Lily's front yard. Lily is not alone, and Materena doesn't know what to do next. She imagines that Lily is with her latest boyfriend and they could be doing the sexy loving. Then again, it could be just one of Lily's friends from work.

And Materena wants to give the lemon tart to Lily right now. If she takes it home, it's going to disappear. Already, when Materena took the tart out of the oven, Pito and the kids came running into the kitchen. She had to shoo them away and promise she'd make them a tart when she got home.

But, this tart in her hands, covered with a tea towel, it's for Lily. Eh, she's going to call out.

But there's a strange sound coming from the house. It's a cry, it's a moan — it's both. Materena opens her ears and she hears Lily shout like . . . eh, like she's getting strangled.

My God, it's the new boyfriend strangling Lily!

Materena's heart is pounding against her chest. She delicately puts the tart on the ground. Okay, what do we do now?

She's going to kick the door open and . . . but first she needs a weapon. Materena looks around her in panic. Ah yes, the shovel. She gets the shovel leaning against the grapefruit tree.

What if the boyfriend has a bush knife, and he's big, and he's muscular? Materena hesitates. Should she go and get Mori?

Should she assess the situation?

Materena tiptoes to the front window. The curtains are pulled close but the window is open. Materena, very slowly, without breathing, and using one finger, makes a little space between the curtains.

There's Lily lying naked on a rug and there's a woman (naked too) on top of her, and they're both wriggling in the position sixty-nine.

Ah well, Lily must be sick of those jealous men who always give her troubles.

Materena is sure relieved that Lily is not being assassinated. Still, she's annoyed Lily's got company. She'll have to let Pito and the kids have this tart, and come back another day to give Lily another tart.

Or she might just get Lily a hand-printed pareu from Rita's fabric shop and send it by the post.

Maco and His Girlfriend

Right after buying Lily two (not one) hand-painted pareus, Materena is on her way to see Cousin Georgette, who is the disk jockey at Club 707, to talk about music. The appointment is in fifteen minutes, so Materena walks faster. She thinks about the day when her cousin Maco introduced his girlfriend to the family.

Maco had had lots of women before he found Georgette. He had had younger women, older women, married women, who all fell for his muscular body and his good-looking face.

The married women gave Maco gifts, like a gold chain or a watch. But none of those women, gift or no gift, kept Maco's interest for more than a month, because Maco always got bored. His eyes wanted to look into other eyes and his hands were eager to caress other *titis*.

Then Maco met Georgette and that was the end of his Casanova career.

Maco has been with Georgette for two years now, and he's still very hooked on her. When they dance, Maco and Georgette are one body and one rhythm, and Georgette drives Maco crazy with her sexy moves.

When Maco announced that there was someone very special he wanted to introduce to the family, his mama, Stella, thanked

God and Jesus. There had been no formal introduction with any of the other women. In fact, few of Maco's girlfriends even made it to his mama's house.

Stella, she didn't appreciate her son's popularity with women. She was always saying to Maco, "You be careful with all those women. One day, one of them is going to curse you. And you stay clear of married women, you hear? You don't need to get another man's woman. You don't need to be that desperate."

She wanted him to settle down, be serious, and give her lots of grandkids to fuss over. She had loved babies since she was a child herself, and no one was surprised when she became a midwife. She never got over that thrill of seeing a new baby . . . Eh, but lately she was a bit *fu* of congratulating others on their grandchildren and not having a grandchild of her own to fuss over.

Ah, Stella was so thrilled with her son's serious announcement. "Ah, finally. Thank you, God and Jesus." She said this over and over again as she cleaned her house and cooked her speciality — coq au vin.

Over the next few days, Stella tried to get a bit of information about that special woman — information such as family, job, and physical description. But the only information Maco was willing to reveal about his serious girlfriend was the name.

Georgette.

"She's pretty?" Stella asked, thinking how horrible that name Georgette was.

"You'll see," Maco replied.

Georgette made her entrance in a sleek new black Honda. Stella, and Maco's papi, Jean, watched Georgette get out of the car, and they were more than a little shocked. Georgette was tall and muscular, and she was wearing tight pants and huge fluorescent plastic loop earrings.

Georgette was very nervous. She was smiling the smile we smile when we're not sure if we're really welcome.

Stella, being very good at hiding her true feelings, managed to hurry to hug Georgette. But deep inside she was thinking, What is this story? She looked over to Jean and he gave her the shocked look back.

Georgette had brought some presents with her. "A few little things," she said shyly. Two bottles of Dom Perignon, pâté de foie gras, crackers, and some expensive cheese — not the Chesdale Stella always got.

Dinner started.

Stella said to herself, Don't get alarmed. Georgette will last as long as the others before her: a very short time. Her baby son was entitled to be silly now and then, although he was going a bit too far this time.

She remembered the other women, the ones she had sometimes met in her house by accident. They had all been very pretty. She particularly liked that Leila, the one before Georgette. She was a real beauty, that one, Maco and Leila would have made gorgeous children together. But Maco must have dumped her for Georgette.

There was no way Stella was going to let that Georgette hang around for more than a day. Tomorrow morning she'd talk some sense into her baby boy's thick head. He had to get rid of that Georgette as soon as possible, before the relations found out about Maco's latest girlfriend. Stella didn't want her relations to laugh at her behind her back. Stella didn't want her relations to laugh at her, full stop. But in the meantime she'd be her hospitable self.

"Are you all right, *darling?*" said Maco, sitting next to his woman.

"I'm fine. I'm fine."

"You want more rice?"

"Yes, please. And more chicken too."

"You're hungry tonight." Maco gave Georgette a sexy wink.

Georgette giggled. Stella blushed, and even Jean blushed a little.

Maco looked at his mother and father. "Okay, you two, we stop the comedy, eh? Yes, Georgette is a *raerae*. She looks like a man, she talks like a man — because she *is* a bloody man."

Then, turning to Georgette, who was laughing, Maco said, "My family's not usually this quiet. For example, once Papi gets talking, he doesn't stop. When nobody wants to listen to him, he talks to the wall, eh, Papi?"

Georgette smiled, this time a real smile. "Ah, there's nothing wrong with talking to the wall. I talk to my pillow sometimes when I need to say words I don't want anybody to hear."

"I talk to the dog. A dog never tells you to shut up," Maco said.

"I'll never tell you to shut up . . . but don't shit me." Georgette was now slowly rubbing her shoulder against Maco's shoulder.

Stella, who was getting annoyed, felt she better say a few words to Georgette. "Ah, this one . . . he's sure going to give you shit heaps of the time. Maco, he's a lazy bugger. I always say to him, 'I hope you're going to find a woman who's not going to mind cleaning up after you.' I'm sure not going to clean up after him all my bloody life. He takes after his father. Oh well, I thought I better warn you."

Georgette put an arm around the man she loved. "If your son is ready to take a big, ugly, hairy fellow like me, then I'm ready to take him as my lover the way he is."

"I like you, Georgette, you've got balls!" By then Jean was quite drunk.

"I'm glad you reminded me of my balls." Georgette laughed, and filled Jean's glass with more Dom Perignon.

Dinner went on until one o'clock in the morning. Then Georgette went home to bed. Not long after, Jean staggered to bed too because Stella had given him the signal to make a disappearance. But first Jean made sure to tell Maco that, Georgette, she was thumbs-up. He had really enjoyed the champagne and the expensive cheese. Stella, she's a bit mean with the money.

Stella, all alone with her son now, flicked his ears. "What's gotten into your thick head, son? Since when do you fancy *raeraes?* God gives you a good-looking face, and what do you do? You go grab a man who needs shaving all over. What are people going to say?"

"Ma, I don't care what people are going to say. The first one I hear laughing, I'm smashing."

"*Aue,* son . . . Leila, she was good for you. Poor Leila, I liked her. Poor Leila. You and that Georgette . . . she's more a George than a Georgette. Anyway, you and her, I mean, him, it's not serious, is it?"

"We get on well," Maco said.

"Georgette can't give you children. You don't want children?" asked Stella, starting to cry. She was crying because her only child wasn't going to give her any grandkids and she was obsessed with having grandkids. Every time she delivered a newborn these days, she said to herself, "I want a grandkid."

Maco tenderly took his mama into his arms. "I just want to be happy, Ma, eh? Please understand."

The relatives were very shocked with that Georgette. They said, "Between them two, who's the man and who's the woman?"

Maco gave James a bruised nose and a black eye for the honor of his Georgette. Apparently James had said to Maco, "So, I hear you're sleeping with a *raerae?*"

And Stella slapped Loma across the face for the honor of Georgette. Apparently Loma had said, "Auntie, I can't believe Maco is a homosexual!"

Maco and Georgette live in the country district now, where

it's a bit quieter. They have a house by the sea. When Stella and Jean visit them on the weekend, Georgette spoils them rotten.

And people all over Faa'a say, "Aren't they lucky, those two."

Now Materena is at the Club 707, but the glass door is closed. She knocks, and waits facing the door. She knows that people walking by are looking at her up and down, but she's wearing a dress and you can see the form of her breasts. Club 707 is a *raerae* club and has quite a reputation for its shows. Not everybody is allowed into Club 707 to watch the shows. You've got to look respectable (no young men wearing thongs and shorts are allowed in, for example) and you've also got to have money. The entry fee is quite high and drinks cost twice as much here as at the other clubs. Rita went to watch a show once with Coco and apparently Coco's eyes were fixed on the dancers, but Rita didn't get jealous, because the dancers were men. And, according to Rita, the club was packed with women yelling, "Take it off! Take it off!" But there were also a few old men quietly drinking in the dark.

Materena knocks on the door again.

Finally, Georgette appears. She opens the door. "Cousin!" Georgette gives Materena two sloppy kisses on the cheeks. "Come in." Georgette is wearing knee-length khaki shorts and joggers with pink socks, and a white blouse tied in a knot at the front, showing off a pierced belly button. They walk to the "office," a little room filled with mirrors, wigs, earrings, and racks of costumes. Materena can see a nurse uniform, a police uniform, a black dress with silver buttons from top to bottom . . .

And there are blown-up photographs of men displayed across the wall. They're all showing off their muscles. Materena recognizes her cousin Maco, wearing nothing more than a piece of cloth on his private parts.

"Right," Georgette says as she gets her notebook. "As you told me on the phone, the friend of your boss is getting married. Do you have a date?"

Materena was using a little *mensonge*. If she tells Georgette the truth, Georgette will tell Maco and then Maco will tell his mama. Then everyone will know! And Materena wants to keep her marriage a secret until she's set a date. "*Non,* I don't have a date, she didn't give me one. But it's for soon."

"It's for this year?" Georgette says.

"*Ah oui.*"

"Well, you came to the right place. I'm the best." Materena nods in agreement. "Music is very important," Georgette continues, clicking her fingers like castanets. "Nobody cares about food at parties. You could serve corned beef with rice and people would rave about the party for years if they've danced all night long, because dancing makes people feel happy."

Materena nods again, although she doesn't really agree with Georgette, but she guesses that in Georgette's world, food comes second to music and dancing.

Georgette goes on about how the disk jockey's aim is to make people go home thinking happy thoughts such as, I feel so young tonight! I feel so beautiful! I want to live! I'm so happy I've married you!

By the time Georgette has finished her speech, Materena wants to hire her on the spot. She can see that for Georgette, being a disk jockey is a passion. And Materena thinks how hard it must be for Georgette to make people want to dance at weddings when she'll never get to dance at her own wedding.

"Okay, thanks so much, Georgette," Materena says at last. "I'm going to highly recommend you to the friend of my boss." Georgette smiles.

Materena is now ready to get down to business. "And how much do you charge?"

"Three thousand francs per hour."

"Ah, you charge per hour? Not per night?" asks Materena.

"I'm available until people will be too tired to dance."

"And you? You don't get tired?"

Georgette looks down for a brief moment. "I love weddings," she says. "I feel very privileged to be part of one."

Fifty Francs

The second relative for Materena to visit is her cousin Moeata.

Cousin Moeata used to be unemployed, but she's got a business now called Chocolate My Love, and the business is thriving because Moeata's chocolate cake is truly succulent. It melts on your tongue and somehow when you eat Moeata's chocolate cake, you get happy.

Materena has tasted Moeata's chocolate cake a few times. Once Moeata borrowed some scissors from Materena and never gave them back. When Materena asked for them, Moeata said, "They're lost, but here's a chocolate cake in compensation."

Moeata's got lots of regular customers, Rita and Georgette, to name a few. Moeata keeps all her money in an old coffee can buried in her backyard.

She's saving for a car, a brand-new one. Materena, on her way now to Moeata's house to ask about the cost of a wedding cake, remembers the story of Moeata and the unpaid debt.

Twelve years ago Moeata borrowed fifty francs from a Chinese girl in her class and she promised to pay the fifty francs back the next day. But when the next day came, Moeata didn't have the fifty francs and she lied that she forgot the coin at home. And when the next day came, she gave the lender the same story. And every single day, the Chinese girl asked for her fifty francs.

"Where's my fifty francs?"

"*Ah hia,* I forgot. I'll pay you back tomorrow."

The Chinese girl who lent Moeata the money made sure to tell everybody about the unpaid debt.

Now, there were occasions in the following weeks and months when Moeata had a fifty-franc coin in her pocket, but . . . well, she just couldn't bring herself to part with it. She wanted to have something in return for that fifty francs — a packet of Twisties, Chinese lollies, things to eat.

Every now and then, Moeata would say to herself, "*Ah hia,* give the fifty francs back," and then she would tell herself, "Ah, don't worry, it's only fifty francs, and she's Chinese, she's got lots of money."

One year passed.

Moeata went to Pomare High School and the Chinese girl went to the Anne-Marie Javouhey College. The fifty francs became history.

More years passed.

One day, Moeata saw the Chinese girl in town, and Moeata made sure to disappear into the crowd. She told herself again, "*Ah hia,* I should just go give her that fifty francs and let's not think about it anymore."

But how do you give back a fifty-franc coin? A ten-thousand-franc banknote, yes, but a fifty-franc coin? And, plus, Moeata believed the Chinese woman wouldn't have recognized her.

And then Moeata applied for a loan for a car, a secondhand car, cheap.

She got the papers at the bank and filled them out cautiously. There was this question: have you ever defaulted on a loan?

Moeata laughed, and circled the answer *non.* Surely that fifty-franc loan didn't count here.

Moeata dropped her loan papers at the bank and within two days she got a phone call from the bank with regard to an interview with the loan officer. Apparently, the loan officer just wanted to ask Moeata a couple more questions before making a decision, because a few of Moeata's answers were a bit unclear.

So Moeata went to the bank.

Someone led her to the office of the loan officer.

Eyes met eyes . . .

And would you believe that the loan officer was the same girl who lent Moeata the fifty francs, that particular fifty francs?

Moeata's first impulse was to run out of the office, but she managed to overcome her shock. She really wanted the money for her car. "Ah, it's you who's the loan officer!" she said, smiling.

"I thought the name was familiar." The loan officer's voice was very cold, very businesslike.

There and then, Moeata got her purse out of her bag. She was so nervous that she dropped her purse and ten-franc coins went flying everywhere on the carpeted floor. Moeata got on her knees and picked up her coins, all the while thinking, Of all the days I need a bloody fifty-franc coin, and all I've got are bloody ten-franc coins.

Moeata had to pay off her debt with ten-franc coins. "Here. That's fifty francs — total." If she'd been white, her cheeks would have been red from the embarrassment.

The loan officer, looking at Moeata straight in the eyes, took the coins and shoved them in her drawer. Then she got right down to business.

Well . . . Moeata didn't get her car loan approved. She says it was because of that fifty francs it took her so long to pay back. How was she to know that the Chinese girl was going to get a job with the bank instead of working at her father's grocery store?

Moeata is busy melting chocolate in the kitchen when Materena arrives unexpectedly.

"*Iaorana,* Cousin!" Materena calls out.

"You're not here for your scissors, are you?" Moeata looks a bit worried.

"Don't be silly, Moeata! My scissors are probably rusted by now. It's been six months since you borrowed them." Materena can't believe Moeata is bringing up the subject of scissors today. "I'm here to inquire about wedding cakes." And before Moeata starts wondering, Materena hurries to clear up the situation. "It's for a friend of my boss. She's getting married this year."

Materena glances at the three big ovens standing side by side, and the three gas bottles. There's enough gas in this kitchen . . . Materena tries to push the thought out of her mind, but she can't. "Do you make sure to turn off the gas every night?" she asks.

"*Non,*" replies Moeata. "But Mama does."

Ah, Materena is relieved. "So, what's the price for a wedding cake?" she asks.

"How long is a piece of string?" Moeata shrugs.

"Eh what?"

"I can't give you a price if I don't know how big the cake is going to be," explains Moeata.

"Well, how about we say the cake is going to be big, like this." Materena draws a square with her hands. "But it'd be good if there's a decoration on it, just so it doesn't look like a normal cake. Perhaps you could write the names of the married couple on it?"

"*Oui,* I could do that. I've got other kinds of decorations too. Red roses are very popular at the moment. Red being the color of love, and people do marry for love — most of them, anyway."

"*Ah oui,* that'd be nice. Okay, put red roses on the cake, then."

"The friend of your boss, she wants roses on her wedding cake?"

"I'm just going to give her the price," Materena says. "But she trusts me. I've told her all about your chocolate cake, the best chocolate cake on the island."

"How would you know, Cousin? I never see you here buying my cakes. The only one you've tried is the one I gave you a while ago in exchange for the lost scissors."

Materena scratches her head. "I was going to, many times, but then I didn't have the money."

"You know well I would have given you credit. You're family." Moeata looks like she's sulking.

"True, but you know me. I don't like to owe people money," Materena says slyly. End of discussion.

Moeata gives Materena the price, and it's twenty-five thousand francs. Materena nods, but inside she's yelling, *Twenty-five thousand francs!* And she's thinking this marriage is going to cost her godmother a lot of money. The problem with Moeata's cakes is that they keep going up in price. Moeata really wants that new car.

But you have to be prepared to pay the price if you want people to enjoy the wedding cake, and Materena has no doubt they will if it's one of Moeata's cakes.

"You think it's expensive?" asks Moeata.

And before Materena has the chance to say anything, Moeata says, "People will spend thousands of francs on music — but who cares about music?"

"Ah, it's nice when people dance. They go home happy."

The chocolate is melted and Moeata moves the family-size cooking pot onto the table. "Who is supposed to be happy at a wedding, eh?" she says. "The guests? Or the married couple?"

"Well, if the —"

Moeata interrupts. "A wedding cake isn't *just* a cake. It's the most important part of the wedding, because it symbolizes the beginning of the husband and the wife's journey. When they cut the cake, they both hold the knife."

"*Oui.*" Materena knows this, but she doesn't understand how cutting the cake is symbolic of a journey.

"They both have a hand on the knife," Moeata explains. "It's not just the wife's hand." Moeata opens the palm of her right hand and looks at it. "It's not just the husband's hand." Moeata opens the palm of her left hand and looks at it. "It's both their hands." She clinches her hands together in a gesture of prayer. "Together. Together in sickness and in health. Together for better or for worse."

Materena thinks that Moeata must have been to a few prayer meetings lately. But it makes sense, what she's saying.

A Little Drive with Mama Teta

Mama Teta is a professional wedding-car driver. She started her business just weeks after she got her driver's license. Initially, Mama Teta had wanted to be a taxi driver, but when she thought about it seriously, she realized that too many people prefer to catch the truck, because it's cheap and there's always a truck available. Anyway, driving newly married couples has turned out to be a much more lucrative business.

Mama Teta's business is doing okay. Materena can't honestly say Mama Teta is the best wedding-car driver in Tahiti, because, well, Mama Teta's driving is a little erratic. However, she is definitely the nicest wedding-car driver in Tahiti. And now Mama Teta is very happy about her niece Materena coming to her house to bring her new business.

"Okay now." Mama Teta claps her hands together. "As you told me on the telephone yesterday, the friend of your boss is getting married?"

"*Oui,* that's right. She's getting married this year and she's just after a price."

"Where is she from?" asks Mama Teta.

"Tahiti." Materena gives Mama Teta a blank look.

"*Non,* not what country, girl! Where does she live? And where is she getting married? I need to know the distance I'm going to drive."

Materena nods, thinking that Mama Teta is like a taxi driver after all. "Well, I don't really know where the friend of my boss lives, but she's getting married at the St. Joseph Church, and I think that she doesn't live too far from the church. But she'd be interested in a tour of Papeete and everything."

"Of course," Mama Teta says. "You've got to have the tour, especially if you live so close to the church."

"*Ah oui.* It's a question of letting people know that you've just got married."

"People like to see a bridal car," Mama Teta says. "They always stop to look." Mama Teta smiles. "There's something magic about a woman in a wedding dress, on her way to the church in a bridal car. She's like a princess."

Materena smiles. "Brides are so beautiful, eh?"

"*Ah oui,*" Mama Teta agrees. "A woman about to get married is radiant, but it's nerve-racking, though, and I've had some real stressed-out women in my car. That's why the wedding-car driver has to be more than just a professional driver." Mama Teta smirks. "Honestly, girl — and you better make sure that the friend of your boss understands — the most important thing on a wedding day is to arrive at the church calm and relaxed."

And in one piece, Materena thinks. She nods.

"One of my brides," Mama Teta continues, "she was so nervous that she started to shake." Mama Teta demonstrates. "I thought she was having a convulsion, and then she started to cry, and her father said, 'You wanted this marriage, so stop crying.' I looked in the rearview mirror — usually I don't do this, but I had to check the situation — and, my bride's father, he was just looking at the view outside, as if he was on a tour bus!" Mama Teta shakes her head and sighs. "Hopeless, that man was.

And so I decided to take action. I started to sing 'Kumbaya, My Lord,' and, my bride, she relaxed like that." Mama Teta snaps her fingers. "When we got to the church, my bride, she was smiling a great big smile."

"Ah, it's good," Materena says.

"So many people think that driving a bride to the church is just about driving, but it isn't, let me tell you. You have to be a bit of a psychologist."

Materena nods knowingly.

"And, plus," Mama Teta goes on, "I offer extras. I'm the only one who offers extras on the island. The other wedding-car drivers, they just drive from A to B."

"Extras?" Materena wouldn't mind finding out what the extras are. "What, for example?"

"Well, I sing," Mama Teta replies.

Materena nods.

"But my best extra," Mama Teta continues, "is that I give a little gift to my bride."

"*Ah oui?* That's very nice of you, Mama Teta."

"Ah, it's only a little something, girl. It's not of great value, but it takes me hours to get that gift. My gift is like a good-luck thing."

"Ah, I'm sure the friend of my boss would appreciate your gift. And what is it? Can you tell me?"

"Well, I can tell you because you're not the one getting married, but don't tell the friend of your boss, because if the bride knows about the gift, then the good-luck thing might not work."

"Don't tell me!" Materena says, then hurries to add, "It might slip out of my mouth. Just tell me the price and include a tour around Papeete."

Mama Teta gives Materena a slightly suspecting look, but then she says the price. Approximate, she says. It will depend a little on whether the boss's friend is from Faa'a or somewhere else.

Materena now has all the necessary information, and she's quite happy about Mama Teta driving her to the church, even if Mama Teta's driving is a bit wobbly when there's a gendarme on the horizon. Materena still laughs out loud when she remembers the story of Mama Teta and the gendarme.

One day, just a little while after Mama Teta got her driver's license, a gendarme started following her, and she wasn't doing anything wrong. She was just taking her son and her grandkids for a little drive and driving way below the speed limit. Sure, Mama Teta was driving a rusty old car, and, yes, a car that made funny rattles and clunking sounds, but she had passed her driving test first go. In fact, Gilbert, the driving instructor, had told Mama Teta many times that he had never seen anyone drive with such confidence as her. Mama Teta, she doesn't hesitate before passing or putting her foot on the brake. She's a quick thinker, which is very important when you drive in Tahiti, because in Tahiti there are lots of unconfident drivers and there are lots of drivers driving without a driver's license.

Ah, true, Mama Teta is a confident driver, but back then that gendarme following her was sending her into a panic attack and making her forget all that she had learned during the two weeks of driving lessons with Gilbert. Here she was, welded to the steering wheel, hands shaking, legs shaking, unable to concentrate 100 percent, unable to think — panicking.

Johno said to his mama, "You're driving like someone who can't see the bloody road, Ma." Then, checking the speedometer: "This is a sixty-five-mile-an-hour zone and you're going twenty-five."

"It's that gendarme following me. He's making me nervous."

Mama Teta was so nervous her hands were sweaty and she had to wipe them on her pareu.

Johno turned around and there was indeed a gendarme following them.

"You want me to drive?" he asked, hoping his mother would say yes, as he was a bit *fiu* of this twenty-five-mile-per-hour drive.

"I don't want nobody else to drive! I've got my driver's license, and why did your old mama have to get her driver's license at bloody fifty-six years old, eh? Because my kids never come and visit me!"

It was the eternal argument. Mama Teta's children didn't come to see her often enough, she wanted them to visit her every day, but the children were always so busy. So Mama Teta had got her driver's license and now she visited her children without warning them of her arrival. Like this afternoon, when she came to take Johno's kids for a drive in the old Citroën. She didn't invite Johno along, he just jumped in. His woman, she didn't like the kids driving with Mama Teta, full stop, especially not by themselves.

All Johno wanted now was for the car ride to end. At his house. It was twenty past five, Josianne would have dinner ready and she was going to be mad if Johno and the kids didn't turn up soon. Like, in five minutes. The kids were restless, tired of the little drive, which was taking such a long time. Because their grandmother Mama Teta was too scared to stop in case the gendarme stopped his car too to ask her questions.

"Ma . . . why are you scared of the gendarmes?" Johno was serious.

"Who said I'm scared! I'm not scared." Mama Teta's voice lowered into a whisper. "Why are you talking nonsense to me?"

"You can talk normal, Ma. It's not against the law. You can even sing!"

"Sometimes you make me so mad, Johno! Who's going to pay the fine if we get arrested? I just want to be careful. Why don't you just shut it!"

Johno smelled panic in the air. "Ma?"

"What?"

"Stop the car — I'm driving."

"What are you saying?"

"I said, stop the car now. I'm driving."

"It's my car, I'm driving." Mama Teta gripped the steering wheel tighter.

It wasn't really Mama Teta's car. It belonged to her niece Lily, who had gone to France with her latest boyfriend. There was a possibility Lily wouldn't come back soon, depending on whether she got sick of the new man in her life. If she didn't, Mama Teta would buy the car for a reasonable price.

Actually, Mama Teta knew Lily was more likely to come back home within two weeks, because Lily is easily bored when it comes to boyfriends. She loves partying too much to settle down. Mama Teta already had her eye on a new white Fiat — but no need to tell Johno all that.

"Ma, stop the car! I want to ask the gendarme why he's following us. There has to be a reason," said Johno.

Mama Teta shrieked, "You leave that gendarme alone! No way I'm stopping my car now. No way."

Johno sighed. No way? Well, we're going to see about that.

Then suddenly Mama Teta accelerated. She had a mean look on her face — she meant business.

"What are you doing, Ma?"

"Going faster. Now shut it. I've got to get away from that gendarme."

Johno sighed again. Did his mama actually think that Lily's rusty, clunking Citroën would lose the gendarme's brand-new car? Yes, she did. Mama Teta was even pressing her chest on the steering wheel — to make the car go a bit faster, no doubt. Faster. Faster. Then came the inevitable siren.

Mama Teta jumped, the kids clapped, Johno was relieved. "You have to stop, Ma," he said.

"I'm not stopping for anybody. I didn't do anything wrong." The Citroën kept speeding away, faster and faster.

"Are you serious, Ma?"

Mama Teta didn't answer.

"Ma!" Ah, now Johno was quite annoyed with his mama.

Mama Teta started mumbling, "There's too many gendarmes here . . . watching us . . . waiting for us to do something wrong so they can lock us away in prison . . . I see them . . . with guns in their pocket . . . to scare us little people. They think they're better than us, in their uniforms. They don't watch the rich people, because the rich people give them money . . . but, us little people, we have to be good, good all the time. That gendarme, he can tell I'm a nobody . . . I'm a little person he can push around for a joke . . . he can scare people with his gun . . . I'm not stopping, you hear? I'm not stopping for anybody."

Johno had to think fast. When his woman got out of control (like his mama was right now), he never tried the talking-sense technique, because that technique didn't work in these situations. He had a better technique, and it was called the shock technique. Johno had never screamed at his mama before. He had told her off a few times but always between his teeth. But right this moment, he had to scare his mama. Shock her. Wake her up. Make her stop that bloody car before she killed them all.

"STOP THIS FUCKING CAR NOW!" It was an order.

And Mama Teta, calm and composed, put her foot on the brake. She made sure the blinker was blinking, and carefully swerved to the side of the road, then she turned the motor off. Not long after, the gendarme parked his car next to Lily's car.

Johno, sweating and trembling, got out of the car to explain the situation to the gendarme. This little drive might cost him a few thousand francs. He had to win the gendarme's sympathy. Surely the gendarme would understand. He had a mother too. And a woman, perhaps. He must know that women, on the whole, do bizarre things.

"Good afternoon, monsieur." Johno was all respect for the skinny little gendarme walking toward him.

"Good afternoon." The gendarme went straight past Johno to the driver.

Mama Teta looked up to the gendarme and did her air of pity. Then she looked at him properly and flashed a big smile like we do when we recognize somebody.

"Good afternoon, monsieur." Mama Teta's voice was singing.

"Madame."

Johno stood still, quite stunned with his mama.

"May I see your driver's license, please, madame?" the gendarme asked.

Again, singing, "Certainly, monsieur . . . here, monsieur." There was a twinkle in Mama Teta's eyes.

The gendarme checked that the woman in the photograph was the woman sitting behind the wheel. Then, obviously satisfied, he handed the driver's license back.

"Do you own the car?" he asked.

And Mama Teta cackled. "Do I own the car? *Ah non,* monsieur. It's the car of my niece and her name is Lily. She's in France now . . . just for a little holiday. Lily, she asked me to look after her car until she comes back. And I'm just taking my son and my grandchildren for a little drive."

The gendarme briefly glanced at the three very silent kids sitting in the back of the car. Then he looked at Mama Teta again. "When is . . . Madame Lily . . . coming back? Any idea?"

"Oh, Lily is coming back very soon." Mama Teta nodded several times.

The gendarme smiled. He pulled his wallet out of his pocket and handed his business card to Mama Teta. She thanked him for giving her his card.

"Would you care to tell your niece to give me a call as soon as she comes back?" the gendarme asked. "There are a few things I need to discuss with her . . . about her car. For example, she must replace the two front tires. This is a rather urgent matter."

Mama Teta put the gendarme's business card in her bag. "Certainly, monsieur, it's a very urgent matter. I told my niece Lily to get a new car. This one is a bit hard to drive. I'm going to make sure that Lily calls you as soon as she comes back." Mama Teta spoke louder every time she said "Lily."

"Thank you for your cooperation."

"Oh, it's nothing, monsieur." Mama Teta made a little movement with her hand.

Johno, even more stunned now, got back in the car, and Mama Teta waited for the gendarme to do a fast U-turn and disappear.

Johno was silent. He had expected his mother to cry, beg the gendarme for mercy, tell him about all her financial problems, her heart problem, her whole life, but she did none of these. She just smiled and cackled.

Mama Teta whistled, then she began to laugh. "*Ah hia hia* . . . that Lily, eh? Playing around with gendarmes, eh? I'm going to give her plenty when she comes back. And that stupid gendarme, thinking I don't know anything. Every time I said 'Lily,' his eyes sparkled, and I bet his thing was hard."

"What are you talking about?" Johno asked.

"Eh, look in the glove box."

Johno opened the glove box. There was a bundle of photographs. The photographs were all of Lily with a man at her side.

Johno flicked through the photographs and there was the gendarme, holding on to beautiful, naughty Lily and grinning with pride like a fisherman who has caught a big fish.

Johno put the photographs back in the glove box and shook his head.

Women . . . they sure do bizarre things.

One-Minute Visit

After a week gathering quotes and thinking about food, drinks, the wedding dress, the wedding rings — all the things that need to be organized before you actually say "I do" — Materena has a headache.

Aue, there's so much to be organized!

But today Materena isn't going to think about the organization. She's just going to think of nothing. Blank the wedding out of her mind. Relax on the sofa. It's so rare she's on her own, but today she's managed it. She looks at the ceiling, enjoying the peace and quiet. She might have a nap or she might just stay in a horizontal position on the sofa with her eyes open.

She's going to do whatever she wants.

Pito is on a visiting tour with Ati, which means he won't get home until dark. The kids are at her mother Loana's house until she gets sick of them and walks them back — in two hours, maybe three if Materena is lucky. She has told the kids they better behave or they'll be in big trouble. She's hoping they will stay with their grandmother till late afternoon.

Materena has cleaned the whole house, everything smells nice, everything has been put away, there are no clothes to wash, no clothes to hang, no clothes to iron, and the sheets have been changed.

Materena feels blissful.

Then Mama Roti's head appears at the louvers. *"Hou-hou!"*

Materena springs to her feet like the sofa is burning hot, and her hands automatically rearrange her uncombed hair. Ah, *fiu!* Materena is so annoyed.

Mama Roti bangs on the door. "What's this locking the door in the middle of the day! What's this pulling the curtains closed!"

Materena is determined to tell Mama Roti that today it's impossible for her to have a talking session. She's going to say her doctor has prescribed rest. She doesn't want to talk.

Materena unlocks the door and Mama Roti barges into the house. There is a woman with her whom Mama Roti introduces as "someone I know." And to the Someone Mama Roti Knows, Mama Roti says, "This is Materena. Pito's half."

Pito's half! Materena thinks, What! I'm a mango now? Ah, that woman! What a nerve! No manners! But Materena can't really be too cranky at Mama Roti, because when Loana talks about Pito to someone, she calls him Materena's shadow.

"I won't stay long, girl," Mama Roti says. "Just one minute. I've got so many things to do. So many things to do, but it's so hot." Then she looks at the floor.

"Eh, what's this? Where's the linoleum?"

"It's at the dump," Materena lies. She doesn't want to hear about that story of how you don't put carpet on top of linoleum again.

"When did you put carpet down?" Mama Roti is now bending over and feeling the carpet with the palm of her hand.

"Four days ago."

Mama Roti gives Materena a suspicious look and makes herself comfortable on the sofa. There and then Materena guesses the visit is not going to be a one-minute visit, it's going to be more like a few-hours visit. Mama Roti fans herself with the palm of her hand. Materena invites the woman Mama Roti has brought with her to sit and gets them a cordial.

The woman sips her cordial and Mama Roti gulps hers.

"Can I have another one?" Mama Roti hands her empty glass to Materena.

Materena goes and gets Mama Roti another glass of cordial. After gulping her second glass of cordial, Mama Roti goes on about how she feels so much better. It's less hot, all of a sudden.

"I bought a lottery ticket last week," she says.

"*Ah oui?*" Materena is not interested at all.

"Girl, if my numbers were three, seven, and nine instead of eleven, four, and two, you'd be facing a millionaire right this second."

"Ah." Materena has heard too many stories about Mama Roti nearly winning the lottery and what she would do with her millions.

On and on Mama Roti goes about how she would have spent her millions. New house, car, a trip to Lourdes, a speedboat for Pito, one hundred thousand francs into Materena's bank account — the one for the kids.

"Thank you." Materena always has to say thank you when Mama Roti distributes the millions of francs she nearly won.

Mama Roti drifts into a reverie, which nobody interrupts. She smiles and sighs. Her friend is still sipping her cordial and looks like she's going to fall asleep, so she jumps at Mama Roti's exclamation.

"And where's Pito!"

"He's with Ati," Materena replies. "They won't be back until late tonight."

"And the kids?"

"They're with Mamie. They won't be back until tonight."

"So you're all by yourself, girl," Mama Roti says. "I'm glad I came to visit and keep you company, but I can't stay long. I've got an appointment in town in an hour — an important appointment."

Well, Materena is sure happy about that important appointment.

But two hours later Mama Roti is still talking.

"Mama Roti," Materena says, "what about your important appointment?"

Mama Roti shrugs, and admits that it's fine if she's late for that important appointment. In fact, it's fine if she doesn't go to that important appointment at all. And the important appointment isn't really an important appointment — it's just an appointment with the dentist. And Mama Roti is not in the mood to have a noisy drill in her mouth today.

"I'll make another appointment with the dentist, he's a good friend, almost family — don't be concerned, girl." Mama Roti pats Materena on the leg.

And now, she says, she's a bit hungry.

Materena goes and makes sandwiches. As she's cutting the tomatoes, she's tempted to escape through the back door and go hide on the roof.

Loana does this. When she hears someone calling whom she doesn't want to see, she hides on the roof and stays there until the person gives up calling and goes away. When Materena was little she used to have to lie to visitors that her mother had just ducked out to the Chinese store. She hated doing this and would always tell the priest at confession. Leilani is the same, she doesn't like lying when Materena is avoiding visitors.

Materena would have gone into hiding on the roof as soon as she'd heard Mama Roti's calling or whistle, but Mama Roti didn't do the polite warning you're supposed to do when you visit somebody.

What if I'd been doing the sexy loving with Pito on the sofa? Materena laughs at the thought of Mama Roti peeping through the louvers and seeing her son in action with his woman.

Mama Roti chomps through her sandwich, and the friend

nibbles hers. Materena wonders if the friend is going to say a word at some stage. She feels she should start a conversation with her, but what if Mama Roti's friend turns out to be worse than Mama Roti in the talking department?

Mama Roti looks into Materena's eyes. "Girl, you look so tired."

"I *am* tired." Materena sighs like she's very exhausted.

"Have some rest." Mama Roti gives Materena the *I understand* look.

She says that she's glad she came to visit, because, in her opinion, if she hadn't come to visit, Materena would have been running around the house looking for something to do.

"At least now you're in the sitting position, girl." Mama Roti makes herself more comfortable on the sofa and begins her tale about how people do too much these days — in her day . . .

Materena drifts off. She's not in the living room. She's . . . she's outside watering the plants. How long she waters the plants, she's not sure.

But Mama Roti's shrieking voice abruptly interrupts her escapade. "You shut your mouth, you! You don't know what you're talking about!"

Mama Roti's friend is up and she's all red in the face. "*I* don't know what I'm talking about! It's you who don't know what you're talking about!"

Mama Roti's friend thanks Materena for the cordial, the sandwiches, and the hospitality, and marches out the door.

"That woman," Mama Roti says. "That shriveled-up prune . . . I've been trying to get rid of her since this morning, but, that empty-headed woman, she wouldn't get the message, she had to keep following me around. Now that she's gone, we can talk about more private subjects."

And so Mama Roti goes on complaining about the Someone

She Knows, whose name is Mama Neno, and how Mama Neno follows Mama Roti too much these days and all Mama Roti wants is a bit of space.

"She used to be my best friend," Mama Roti says, "but it doesn't mean she can suffocate me."

And then Mama Roti explains to Materena that she and Mama Neno were very close friends when they were young girls, until Mama Neno got involved with this horrible man. But Mama Neno's horrible man had just recently died, and so she decided to rekindle her friendship with Mama Roti.

Materena listens to Mama Roti and waits for her to get tired of talking about Mama Neno.

Mama Roti finally stops talking. She looks at the carpet. She looks at it for a very long time and Materena wonders why Mama Roti is looking at her carpet like she's seen that carpet before.

"Girl, what's happening?" Mama Roti's eyes are still on the carpet.

"What's happening?" Materena has no idea what Mama Roti is talking about.

"That new carpet." Mama Roti points to it. "When women change things around the house, it means there's something in the air."

"Mama Roti, I was just *fiu* of the linoleum," Materena says.

"Are you sure this is the reason?"

"Of course!"

Mama Roti's eyes are now trying to penetrate Materena's mind. "The linoleum has been in this house for as long as my son has been in this house. And now there's no more linoleum, and to me it means that there's going to be some changes around here."

Materena smiles a real smile. "Mama Roti, I'm happy with your son."

"He's a good man, my son," Mama Roti says.

"*Ah oui.*"

"He works."

"*Ah oui,* that's good," Materena says.

"He drinks a bit every now and then," Mama Roti goes on. "But at least he's not violent when he drinks. He just talks a lot of nonsense."

Materena nods.

"I've raised him very well."

Materena nods again and looks away.

Heritage

Mama Roti ended up staying for another two hours, talking nonstop about her wonderful son and boring Materena more and more by the second.

When Mama Roti finally realized that she had taken enough of Materena's time (five hours in total), she rose to her feet to leave, but she had one very important question to ask.

"Girl, are you sure everything is fine between you and my son?"

"*Oui,*" Materena said firmly. "Everything is fine between your son and me."

Mama Roti nodded but didn't look too convinced. She left sighing.

Now, the following day, she's back again! There's no way Materena can handle her mother-in-law again today — plus, Pito and the kids are home, they can look after Mama Roti.

So after a quick kiss to her mother-in-law, Materena escapes to Loana's under the pretext that she's giving her mother some lemons.

Mother and daughter kiss each other, then Loana takes the plastic bag from Materena and says, "Thank you for the lemons, girl."

"The health is good?" Materena already knows the answer, but she always inquires about her mother's health, it is the ritual. And Loana always says, "The legs are a bit stiff when I get up in the morning."

But today is different. "I was about to come and see you," Loana says, "because I signed some papers, and there's a story I have to tell you." She puts the lemons away in the fridge. "It's about your great-grandmother, how her children didn't come from her husband but from another man."

Materena sits at the kitchen table, but Loana would rather tell the story in the bedroom. She needs to lie down a little.

Loana lies on the bed, a pillow under each leg. Materena sits on the floor, her back pressed against the wall, and she checks the paint peeling off the wall.

"My mother's mother's name was Rarahu," Loana begins, her eyes fixed on the ceiling. "And according to talk she was quite a beautiful woman. It would have been good, girl, if there had been a photograph of that woman, but in the old days, people from the Tuamotus didn't have photographs of themselves. There was no photographer on the atoll, you had to come to Tahiti to get a professional photograph, and, Rarahu, she never left the atoll of Rangiroa. She was born in Rangiroa, she died in Rangiroa, she had only ever lived in Rangiroa. Anyway, her beauty has nothing to do with this story."

Loana clears her throat. "Rarahu was sixteen years old when she married Mareco Tetu. It was an arranged marriage. She had no choice, he had no choice, because they were both afraid of their parents. So they went to the church, did the whole ceremony. It was a grandiose marriage. Rarahu was veiled, meaning that she was a virgin, that she'd never played hide-and-seek in the coconut plantation.

"After the marriage, Rarahu followed her husband back to his parents' old colonial-style house, and people expected her to fall pregnant within three months, at least. But six months passed and Rarahu's belly was still flat. That was because Mareco was sleeping on the floor. He was sleeping on the floor because he wasn't fit to love a woman. He was only fit to love a man. Mareco himself confessed this to his wife."

Materena arches her eyebrows. She understands now how Rarahu got children from another man.

"I know you're thinking: No wonder the woman got herself another man *illico presto*," Loana says. "*Oui,* Rarahu left her husband — but ten years after being married to him.

"She fell in love with Nonihe, who had come to Rangiroa from Rapa Nui to work in the copra plantation. And he fell in love with her too. So she packed her bags and moved into a hut with him. They were poor, but they were happy, or so the talk said. Nonihe was a good man.

"Rarahu had four children with Nonihe, but Nonihe couldn't recognize them, since Rarahu was still married to Mareco.

"And on her deathbed, she made each one of her kids swear that they would never go after the Tetu heritage. And the children swore that to their mama.

"And now, girl, I've signed the papers, and so that story is settled forever. Celia didn't sign. She wants her kids to be able to claim some of the Tetus' heritage. But, I tell you, girl: when you take what doesn't belong to you and you know about it, you get bad luck."

"Was there a lot of land?" Materena asks.

"Acres."

"In Rangiroa?"

"Rangiroa, Apataki, Tikehau too."

Materena thinks about all those acres . . . "What happened to Mareco?"

"He died a lonely man."

"Did everyone in the village know he was —"

Loana interrupts Materena before she says the word. "*Non,*

only his wife and her best friend, and now us." Materena thinks about all those acres again, that's a lot of land . . .

And Loana repeats, "When you take what doesn't belong to you and you know about it, you get bad luck, and not just you, but your kids, your grandkids, your great-grandkids, on and on. I tell you, girl, we're much better off without all those acres. You don't muck around with things like this. You don't want the land to eat you."

Materena shivers and her eyes wander to the framed black-and-white photographs displayed on the wall. There's a photograph of an eight-month-old baby in the arms of a young woman, and standing next to the woman are a nun and two children, boys. The baby is Loana. Materena has asked her mother about the people in the photograph, but Loana couldn't say who those people were. But Loana has framed that photo because it is the only baby photo she has of herself.

Then Materena's eyes move to another photograph — the photograph of a man. It is her grandfather Apoto. He's tall and lean. He's got white skin and his nose is pointed. And next to him there's a photograph of a plump woman, she's brown and her nose is large. It is Materena's grandmother Kika.

And Materena looks at her mother.

She looks at the wide nostrils and the pointed chin. And she thinks about the story of Apoto and Kika, the story her mother Loana has told her.

"My father left my mother when she was three months pregnant with me, but before he sneaked into the schooner *Marie Stella,* he made sure to tell the whole village that the child inside Kika's belly wasn't his doing. He said, 'Someone else planted that child — maybe the Chinese man.' He needed an excuse to justify abandoning his pregnant wife and their five-year-old daughter for another woman.

"And just my luck that I was born with slanted eyes.

"But I didn't grow up thinking my father was the Chinese man; my mother, she often said to me, 'Loana — your father is Apoto Mahi.'

"But . . . when I became a woman, doubt began to bother me. I realized that it isn't unusual for a married woman to get pregnant by another man. I saw things, things of life. Even when my father died moaning, 'Loana — Loana, my daughter,' I still had that doubt in me.

"I remembered the Chinese man. He was always nice to me, always giving me lollies behind his wife's back, and to my mother unlimited credit. And the Chinese man's wife didn't like my mother, and vice versa. They never spoke to each other.

"Things like that I remembered. And, Celia, she used to say we didn't look like sisters, that she looked so much like Apoto, and I, I looked like no one in the family.

"After Apoto died, I got a letter about my heritage — my land.

"I didn't want to accept, but I was a bit tired of moving from one relative's house to another relative's house. Your godmother, Imelda, used to always say to me, 'Cousin, my house is your house. Stay as long as you want.' But I wanted a place of my own. My piece of land. And I kept thinking about that bad-luck thing, which I heard from Kika. She'd say, 'That person is not allowed to get the coconuts from this land because this land doesn't belong to him and he knows it. Well, bad luck will come to him.'

"And, sure enough, bad luck always did. Or should I say bad crop?

"But one night, Mama came into my dream and said, 'I've only ever loved Apoto and he gave me you.'

"So I accepted my heritage, and later on I found out that my slanted eyes came from an ancestor who was a Filipino."

Loana has fallen asleep, and Materena quietly stands up. She kisses her mother on the forehead and looks at her. Then she looks at the grainy photograph of Apoto. There is no resemblance whatsoever between Loana and Apoto. But Materena realizes that not all children resemble their father.

Moana, for instance, he looks nothing like Pito, with his freckles, green eyes, and golden hair. And, Leilani, well, she is very much a young version of her grandmother Loana. In fact, now that Materena is analyzing the resemblance of her children, Tamatoa is the only one who looks like Pito. And Materena thinks about how things could have turned out different for her if Tamatoa wasn't the stamp of his father when he was born.

Ah yes, Materena remembers now how Pito scrutinized his newborn son for hours. And then Pito compared his newborn son to a photograph of himself when he was a newborn. And Pito was happy to say, "Jeez, that fellow looks just like me when I was born."

And only last month, Materena's cousin Rita was saying to Materena how Tamatoa was looking more and more like Pito and how she hoped the resemblance would only ever remain in appearance.

Materena wishes God had made Loana resemble her father, even just a tiny bit. Loana's life would have been much easier had Apoto accepted her as his daughter when he was alive and not just when he was dying.

But who knows with these things.

Materena quietly leaves the room and goes to the kitchen to make a pitcher of fresh lemonade. Ah, she might as well wipe the benches too.

She's in no hurry to head home.

A Postcard from France

After two hours pottering around in her mother's kitchen, including rearranging and cleaning her fridge, Materena goes home, hoping Mama Roti has gone. She has.

"How come you were so long?" Pito asks. "It doesn't take two hours to go give someone a bag of lemons."

"Mamie wanted to talk a little," Materena says. "And your mama? She stayed long?"

"She was only here for fifteen minutes, and she was a bit bizarre."

"*Ah oui?*" Materena says, thinking, Your mother is always a bit bizarre.

"She asked me bizarre questions about the carpet and what it meant."

"And what did you say?" Materena asks.

"I said, 'It means Materena was sick of the linoleum, that's all it means.'"

Materena cackles.

"She came to give me this." Pito shows Materena a postcard. It has a picture of the Eiffel Tower on it. "It's from France," boasts Pito.

"From France?" Materena, very intrigued, reads the postcard.

Iaorana, Pito, e aha te huru? Yes, I'm still living in France.
I haven't been back to the fenua for sixteen years now. I miss the
corned beef! I miss the fenua too, but my life is here now. How are
you doing, Pito? Maybe you don't remember me. Tihoti

"Who is that Tihoti?" Materena asks Pito.

Pito doesn't remember yet, but he's trying to. He searches his memory, and after a whole hour of this, the name Tihoti Ranuira finally connects.

Tihoti Ranuira. They did military service in France together.

Pito did military service in France because he didn't want his mama embarrassing him like she embarrassed his brother Frank. Frank did military service in Tahiti and Mama Roti would go to the barracks and call out to the guardian that she had home-cooked food for her son and to go get him. She believed the food at the barracks was poisoned. She would also stand by the side of the road to cheer her son as he ran past with his platoon. Pito's brother suffered.

When Pito announced to his mama that he had enlisted himself to do military service in France, she panicked. Mama Roti tried all kinds of tricks to make her youngest son stay. She lied that she had an incurable disease, she threatened never to speak to Pito ever again, but at the age of eighteen, Pito felt he really needed some time away from his mama. Two years.

Materena knows the story, Mama Roti has told her many times how afraid she was that her son would fall for a *popa'a* girl and then decide to live in France. The day Pito came back from France was a very happy day for Mama Roti.

Yes, Pito came back, but Tihoti stayed in France. Pito says Tihoti felt there was nothing for him in Tahiti, no family ties, no prospects, no woman, nothing. His future was in France, in the army. Tihoti wanted to be a colonel.

Materena is surprised Pito has never talked about Tihoti. Two years is a long time to spend with someone, how could you just forget them? Pito insists that he and Tihoti weren't close like inseparables — they just happened to be from the same island. They talked Tahitian, they sang Tahitian songs, and Pito played the ukulele.

"He was a bit . . ." Pito searches for the proper word to describe Tihoti. "He was a bit . . . well, he wasn't one hundred percent normal."

The postcard is a shock to Pito. Why would anyone contact somebody after so many years?

In Materena's opinion that particular friend must have felt lonely for him to suddenly write to Pito. And Pito should be honored his friend remembered him in his moment of crisis.

But, according to Pito, his friend from the military days wasn't going through a crisis at all when he wrote the postcard. *Non,* his friend probably just drank a bottle of wine and did some remembering about the old days, or maybe he found a picture from the military-service days and the past came back to him.

"It doesn't matter why he wrote to you," Materena says. "You've got a postcard." It means Pito is an important person and he must respond.

"And what am I going to say?" asks Pito.

"Whatever comes into your head." Materena is already looking in her pandanus bag for the special writing paper and the pen she uses to write notes to the children's teacher. She gives them to Pito, who sits at the kitchen table. Materena remains standing and pretends to be busy. She fusses over a pot, she puts a plate away, and she eyes the blank page.

Eventually, Pito writes one word, two words, five words, two lines. He scratches his head, he looks at the ceiling, he looks at the plants outside, he looks at the paper, he reads his two lines and shakes his head.

He's having difficulties, the words are not coming into his head, and Materena understands the situation. The kids are mucking around in the living room, and she knows it is much easier to write when there's silence. She writes her notes when everyone has gone to bed. Pito could wait for that time, but Materena wants him to respond to his friend now.

Because with Pito, later can mean never.

And Materena wants Tihoti to get a letter from Pito. She feels a bit sorry for him. Not wanting to come home — it's sad. Tihoti's only link to Tahiti is Pito.

Materena marches into the living room. "Eh, kids. Go play out the back. Papi is writing a letter to his friend in France."

"Papi's writing a letter?" Leilani is rather amused.

"Papi's got a friend in France?" Tamatoa whistles, he's impressed.

"Papi's got a friend in France and he's writing a letter to him?" Moana marches to the kitchen to see his father writing.

"Out the back!" Materena hoots the children outside.

She goes back to the kitchen and fusses over the frying pan. Pito seems to be inspired, he's furiously writing. But then he's furiously scrunching the paper.

"It's no use," he says.

Materena knows just what to do, and she's now unplugging the radio. Then she gets batteries and a blank tape from a box in the bedroom. Materena always has a blank tape available for when she's in the mood to record herself singing.

Materena also gets Pito a cold beer, that way he'll be more relaxed.

Pito is now comfortable, sitting on a chair under the tamarind tree with the radio on his lap and a beer in his hand.

He presses the record button and takes a long slug of his beer.

He's ready now. "Of course I remember you. What do you think, eh?"

Long silence.

"Are you still skinny like a nail?"

Long silence.

"Eh, fourteen years, it's a long time. I don't know what I'm supposed to tell you, mate."

After three beers, Pito's tongue loosens up. He doesn't hear the giggling of his children, who are hiding behind the tamarind tree. Materena waves them away. The last thing Pito needs is an interruption. He's talking to Tihoti and Materena is happy.

Pito reminisces about the barracks, the slop they ate, the jokes they did on the commandant. He talks about speedboats, fishing, his work, and the beer they will share one day with Ati. Pito talks until the tape runs out. All that talking has tired him. He says he's going to have a lie-down.

While Pito rests, Materena quietly listens to the tape. She's very annoyed Pito didn't talk about his family — his woman, his kids — yet he mentioned Ati.

Well, she's going to rectify the situation. She erases about two minutes of Pito's talk, but she's going to do a little practice before recording. "Tihoti," she says out loud, "*iaorana*. My name is Materena and I'm Pito's wife." Materena shakes her head. She can't introduce herself as Pito's wife, since they're not married yet. She starts again. "Tihoti, *iaorana*. My name is Materena and I'm Pito's future wife." Materena is not happy with this introduction line either. She can't say that she's Pito's future wife, since there's no date for the marriage yet. Materena is at a loss as to how she should introduce herself to Tihoti, especially since Pito didn't mention her and the kids. But Materena realizes that women are usually the ones who talk about their family, their kids. Men, they talk about their mates and their sports.

Materena has her introduction line worked out now. She calls to the children to come into the kitchen. After she calls them several times, the children come. She explains the situation. The children nod. Yes, they understand the situation.

Materena places the radio in front of her and leans forward. "Tihoti — *iaorana.* My name is Materena, and I've been with Pito for nearly thirteen years now, and we have three children. I'm a professional cleaner and it's very nice you sent a postcard to Pito. It's the first time he's received a postcard, plus, all the way from France too. Pito, he's very happy . . . he's happy you remembered him. Now, when you come back to the *fenua,* our house is open to you, and your family too is welcomed to our house, your woman — your children. Now here are Pito's children to say hello to you."

The next day, on her way to work, Materena stops by the post office in Papeete to send Tihoti his package, which comprises the tape, three cans of corned beef, and four blocks of coconut-scented soap. She hopes this package will make Tihoti feel as if they all know of him.

As if Pito talked about him all the time.

Totem

It's true, Materena was quite upset when Pito didn't mention her and the kids on the tape to his friend Tihoti. But look at Pito now, sitting at the kitchen table with his children, telling them about his totem. It's so beautiful to see. Materena, mixing a cake, is feeling very moved by this family gathering.

Pito's totem is Piihoro, a giant black-and-white dog with a long tail. Piihoro came from the island of Raiatea and his first mission was to look after the rare black pearl. For Piihoro to come to the rescue, you call out: "Piihoro, eh, I'm Tehana blood. You're my totem — come to me." And Piihoro will make an appearance in a second.

Pito has never needed, so he stresses to the kids, to get in contact with Piihoro. But one of his cousins was walking around the streets of Papeete one night when a gang of hoods confronted him. Pito's cousin called out, "Piihoro, eh, I'm Tehana blood. You're my totem, come to me." Soon after, the no-goods began to yell like lunatics and they ran off at one hundred miles per hour, calling out for their mamas.

Materena chuckles. "Eh, Pito," she says sweetly, "your cousin — you're sure he wasn't a bit drunk that night?"

"You're telling me the story of my cousin is a lot of inventing?" Pito is on the defensive.

Materena keeps on mixing her cake. There are days when it's best just to listen to Pito's talk and make no comments.

Pito goes on about how we, the Polynesian people, all have a totem, but not many of us know what our totem is, because when the white people arrived, totem talk became forbidden.

One of Pito's aunties has a newspaper clipping about Piihoro in her family album. Pito is going to get it for the kids to read, although there's no guarantee that his auntie is going to lend that newspaper clipping, because the last time she lent something out of her photo album to a relative, it never came back.

"What is your totem, Mamie?" Leilani asks.

Materena confesses that she doesn't know what her totem is but she's going to inquire about it tomorrow.

But as soon as the cake is in the oven, Materena hurries to Loana's house. She's too curious to wait for tomorrow, and she wouldn't mind her totem being a creature of the sea, because she loves the sea.

Loana is raking when Materena arrives. They kiss each other. Materena asks her mother about her health, and Loana complains about her legs being a bit stiff when she wakes up in the morning. Then Materena compliments her mother on the garden and Loana complains about the lack of rain.

Now Materena can reveal the real reason for her visit. "Mamie, I've come to ask you about my totem."

"Eh, what? What is this question about your totem?" Loana looks surprised.

"I'm just curious because Pito told the kids about his totem and I want to tell the kids about mine."

"What is Pito's totem?" Loana says, squinting.

"It's a dog, a giant black-and-white dog called Piihoro." Materena knows her mother is going to make some comment about Pito's totem being a giant dog.

"It can't be just a dog," Loana says. "It has to be a *giant* dog."

Materena ignores her mother's comment. "And my totem, what is it?"

"I don't know." Loana's answer is firm. But then she goes on about how she knows that the totem of her father is the shark, but, since the totem can only be passed from the mother, Materena's totem can't be the shark.

"How come the totem can only be passed from the mother and not the father?" Materena is perplexed.

"What do you think?" Loana says.

Materena shrugs, so Loana spells out the reason. The totem can only be passed from the mother because a child is sure to be that woman's child but not necessarily that woman's man's child.

"Ah." Yes, now Materena understands.

Loana thinks awhile, then says, "Your totem could be the turtle." Loana tells Materena about how her mother was so fond of turtles that she would never eat the turtle. One day, there was a feast and they served barbecued turtle in coconut milk, and Kika said, "I can't eat the turtle." And someone immediately said, "Yes, of course you can't eat the turtle."

Materena hurries to declare that she too is very fond of turtles. There was a documentary on the TV not long ago about a turtle laying eggs, and the camera was focused on the turtle's face. Materena saw the tears, the silent tears of suffering, and tears came to her eyes too, she felt the turtle's pain. And then, when the turtle struggled back into the sea, Materena said, "Go on, turtle — courage."

Loana nods. She informs Materena that she too watched that documentary and it made her cry. In fact, Loana goes on, any woman who's given birth would have related to the turtle's pain and cried. You don't need to have the turtle as your totem to feel sorry for the turtle.

Materena is very happy her totem might be the turtle.

She excuses herself to Loana, explaining that she's got to hurry home because there's a cake in the oven, but how about Loana comes for dinner soon? "Eh, Mamie?" asks Materena. "We eat together tomorrow?"

Loana looks up to think a little. "Okay, I'm pretty sure I'm free."

"See you tomorrow, then." And with this Materena runs home.

Pito and the kids are still in the kitchen waiting for the marble cake to be ready. Materena checks it, but there's still a bit more cooking to go.

And then, standing next to the oven, Materena proudly announces that her totem is the turtle.

"The turtle!" Pito laughs his head off.

According to him, from the time you called out for help to the arrival of the turtle, one hundred years would have passed. Materena reminds him of the rabbit-and-turtle story. The turtle won the race, didn't it?

"It was a tortoise, which is different from a turtle, and, anyway, it's only in *popa'a* stories that tortoises or turtles win and rabbits lose."

Pito asks the kids what totem they would rather call out to, the fast giant dog or the slow turtle. There's hesitation at the kitchen table. The kids look at each other.

"Eh, you don't have a choice, anyway," Materena says. "You can only call out to the turtle."

"How come we can only call out to the turtle?" the children ask.

"Because the totem can only be passed from the mother and not the father," Materena says.

And Pito wants to know how come the totem can only be passed from the mother and not from the father, and Materena repeats what her mother told her.

"It's been like that for hundreds of years," she adds. "It's not a new rule and you can't change that rule. So Piihoro is not your totem after all."

"Ah." Pito doesn't look too happy with this information.

He now inquires about the cake.

But there's no changing the subject. Everyone wants to know what Pito's totem is, and Pito seems uneasy and annoyed.

His answer, which finally comes after a long silence, is abrupt. "It's the gecko."

The children shriek.

"Ah, be careful, you lot," Pito snaps. "You don't want the gecko to fall on your head in the middle of the night. Show respect."

And Materena is chuckling as she takes the cake out of the oven. She's chuckling because Pito is not fond of geckos at all.

He always keeps a flashlight under the bed, and when he hears the clicking sound of a gecko, he gets that flashlight real quick and shines it on the ceiling to check if there's a gecko up there. Right above his head.

And when there is a gecko sleeping on the ceiling right above his head, Pito either tries to shoo it away with the broom or he moves the bed to the other side of the bedroom. Most of the time, he wakes Materena up to help him move the bed.

A while later, there's a gecko on the ceiling, and Pito grabs the flashlight from under the bed. Then he wakes Materena up to help him move the bed to the other side of the bedroom.

Materena, who has been sleeping a deep, beautiful sleep, is furious. "How can you be afraid of a gecko? It's your totem!"

"Eh, my totem and that fat gecko, they're not the same, okay?" Pito is illuminating the gecko with his flashlight.

He goes on about how it's not his fault that he's afraid of geckos. It is the fault of his mama.

Mama Roti was seven months pregnant with Pito and resting

in the living room when a fat gecko fell from the ceiling and landed on her uncovered belly. She opened her eyes, saw the gecko, and screamed her head off.

In Pito's opinion, he was born with the fear of geckos in him.

The bed is on the other side of the bedroom now and Materena hops back in and makes herself comfortable. But Pito is standing, still illuminating the ceiling.

"You and the geckos better start living in harmony," Materena says.

Pito turns off the flashlight and gets into bed.

"*Oui,* it's true. I have to fight my fear of geckos," he says. "I can't go on checking the ceiling every single night of my life."

"Ah, *oui alors,*" Materena agrees. It's daunting going to bed never knowing if you're going to get woken up in the middle of the night because there's a gecko on the ceiling.

Materena is just drifting off when Pito wakes her again to make an announcement. He's getting himself a tattoo. He's been thinking about this for weeks — a tattoo on him — but he wasn't sure what it should be. Until now.

Materena hopes it's not a dragon spitting fire — that makes you look like you've had a visit to the prison. When Mori had that green and red dragon spitting fire tattooed on his chest, his mama went crazy. She believed that the dragon made her son look like he'd had a visit to the prison, which he had, but there was no need to tell the whole population.

There's no way Materena is letting Pito have a dragon tattooed on him.

"I'm not giving permission for you to have a dragon tattoo," she says.

"Eh what!" Pito exclaims. "Did I ever talk to you about dragons?"

"Ah, the tattoo is not a dragon?" Materena is relieved.

"I don't want a dragon," Pito says. "I'm not Chinese."

"You don't need to be Chinese, look at my cousin Mori."

"Your cousin Mori and I, we're not the same," Pito snaps. "And what is this permission business, eh? I don't need your permission. When you had that perm, did you ask my permission? *Non.* You went straight to the hairdresser, and when I saw you, I didn't recognize you, I thought you were a sheep."

Materena takes a deep breath. "A perm, it's for a few months. A tattoo, it's for eternity. What kind of tattoo are you going to have?"

She hopes it's not a heart pierced with an arrow. Her cousin James got one of them and it looks ridiculous.

Pito reveals that his tattoo is going to be a gecko.

And Materena thinks, Ah well, maybe the fear of geckos is going to disappear for good once Pito tattoos one of them on his body.

"And where are you going to put that gecko?" she asks.

Pito's gecko is going on his thigh, and this doesn't make sense to Materena.

"What's the point of having a tattoo if it's to hide it?"

"My tattoo, it's not to show off, it's . . . it's . . ." Pito searches for the right words.

Five minutes later: "It's like my identity."

Materena slowly nods. She's going back to sleep, but she's remembering her godfather Hotu's tattoo. He has a tattoo on his right shoulder. It is the name of the woman he loves — Imelda.

Hotu was fifteen years old when he had that tattoo done, and he went to show it off to Imelda. They weren't together at the time. Imelda got angry with Hotu. She said, "Ah, now that my name is tattooed on you, I'm forced to accept you."

Materena wouldn't mind having her name tattooed on Pito. Right underneath the gecko. There are no reasons why Pito shouldn't tattoo my name on his body, Materena thinks. I'm his wife.

"Pito, and my name? Can you tattoo it on you? Next to the gecko?" Materena is caressing Pito's thigh.

"I'm not tattooing any name on me," Pito says. "Just my gecko."

"Fine." Materena turns her back on Pito. "Maybe you're going to stop being afraid of geckos once you get one tattooed on you. But you don't know, eh? Your tattoo might attract geckos to come your way, crawling up your legs to say hello to their mate, sleeping on your thigh."

Materena waits for Pito to yell at her, but he just pulls the quilt over himself.

Brooming

Materena is now setting the record straight with Loana about Pito's totem. It is not a giant dog at all but a gecko. Loana's come, as discussed, to share a meal with her daughter, her daughter's man, and her grandchildren. As Materena gets the baked chicken out of the oven and calls Pito and the children, she whispers to her mother that it's best she doesn't tease Pito about it.

"Why would I tease him?" Loana snaps. "A totem is a totem! Think before you speak, Materena!"

Okay, Materena can see that her mother is in a slightly snappy mood tonight, so she serves her a nice glass of wine.

Loana and Materena are still at the kitchen table, drinking, with the kids in bed, when Ati makes an appearance.

Ati is Pito's best friend. Ati used to regularly visit Pito, but recently he got involved in politics. These days Ati is so busy with Oscar Temaru's independence party that he doesn't even have time to look for a woman.

Now, there's something you must know about Ati.

Ati was crazy about a woman a while ago and there was talk of a church marriage, but Ati's woman went out dancing at the Zizou Bar one night and met a legionnaire. Within two months of the meeting and after many secret rendezvous, the pair got married and flew to France.

Ati only became cranky at the *popa'a* after that episode. They hadn't bothered him much before.

Ati started to hang around with a few mates outside the Zizou Bar to pick fights with the *militaire.* Pito didn't participate because he didn't want to be seen hanging outside that bar.

Ati got in trouble with the gendarmes a few times and then his mama got really cranky at him and made him swear on top of his dead grandmother's head to stop picking on the *militaire.*

And it was then that Ati discovered politics and joined Oscar Temaru's independent political party.

The Oscar Temaru political party has organized an independence rally for tomorrow afternoon. They're all going to grab their brooms and go sweep the road. The sweeping is supposed to symbolize getting rid of those French *popa'a,* those invaders, those wicked people.

This is the reason Ati is here tonight. When Pito appears from reading his latest Akim comic, Ati asks Pito to be involved with this very important rally. Pito says, "Mate, I don't even sweep around the house, and you want me to go and sweep the bloody road?"

Ati asks Materena, who says, "Ati, you don't think I do enough sweeping as it is?"

And so Ati asks Loana, because it is his job to get as many sweepers as he can for tomorrow.

Loana looks deep into Ati's eyes. "Ati, you tell me why I should grab my broom and go sweep the road with you lot tomorrow, and then I'm going to give you my decision."

Materena, who is sitting opposite Ati at the kitchen table, makes signs to him to change the subject. It's not recommended, talking politics with Loana, especially the politics of independence.

Loana worships Gaston, the president of the territorial government. She queued three times to see him at the Territorial Assembly sixteen years ago. The first day she got there, it was five thirty in the morning and there were already about twenty-five people waiting to see Gaston. In those days, if you wanted to see Gaston, you just went to the Territorial Assembly and waited in line, no appointment was required.

Anyway, Loana didn't get to see Gaston on the first day. On the second day, she got to the Territorial Assembly at four thirty in the morning, but again she was too late. So on the third day, she arrived at three o'clock and she was granted a meeting with Gaston for nine o'clock.

Loana explained to him her trouble, which had to do with a legal bill she couldn't pay. Gaston got on the phone to his secretary and the secretary issued a special paper to Loana to give to the lawyer.

And since that day, Loana has worshipped Gaston. She's even got a few election T-shirts with a picture of her hero on them.

There's no way she's going to grab her broom and go sweep the road for Oscar Temaru, even if he is a distant relative — because she promised herself to remain true to Gaston till her death. And, anyway, Oscar irritates her.

Materena knows talking about Oscar's party to Loana is only going to end up in a heated argument, and Materena doesn't want a heated argument in her kitchen.

She wouldn't have minded so much if it were the afternoon and they were drinking cordials, but it is nine thirty at night — and they've been drinking lots of cheap red wine.

Ati takes a long slug of his red wine, Loana takes a long sip of her red wine. Materena is still trying to get Ati's attention, but he ignores her.

Pito says, "Relax, Materena."

Ati fires away. "When *pai* France needed patriots during the two World Wars, eh, we volunteered, yes, we volunteered to defend *la patrie*, because that is what you do when *la patrie* needs you — true?"

"Ati," Loana snaps, "just talk, don't ask me questions."

"*Oui,* I was saying, *la patrie* called out for help and we responded, and by the thousands, but when it was us who called out to *la patrie, la patrie* did the deaf trick on us."

Ati goes on about how when it was officially announced that Mururoa Atoll was chosen as the nuclear testing base in 1963, the Polynesian people said no. France told us that Tahiti would play an important role in the project. Again, we said no. The Port de Papeete would be modernized. No.

Everything would be of great value to Tahiti. *Non — aita! Aita!*

According to Ati, we never wanted the bomb. We formed parties to express our discord and anger. And every day more and more people joined the protest, and more, and more . . . But one day, President de Gaulle (Ati calls him *titoi* de Gaulle) made use of a twenty-seven-year-old law that "forbade all associations or groups whose aim is to assault the National Territory."

Ati puts his head down and sighs. "And these bastards exploded their bomb in our country." Ati lifts his eyes to the ceiling. "Our country!"

Another sigh from Ati. "France gave us money to shut our big mouths . . . and too many of us accepted, and since then we're all *foutue.* The whole lot of us. *Foutue.*"

But.

Ati smiles and explains that he has a vision (which he got from Oscar), and that is to get rid of all the *popa'a* and to live like we used to live, yes, we will plant our own food, we will fish, we will live simply. Happily. Independently.

Ati bangs his fist on the table and gulps more wine.

There's a long silence and everyone is waiting for Loana to fire back. Materena gets busy putting the flagon of wine away on top of the fridge.

Loana looks at Ati as if she were a schoolteacher, and he her student. "Ati, your mother, she still cooks for you and she's still cleaning up after you, *oui?*"

"*Oui*, and . . . ," Ati begins, puzzled. "What does my mama have to do with independence?"

Loana gets to her feet. It's late and she's going home, but there's one thing she must tell Ati before she leaves. "Independence, my arse."

Loana is gone and Materena clears the table, except for Ati's glass. Pito, he's got a beer. Ati and Pito are now talking about boats and fish, their usual topics of conversation, but Materena knows that when she's not around, Ati and Pito talk about women. Well, Ati does the talk about women and Pito listens. It's late and Materena would like Ati to go home, and so she grabs the broom and begins to sweep underneath the table. That is the polite way to let people know that they should make a disappearance. Nobody's feelings are hurt then. The broom touches Ati's feet, meaning, can you go now? But Ati lifts his feet up and smiles at Materena.

"You know what your mother said about me living with my mama," he says.

"*Oui, Ati.*" Materena doesn't sound interested.

"I'm not going to live with my mama for the rest of my life," Ati continues.

"Good for you," Materena replies absently. She likes Ati, but she sometimes finds him a bit annoying, with all his stories about women. At least he doesn't come around as often as he used to.

"As soon as I find myself a woman" — Ati goes on looking at Materena — "a woman I really care about, I'm going to marry her."

"Eh what?" Materena is so shocked to hear Ati mention marriage. "You? Married?"

"*Oui*. As soon as I find the right woman for me," Ati says.

Pito coughs, and gulps his beer. Materena puts her broom away and sits at the table, facing Ati.

"Are you serious, Ati?" she asks.

"*Ah oui,* Materena. I want kids, I want my own house. I want a wife."

Pito shuffles his feet uneasily.

Materena rests her head in her hands and looks at Ati straight in the eyes for a long time. She didn't know that side of Ati existed. The Ati she knows is a man who can't stay with a woman for more than two weeks, a man who doesn't want kids, a man who likes to show off his speedboat to Pito. She's never understood Ati's popularity with women, as she doesn't find him that nice to look at, but tonight, as her eyes meld into Ati's eyes, she can see why women would throw themselves at him. And she's thinking, Eh, he's not bad-looking at all, Ati. She chuckles inside as she remembers the wink Ati gave her that first day when he came to the snack with Pito. It is such a long time ago. She was sixteen years old.

"I just have to wait to meet that woman," Ati says.

"You will meet that woman." Materena gives Ati a tender smile. "And Pito?" she asks. "Is he going to be the best man?" She certainly wouldn't mind Ati being the best man at Pito's wedding.

"Woman," Pito snaps, "the way you're talking, Ati is getting married tomorrow."

"Pito?" Ati asks. "You want to be the best man at my wedding?"

"What is this?" Pito looks like he can't believe his ears. He gets up. "I'm going to bed."

Ati rises to his feet to leave too.

"Ah, come on, Ati," Materena says. "Stay. You don't have to go just because Pito is going to bed."

"It's okay, Materena, I'm going to my cousin's house for a birthday party." Then, looking at Pito: "You want to come too, or are you going to bed?"

"Sure." Pito isn't tired anymore. "I won't be long," he says to Materena.

Materena, smiling, waves Pito away.

It's the Rope Around the Neck

It is nine o'clock the following morning. Materena is walking past the church on her way home from the Chinese store, and there's a wedding going on there. Materena goes up to the church and peers through the louvers.

The bride is young and beautiful. Her wedding dress must have cost a lot, there's about twenty yards of lace and she's veiled. These days a veil doesn't mean virginity, of course. Her mother probably insisted on it.

The young woman whispers into the microphone her sacred vows to love, cherish, and obey the man standing beside her. The priest pronounces the two people husband and wife. Before God, before the law, before him. Husband and wife give each other a shy kiss, no doubt they'll get more passionate later on. Holding hands, and walking slow steps, they make their way out of the church. Most of the women in the congregation are dabbing their eyes. One woman sitting at the front cries loud tears — the bride's mother, for certain.

Petals of roses and grains of rice greet the newly wed couple outside.

Materena thinks she should probably go home now. Pito will be waiting impatiently for his hangover cure of roast-beef slices and lemonade, and, besides, she's wearing an old pareu and an oversize T-shirt, and people are starting to give her strange looks.

But the church is a public place and she's not being a nuisance. She just wants to see the married couple drive off in their bridal car.

"Materena! Materena, girl!"

Materena looks at the woman sitting at the steering wheel of the bridal car. "Eh!" she calls out, recognizing Mama Teta under the makeup. "It's you, the driver?"

"What's happening with the friend of your boss?" Mama Teta calls back. "What's taking so long? Is she still getting married, or has she pissed her man off?"

Materena can't believe Mama Teta's language sometimes. "The marriage is for very soon!" she calls.

The bride and the groom make their way to the bridal car, and Mama Teta is back in business. She toots the horn and the crowd cheers.

Materena waves good-bye to the happy couple, thinking, Soon it's going to be Pito and me in that bridal car.

Last night, after Ati told Materena about his desire to get married, she got really fired up about the wedding. She fell asleep thinking, Ati, he just *can't* get married before Pito.

Materena hurries home. As soon as she gets there, she's going to say to Pito: "When do you want to go to church to marry me?" She'll get the date and then she'll advise everyone of her marriage, starting with her mother.

Pito is not pleased she took so long to go to the store. "Did you go to France for that lemonade?"

Materena laughs. "*Ah hia hia,* stop your complaining."

Pito's on the sofa resting his eyes, a wet towel on his forehead — his head is sore. Materena tends to him lovingly, pouring his lemonade and serving him his beef slices.

Materena looks at Pito, who's hammering into the beef slices. "Pito." Her voice is so tender.

"Don't ask me to do anything," Pito growls.

Materena suggests that she make him an omelette. She knows Pito is always very hungry after a night on the booze. She also knows that it is no use to talk about serious matters with Pito when he's hungry and with a hangover.

"*Ah oui,* okay, thanks," Pito says.

Materena's in the kitchen beating the eggs for Pito's omelette when the bridal horn sounds again in the distance. She stops beating the eggs, smiles, and says, "Happiness to you two."

Pito's comment is loud and clear. "You bloody fools! Go hang yourselves!"

He goes on about how marriage is not for him: "Marriage — it's the rope around the neck," he grumbles.

The rope around the neck! Materena shouts in her head. This is what marriage means to you? The rope around the neck?

Materena, very angry now, cooks the omelette and eats it herself, thinking, The day I want that wedding, Pito better marry me! The day I want that ring on my finger and that marriage certificate on my wall, I'm not going to take no for an answer! And the children can pay for a wedding reception for their hardworking mother. I deserve a reception at the hotel by the beach — with a live band.

Pito calls out to Materena, "Eh, what's happening with that omelette? Did you go to the farm to get the eggs?"

Materena finishes the omelette and gets up.

"Materena!"

She washes the plate.

"Materena, darling!"

"Ah . . . *mamu.*" Materena goes outside to rake some leaves.

The Old Girlfriend

Materena is still outside raking the leaves (angrily, so angrily that the children are staying out of her way, quietly playing marbles) when she feels Rita calling out to her: Materena, Cousin!

Go to the telephone booth! I desperately need to talk to you! Rita's call is strong, very strong, and sad too. This is definitely not a happy calling. Materena puts her rake down. Sometimes you've got to put your own trouble aside. Materena hurries inside the house.

"Where's my omelette, *chérie?*" asks Pito, still resting his eyes on the sofa.

Materena fires a cranky look at Pito, gets her purse, and changes her T-shirt, and she's off to the telephone booth.

There's a young man in the telephone booth, and Materena sits on the curb and waits. Ten minutes later, the young man is still talking and Materena is starting to get annoyed. Always when you need to make an urgent call, she thinks, there's somebody in the telephone booth. Materena gets up to stand by the telephone booth. That way the young man will know she also needs to use the telephone. The young man looks at Materena and turns his back to her.

He puts more coins in.

Materena opens the door. "Are you going to be long? I need to call my cousin, it's urgent."

The young man turns around. "I'm talking to my girlfriend!"

"How long are you two going to talk for?" Materena is asking nicely so that the young man won't think that she's trying to kick him out of the telephone booth.

The young man looks like he can't believe his ears. "Why? You own the telephone?"

"Just give me an approximate time," Materena replies, keeping calm.

"I'm going to talk until I'm sick of talking!"

And the young man says to his girlfriend, "There are some people in this world. No respect for the people who are on the telephone."

The young man closes the door on Materena.

Materena realizes that there is no point in waiting for the telephone to be available, because when a young man talks to his girlfriend, the conversation can go on for hours. Why don't they just meet somewhere to talk? thinks Materena, and stomps off.

Materena hurries to the airport, where there is more than one telephone booth available, and she's remembering that movie she saw on the TV a few weeks ago.

The movie began with a man who had a gun in his mouth, about to pull the trigger, but the telephone rang. The man looked at the telephone and waited for the ringing to stop so that he could concentrate on killing himself. But the telephone rang and rang and rang. The man couldn't stand the ringing any longer. He answered with the gun still in his mouth.

It was an ex-girlfriend from a long time ago, calling him for help. "Please help me find my son," she said. "He's seventeen years old soon and he ran away."

The man said, "Excuse me? Who am I talking to?" The woman gave her name and the man immediately remembered her.

"He's your son too," the woman cried. "I beg you to help me." The man who had wanted to commit suicide took the gun out of his mouth and put it on the desk.

Materena is all puffed when she gets to the airport, but there's no time to catch her breath. She immediately barges into a telephone booth and dials Rita's number, but Rita is not answering. Rita's telephone is still ringing when Materena remembers the code. Rita came up with the code about three months ago. When Materena calls Rita, she must let the telephone ring three times, then hang up. She must do this twice in a row and then Rita will know it is Materena calling her.

Coco has a code too. A few people have a code, like Lily and Georgette, but Rita's mama and Rita's boss, they don't have a code.

Materena calls Rita using the code and Rita answers her telephone.

"'Allo, Materena." Rita sounds a bit sad.

"Rita, is everything okay with you?" All kinds of ideas come into Materena's mind. Rita's got cancer. Rita lost her job.

"I'm not fine, Cousin. We bumped into Coco's ex last week," Rita says.

"Okay, Cousin." Materena puts more coins in. "Tell me the story."

Last week, Rita and Coco stopped in town to look for Coco's mama's birthday gift, and they were supposed to just go to the Chinese store for a little bit of shopping. Rita and Coco were walking hand in hand when a woman marching past called out, "Eh, Coco! It's you?" And Coco exclaimed, "Eh, Sylvie! Are you fine?" And Rita got all tense because she knows about that Sylvie.

Sylvie opened her arms to Coco and gave him two big sloppy

kisses on the cheeks. And to Rita she gave a cold "how are you," all the while looking at Rita up and down. Rita was really annoyed that she was only wearing a pareu and an oversize T-shirt. She wished she was wearing her best clothes.

Rita gave Sylvie a cold "how are you" back and looked at her up and down too. She was really annoyed to see that Sylvie was wearing her best clothes and makeup, and nice shoes. That show-off bitch, she thought. If she was wearing an old pareu like me, she would have zoomed past — no stopping.

Sylvie was an ex-girlfriend of Coco, but not just any kind of ex-girlfriend. Coco and that woman had intended to get married, or so Coco's mama told Rita one day.

Sylvie lived with Coco for six months, and, according to Coco's mama, Coco and Sylvie were very good together. They never had arguments, they laughed, they joked around, and Coco's mama was happy because Sylvie made her son happy. And, plus, Sylvie was a good girl.

Yes, there was talk about marriage at the church.

But one morning, Sylvie packed her bags and disappeared, no good-bye, no nothing. When Coco's mama left the house to go to the Chinese store, Sylvie and Coco were talking in the living room, and by the time she came back, which was several hours later, as she bumped into three cousins on the way home, there was no more Sylvie.

Coco's mama thought Sylvie had gone to visit her mama. And when Coco told her the news, it was a real disappointment for her.

She tried to get an explanation from Coco because, to her mind, people didn't separate just like that. There had to be some fighting, some arguing, some tears, before the end. But every time she interrogated Coco, he would snap at her, "Ask me again and I swear I'm going to pack my bags too."

Coco was devastated. He lost his appetite for two whole weeks.

He watched the TV, and when the movie was funny he didn't laugh, and when the movie was sad, he sobbed.

Now here was that Sylvie in the flesh, chatting with Coco while Rita stood still like a coconut tree, smiling and not smiling.

Sylvie briefed Coco about her life since their separation. She'd been a dancer touring the world, married a wealthy American, divorced the wealthy American, moved to France and lived there for two years, then decided to get back to the *fenua* for a little while before heading off to Honolulu.

Coco nodded and smiled, and Rita felt like smacking him for that nod, that smile, and these big eyes staring at Sylvie's breasts, popping out of her décolleté.

Then Sylvie had to show off to Rita that she knew Coco very well.

"And you're still sleeping on the left side of the bed?" "And you're still trying to count the stars at night?" "You still like having your hair braided?" At each of Coco's affirmative answers, Sylvie exclaimed, "You're still sleeping on the left side of the bed!" "You're still trying to count the stars at night!" "You still like having your hair braided!"

Rita's ears were ringing and she clicked her tongue. And when Rita clicks her tongue, it means someone is getting on her system, and if that someone doesn't disappear real soon, Rita is going to do something irrational. So Coco said, "All right, then, Sylvie. We've got to go now."

Again Sylvie gave Coco two sloppy kisses and held on to him like he was her man, like the past was the present. She closed her eyes and dreamed, so Rita concluded, about the time when she was Coco's woman. Then she hurried away and soon disappeared.

Of course Rita wasn't in the mood to keep searching for Coco's mama's birthday gift (she wasn't in the mood in the first place, but after Coco's chitchat with Sylvie, she was even less in the mood). What Rita wanted to do was go home, shampoo her hair, massage her body with oil, and put on her best dress and a bit of rouge on her cheeks and lots of rouge on her lips.

Rita realizes that the past is the past and some part of the past is allowed to remain secret, but she really wanted to know why Sylvie left Coco. He mustn't have done anything bad to her, because if he had, Sylvie would have walked straight past him, her head held up high like she'd never known him in her entire life. But she jumped on him, she looked at him with . . . with loving eyes.

Rita wanted to make inquiries about Coco's separation from Sylvie. Why did Sylvie pack her bags? Why did she leave him?

But Rita waited for after dinner to dare inquire, because after dinner Coco is relaxed, he's willing to answer any questions.

So right after dinner, as Coco was enjoying his vanilla ice cream, she inquired.

And Coco said, "We just left each other."

And Rita wondered if there was any regret in Coco's heart. She wanted to ask him, "And do you regret?" But it's best to avoid asking such questions. Rita had to bite her tongue and concentrate on the ice cream on her plate.

That is the whole story, and now Rita is waiting for Materena to comment.

Materena is thinking.

She's thinking about how Rita gets upset when Coco looks at another woman. Even when the woman is in a movie, Rita gets upset. She turns the TV off and tells Coco that the next time he wants to do the sexy loving, he can go to Hollywood and find that woman to take him to the seventh sky, because Rita sure isn't going to be available. Coco can't look at another woman in a magazine either.

So, Coco looking at an ex-girlfriend . . .

And Materena is thinking about her cousins Lily and Loma. When Lily broke up with her fireman boyfriend because she got bored with his body and his fits of jealousy, he went out with Loma. Well, every time Loma bumped into Lily, Loma would give Lily dirty looks or pretend she didn't know her. But then the fireman broke up with Loma because she would only do the kissing and he was so on fire after all the things Lily used to do to him that he was desperate to do more than tender kissing.

And Loma is still giving Lily bad looks.

"Rita" — Materena is carefully weighing her words — "just you be thankful Sylvie isn't a cousin and you don't have to bump into her every time you go to the shop or to Mass."

There's a silence.

"Ah, true," Rita finally agrees. "Coco's with me and that's all I need to know, eh, Cousin?"

"That's all you need to know," Materena confirms.

"*Merci,* Cousin," Rita says, sounding close to tears. "You're such a good friend, I feel so much better after talking to you."

"It's okay, Rita," Materena says, "you make me feel better too when I'm down."

After a few more words of friendship, the cousins bid each other good-bye, say see you soon, I love you, etc., etc.

And Materena, walking home, is feeling much better too. Well, it's a beautiful morning, after all, a perfect day to take the kids to that beach that used to belong to the Mahi people, dig mussels (Materena loves mussels), and forget about the whole marriage nonsense. All of this is in the past.

Mussels

It's twenty past one in the morning and Materena is sitting at the kitchen table.

She can't sleep.

At six o'clock she's going to get the bread at the bakery and then she's going to make the coffee. Materena yawns. She's tired but she can't sleep, and there's no point lying in bed with the eyes open.

She could go scrub the bathroom for an hour, only she's too tired to scrub but not tired enough to sleep a deep sleep — the kind of sleep when you think of nothing. Materena sighs a long, heavy sigh.

She's worried. Today at eleven o'clock, she's going to court, and God knows what can happen to you when you go to court. Eh, you can go to prison. Many of her cousins have been to court and proceeded straight into the gendarmes' van. Direction — Nuutania Prison. Her cousin Mori, for instance, he borrowed a canoe, and the owner of the canoe sued him, and Mori spent two days in prison.

Materena is going to court because the gendarme caught her on private property.

Here's the story.

Behind the airport there's some land next to the sea. That

land behind the airport used to belong to the Mahi tribe, but an ancestor exchanged it for a few quarts of red wine. The exchange was carried out under private seal, so nobody knows the name of the *popa'a* who got the land for cheap. It's not for certain that he was a *popa'a,* but back then (when the Mahi people lost the land behind the airport) the *popa'a* people did a lot of exchanging with the Polynesian people — under private seal.

Materena loves that place behind the airport. She's been there six times. There's *aito* trees for shade, there's white sand, and there's the calm sea that is safe for the kids to swim in. Above all, there are lots of mussels, and Materena loves mussels. Mussels fried with garlic and onions or raw mussels with a squeeze of lime juice.

Whenever she feels like eating mussels, Materena packs bread, limes, cordial, cans of corned beef, a bucket, a can opener, and a knife and heads off with her kids to that special place. It takes them about twenty minutes to walk from the house. When they get to the landing strip, Materena makes sure the traffic light is green and there are no planes in the sky, then she gives the children the run signal. They always race across the landing strip. Materena stays behind the kids and yells, "Hurry, kids!"

As soon as they get to that place, the kids go for a swim (they're not allowed to go past the rock where the warm, shallow water ends and turns into dark blue water) and Materena gets busy digging mussels. She sits in the knee-deep water and digs her fingers into the sand. She always gets a mussel, but she only takes enough to fill up the bucket.

And it happens that Materena feels the presence of the people who used to dig mussels there, the people way before her time — her ancestors and their friends. They're sitting in a circle and they talk and they laugh, all the while digging mussels.

Since discovering it, Materena had hoped to be digging mussels at that special place for years to come.

But a gendarme paid her a visit in his police car.

Moana spotted the police car first. He hid behind his sister and shrieked, "Mamie, the gendarme!" And Leilani covered her flat chest with her hands, as she wasn't wearing a T-shirt.

Materena stopped digging and hurried to the shore, where the gendarme was waiting for her.

"*Iaorana.*" Materena smiled at the gendarme.

The gendarme just looked at her.

"Bonjour, monsieur." Materena thought that maybe the gendarme didn't appreciate the other greeting.

Again, the gendarme just looked at her, so Materena looked at him. There and then she figured out that the gendarme was in a bad mood. His eyes were angry — maybe he'd had a fight with his woman.

"What are you doing here?" he asked, in a bad mood.

"My kids, they swim." Materena showed the gendarme her kids. "And I look for a couple of mussels."

The gendarme was more interested in what was inside the bucket Materena was still holding than in her kids' swimming. "Are you aware this is private property?"

"Private property?" Materena asked, as if she didn't know what the gendarme was going on about.

The gendarme took a black booklet out of his pocket.

"Name?" The gendarme clicked his black pen.

"Materena Loana Imelda Mahi."

"Address?"

"Faa'a PK 5, behind the petrol station."

The gendarme furiously wrote the information down. "Occupation?"

"I'm a professional cleaner." Materena's voice was louder.

The gendarme looked at Materena and wrote *cleaner.* "Marital status?"

Materena grimaced. Talk about digging the knife in the wound!

"Marital status?" The gendarme sounded impatient.

"Monsieur," Materena replied, "I'm not married today because —"

The gendarme interrupted. "Either you're married or you're not. Marital status?"

"I'm not married."

"Are you a single mother?" The gendarme glanced at the children, who were still in the water.

"*Non!*" Materena didn't know why she had to shout. "*Non,*" she repeated, this time in a lower voice. "I'm still with the father of all my children."

"So you're in a de facto relationship," the gendarme said.

"Yes, monsieur."

"Couldn't you just tell me this earlier?" The gendarme looked so annoyed. "I haven't got all day to play guessing games."

He scribbled the words *de facto* and then ordered Materena to vacate the property — immediately.

"And this is private property," he said as he was leaving. "Do you know what *private property* means?"

Materena hesitated. "You can't go on the property."

"It is against the law to trespass on private property," he said. "Just you remember this. Vacate the property immediately."

He tipped his hat and left.

As soon as the gendarme's blue car was out of sight, the children got out of the water and raced to their mother. Materena explained the sad situation to them and immediately began to pack.

"That gendarme!" Tamatoa shouted. "Who does he think he is! If Papi was here . . ."

"You don't tell the gendarmes what to do," Materena said.

"They tell you what to do. If you tell them what to do, you get a court summons in return." And very seriously, she added, "The gendarmes are the law."

"But we weren't doing anything against the law," Leilani said. "The sea doesn't belong to one person. It belongs to everybody."

"God owns the sea." Moana waved to the sea.

"We walked on the private property before we got to the sea," Materena explained.

"But," Leilani continued to argue, "when the gendarme came, we weren't on the private property."

Materena, already on edge, snapped. "Leilani, it's not the moment to show off, okay? We're going home."

That evening Materena told Pito what had happened behind the airport.

"Why did you give your name to the gendarme?" Pito was angry. "You never give your name to the gendarmes. You make up a name. And why did you give your address?"

In Pito's opinion, and he was speaking from personal experience, if you don't give your name to the gendarme, the gendarme can't do anything. He can try to find you, but nobody is going to give him information, because, Tahitians, they don't talk to the gendarmes. They only talk to the *mutoi*.

"And what are you doing crossing the landing strip, anyway?"

"We only cross when the light is green," Materena said.

"Eh, sometimes the traffic lights don't work properly."

Materena also told Loana what happened behind the airport.

"What are you doing digging mussels there?" Loana was angry too. "I told you the mussels there are poisoned, cursed, and no good to eat."

Once Loana ate mussels from the airport and she nearly had to have an emergency operation.

"That gendarme," Loana continued. "I'm sure his woman gave him trouble in the morning and he had to take out his bad mood on you. Eh, maybe his woman left him for a younger man — a Tahitian."

Three days after the encounter with that bad-mood gendarme, Materena received a court summons.

She showed it to Pito.

"Ah, it's nothing," he said.

But Materena was in shock. "I can go to prison for this?"

"Nobody goes to prison over a bucket of mussels." Pito laughed and carried on reading his Akim comic.

Materena showed the court summons to Loana.

"Don't you worry about it, girl," she said.

"I can go to prison for this?"

"Let them try a little. They don't know my name. We're going to see Maeva and she's going to fix the situation pronto."

Maeva was definitely the woman to see — she knew about the law. Maeva is a distant cousin of Loana, from her mother's side. Maeva is a secretary of the boss of this big company, but she should have been a lawyer. She took the government to court a few months ago over Crown land in Rangiroa and she won the case. The story was in the newspaper. There was a picture of Maeva, barefoot and carrying her pandanus bag, on the front page with the thirty witnesses she got to speak at the tribunal of Rangiroa. One by one, these witnesses told the judge — who had flown from Tahiti for the case — a story about their land.

Loana and Materena went to see Maeva at her office. Maeva listened to the story as she typed a letter. She was very busy that day. "This is what I think," she said, typing her fast typing still. "There was a private-property sign and Materena ignored it."

Loana was about to explain that Materena ignored the private-property sign because the land used to belong to the Mahi family but an ancestor sold it for a few quarts of red wine, but Maeva held up her hand — meaning, I haven't finished.

"I know about the quarts of wine," she said. "We all lost land over quarts of wine, and the land we lost over quarts of wine is not the issue here. The issue here is that there was a private-property sign and Materena ignored it. Is the sign really visible?"

"Well, it's nailed to a tree," Materena replied.

"How high?"

Materena wasn't sure what Maeva was asking her.

"Is the sign nailed at eye level?"

"*Non,* it's higher."

"Do you have to lift your head to read the sign?"

"*Ah oui.*"

"Do you always lift your head when you see a tree?"

"*Oui,* to see if there's anything ripe in that tree."

"We're talking about an *aito* tree here, *oui?*"

"*Oui.*"

"And there's nothing ripe in an *aito* tree."

"Well, the *aito* doesn't have fruit."

Materena was getting more and more confused.

"So when a tree doesn't have fruit, you don't look up — correct?"

"True."

Loana made an interruption. "Why are we talking about trees?"

"We're talking about trees because the sign, which is the core of this story, is nailed to a tree." Maeva looked at Materena. "Describe the sign to me."

"Well . . . there's a black board and the writing is in white."

"How big is the board?"

Materena shows Maeva with her hands.

"Okay," Maeva said. "It's not a big sign. And the letters — are they capital letters?"

"*Non* — normal."

"Is the sign only written in French?"

"*Oui.*"

Maeva nodded. "Did you see the sign the first time you went there?"

"*Non.*"

"How come?"

"You can't see that sign if you don't look for it."

"Why is it that you can't see the sign?"

"It's a bit hidden by the branches."

"Did the gendarme ever point out the sign to you?"

"*Non.*"

Maeva stopped typing and swung her office chair to face Materena and Loana.

"Okay. You go take a photograph of that sign. Make sure you can't see the whole sign in the photograph. Don't you two cut the branches to make that sign more visible."

"That's all we do?" Loana asked.

"*Oui.*"

Loana had thought her cousin was going to tell them to argue about a particular article in the law that said that when the land is sold over a few quarts of red wine, the original owners of the land still have the right to the land in some way.

"That's really all we do?" she asked again.

"Can I go to prison for this?" Materena asked.

Maeva did her serious-business look. "Girl, if you go to prison, your story is going to be on the television. Nobody can be accused of trespassing on private property when the private-property sign is not visible."

So Materena and Loana went to take a photograph of that not-visible sign.

They also went to the courthouse three days ago to familiarize themselves with the environment — Loana's idea. They sat at the back and watched and listened. There was a young man who stole a TV — he got convicted. There was a young man who stole a car — he got convicted. There was another young man who stole a hi-fi system — he got convicted. The judge spoke harshly to these young men, like he was *fiu* of dealing with thieves. There were mamas and grandmamas crying all over the place. One man (the one who stole the car) yelled out, "I'm innocent!"

And the judge said, "Get a job — and pity your mother for a change."

"You can't compare yourself to them," Loana reassured Materena once they were outside the courthouse. "They're hoodlums and you're a hardworking mother. You're going to get dressed nice — you have to look respectable. Those hoodlums, they didn't even comb their hair."

Loana advised Materena to take the kids to the tribunal because apparently the judge always feels sorry for you when you've got kids, but Materena refused. The kids, they're going to school.

The kids don't know about the court summons.

Materena's boss doesn't know about the court summons.

And Pito can't take a day off, because he's had so many (due to hangovers) that he might lose his job.

Materena and Loana are in the truck now, on their way to Papeete. It's nine thirty, there's plenty of time, but Materena wants to be in the tribunal way before eleven o'clock because it's best to be in the tribunal early. Then you don't keep the judge waiting.

Materena is wearing a dress, and her hair is plaited in two plaits. There's no rouge on her cheeks, and there's no flower behind her ear. There's just the dress and the bleached white, flat shoes. And the pandanus bag.

The rock-and-roll music in the truck is annoying her. It's too loud. But you don't tell the driver what music he can play in his truck.

"You've got the photos?" Loana asks in Materena's ear.

"*Oui.*"

"You're sure?"

"Yes, Mamie."

But Loana wants to see the photographs with her own eyes, so Materena gets the photo holder out of her bag. There are thirty-six photos of the tree and the PRIVATE PROPERTY TRES-PASSERS WILL BE PROSECUTED sign that you can't really see. They used a whole roll of film. Loana flicks through the photos. She's satisfied now, she puts the photos back in the holder. Materena puts the holder back in her bag.

"Don't you get nervous." Loana puts her comforting hand on Materena's shoulder. "Stay calm."

"Yes."

"Because when you get nervous, you say a whole lot of nonsense."

Materena, looking out the window, nods.

"Like how you've gone to that place six times," Loana goes on. "I told you not to go there. *Ah hia hia,* the children, we think once they're grown-ups, we don't have to worry about them, but the worrying never stops."

Materena keeps looking out the window.

"Stay calm," Loana says.

"I'm calm."

"Don't be afraid of the judge. He's just a person. Just imagine him on the toilet. He's somebody, but he's not God. Ah, if I had the money, I would have hired a lawyer to defend you. A lawyer has to be better than you defending yourself. A lawyer knows the tricks and the rules. All you've got are photos."

"I can defend myself." Materena strives to sound confident.

"Don't cry at the tribunal," Loana says.

"I'm not going to cry."

"When we cry, it's like we're guilty. The judge doesn't like it when we cry in front of him. He prefers it when we stay calm."

"Yes." Materena wishes her mother would keep quiet. She's concentrating here.

"Don't forget that when you speak to the judge, you have to call him Your Highness."

"Yes, I know." What is the boss going to say when she finds out about the conviction?

"And don't talk to Your Highness the way you talk normally. We don't say 'eh' to Your Highness."

"Yes." Pito, he can't even cook rice.

"Look at the judge in the eyes."

"Yes." Materena's voice is now a sad murmur. And my poor kids, eh. No way I'm going to prison.

"Do you think you're a pilot?" the judge asks.

Materena is standing before him, her head held up high but not so high that the judge would mistake respect for arrogance. She's surprised about the question. She thought the first question Your Highness was going to ask her would be, "Did you see the private-property sign?" She would then have said, "No, Your Highness, because the sign is not very visible, and I've got proof, I've got photos."

Does she think she's a pilot? Of course not! Why would she think that she's a pilot? Is Your Highness trying to trick her?

"*Non,* Your Highness." Materena hesitates. "I don't think I'm a pilot."

"Er, it's Your Honor," the judge says. Then, "Imagine you and the children are on the landing strip and a plane has to land." The judge looks into Materena's eyes. "Are you imagining?"

Materena wants to tell Your Highness (Honor) that they

only cross the landing strip when the light is green, and the light is still green by the time they reach the other side. Also, she always checks the sky for planes, she knows that sometimes planes have to do an emergency landing and the pilot doesn't have time to contact the traffic controllers. It's a risk to cross the landing strip, Materena realizes that, but it's safer to cross the landing strip than it is to cross the road.

She can't imagine herself and the kids on the landing strip when a plane has to land. But she's not going to argue with Your Highness.

"Yes," she says. "I'm imagining."

There's a moment of silence.

"Anything can happen," Your Highness goes on. "The pilot might try to divert the plane and in doing so crash the plane, killing hundreds of people . . . or he might choose to run you and your children over. Are you imagining?"

Ah yes, Materena is imagining now, and she's not feeling good.

"And I do not count the fact," Your Highness says, "that you are endangering yourself and your children by swimming at the airport. Underwater electrical cables, for example."

Materena gives Your Highness a shocked look. "Underwater electrical cables? It doesn't say on the private-property sign that there's underwater electrical cables."

"So you *knew* about the private-property sign." The judge looks a bit angry now.

Materena too, she's angry. She's not thinking about her defense. She's only thinking about how her kids and she could have been electrocuted.

"Monsieur," she says, "I know all about electrical cables. My brother, he was an electrician once. I know you don't mess around with electrical cables, and I never do mess around with electrical cables. We can die when we mess around with electrical cables. Now, monsieur, that sign doesn't say anything about the electrical cables."

Materena is forgetting to call the judge Your Highness or Your Honor. "*You* imagine a little, eh? My kids, they're swimming and they get electrocuted because nobody told me about the electrical cables. Imagine how I'm going to feel. I'm going to feel like I killed them. I'm never ever going near that place again. And, monsieur, that private-property sign better be fixed . . . I'm glad the gendarme sent me a court summons."

Ah yes, she's blessing that man now. She's taking back all the bad talk she and Loana did about him — how his woman left him for a younger man because he's a cranky old bastard, etc. And then Materena starts crying. She tries to fight the crying, but the revelation about these underwater electrical cables — it's too much of a shock.

"I'm happy we didn't get electrocuted." Materena is now wiping her eyes with the palm of her hand. "Give me one hundred thousand francs, give me a million francs, I'm never ever going to that place behind the airport."

Case dismissed.

Teacher

What a shock about those electrical cables . . . her children came so close to being killed . . . Materena is still crying as she walks to the market past the clothes shops, wiping her tears with the back of her hands.

"Mamie," she says, "I'm going to buy the kids a surprise." By *surprise,* Materena means a family-size packet of chocolate cookies — something nice to eat that her kids don't often have. She might even buy a big, juicy watermelon on top of the surprise. "I can't believe . . ." Materena stops talking to look at her mother, standing still, with a pained expression on her face. "Mamie?"

Loana hurries to hide behind a rack of clothes reduced by 50 percent, with Materena following.

"Look at that man," Loana whispers. "There, walking slow steps, a pandanus bag on his arm."

Materena looks at the old man and looks at her mother. Is she supposed to know that old man?

The man stops to sit on a bench and roll a cigarette. He doesn't notice the two women standing next to the rack of clothes reduced by 50 percent — eyeing him. He gets a book from his pandanus bag and reads, all the while smoking his cigarette.

Materena waits for her mother to tell her who the man is. Loana knows a lot of people and it isn't unusual for her to bump into a number of them when she's in town. Materena is used to her mother chitchatting for long minutes at a time with someone she knows or used to know, or someone who's a bit related to her.

"That man was my teacher." Loana is still whispering. "He's an old man now but he was a young man when he taught me all those grammatical rules and mathematical formulas."

"In Rangiroa?" Materena is whispering because her mother is.

"Of course in Rangiroa," replies Loana, now talking with her normal voice. "I didn't go to school in Tahiti. I only went to school in Rangiroa."

"Ah — well, go say *iaorana*."

"*Oui,* I'm going to say *iaorana* to him. I'm sure he's going to recognize me, I was his best student."

But Loana doesn't go over to her teacher. She just hides behind the clothes rack.

"Go on." Materena is puzzled. Usually when her mother wants to have a little chitchat with someone, she just marches over to that someone and calls out, "*Iaorana!*"

"He'll think I'm somebody now, you see," Loana says.

"Mamie, you raised us kids. You *are* somebody."

"*Non,* it's best he doesn't know I clean houses." Loana's voice is a sad murmur now. "It's best Teacher thinks that Loana Mahi, the daughter of Kika, is somebody — a secretary or a teacher."

The man has finished his cigarette and slowly rises to his feet and walks away — he's gone.

Tears well in Loana's eyes. "My teacher, eh."

In the truck, on the way home, Loana talks more about her teacher, she talks about the days when she was at school.

"In my day . . . it was forbidden to speak the native language on the school grounds. We speak *miri-roa* in Rangiroa, it's like the Tahitian language but a bit more singing and with a few different words.

"*Oui,* we had to speak the French language, but it's a bit difficult to play in a foreign language, so at every lunch break Teacher would always catch a student breaking his command, and, that student, well, he got the porcelain shell. His mission: find another *miri-roa*-language user and pass the porcelain.

"The porcelain shell transformed you into a person with a contagious skin disease. Everybody would run away from you, tell you to go to another direction, call you *tiho tiho,* the informer. Only the tough ones continued to play, and speak the native language, without fear of getting the porcelain shell. Their warning: 'You give me that shell and you're going to get it after school.'

"When the first person to have the porcelain shell was a tough, he would get rid of it in a rapid second. He would walk up to somebody and say, 'Take this or you're going to get it after school.'

"That was how I would get the porcelain shell, girl.

"One day I told Teacher, 'It's much easier to play in *miri-roa.* The French language, it's for inside the class.'

" 'Loana,' he said, 'I'm the teacher and I'm telling you, the French language is to speak as soon as you enter the school yard. Do you think I'd be a teacher today if I didn't force myself to speak the French language every day, more than my own language?'

"Some days, when the porcelain shell wasn't passing around as much as Teacher expected, everyone got special punishment: weeding, and scrubbing the grapefruit leaves.

"And writing *I must speak French at school* one hundred times."

Materena nods. She can relate to her mother's story. It was also forbidden to speak Tahitian on the school grounds in Materena's school days, and she remembers the nuns pacing the school ground, their ears wide open for a foreign word. Things have changed now, and the Tahitian language is being taught at school.

"He was a devoted teacher, that man," Loana says. "He was always arguing with the parents for allowing their children to miss out on school — the girls to help with the cleaning, the boys to fish and work copra.

" 'Paper is the future!' he often said. And one of the parents would always respond, 'Coconuts — always plenty on trees. Fish — everywhere in the ocean. A girl, she needs to learn how to cook.'

"Teacher had a vision: to see more Polynesian teachers, so many they wouldn't need to come from France to teach us. In his vision, there was even a Polynesian governor, and, who knows, he could be from Rangiroa!

"People laughed at his vision. Some said, 'The other teacher was better. He didn't interfere with people's lives. He didn't try to change us.' And, 'That teacher, he's a dreamer. He should go back to Tahiti.'

"Teacher was obsessed with getting his students to pass the school certificate, but every year all he got were failures. One year, a few years before I was in his class, he seriously considered giving up teaching, but his wife threatened to leave him. She told him he didn't study all these years to become a postman.

"There were only two classes in the school. One class for the little kids and one for the big kids. Teacher was my teacher for three years, and during that time he discovered that I had — and I don't mean to show off to you — I had an amazing memory."

Materena hugged Loana. "Mamie, you still have an amazing memory. You always remember people's names and words they told you, even if it was ten years ago."

Loana cackles, but not loud. She doesn't want the other passengers of the truck to think she's mocking them. They are German tourists with sunburned noses, thongs, and cameras hanging at their necks. They just look out the window.

"Girl," Loana says, "the reason my memory is good is because your grandmother didn't like to repeat herself. She would tell me her orders once and I better register them . . . Teacher only had to tell me a grammatical rule or mathematical formula once for me to register, whereas with the other students, he had to repeat and repeat, and sometimes he would fall on his chair and rest his head on the table for a while. Other times he smashed his cane on the board and left the room to go have a cigarette outside . . . I can see him, eh, my teacher. His hands are white from the chalk. His face is brown-red from the frustration. He's having his cigarette outside, and there's total silence in the class."

Loana smiles. "You know, girl . . . Teacher personally selected me to recite the welcoming speech to the governor of Tahiti when he came to Tiputa to inaugurate the new quay."

"*Ah oui?*" Materena is truly impressed.

"*Ah oui,* girl. Teacher selected me because of my amazing memory. The village approved of the selection, except for a few mothers who believed their child was a better selection. They went to confront Teacher about that matter. He gave them two seconds of his attention, then showed them the door."

Materena laughs. She imagines these women in Teacher's office, complaining and carrying on about how their kid is better than Loana. It's a natural thing to think, and Materena understands.

"Teacher said to me, 'Loana, the whole village will be watching you. Don't make me regret my decision.'

"The welcoming speech was quite short. 'Welcome to Tiputa, Monsieur le Governor! We are honored . . .' More words like that and some words that didn't make sense to me at all.

"Days and days I lived for that speech, reciting it over and over again, morning, afternoon, and night. Mama exempted me from all duties, she wanted that speech to be planted in my head. She couldn't help me with the speech because, your grandmother, she didn't speak French, except for a few sentences like, 'Is this an owl I perceive in the forest?'

"Girl, I was shaking with nerves when I got onto the podium . . . then all the people disappeared — Mama, Teacher, and the governor of Tahiti included.

" 'Welcome to Tiputa!' I began, and before I knew it, the crowd was applauding.

"I was the star of the inauguration. Eh, I danced with the governor! And I sat beside him at the table of honor! And you know what Teacher said to me?"

"He said it's good?" Materena asks.

"He said, 'Loana, when I retire, you're going to replace me.'" Loana looks out the window. "But here I am, past fifty, and I still don't have my school certificate."

Materena knows that Loana doesn't have her school certificate because she left school three months before the school-certificate exam to come to Tahiti with her mother. Her mother's man was in Mamao Hospital, very ill. But her mother ended up dying (of a heart attack) instead — and her man, he went back to his island, leaving Loana alone in Tahiti.

And Loana has been cleaning houses ever since.

Materena tenderly holds her mother's hand. She remembers when she sat for the school certificate, how Loana really got involved with her studies. She pinned notes all over the house and Materena couldn't go anywhere in the house without being confronted with a grammatical rule or mathematical formula, not even in the toilet. Those notes drove Materena crazy, and she escaped into the garden, but then Loana decided to pin the notes on the trees, the potted plants, and the wire fence.

Loana also decided that Materena was going to sing a song for the oral exam instead of reciting a poem, and the song would of course be a church song, as, in Loana's opinion, Materena was bound to score twenty out of twenty with a church song.

The day of the exam results, Loana was sick with nerves, and Materena couldn't just tell her mother the result as it was — pass or fail. Loana had to have signs — wave her pareu this way for *pass* and wave the pareu that way for *fail*. It was all so complicated.

Well, Materena passed the exam and Loana went around the neighborhood to show off her daughter's framed school certificate. Materena's framed school certificate is still proudly displayed in Loana's living room.

Materena thinks about how her mother should be proudly displaying her own school certificate.

"Mamie," Materena says.

"Yes, girl."

"You can get that paper now. I can enroll you. There are classes at the Pomare High School for the school-certificate exam, and you can get that paper — easy. You're very intelligent."

Loana half smiles, and shrugs.

"Eh, Mamie," Materena goes on, "there's no law that says you can't sit for the school-certificate exam at fifty-two years old. Look at Mama Teta, she got her driver's license at fifty-six."

"It's thirty-eight years ago I needed that paper," says Loana. "Not today."

Belief

Poor Mamie, eh, thinks Materena, hiding the family-size packet of chocolate cookies in the fridge. Eh-eh, Mamie . . . Materena sits at the kitchen table. She needs to recover a little from the day — the court, her mother's teacher. Sometimes too much happens in one day.

But wait a minute, Materena tells herself, did she thank her mother for having come with her to court? *Non!* Materena springs to her feet and hurries to her mother's house.

Loana is in the living room pinning patterns to a quilt. "Eh?" She cackles. "You again?"

Materena throws her arms around her mother (she won't bother asking her about the health this time), all the while thanking her for her support in court, for all the food she put in her stomach, for everything.

"*Chérie,*" Loana says, "it's all right."

More hugs, until Loana gently pulls away, she has a quilt to finish, she says.

"Who is the quilt for?" Materena asks.

"It's for Father Louis. It's a farewell gift to him from your auntie Celia. You know he's going home to Quebec to retire?"

"*Ah oui?*" Materena says. She's sad. She likes Father Louis. He's funny. "And who is the new priest?"

"I don't know, but he better not be too young and too handsome."

Materena nods, all the while helping her mother pin the patterns onto the quilt. The base fabric is white with patterns of green breadfruit leaves, red hibiscus flowers, yellow frangipani flowers, and light blue doves. Once all the patterns are pinned, Loana will hand stitch them. When she starts that she will require total silence — Loana can't talk when she's stitching her quilts. She needs 100 percent concentration. But right now she can talk.

"We, the Polynesians, have always been a religious type of people, girl. In the old days, and I'm talking about the old days, a long time ago," Loana insists, "we prayed before everything we did. We prayed before eating, working on the land, planting our gardens, building our houses, throwing the net, and before we began and ended a voyage. We prayed nonstop, girl.

"We had a god, or, I should really say, gods," she continues, "but the most important god was Ta'aroa. You know about Ta'aroa? The legend?" Loana asks.

Materena shakes her head. She doesn't know the legend of Ta'aroa. She only knows the story of God. God who forgives, God the greatest, Jehovah.

"Here's the legend, girl. You can tell the kids."

Loana neatly places a pattern of a dove on the fabric and straightens it a few times with the palm of her hand.

"A long time ago," begins Loana, "there was Ta'aroa. He was his own creator and he lived all by himself in a shell. The shell looked like an egg. This egg was in the space and there was no sky, no earth, no moon, no sun, no stars. There was nothing, girl.

"Ta'aroa was a bit bored in his shell, so one day he broke it and got out to see what was outside. Outside was dark, outside was nothing. There and then Ta'aroa realized he was alone, all alone.

"He shattered his shell and created the rocks and the sand. With his vertebrae he created the mountains. The oceans, the lakes, and the rivers came from his tears. He gave the fishes and the turtles scales using his nails. With his feathers he created the trees and the bushes. And Ta'aroa made the rainbow using his own blood.

"Then Ta'aroa decided to create man . . ."

Loana's voice dies down to a murmur.

"This is what the legend says, anyway," Loana says, looking at the statues of the Virgin Mary displayed in her living room. "But it doesn't mean the story about Adam and Eve is an invention.

"We made *to'o* images of our gods. We used wood or rock, and there were feathers attached to the image, red and yellow feathers. These feathers were the emblem of divinity."

Materena's ears are wide open. She likes when her mother talks about history. Loana knows about history because when she and Imelda meet for a little chitchat, Imelda always talks about history and Loana likes to listen. Imelda's vast knowledge of history comes from the many old people she's befriended over the years. She always says, "You want to know about the past? Well, talk to the old people."

"The image was kept in the house of God," Loana says. "And when we needed to communicate with God, we would appeal to Him to grant us His presence — by entering the *to'o*, His image.

"We had to have ceremonies, and long too, I'm talking days, for God to come to us. Whereas now . . . all you need to do for God to listen to you is say, 'God — I really need to talk to you.'" Loana sighs. "It's good to believe."

Materena agrees with a slow nod. She thinks, Yes, it's true, it's good to believe — in something.

They pin the patterns in silence for a while, humming church hymns.

And Loana asks, "You know how we became Christians? The Mahi family, I mean. I don't know how my family from my mama's side became Christians. You know the story of the mango tree?"

Materena doesn't know that story.

"Are you sure I've never told you that story?" Loana looks at Materena in doubt.

"I'm sure, Mamie. I'm one hundred percent sure."

"You should know the story of the mango — and tell it to your kids . . . Well, here's the story of how we became Christians.

"Your great-grandmother was lying on the mat by her mango tree one day when the priest came to pay her a visit. She greeted him coldly because she wanted nothing to do with him, and that woman wasn't the kind to have her resting interrupted — a bit like me.

"The priest, well, he ignored her coldness and went on about how beautiful the day was. Great-Grandmother told him the sun was going to disappear soon — look at the sky, see the gray clouds, feel the rain coming. The priest maintained the weather was going to remain charming until the end of the week. 'Who told you?' she asked. 'Your God?' He replied, 'Yes.' 'What is it you want at my house?' she asked the priest.

"Spread the goodness of God, was what he wanted to do. 'Your God, it doesn't interest me, now go your way,' Great-Grandmother said.

"She stood up and faced the man in the black robe. 'You come here and burn our prayer-meeting houses, and destroy our *marae,* you come here and tell us our God doesn't exist. Your God you can keep for yourself, I don't want Him.'

"She lifted her eyes to a mango and down it fell, onto the

priest's head. He stumbled, and for a brief moment, it looked like he was going to faint. 'Out of my land,' she said to him. 'I've spoken.'

"The priest lifted his eyes to the tree and said to it, 'As of today, you will produce no more fruit.'

"The following morning, the mango tree was ashes, and the next day, your great-grandmother, she became a Christian, a Catholic, and right until her death she blessed the day God, the real God, came into her life."

Materena looks at her mother, thinking that the priest probably sneaked back to the mango tree during the dark with a box of matches and some firewood.

But she says, "It's true?"

"Oh *oui,* girl, I'm not inventing."

They get humming again and soon every single pattern is pinned onto the fabric. And it is time for Loana to start stitching. Materena rises to her feet, she's going home.

Mother and daughter hug, and kiss each other on the forehead. And on her way home, Materena thinks about God. God, and Loana.

Loana was raised within the walls of the Church — every night she and her mother would go to Mass and then to the singing rehearsals. The whole village went to Mass and singing rehearsals, especially when it was the priest and not one of his *diacres* who was celebrating the Mass.

The whole village was on its best behavior when the priest was in the village. But as soon as the priest went away to attend to the needs of other atolls, fights and arguments would break out here and there in the village. Mostly about women and coconuts. And ten-year-old Loana would help her mother wash the priest's robe — a great honor.

Between her twenties and her thirties, Loana forgot God as

she drifted from man to man in her search for Love. But her cousin Imelda slowly drew her back to God. And since, Loana's life has been much easier.

She often says, "I thank my faith."

Nowadays Loana goes on weekend retreats with the nuns. She reads at the Mass too sometimes, when her sister asks her to. Materena usually helps her mother with the reading. She listens to Loana practice over and over again, she even records the reading so that Loana can relax, knowing her reading is perfect — that she's got the right tone of voice and she's not speaking too fast or too slow. And Materena goes to Mass to listen to her mother read a paragraph out of the Bible to the congregation, to show her support. Once, in the earlier days of her reading at the Mass, Loana got sick with nerves and went to hide behind the church. And so Materena read for her mother, and Celia got angry with Loana.

She shrieked, "That is the last time I'm giving you the opportunity to read at the Mass!"

But Celia forgot her anger with Loana because she needed her younger sister to do something for her.

Like make that quilt.

Materena is still thinking about God as she walks home.

Someone toots the horn and Materena waves absently — it must be a relative.

Materena used to test the existence of God. If that woman there looks in my direction, God exists. If that baby there starts to cry, God exists.

One day, she asked her mother if God really existed. Loana didn't say yes, she didn't say no.

She just said, "One day, girl, you're going to be thankful there's a God for you to believe in."

And it is true, Materena is thankful there's a God for her to believe in. But she prays to the Virgin Mary, Understanding Woman, more than she prays to God.

In fact, Materena only prays to the Virgin Mary, Understanding Woman. Her most frequent prayer is about not outliving any of her children, because children, unlike men, are irreplaceable.

Children, unlike men, show you that they love you.

The Story of the Coconut

With a quick cranky look at Pito, lying still on the sofa like a coconut tree, Materena, a coconut in her hand (for the coconut milk), greets her mother at the door.

"*Iaorana,* Mamie!" Materena sings, kissing her mother on the cheeks.

"*Iaorana,* girl," says Loana, then glances toward the sofa. "Eh, *iaorana,* Pito."

"*Iaorana.*"

Loana looks at her daughter and raises her eyes, meaning, does he ever do anything? Materena shrugs, meaning, *non,* you know your son-in-law, he likes the horizontal position.

Allez, let's go to the kitchen, but first Loana has to kiss her grandchildren, especially her youngest one, Moana, who hasn't learned to answer back yet. The sweet eight-year-old follows his mother and grandmother to the kitchen.

And now he's looking at the coconut, which Materena is about to crack open with a machete. Loana, who has been invited for lunch, takes the coconut from Materena and holds it out in the palm of her hand.

"Look at that coconut, Moana."

Moana stares at the coconut.

"What can you see?" Loana asks.

"I can see dots."

"How many dots can you see?"

"Three." And, pointing to each dot, Moana adds, "One here, one here, one here."

Loana smiles. "And do you know what these dots represent?"

Moana shakes his head.

"These two dots here — side by side — represent the eel's eyes," Loana says.

Moana looks closer at the dots, then he lifts his eyes to his grandmother. "Eel's eyes?"

"*Ah oui,* Moana. And this dot here all by itself represents the eel's mouth. Do you know about the legend of the coconut?"

No, Moana doesn't know about the legend of the coconut.

Loana says she is going to rectify the situation, as, in her opinion, everybody should know about the legend of the coconut. It is such a great legend.

"A long time ago," Loana begins, "long before the airplanes were invented and long before the television was invented, there was a princess called Hina.

"When Hina turned sixteen years old, her father told her that she was to marry the prince of Lake Vahiria. Hina looked forward to meeting that prince, but when they were finally introduced, she saw that, as well as being ugly, the prince of Lake Vahiria was an eel. She was horrified and swore to herself that she was never going to marry that repulsive eel.

"But the eel lost his heart to the beautiful princess within a second. He would not take no for an answer, so Princess Hina decided to have him killed. She appealed to God Maui for help. God Maui captured the eel, cut him into three slices, and wrapped the head of the eel in tapa cloth. He gave it to Princess Hina with strict instructions to immediately bury it in the familial *marae.*

"But Princess Hina forgot all about Maui's instructions and

went for a swim in the river on her way home. Not long after, the earth began to tremble and a tree sprouted — a strange-looking tree resembling an eel. On her way home, a voice cried out, 'One day, Princess Hina, you're going to look into my eyes, you're going to kiss my mouth. You're going to love me.'

"Princess Hina, she just laughed.

"Years passed and a terrible drought hit the islands of Tahiti. People everywhere were dying from thirst. Hina went back to that strange-looking tree. One of her servants picked up one of its round fruits and peeled it. Princess Hina saw the three dots and remembered the eel's words. The servant pierced a hole in the dot, and Princess Hina pressed her lips on the eel's mouth and drank the sweet water. There and then she realized how much the eel had loved her, and loved her still."

Moana wants to hold the coconut, and Loana puts it in his hand.

"This is the legend of the coconut," she says. "Tell it to your kids."

Moana feels sad for the eel. He caresses the coconut. "Just because the eel was ugly. Poor eel, eh."

Loana goes on about how beauty, the real beauty that lasts forever, comes from within. The eel was, perhaps, ugly, but his heart was beautiful and pure. His love for Princess Hina was true.

"Poor eel." Moana is now kissing the coconut. "Poor prince."

Pito, still lying on the sofa like a coconut tree, calls out, "Hina didn't want the eel because he was an eel — full stop!" In Pito's opinion, the prince of Lake Vahiria would have been better off mixing with his own kind. There were, for sure, lots of keen and pretty eels swimming about in the river, waiting for the prince's signal. The eel was stupid, wanting a human for his woman.

Moana doesn't feel sorry for the eel anymore. He gives the coconut back to his grandmother. "Stupid eel."

And now Moana is going to play outside and Loana is going back to her house. She's lost her appetite. She rises to her feet and grabs her bag.

"Ah, come on, Mamie," Materena pleads. "Don't pay attention to what Pito says."

Giving her mother her best *I beg you* look, Materena continues. "I went to the market at five o'clock this morning to make sure your *ature* was fresh."

Loana sits down again.

"Can I get you a glass of wine, Mamie?" Materena asks.

"No, it's too early. Later."

Materena is really annoyed with Pito. The trouble with Pito is that he can't understand legends, so he has to ruin them.

Last time she visited, Loana told the legend of the breadfruit to Leilani. The legend is about a man who transforms himself into a breadfruit tree in the middle of the night so that his woman and children have something to eat. That legend was another story of love, as Loana likes legends about love, just as she likes movies about love and songs about love. Just like Materena.

Pito had to add his grain of salt then too. "What is this transforming yourself into a tree?" he called out from the sofa. "What use can you be to your woman and children if you're a tree? Isn't it better for a man to go hunt some wild pigs or fish to feed his family!"

Of course Loana got cranky and went home, but today she must stay, because the *ma'a* Tahiti is in her honor.

Materena gets the coconut and she's about to crack it open, but first she feels she should talk to Moana. Explain the legend to him a bit better.

"Moana, darling!" she calls out.

Moana immediately responds, "*Oui,* I'm coming, Mamie."

Materena gets him to hold the coconut and sit. "Now," she begins, "you know your friend Albino."

"Yes," says Moana, "but his name is Vetea." Vetea is Moana's best friend from school. Moana talks about him a lot, how his friend Vetea always gets teased at school for being an albino, and Moana got a bruised nose once for defending him. "Why are you talking about my friend Vetea?" Moana asks.

"Imagine, a little," Materena goes on. "Your friend Albino, I mean, Vetea, falls in love with a girl, but she doesn't want him because he's an albino. How are you going to feel?"

"Eh, I'm going to be cranky at that girl!" Moana exclaims.

"And would you tell Vetea that he should just look for a girl who is an albino, just because he's an albino?"

"No," replies Moana softly.

"And why not?"

Moana hesitates. "Because God made us equal?"

Loana is seriously nodding now, she's very pleased with her grandson's answer.

And so Materena's explanation is over. "All right." She kisses Moana on the forehead. "You can go and play outside. Give me the coconut."

Moana kisses the coconut and gives it to his mother.

And Materena expertly cracks it open with the machete.

Lunch is over, and all the food that was on the table got eaten: the raw fish, the baked breadfruit, the taro, the sweet potatoes; and now everybody is feeling like a little lie-down, but Loana wants to help Materena clear up the table before she goes home.

"Don't worry about it, Mamie," Materena says. "You just go home and have a rest."

"Thanks for the lunch, girl." Loana kisses her daughter on the forehead.

"Eh, what's one lunch compared to all the food you put in my stomach over the years?" Materena replies.

After a few more kisses, Loana leaves and Leilani decides to go with her grandmother to keep her company. The boys go outside for a game of marbles, and Materena retreats to her bedroom. She's a bit upset and couldn't care less about the mess in the kitchen.

She's in bed now. She pulls the quilt over her head as if to escape. The lunch was good and everybody chatted away, but Materena did not say one single word to Pito. She didn't even look at him. It was like he wasn't sitting on the other side of the table.

And here is Pito now, coming into the bedroom.

"Go on your sofa." These are Materena's first words to Pito in the last two hours.

Pito hops into bed, and now he's trying to get under the quilt.

"You've got to be joking," Materena says.

"Ah, come on, darling," Pito says.

"Why do you always have to ruin Mamie's legends?" Materena's tone of voice is definitely not friendly.

"What!" Pito exclaims. "Is this why you're cranky at me?" He tries to pull the quilt away, but Materena grips it firmly.

"The trouble with you," Materena says, "is that you don't understand anything when it's about love, you only understand things when they're about a whole lot of nothing!"

Pito whistles. Materena jumps out of bed and marches to the kitchen, and you can hear the banging of pots and pans miles away.

Tupapa'u

Later, when Pito goes into the kitchen to get his Akim comic, he finds Materena looking very serious while she's washing the dishes.

"You're still cranky with me?" Pito cackles.

No answer from Materena.

By nighttime Materena, defrosting the fridge, is still not talking to Pito. But now he starts to whistle, and Materena knows very well it's best to whistle only during the day.

When you whistle at night you're calling the *tupapa'u* — wandering spirit — to come pay you a visit. Materena knows a story about a woman who liked to whistle at night while she supervised the cooking on the fire. One night, a *tupapa'u* with beef legs came to pay her a visit. The woman jumped with fright and landed straight in the cooking pot. She became mad after that experience. She never whistled again, not even during the day.

Materena never whistles at night. Her kids never whistle at night. But Pito, yes.

He's whistling louder and Materena can't bear it any longer. It's not like she's afraid of *tupapa'u,* but she doesn't want a strange apparition.

"Pito — stop whistling." There. Materena has just broken her silence.

Pito keeps on whistling. He's in the mood to whistle and nobody is going to make him stop. He will whistle till he's sick of it.

According to Materena, there are good *tupapa'u* and there are bad *tupapa'u*. When the air circling you is hot — it's a good one. When the air is cold and there's a foul smell — it's a bad one. Watch out.

Bad *tupapa'u* are usually dead people who don't want to be dead, and they're angry with everyone who's alive.

The good *tupapa'u,* they just wander around until they're ready to go where they are supposed to go. They come into your house and do tricks on you, little tricks like moving something around, and they watch you looking for that something, they listen to you say: "I thought I put the washing powder on the kitchen table. Where is it now?" — and they laugh. For them it's a joke.

The bad *tupapa'u* do worse tricks. They come into your head. They make you scared. They want you to do strange things.

"Pito, stop whistling!" Materena is ordering him.

"Materena, you just concentrate on your fridge." Pito flicks a page of his comic.

Wandering spirits come to you even if you don't whistle, but when you whistle it's more guaranteed that they will come pay you a visit. They can talk to you too.

Materena remembers when she was about eight years old. She was helping her mother make a *tifaifai* quilt when a foul smell penetrated the living room.

Loana stopped stitching and looked around. "Go your way," she said. "I didn't invite you into my house."

The *tupapa'u* didn't go away when Loana stood up and faced the wall.

"What?" Loana rolled her hands into fists. "What do you dare tell me? This is not my land? Speak up, I can't hear you!"

Materena gripped the quilt, scared; her mother looked like she was possessed.

"I'm Mahi blood! This land belongs to me! My father is Apoto Mahi!" Loana was yelling by then.

Materena wanted to go get the crucifix, she knew *tupapa'u* couldn't stand the sight of Jesus Christ nailed to the cross, but she was too scared to make a movement.

Loana went to open the door and, pointing outside, she said, very calmly, "Leave now or I will curse you — you will wander for the eternity. You will never see the face of God."

Cold air rushed behind Materena's neck — then the door slammed. Loana got back to her quilt.

"Girl," she said, "don't you worry — he's gone."

Materena shivers. Pito's whistling is even louder now.

"Pito — please stop whistling." Materena is begging him.

She tells him the story about her mother and the *tupapa'u*. Pito just laughs. In his opinion Loana had a bit too much to drink that night and had a hallucination.

Materena tells him the story about the beef legs. Pito laughs even more. In his opinion, that story is fabricated — it's a story mothers tell their children when they muck around too much at night. "I'm going to call the beef legs." Pito heard that sentence a few times from his mother. But she never called the beef legs, since there's no beef legs to respond to the calling.

In Pito's opinion, *tupapa'u* don't exist. They are in the imagination. When you're dead, you're dead — you become ashes, it's finished.

"And what about my cousin Mori when he saw a hairy man come out of a grave as he was walking past the cemetery one night . . . ?" Materena is beginning to feel a bit cold.

Pito laughs again.

"And the white lady who hitchhikes by the side of the road and sometimes she comes into your car without you even stopping — you look into the rearview mirror and there she is, on the backseat, smiling at you?" This is another one of Mori's stories. By now Materena's really got the shivers.

Again Pito laughs. "Your cousin Mori, he's the king of invented stories."

Pito goes on about how he's been in a car many times at night and the only people he's seen hitchhiking were hoodlums.

Pito whistles a happy tune and shakes his shoulders.

Materena goes back to her defrosting. "Keep whistling, Pito. But don't say I didn't warn you that a wandering spirit will come pay you a visit."

Then an idea comes into Materena's mind. "Pito."

Pito looks up because Materena is now whispering and only two seconds ago she was almost shouting.

Materena drops the sponge. Her eyes are wide open, like she's afraid. "Pito . . . look behind you, there's . . . there's . . ."

At that precise moment, a ten-pound breadfruit crashes onto the tin roof, and cold air (from the open fridge) penetrates Materena's skin.

She jumps on Pito. Pito falls off the chair. And Materena and Pito are on the floor.

"You stupid bitch woman!" Pito is all pale now. "What were you trying to do? Scare me?"

First Day Here

That Pito, Materena says in her head, walking to the Chinese store. He likes to think he's so tough, but he's not tough at all, he's afraid of geckos, he's afraid of *tupapa'u* . . .

Materena can see Pito's face again. He was so pale! Ah, if she were to put the news on the coconut radio, there would be laughing all over the place. It would be her revenge for all the bad things Pito did to her . . . like proposing to her when he didn't mean it.

Bastard. If Materena were mean . . . but she's not, this is the problem. She's tempted to spill the bucket, though, bumping into Cousin Mori and other cousins . . . And here's Cousin Teva.

Drinking alone, with his head down. That is very different.

Materena walks up to him. "Teva," she says, "are you all right?"

He's holding a picture of a young woman. The young woman looks very serious as she grates a coconut.

"It's Manuia," Teva says.

"Ah. She looks strong." Materena has heard about Manuia and how Teva was going to marry her.

"Manuia got married last month." Teva starts to cry. "Mama sent me the news."

Materena puts a reassuring arm on Teva's shoulder. She's got mixed emotions. She feels sorry for him, but she also thinks that he deserves to cry. He's come to Tahiti with plans and done nothing about them.

This is the story of Teva's arrival in Tahiti as Loana told it to Materena.

He is seventeen and leaving his island for the first time.

He's leaving Rangiroa for Tahiti, where people can earn lots of money — easily.

Many of his relatives have gone before him and they are all doing fine. None of them have come home, because they are doing so well. But he will, in two years. He has a plan. Work very hard, very long hours, save most of his pay, then come home in five years' time and start a business taking tourists spearfishing on the new speedboat he can afford to buy. And, of course, marry Manuia from the village and have beautiful children with her.

He promises his mother these things. She says, "Son, once you taste life in Tahiti, you're not going to want this slow, simple life in Rangiroa. You're not going to want to be a fisherman."

And now he is going aboard the *Temehani,* which will take him to Tahiti. He watches his mother, his father, his sisters and brothers, standing on the quay, waving. He waves back until he can't see them anymore.

He waves for a long time.

Then Teva sits on the deck and hides his face in his hands.

Cousin James picks Teva up in Tahiti. Teva hardly recognizes James at first. James has a big gut, a wild beard, and messy hair. He used to have iron muscles from hunting big fish. He used to look clean and healthy. Now he's a slob. Teva looks at the tattoo on James's arm. It is a tattoo of a heart and the heart is pierced with an arrow and Teva wants to laugh, but he knows that it isn't a good idea to laugh at James's tattoo.

They kiss and hug. Then they walk toward a rusty old Peugeot. "Is this your car?" asks Teva.

James raises his eyebrows. It means, of course it's my car, what do you think, that I don't have a car? Do I look like someone who doesn't have a car to you? Of course it's my car, and it's a good car.

Teva is surprised about James's car. The rumor in the village was that James had a new red Honda that could speed faster than Liu Song's speedboat.

It takes a while to make the old Peugeot start. Then the car propels itself forward, rattling and squeaking as it goes. Teva wants to laugh, but he knows it's not a good idea to laugh at James's rusty Peugeot. And, plus, James is older, so he needs to show a bit of respect.

"What have you got in that bag?" James asks.

"Clothes."

"You've got nice ones for going out . . . for hunting good-looking women?" asks James, looking at a woman waiting to cross the road.

"I'm here to work, Cousin." Teva is serious.

Cousin James laughs a mocking laugh. "Work! There's no work here! Who told you there's work here! The economy is stuffed, Cousin. You know a bit about the economy?"

Teva admits that he doesn't know one bit about the economy.

"Well, I'm telling you, Cousin, the economy's stuffed."

"You work?" asks Teva.

"When it suits me." James furiously toots his horn at the car in front, which is moving too slowly. "Get off the fucking road!" he yells as he accelerates to pass the white Fiat.

Teva looks at the woman who is driving the Fiat, her chest pressed to the steering wheel like she can't see the road, and he feels quite uncomfortable, because the woman is a mama and back home you just don't yell at the mamas. Only the papas can yell at the mamas — not the young people.

James looks at the driver of the Fiat too as he passes. "*Putain,* it's Mama Teta! What is she doing on the road? She's a bloody public danger."

Then James passes a truck and Teva is holding on to his seat.

"I don't like people bossing me around." James continues the discussion about work. "I won't eat nobody's merde. Give me two million francs . . . give me five million francs, I'll still refuse. Got my pride. What about you? You eat merde if your boss asks you?"

"*Non.*"

"Good," James says. "Don't make me sorry we're related."

Teva looks out the car window and thinks about Rangiroa.

Finally they arrive at Noelene's house. Her house needs two coats of paint, at least — the place is a wreck. As soon as Teva gets out of the car, big Mama Noelene smothers him with kisses. And then she cries for the whole neighborhood to hear, "*Aue,* welcome . . . welcome to my home . . . welcome, my nephew from Rangiroa!"

Teva says, "Thank you, Auntie."

When Teva's mother asked Noelene about him staying with her, Noelene promptly sent a message back: *Your son is my blood. He can stay at my house. I have a big house.*

"The family is fine back home?" Noelene takes Teva's bag.

"Petero died last week."

Noelene is shocked. She didn't know Petero had died. If someone had taken the time to send her the news, she might have caught the plane — for the first time in her life — to be at her uncle Petero's wake and funeral.

"How did he die?"

"Sleeping."

"It's a good way to die," Noelene says.

More talk inside the house, but James joins his mates drinking under a mango tree, watching cars drive past.

The house is clean and it smells of bleach. Teva guesses his auntie Noelene cleaned up the house good for him. When a relation from another village comes to visit Teva's family, his mama goes crazy for hours making the house cleaner than clean, and nobody is allowed in the house until the relation arrives, and the relation always makes a comment about the house being clean.

So, with respect, Teva says, "Your house is very clean, Auntie Noelene."

"You call this house clean?" Noelene admires her bleached walls.

"*Oui*, Auntie, your house is very clean." Teva knows that a compliment like this one has to be repeated.

Noelene complains that usually the house is a bit cleaner, but she's always so busy. She smiles and says, "You sleep in the living room until James's two good-for-nothing friends remember they have a mother. I get so mad with James. He's always inviting friends to stay at my house, and his friends don't work! Who puts food in their mouth, eh? Me! I told James his two good-for-nothing friends have to go soon, before I throw them out myself. Are you hungry a bit?"

Teva feels embarrassed. His mother never asks that kind of question. She just puts the food in front of you and eats with you. Teva is hungry, but if he says yes, she might think he is a good-for-nothing. If he says no, he's going to stay hungry.

"I'm not hungry, yet."

Noelene gets mad. "You're telling me you don't want to eat my food? Come. We go eat. My food is not special, but when Auntie Noelene gets her pay, I'm going to cook special food. Just for you."

Teva sits at the kitchen table and digs into the corned beef.

"Why did you come here?" Noelene sighs, and rolls a cigarette. "There's too many good-for-nothing people living in Tahiti . . . I hope you're not going to turn into a good-for-nothing. Don't you make me sorry we're related, eh?"

Teva nods.

"If you don't find a job soon, you'll have to go home. When you wait for the job to fall out of the sky, you become a good-for-nothing nuisance."

Teva is glad James is calling out to him, and he gets up.

"Remember what I told you." Noelene grabs Teva by the hand. "If you don't find a job soon, you go home. And don't listen to those good-for-nothings drinking outside. And don't you turn into a good-for-nothing on me. There's enough good-for-nothings in my life."

Teva hurries outside.

James waves to him. "What're you doing? The beer is getting warm."

Teva sits next to James, who affectionately pats him on the shoulder. Then he addresses his assembly.

"See him?"

"Yeah . . . we see the kid." James's friends are already drunk.

"He's my cousin," James says. "Make trouble with him and you're going to be sorry. You're going to talk like girls . . . no more balls . . . gone with my knife." James pulls a hideous face and the drunken good-for-nothings lower their eyes.

"Tell me, James, what is the kid doing here?" one of them asks.

"Looking for work." James takes a long slug of his Hinano.

The assembly roars with laughter. "You mean your relation doesn't know there's a problem with the economy? Doesn't know you need to have gone to university to sweep the road? What can you do, kid?"

Teva shrugs. What can he do? Teva can do anything. Free dive down to the black coral, kill big sharks who would steal his fish, spot a school of fish a mile away, find his way back to the shore on dark, stormy nights. Teva from Rangiroa can do anything.

The assembly is waiting for him to answer. Teva shrugs again. What can he do? It will take too long to tell.

"You don't know?" asks the assembly.

James puts his hand in the air. "Leave him alone. This kid . . . he's different from us. Maybe he'll surprise us all. We used to be like him."

Then James hands his young relation a cold beer. Teva drinks slowly.

"He drinks like a girl!" The whole assembly is laughing. "Men don't sip, drink it in one go, boy! Can't drink like a man . . . can't be a man!"

James puts an arm around his cousin. "First day here. He'll change."

"Teva." Materena takes her arm off her cousin's shoulder. "A woman can only wait for so long, and you've been here for over two years now."

Teva nods and continues to cry.

"You don't think this is a sign for you to go home?" asks Materena.

"What for?" Teva says between the tears. "Eh? What for? It's too late now. Manuia is married, she belongs to someone else, she did this to hurt me, it's her revenge."

"She got married because she was *fiu* of waiting for you," Materena snaps. "What did you expect? For Manuia to wait for you all her life?" Then, tapping the crying young man on the shoulder, Materena advises him to get on with his life, beginning with getting himself a job and then going home to his close family.

And with this advice, Materena leaves so her cousin can do some serious thinking — she has some shopping to do. And a bit of cleaning, and hopefully a bit of resting too, seeing that she has the day off today.

The Electricity Man

Materena is about to have an afternoon nap when she hears a whistle outside. Who's that? she asks herself. She gets out of bed, pops her head out the shutter discreetly, and next minute, she's rushing outside, panicking.

Now, positioned in front of the electricity box, she's asking the electricity man what on earth he is doing.

He tells her he's disconnecting her electricity.

"You can't disconnect my electricity," Materena says, "are you crazy?"

The electricity man explains to Materena that he's not the boss of the company and his job is to disconnect the electricity when people don't pay their account.

"You didn't pay your account — it shows on the computer, okay?"

But it is not okay with Materena, and she's still standing in front of the electricity box like a security guard. She doesn't want her electricity cut off. *Dallas* is on the TV tonight and she *never* misses *Dallas*. She tells the electricity man she did not receive the disconnection notice.

"You can't cut my electricity." Materena gives the electricity man a defiant look.

The electricity man gives Materena a defiant look back. "You think I can't cut your electricity just because you say 'You can't cut my electricity'? When you pay your account — in full — I come back and connect your electricity. Now move aside . . . I've got work to do."

But Materena is not going to move aside, and the only way for the electricity man to access the electricity box is to push her out of the way, but she is an angry woman, a big angry woman.

"I always pay the electricity account as soon as I get the disconnection notice," she says. "And I didn't get the disconnection notice. When are you going to believe me, eh?"

The electricity man laughs a forced laugh. "I could write a book about all the invented stories people tell me to make me stop disconnecting their electricity. You know, I tell those invented stories to my *copains* when we meet on Friday for a beer, and my *copains* always laugh. My mates like those invented stories. They say, 'Eh, mate, how about a disconnection story for us tonight?' but" — the electricity man widens his eyes — "but I'm *FIU* of those invented stories!"

Materena widens her eyes too and replies, "I'm not telling you an invented story. My story is nothing but the truth!"

The electricity man points a finger at Materena. "You know what? When a call comes on my radio, I always pray no one is going to be home. But it seems to me that most people who don't pay their account have nothing better to do than stay home to watch the TV, drink, sleep. Too busy to work."

Ah, he's stepping out of line here. Materena narrows her eyes. "I work, but my boss was sick today and she didn't need me cleaning her house. She gave me the day off. I work, okay?"

The electricity man and Materena look into each other's eyes.

"Okay, I tell you why I didn't pay my account," Materena says. "I usually pick up my man's pay on Friday afternoon. The girl at the office, she knows me well. She gives me the envelope and I sign the register, there's no problem. But last Friday I had to visit my mamie, she was a bit sick. I went to show her the kids to make her a bit happy, you know? When I came home, it was past nine o'clock and my man was blind drunk. He got mad at me because there was nothing for him to eat. My man is a lazy bastard. I tried to tell him about the electricity account, but he got cranky, he doesn't like me playing the boss. It's his job to think about the electricity account. I told him, 'Sure, you're the boss, what about fixing the electricity account, eh?' He went for me. I grabbed the kids and we ran to Mamie."

Materena's story is a whole lot of inventing (since the electricity man refuses to believe that she didn't receive the disconnection notice, which is true). She hopes the electricity man is going to feel sorry for her now. She really doesn't want her electricity cut off — it's a nuisance.

Materena has had her electricity cut off twice. The first time it was because Pito drank his whole pay (that was before she started to pick up his pay) and Materena couldn't bring herself to ask Loana for a loan, not wanting Loana to get cranky with Pito.

The second time, it was also because Pito drank his whole pay (that was also before she started to pick up his pay) and Materena dared go ask Loana for a loan. She no longer cared if her mother got cranky with Pito. But her mother had gone away for the weekend to a religious retreat at Taravao, and Rita ended up lending Materena the money. Well, Rita didn't really lend the money. She just saw the candles and gave Materena, who was breast-feeding Moana, ten thousand francs and said, "Here, that's for my godson's diapers."

Materena thinks maybe she should try to make the electricity man feel bad.

"Eh, you don't feel bad doing this to your own people?" she says.

"*Non,* I don't feel bad, and I told you I'm not the boss of the company. If I don't do my job properly, I don't have a job. It took me months and months to score this job. It's a good job."

The electricity man unexpectedly pauses to ponder, leaving Materena time to get into the argument.

"The other electricity man was better than you," she says. "He understood my troubles. He told me: 'No worries, woman, I give you a couple more days to get the money organized.' I can get the money tomorrow. My mamie, she's got piles of money at the Socredo. Tomorrow morning I'll go talk to my mamie then I'll come and see you at your company."

A bit of flattery doesn't hurt, but it doesn't look like the electricity man is buying it.

"Move," he says.

"I'm not moving," Materena replies.

The electricity man puts his right foot forward. "Move, I say."

Materena also puts her right foot forward. "What do you think you're doing?"

The electricity man puts his left foot forward.

"Don't even think about it." Materena also puts her left foot forward.

The electricity man pushes Materena out of the way.

And Materena pushes the electricity man out of her way. "Don't mess with me, young man."

The electricity man stares at Materena. "Move."

"*Ah non.*" Materena folds her arms, and her feet are firmly planted on the ground.

The electricity man puts his hands up. "Okay then . . . don't move . . . I'm going to write a special report about you and I'm going to give that special report to my boss . . . and you know what that means?"

He doesn't leave time for his difficult customer to answer.

"It means you're not going to be able to iron your dress for Sunday Mass ever again, because I'm going to make sure your account disappears from the computer. I have a friend who works in the computer department, it's very easy to make names disappear. How do you think the company knows you haven't paid your account, eh? Because of the computer! My friend is a computer expert, he clicks one button and *ffffrrrrr*, you don't exist. If I write the special report . . . no more electricity for you . . . even if you pay your account in full. Count how many candles you have to buy at the Chinese shop. Your house — the only house with candles. Think a bit. People are going to laugh at you . . . and what about your husband, eh? What is he going to say when I tell him it's your fault he can't have cold beers in the fridge?"

"My husband!" Materena looks at the electricity man as if he's just said something really absurd. "He's not my husband. Would I marry someone who's a lazy bastard?"

"Eh, I don't care if he's not your husband," the electricity man snaps. "I don't care if he's your lover, your secret admirer, all I care about is the electricity account and the disconnection. Move, and let me do my job, if you don't want me to go and write that special report today."

Materena gives the electricity man a suspicious look.

Can an electricity man write a special report? Isn't this the job of the boss of the company? The job of the second-in-charge boss, even? Can an electricity man organize someone in the computer department? Candles for the rest of my life?

Materena moves away from the electricity box. "All right, do your job. You don't need to write a special report to the boss of the electricity company. And where's my disconnection notice? I always pay as soon as I get the disconnection notice. It should be against the law to have your electricity cut off without a dis-connection notice."

Materena goes inside the house and rushes to her bedroom to check her bill box, where she keeps her bills (electricity, school fees, rates); perhaps she did receive the disconnection notice, after all, but was so caught up with her wedding preparations that she forgot.

Ah ha, and what's this? An unopened envelope from the EDT? Materena rips it open, and there it is, the disconnection notice, in black-and-white, addressed to Mademoiselle Mater-ena Mahi. Merde, now Materena feels like an idiot. She wonders if she should apologize to the electricity man . . . Actually, it might not be a good idea, he might use her apology against her later on.

Materena rips up the disconnection notice and hears the elec-tricity man start talking. She goes to the shutter and discreetly pops her head out.

The electricity man is talking to Cousin Teva, and Materena listens to what he has to say.

"Maybe I don't look tough enough. When you look tough, when you've got muscles, people respect you. I'm skinny. I'm young."

"You're not that skinny," Teva says.

"And that big woman, trying to flatter me," the electricity man continues. "I know all about flattery. When you flatter it's because you want something. Ah yes, there's always a reason with flattery. When Suzie wants me to do something, she flat-ters me about my muscles or my eyes. And when she doesn't want anything from me — well, I can wait for the flattery to come my way.

"It's not my fault ninety percent, perhaps even ninety-nine point nine percent, of people who don't pay their electricity account are people like me. Tahitian. I rarely visit the *popa'a* houses, and when I do, it's a misunderstanding between the man and his woman. The woman thought her man paid the account and the man thought his woman did. And then they pay the account and I reconnect the electricity and the *popa'a* apologize for the disturbance. The *popa'a* make me feel like I'm an important person. A person you shouldn't disturb.

"But my own people — *ah hia* — they give me a hard time and expect special treatment. They swear on some ancestor's head that they paid the electricity account in full. And when I ask to see the official receipt, they want to dong me. They swear on some ancestor's head that the invented story is nothing but the truth. And when I ask them to swear on the Bible, they want to dong me.

"My own people are the most difficult customers, *ah oui.* And the worst payers too.

"The problem with Tahitian houses is that your relatives are free to come in and use the telephone, watch the TV for hours, eat everything in the fridge, drink all the Coca-Cola, use the washing machine, borrow clothes. It is an insult to lock your house. What if one of your relatives really needs to borrow something urgently? And then you've got no money to pay the bills.

"The problem with Tahitian people is that we have too many relatives who don't have a job, and just too many relatives."

Teva finally speaks. "It's nice to have relatives."

"Sometimes," the electricity man says, "not all the time . . . I'm finished here now, I've got eight more houses to go to. Wish me good luck."

"Good luck."

Materena waits for the electricity man to leave and then opens her door to Teva, standing still outside. "Cousin, what is it?" She's not really in the mood for further discussion about the woman Teva wishes he had married.

But the reason Teva is here is to thank Materena for her time before, and tell her that he's feeling much better now, and that, *oui,* he will be going home to his family soon.

That's all he came to say.

Colorful Imagination

The electricity has been reconnected now and all is well for Materena — especially with her clever daughter Leilani coming home from school with a Colorful Imagination Class Merit Award. Leilani got that award for a story she wrote.

Leilani's story is about a ten-year-old girl who loses a thong while sitting on a pontoon. The girl is admiring the sunset when one of her thongs slips away from her foot and gently lands on the water. The girl can't swim, so there's nothing she can do to save her beloved thong, she just has to watch as the thong drifts toward the horizon. She's very sad because her best friend bought her those red thongs.

That night, the girl dreams the thong came back with the current, but the next morning, when she hurries down to check the shore, there's no thong there. Just an old woman gutting fish.

"Why are you crying?" the old woman asks. The girl reveals the reason for her sadness.

"*Aue . . . ,*" the old woman sighs. "It's not the first time the sea has taken a thong, but don't cry, girl, the sea will bring your thong back one day." The old woman says she knows of a young girl who also lost her thong in the sea and found it twelve years later, buried under branches at Papara Beach.

Materena likes the story. She understands.

There are books everywhere in Materena's boss's house. The first thing Materena does each morning is go around the house picking up books and putting them back in one of the bookshelves — wherever there's a space available. Every now and then, Materena flicks through the pages and reads a few lines, but the words are too complicated. There's a paragraph she read once, it was all about the sky, how the clouds were like cotton balls and everything.

Leilani's story is simple, and half-true and half-invention. Leilani lost thongs last year, but she wasn't sitting on a pontoon, she was sitting in the truck. She just got off the truck without her thongs — brand-new thongs too. And Materena got real cranky at Leilani.

Materena feels bad now about how she overreacted that day. Perhaps she'd been in a bad mood already and Leilani losing her brand-new thongs made her bad mood worse.

Materena puts Leilani's story and merit award in her never-to-throw-away box of things. Leilani is going to want to read her story to her kids and display her framed merit award in her house for everyone to see and comment about.

It is clear to Materena that her daughter is destined to become a writer.

Materena goes and says this to Pito, who's practicing on his ukulele outside.

"Be careful about saying things like that," says Pito. "Just think about your cousin James." He doesn't even stop practicing on his ukulele.

"What about my cousin James?" Materena asks.

"Where's his canoes, eh?" Pito says. "They only exist in James's dreams. Now James is angry because he's not building canoes and his mother is angry because he doesn't have a job."

One day, James helped his uncle Hotu build a canoe, and the uncle said, "James, it's a good canoe you've built." And James told his mama about what his uncle had said. And his mama decided that James was going to build canoes. She couldn't stop raving about how, her son, he was going to build canoes, and not just any kind of canoes, but the best in the world! "You're going to build canoes," she kept on saying to her son. "My son is going to build canoes," she kept on saying to the whole neighborhood.

"Don't compare my cousin James to Leilani."

Materena is not happy with the comparison. The way she sees it, dreams don't come to you — you have to make them happen. That James, he thinks his canoes are going to fall out of the sky, and he's dreaming about his canoes, but all the while he's drinking by the side of the road and counting cars. Dreaming dreams isn't going to turn dreams into reality.

Leilani can become a writer. There's no stopping her.

"What if Leilani says she wants to be a pilot, are you going to tell her it's possible?" asks Pito.

"*Oui.*"

"The president of Tahiti?"

"*Oui.*"

"The president of France?"

"*Ah oui!* Of course!" This statement comes from the bottom of Materena's heart.

Pito shakes his head. Materena goes back inside the house to get Leilani's story. She wants Pito to read it.

"Later," he says.

Right this moment, he's too busy fooling around with his ukulele.

That night, Pito reads Leilani's story in bed. Materena expects him to say, "Eh, this story is good," because the story *is* good. Pito frowns as he's reading the story. Then he grimaces, and when he finishes he goes on about how the story doesn't make sense to him. What's all this fuss over a thong? You cry when a person dies, you don't cry because you lost a thong. And why didn't that silly girl jump into the sea to get her thong back instead of just watching it slowly drifting toward the horizon, like a martyr?

Materena reminds Pito that the girl can't swim.

"*Ah oui,*" Pito says. Still, the story doesn't make sense to him. It's not like you can't get a replacement thong at the Chinese store.

Materena is getting more annoyed by the second. That Pito, she thinks. He understands nothing when it's not about his Akim comics.

She puts the story back in the never-to-throw-away box and turns the light off. She gets into the bed, making sure to stay on the far side because she's cranky at Pito.

"Materena," Pito says a while later.

"What?" she replies.

"Leilani — did she tell you she wants to write books?"

Materena's answer is almost a murmur. "*Non.*"

But Materena knows the kids don't always tell her everything. They've got secrets.

So next payday, Materena buys Leilani a diary, a leatherbound diary with a key. "Here," she says, casually giving Leilani the leatherbound diary.

And before Leilani has a chance to comment, Materena adds, "It was on special at Hachette Pacific and I thought it might be of use to you. If not, well, just give it to one of your friends."

Whatever You Want to Be
Is Fine with Me

Materena knows that nobody else should read a diary except the person who writes in the diary. But she's only going to read the first line, the first two lines, the first three lines, no more. Materena just wants to check how many pages Leilani has used in the diary she gave her. She might need a new one. Materena might also check if Leilani has ever written about her hardworking and loving mother.

And if the diary is locked, then Materena won't insist.

So Materena goes into Leilani's bedroom and closes the door. She looks under the pillow, the mattress, in the desk drawers. The diary is hidden underneath the Bible that Loana gave Leilani for her Communion.

Materena looks at the door with anxiety. But Leilani is out with Loana, sweeping the church. Every sixth Saturday it is Loana's turn to sweep the church, and usually Materena goes and helps her mother, but this morning Leilani offered to go in Materena's place.

Leilani's diary is not locked. So Materena opens it and reads the first two lines.

I know Mamie would like me to be a writer because I got a Merit Certificate for Colorful Imagination, but, God, what I really want to do is to serve you. Deep in my heart, I feel a strong desire to be a nun . . .

Materena snaps the diary closed. Because the writing is about God, she feels it is a sin to read Leilani's diary.

Materena, a bit shocked, sits on Leilani's bed and thinks about her cousin Heipua.

When Heipua announced at twenty-one that she wanted to be a nun, nobody was surprised.

That Cousin Heipua, she liked to be in the church.

She went to two Sunday Masses, the morning and the night Mass. She also went to the daily Masses at six o'clock in the morning, with all the old people.

And in her bedroom, Heipua had many statues of the Virgin Mary, Understanding Woman, even glow-in-the-dark statues and a statue with a beating red heart that plugged into the power socket. When she was a little girl, Heipua once said that the Virgin Mary, Understanding Woman, smiled at her. Nobody thought it was a child's imagination.

At sixteen, Heipua had pinned posters of Jesus Christ to the wall. Her other sisters' posters were all of actors and singers. One of the sisters said, "Eh, you don't think Jesus Christ looks a bit like an actor, with his long hair?"

Heipua got cranky.

Heipua never paid attention to boys, unlike her sisters, who would jump over the fence in the middle of the night to go and meet boys. Heipua, she just stayed home and watched the TV or prayed. She was a very serious type.

And she had special powers.

She visited the old and the sick at the hospital, and she only had to hold their hands for them to feel better. Sometimes she sneaked into the maternity ward to look at the newborns.

She had to sneak because the woman in charge of visits to the hospital didn't like Heipua to look at the newborns. The woman preferred Heipua to look at the dying people.

Heipua wore long dresses to the ankles, and her hair was always braided in two heavy plaits. She had glasses for the sight too, her eyes were a bit damaged from reading the Bible all night long.

One night, just after she turned twenty-one, Heipua said, "God spoke to me."

Her mother hurried to pass the news on to the coconut radio. Nobody said, "What is this fairy story?"

And then, two days after God spoke to Heipua, she announced her desire to be a nun. Her mother hurried to pass the good news on to the coconut radio, and again nobody said, "What is this fairy story?"

Heipua's mother was honored one of her daughters was going to be a nun. She said to her other children, "You — you're just going to be good-for-nothings."

Heipua spent a week with the nuns at the mission. She returned home more certain than ever that her destiny was to serve God. She said, "The nuns are normal women except that their man is God, and their children are the whole population."

She wanted to join the mission there and then, but the nun in charge of the mission advised Heipua to seriously think about her vocation for the following two months. "Once you're a nun," she said, "you're a nun forever."

So Heipua did her serious thinking at the church. She went to the early Mass, and instead of going home after the Mass, she stayed at the church until late afternoon — to pray.

One afternoon, a young man of about Heipua's age began to pray at the church too. They didn't speak to each other. He came back to the church the following day and the next. They said hello to each other.

The young man was praying to be a priest.

Well, within two weeks, they were kissing and caressing.

Heipua didn't change her appearance (she was still wearing her long dresses and her glasses for the sight, and her hair was still braided in two heavy plaits), so nobody suspected that anything more than praying was happening in the church.

Aue, those two resisted the temptation, but when there's physical attraction, it can be difficult not to surrender. And the inevitable happened. After the kisses and the caresses came the fornication. It was the first time for him too.

And Heipua got pregnant.

Aue, the shame and the embarrassment for her mother. She wanted to move to another town, another island, another country, even. She knew well that people were talking behind her back, mocking her, joking about how maybe her daughter's pregnancy was an immaculate conception.

Yes, it was a shock, Heipua's pregnancy.

Heipua's mother threw her out of the house.

And Heipua went to the young man's house with her bags and her statues.

When his mother opened the door, Cousin Heipua explained the situation. The shocked mother said, "What? What is this story? My son is going to be a priest!"

Then she called out to her son, and he immediately responded to her calling. She said, "This girl tells me that she's pregnant from you. Is this true?"

And he said, "I never saw her before, Mamie."

The mother slammed the door on Cousin Heipua.

Heipua, she walked around the streets not knowing what to do next. Night began to fall and she sat on a rock and waited for the day to come. And when the day came, she caught the truck to Papeete.

Two months later, a relative saw her at a bar in Papeete. She was drinking with a sailor, drinking and laughing and acting (so the relative repeated on the coconut radio, we don't know what the relative herself was doing at the bar) like a prostitute.

Heipua should have been way into her pregnancy, but there was no belly to show for it. Something must have happened to the baby, but nobody knew what, exactly.

Her mother spat, "Ah, she'll end up in a hole." Because, according to her, when you do wrong by God, you get punished.

But only last month Heipua's mother received a letter, a letter from France. Heipua sent her the letter. In the letter, Heipua wrote that she was now living in France and that she was a nun. Her name was now Sister Louise.

There was a photograph of Heipua dressed in the nun uniform, her hands in prayer, standing next to a tree.

But nobody knows if the photograph tells the real story. Nobody knows if Heipua rented the uniform at one of those stores where you can borrow any kind of uniform you want, but they all want to believe that Heipua is Sister Louise and that she's very happy.

And, as for the young man, there hasn't been a Polynesian priest for the last fifteen years. It would have made the front page of the newspaper.

Perhaps what Heipua did to that young man pleased him so much he decided to abandon his idea of being a priest. Or perhaps he's a priest in another country.

This is the nun story of Heipua, and now Materena is thinking about her own nun story.

When she was about eleven, she told her mother that she wanted to be a nun.

"What!" Loana said. "Did God speak to you?"

Materena admitted that God hadn't spoken to her.

Loana then asked Materena how come she wanted to be a nun, and Materena said, "I don't know. But when I see a nun, I say to myself that I would like to be a nun."

Loana advised Materena not to put this revelation on the co-conut radio, and to wait a few more years before seriously thinking about becoming a nun.

"You might change your mind," Loana said, "when the hormones start kicking in."

And, sure enough, when Materena turned fifteen the hormones started to kick in, and she no longer thought about being a nun every time she saw one.

But could it be that Leilani . . . ?

Materena has always hoped that her daughter would become a writer, since she is so good at writing stories, but above all Materena's main concern is for Leilani to be happy. To have a nice husband who loves her very much, a husband who says nice things to her. Well, he doesn't have to be a husband, as long as he's a good person and he makes Leilani happy. But if Leilani wants to be a nun . . .

Materena doesn't mind it one bit. There are many happy nuns.

And now Materena and Leilani are alone in the bathroom. Leilani is brushing her teeth and Materena is pretending to look for something in the cupboard under the sink.

"Ah, Leilani, my girl," Materena says. "Have you thought about what you'd like to do when you grow up?"

But before Leilani has a chance to answer, Materena, her head still in the cupboard under the sink, adds, "It's just that I heard on the radio that it's good for the parents to know what their children want to do. Because maybe the parents can help."

Materena stands up and mother and daughter look at each other in the mirror.

"So? Any idea?" Materena is asking lightly so that Leilani won't think that this is an interrogation.

"I'm not quite sure, Mamie." Leilani still has toothpaste in her mouth.

"Okay then," says Materena. Then, in a very serious tone, "But always remember that whatever you want to be is fine with me."

Leilani nods and smiles.

Squashed Banana

It's been a while since Materena took the kids to visit their grandmother Mama Roti. She was so busy with the wedding and everything — and what a waste of time that was! Anyway, today seemed like a good day to visit. Materena didn't particularly want to, but it's one of those things. It's for the children.

Right now Mama Roti is resting on the *peue* mat outside, complaining about her back to Materena. And all the while Materena is thinking about her escape. Materena has been at Mama Roti's house for fifteen minutes and she wants to go home, but Mama Roti has so much complaining to do. She needs ears.

"*Aue,* my back, eh. I'm not as young as I used to be. My back is going, everything is going, *aue* . . . Eh, one of you kids! Bring Mama Roti a piece of bread and a banana." She hurries to add, "A ripe banana, not a green banana!"

Less than a minute later, Moana brings his grandmother a piece of bread.

"And where's the banana for Mama Roti?" Mama Roti asks.

The banana for Mama Roti is in the bread.

Mama Roti looks inside the bread and rolls her eyes. "Eh, I asked for a squashed banana inside my piece of bread?"

Moana looks at his feet and shakes his head.

"What did I ask for?"

"A piece of bread and a banana?"

"You coconut head, *va*." Mama Roti impatiently waves Moana away. Then she throws the piece of bread with the squashed banana to the chickens and the dog. Materena gives Moana a little caress, and to Mama Roti she gives a cold, angry look. But Mama Roti's head is already turned the other way.

Materena is cranky. She gets up. She's going home.

"You're leaving already, girl?" Mama Roti asks.

"I just remembered I've got a chicken in the oven."

"Ah, okay, girl."

Materena kisses Mama Roti very lightly (usually there's a hug). She calls out to Tamatoa and Leilani that it is time to go home, and they come rushing, glad to go home. Tamatoa and Leilani don't really like to be at Mama Roti's house. There are too many things they're not allowed to do.

They're not allowed to be in the house when Mama Roti is not in the house, because she thinks they're going to break something behind her back. Also, Mama Roti prefers the kids to play outside because, in her opinion, kids shouldn't be in the house when the sun is shining. She never used to let her kids hang around inside the house when the sun was shining, which is probably why Pito can spend a whole day on the sofa now when the sun is shining. And the kids are not allowed to run around in the garden, because Mama Roti thinks they're going to stomp on her plants. They're not allowed to play with the ball, because the ball is bound to break Mama Roti's louvers.

They're home now and Materena is still cranky at Mama Roti. Moana is only eight years old, and you don't talk to your grandson that way. Still, Materena is trying to excuse Mama Roti. Perhaps her back was hurting, for real. And she's a bit old.

"Eh, but you don't call my kids 'coconut head,'" Materena mutters.

As far as Materena is concerned, she is the only person who can call her kids "coconut head." That Mama Roti, Materena thinks as she gets into peeling potatoes, she's got no manners at all. Right this moment, Materena is glad that her last name isn't the same as Mama Roti's. She's certain that people who know Roti Tehana think that she's a rude woman, and Materena certainly doesn't want to be associated with her.

The following day, Mama Roti arrives unexpectedly (as she always does) with a banana cake.

"Hello, girl!" she says to Materena. She's all bubbly.

Materena's *hello* is bubbly too, but only just. Mama Roti goes on about how all the bananas in the bunch turned ripe on her overnight, so she decided to bake a banana cake.

"Ah." Materena doesn't sound too interested in Mama Roti's banana cake. She keeps on sweeping the kitchen.

"Will I cut you a slice?" asks Mama Roti.

"Not right now, Mama Roti. A bit later on."

Materena can't eat Mama Roti's banana cake right now. She's still angry with Mama Roti. When Materena saw her, the words *coconut head* rang in her ears. And Materena doesn't think that she's overreacting. Her cousin Giselle, for instance, when Ramona's *maman* said to her, "What a ridiculous name that name Isidore Louis junior is. It's so ridiculous it makes me want to laugh," well, Giselle threw an ashtray at her.

All Materena is doing to Mama Roti is refusing a slice of her banana cake because she's angry and because she's never thrilled to eat Mama Roti's cakes. Mama Roti puts too much sugar in her cakes.

Mama Roti sits down and babbles on about the heat, the mosquitoes last night, and the ripe bananas.

"It's bizarre, eh?" she says. "All my bananas turning ripe during the night?"

"It's bizarre," Materena says.

"And where's the kids?" Mama Roti asks.

"In their bedrooms, I think."

"With that sun!"

Materena sighs between her teeth.

And Mama Roti calls out, "Eh, you lot, come quick, your Mama Roti baked you a banana cake and the bananas are from the bunch of Mama Roti!"

But only Moana calls out, "I'm coming!" Usually Materena would be rushing into their bedrooms to order the kids to hurry up and come eat the cake Mama Roti baked for them. The order would have been discreet, of course, as it's best that Mama Roti doesn't know that her grandkids have to be forced to eat her cakes.

But today Materena is just going to keep on sweeping.

Mama Roti cuts a slice of her banana cake and Moana eats the whole slice.

"Your banana cake, it's very good, Mama Roti," he says.

Mama Roti cackles and throws her arms around Moana. She holds him tight and sighs. "Ah, you know how to make your old grandmother happy, eh." She kisses Moana's forehead. "My little duckling, my little chicken, my little treasure."

Materena goes to Tamatoa's bedroom. He's reading an Akim comic in bed. She orders him to go and eat the banana cake his grandmother baked.

"I don't like Mama Roti's cakes." Tamatoa flicks a page.

Materena clips his ear and mutters, "Get off that bed now and go and eat Mama Roti's cake, and if you tell her that her cake isn't good, you're going to have to deal with me later on."

Then Materena goes to Leilani's bedroom. Leilani is cutting pictures out of the newspaper.

"Girl," Materena says quietly, "Mama Roti baked you lot a banana cake. Go and eat it."

"Otherwise?" Leilani looks at her mother.

Materena shows her the palm of her hand, and Leilani puts her scissors away and gets up.

"And don't tell Mama Roti that her cake isn't good," Materena says.

"Okay. I'll tell Mama Roti that her cake is superb." Leilani smiles at her mother. The last time Materena ate Mama Roti's cake, which was a butter cake, she had to rush to the bathroom and spit the piece of cake out.

Materena cackles, and smiles back at Leilani. "You don't have to say to Mama Roti that her cake is superb. Just say it's good."

Marae

There's a school excursion to the *marae* and Tamatoa asks his mother to sign the school note and to give him the money.

"You're sure you want to go to the *marae?*" Materena isn't even looking at the school note.

Ah yes, he wants to go, the whole class is going and the teacher said everybody should go, because *marae* are part of our history.

Materena asks for a pen and Tamatoa goes off to find one.

She thinks about the excursion, she's uneasy. Tamatoa likes to fool around too much. At Mass, he's always coming up with some plan to disturb his brother and sister, and everyone sitting nearby — instead of sleeping quietly, like Leilani and Moana do. He pinches, he kicks, he whispers jokes, he makes fun of the priest. Sometimes he's so bad Materena ends up sending him outside. Most of the time, though, she just whacks him on the head or flicks his ears or threatens to make him sit next to her auntie Celia if he doesn't behave.

How is Tamatoa going to act at the *marae?*

Tamatoa comes back with the pen, but Materena isn't ready to sign the note yet.

"You know the *marae* is a sacred place?" she asks.

Ah yes, of course he knows. They studied *marae* in class and there's a whole page about *marae* in his schoolbook — he's going to read it tonight. Materena asks to see that page. Tamatoa drags himself to his schoolbag and drags himself back to the kitchen with the book. Materena commands Tamatoa to read her the page, and he falls on the chair beside her and sighs.

" '*Marae* are sacred sites, and there are six types of *marae,*'" he begins.

Then Tamatoa looks at his mother.

"Don't look at me," Materena says, "look at your schoolbook."

" 'The first type is the *marae* built in Opoa and dedicated to the god of war,'" Tamatoa continues. " 'It is an international *marae,* as chiefs from many archipelagoes were linked to that *marae.* The second type is the national *marae,* with a high priest associated with a prince — human sacrifices could be done on a national *marae.* Then there are the local *marae,* for villages run by a chief with a high priest. No human sacrifices could be done on that kind of *marae.* Then we have the ancestral *marae,* built on the land of each family; the social *marae,* dedicated to the gods of great importance; and, finally, the *marae* dedicated to specialists such as doctors, canoe builders, and fishermen.'"

There's more to read, but first Tamatoa wants to make sure that his mother wants to hear more about *marae.*

Materena gives Tamatoa her most serious look. "Of course I want to hear more. But first I want to know, what kind of *marae* is the *marae* Arahurahu?"

"What's the *marae* Arahurahu?" Tamatoa shrugs like he couldn't care less what kind of *marae* the *marae* Arahurahu is.

"It's the *marae* you're going to visit!"

"Ah."

Well, Tamatoa doesn't know what kind it is — it could be a local *marae.*

He continues his monotonous reading. " 'Here follows a list

of ceremonies that would take place on the *marae:* The beginning and the end of a war. The king's recognition of the power of the gods. The maturation of the year. The reparation of the sins committed by the priests — such as violating their sainthood by doing domestic work, making mistakes during rituals, demonstrating gluttony as they ate the head of a turtle. These offenses committed by the priests could bring bad luck on the priest himself, the population, and the island. Therefore the guilty had to recognize his fault and be punished by being reduced to common social status. There was a ceremony at the *marae* for every single important event linked to the royal family: birth, illness, and death.'"

Tamatoa snaps his schoolbook shut. "That's it," he says.

Materena decides to add a bit of information.

"Open your ears." Again, she gives Tamatoa her most serious look. "Even if the *marae* isn't used nowadays, the spirits who guard the *marae,* they're still in action. They circle the *marae* and make sure all the people that visit the *marae* show respect. The spirits' eyes are wide open and their ears too are wide open. Beware of upsetting these spirits, because there's always payment."

Materena tells Tamatoa about a man who pissed on the *marae.* Two weeks later he died in agony, his penis swollen with pus. (Her cousin Mori told her this story.)

Tamatoa widens his eyes.

Materena tells him about the kid who spat on a *marae.* Barely two minutes after the spitting, the kid suffered a convulsion, with white foam and spit dribbling out of his mouth. He died on arrival at the hospital, suffocated by his tongue. (Her cousin Mori also told her this story.)

Tamatoa widens his eyes even bigger.

Materena tells him that under no circumstances should he take anything from the *marae.*

She tells him there was this tourist, and he took a stone from a *marae.* He wanted to show it off to his family back in his country. That night, he was woken up by a horrible nightmare in which he saw himself plunge to his death from a cliff. A voice commanded the tourist to take the stone where it belonged. *Take the stone back where it belongs, take the stone back where it belongs,* it said. The tourist ran all the way to the *marae* that same night, and the following day he caught the plane back to his country. (This story is common knowledge.)

Tamatoa's eyes are nearly popping out. "It's true, everything you're telling me, Mamie?"

"Just show respect to the guardian spirits. They are out there, it's not an invention." Materena signs the note.

Then she gets the coins from the money can and puts the note and the payment in an envelope.

Tamatoa stayed in the school truck. He told his teacher his stomach was playing up a bit on him, but the truth was that Tamatoa didn't want to walk around the *marae.* He was scared.

And Materena isn't angry about the excursion money she paid for nothing.

"It's best we leave the sacred places alone," she says to Tamatoa.

Circumcision

Pito was twelve years old when he got circumcised. His father took him to the hospital and for a whole week Pito couldn't wear shorts because his *moa* was bruised and swollen. He had to wear a pareu.

And now Pito wants to take Tamatoa to the hospital for the circumcision, but he can't do it without Materena signing the authorization paper, so he's asking her to sign it.

"Pito, you're not taking my son to the hospital, his *moa* is fine as it is." Materena continues to hang the clothes on the line. She's not even going to look at the authorization paper.

Pito goes on about how a circumcised *moa* is much easier to look after because you don't have to pull the skin up to wash it. It's more hygienic and the *moa* doesn't stink. And, according to Pito, Tamatoa will be very grateful if she signs the authorization paper for him to get circumcised. No man wants to be stuck with an uncircumcised *moa*, except, perhaps, the *popa'a*.

"There's no need to bring the *popa'a* into this." Materena gives Pito a furious look.

"*Ah oui,* sorry," Pito says. "I always forget that your father is a *popa'a*. The circumcision is a man's business," he goes on.

"*Ah oui,*" Materena says. "We're going to see about that."

Pito decides to give Materena a little bit of a history lesson about how in the old days, fathers would take their sons to the *tahua'a tehe,* the circumcision specialists, without the mothers having to put in their grain of salt.

"Well, that was the old days," Materena says. "Now it's the new days. Now we have the authorization paper for us mothers to sign if we want to."

Pito curses the authorization paper and calls out to Tamatoa to come outside.

From the living room Tamatoa's voice calls back, "Papi, we're playing marbles and I'm win—"

"Here. Now!" This is Pito's serious-business voice, and Tamatoa is by his father's side within seconds.

"You want to be a man?" Pito asks him.

Tamatoa doesn't understand the question. He does his googly-eyes expression.

"What?" Pito snaps. "You don't want to be a man?"

"*Ah oui,* I want to be a man," Tamatoa hurries to answer.

"You know about the circumcision?"

"*Oui.*" Tamatoa is a bit pale now.

"You want to be circumcised?"

Tamatoa looks like he's having trouble swallowing.

"You want a *moa* that stinks for the rest of your life!" Pito exclaims, annoyed.

"*Non,*" Tamatoa mumbles.

"So you want to be circumcised, then."

Tamatoa's answer is a murmur. "*Oui.*"

"Well, ask your mother to sign the authorization paper." Pito gives his son the authorization paper and the pen.

"Mamie, can you sign the authorization paper?" Tamatoa doesn't sound convincing at all.

Materena looks at her son and sees the fear in his eyes. She can guess that Tamatoa is thinking that she's going to give in to Pito, because she has done it so many times. It's true that she has given in to Pito many times, but it is not going to happen today.

Materena is thankful there's an authorization paper. She's sure a woman invented it.

"There's no need to ask me to sign the paper, Tamatoa," Materena says. "My answer is no. The day you can look after yourself, then go do whatever you want with your *moa*. Until then, your *moa* is my business."

Tamatoa smiles discreetly at his mamie and passes the authorization paper and the pen back to his father. "Can I go now?"

Pito waves Tamatoa away. "Yeah, go. But every time you get called *moa taioro,* you'll be able to thank your mother for it."

Leilani calls out from the kitchen, "Is Tamatoa getting circumcised?"

"Mind your own business, Leilani!" Pito calls back.

Leilani comes out and asks her brother if he's getting circumcised. Tamatoa informs his sister that he would like to be, but Mamie doesn't want to sign the authorization paper.

"It's just that, my friend," Leilani says, "her brother got circumcised and the doctor did a mistake and now my friend's brother's penis is like that." Leilani shows the size of her friend's brother's penis. It is about one inch. "He's twenty years old now," she continues, "and he can't get a girlfriend."

"Is this what you talk about at school? Penises!" Materena is half-serious and half-laughing.

"*Non,* Mamie," Leilani says, all embarrassed now. "My friend, she just told me."

"I'm never going to get circumcised!" Tamatoa puts his hands on his penis area.

Pito, crunching the authorization paper, looks like he doesn't know what to say. Eh, he's going to get himself a cold beer.

Materena turns to Tamatoa. "Well? What about a game of marbles with me? Go on, go and get the marbles. It's better to play outside than inside the house. And get your little brother too."

Materena likes playing marbles with her boys. She used to play marbles at school, but she always lost. Some people can shoot their marbles straight into the hole and some people can't. It's a mystery to Materena.

Her cousin Lily was very good at playing marbles at school, before her hormones started racing. She never really shot her marble straight into the hole, but her marble was always the closest to it. Lily's success might also have had something to do with her only playing marbles with boys and them being a little bit distracted by her long, muscular legs.

Materena played marbles with boys too, but her marble was never the closest one to the hole.

Materena's not expecting to win today. She's not playing to win. She's only playing for something to do with her boys.

Tamatoa distributes five marbles to each player. Materena is given the honor of flicking her marble first.

So, her eyes focused on the hole, her concentration 100 percent, she flicks her marble. Materena's marble does a zigzag and shoots straight past the hole.

"Not bad, Mamie," the boys say.

"Materena, you don't do it like that." Pito has wandered back outside clutching a beer. He advises her to watch him in action. Apparently he was the best marble player at school, and he's sure his record is still unbeaten.

"Watch the professional." He puts his beer down, then rolls the marble in the palm of his hand. He flicks, and his marble shoots in a straight line toward the hole. Pito's marble rolls neatly into the hole and Pito smacks his hands.

"I'm such a crack shot," Pito says.

The boys have their go. Moana's marble misses the hole and

he just shrugs. Tamatoa's marble also misses the hole and he kicks the ground.

It is Materena's turn again. She rolls the marble in the palm of her hand. She does this for quite some time and Pito asks her if she's going to shoot today or tomorrow.

"Pito, I'll shoot when I'm ready," she replies.

She flicks her marble. It zigzags and goes way past the hole.

"It's better than your last shot, Mamie," says Moana.

But Pito shakes his head. "Materena, you don't do it like that."

The boys have their go, then it's Materena's turn again. She flicks and the marble shoots straight past the hole.

"Your marble is getting closer to the hole," says Moana, looking at his mother with pity.

Pito rolls his marble in the palms of his hands and spits into his hands. He's about to shoot his marble when Materena starts to whistle a happy tune. Pito complains that he can't shoot when there's whistling around him. It affects his concentration.

"Pito, eh," Materena laughs. "It's not a marble competition. You're not going to get a medal."

"Why are you whistling? Are you whistling to make me lose my concentration?" Pito looks into Materena's eyes as if he's trying to read her mind.

"I'm whistling because I feel like whistling," Materena says.

"Whistle after my marble is in the hole," Pito says.

He flicks his marble — of course, straight into the hole.

"I'm the best." Pito snaps his fingers.

It is now Materena's last marble and she's glad the game is almost over. She's got work to do.

"Materena —," Pito says.

She holds up her hand, meaning she's not interested. Pito goes on anyway. In his opinion, Materena shouldn't attempt to flick her marble straight into the hole — it's an unrealistic goal. She should instead concentrate on flicking the marble as close to the hole as possible.

"Ah really?" Materena says. "We'll see about that."

Materena doesn't roll the marble in the palm of her hand. She doesn't focus her attention on the hole.

She just flicks.

The marble shoots straight into the hole. Materena cannot believe her eyes. Her boys run to her, shouting, "Mamie's marble, it's in the hole!"

Leilani pokes her head out and yells, "What's in the hole?"

"Mamie's marble!" Moana yells back.

"Ah." Leilani goes back to whatever she was doing.

"How did you do that?" Pito asks Materena.

Materena winks. "Ah, I've got a technique too. You're not the only one with a technique."

Pito would like her to do it again.

"Another time," she says. Materena knows that when you shoot one like that, you don't try to do it again. She also applies this rule when she plays bingo. As soon as she wins, she collects her prize and goes home. There's nothing like quitting a game with a win.

Materena bows gracefully to her cheering sons as Pito gives her a suspicious look that says, *it's really bizarre, your marble going in the hole like that.*

"Mamie's a champion," Tamatoa calls out, pumping a fist, and Materena smiles at her eldest son, thinking, He's still only a kid.

Ah, the circumcision business, Materena thinks again, looking at her son, fast asleep now. It's a lot of *connerie.*

The day her brother got circumcised, he started to act tough and talk back to their mamie. He was much more polite before he had his *moa* operated on.

The same thing happened with Pito, so Mama Roti lamented to Materena. Apparently Pito used to be a really sweet boy who would do anything for his mama, and he would cuddle her all the time, but then his papi took him to the hospital to get circumcised and Pito became a tough. There were no more cuddles for Mama Roti. Pito was too busy flexing his muscles in front of the mirror.

But not all boys change after the circumcision.

Mori, for instance, he's still very sweet to his mama. When he walks past a garden and there are lots of beautiful flowers, well, Mori goes and picks them. Then he makes a lovely bouquet and gives it to his mama with the words "For my beautiful mama." Some days Mori's mama says, "Ah, my son, bless the day I gave birth to you." And some days Mori's mama says, "Stop stealing flowers and go get a job."

Materena brushes her fingers through Tamatoa's hair and kisses him on the forehead.

It is past eleven o'clock and she's kissed her kids already, when they went to bed at eight. But she always gives them a kiss on the forehead before *she* goes to bed. Just to make sure.

The Swimming Pool

It's hot and humid and ants have invaded the kitchen.

Materena places the sugar bowl into another bowl, half-filled with water. The ants get into the bowl and drown. It's going to rain soon, but for the moment the heat is unbearable.

It's the weekend. Tamatoa and Leilani are arguing in the living room about a pencil that Tamatoa took without asking permission, and Materena is trying to ignore their shouting.

"Give my pencil back!"

"When I'm finished!"

There's more shouting and Materena's nerves snap.

She grabs the wooden spoon and marches into the living room. Tamatoa and Leilani are on the ground. One is punching and the other is biting. They see the wooden spoon and within seconds they are on their feet, running back to their rooms. Still, Materena manages to whack a couple of legs.

It's so hot!

She's back in the kitchen now.

"What can I do?" Materena is talking to herself. "Ah, I'm going to make lemonade for the kids." She gets a bottle of cold water and two lemons from the fridge. She pours the cold water into the pitcher and fills the bottle up again with tap water for another round of lemonade later on. She cuts the lemons and squeezes them into the pitcher until there is no more juice left. And as she's mixing the sugar, she notices a few ants floating about. She scoops them out and once again complains about the heat.

"Where's that rain!"

She calls out to the kids, but only Moana responds to the calling. He arrives with his pencil and drawing paper.

"Have you been drawing?" Materena asks him.

"Yes, and I'm drawing a swimming pool."

"You're a good boy." Materena is smiling and thinking how strange it is for Moana to be drawing a swimming pool. He usually draws trees. Trees and animals.

"And why are you drawing a swimming pool?" She's interested to know.

"Because I'm hot!"

Moana drinks his lemonade and goes back to his room to finish his swimming pool.

And Materena decides to build a swimming pool.

She's still got those bathroom tiles sitting around — the ones that Lily offered to give away to the first person who went and got them when she retiled her bathroom.

Materena gets a piece of paper and a pen and sits at the kitchen table to draw her swimming pool. It's square. One yard by one yard, and twenty inches deep. Materena studies her plan for a while and concludes that her swimming pool is more a pond than a swimming pool.

Well, a pond is better than a washtub, Materena thinks.

The pond is going to be out the back, next to the frangipani tree, and Materena gets the shovel. Pito, who's practicing on his ukulele outside, shakes his head as Materena walks past him, the shovel on her shoulder.

"What are you doing with that shovel?" he asks.

She explains the situation and Pito laughs.

"So, you're a pond expert now?"

"I never said I was a pond expert." Materena wishes Pito would just concentrate on his ukulele.

"But you know what you're doing?"

"Oh *oui!*" And to prove to Pito that indeed she knows what she is doing, Materena begins to dig furiously.

Pito calls out to the kids to come and look at their mother, who is building a pond, and within minutes the three kids are at the scene.

"You're building a pond?" Moana asks.

Materena nods.

Moana's eyes widen with excitement, and he starts taking his clothes off. "When is it going to be finished?"

"Soon." Materena is very confident.

Pito snorts, prompting Tamatoa to snort too. Circumcision or no circumcision, Materena has been noticing some changes in Tamatoa lately. Eh, it's the age. But it makes her feel just a bit sad.

"I better not see your behind in Mamie's pond, Tamatoa," Leilani warns him.

"And the pond is going to be big?" Moana asks.

"Big enough for you, Leilani, and me," Materena replies, looking straight into Tamatoa's eyes.

She keeps on digging. There's sweat on her forehead, sweat under her armpits, sweat between her legs. She'd never known digging a pool would be so difficult. She keeps on digging and hums a happy tune to give herself energy. Materena can visualize the pond when complete. In her opinion, if you believe in yourself, you can't fail. And she believes in herself. She wants that pond very much.

She's got the hole, and now it is time to place the tiles in it. She goes and gets the tiles, stacked at the back of the house. Leilani and Moana follow her. There are over one hundred tiles — plenty. Moana and Leilani immediately propose to help, and the three of them carry the tiles back to the hole.

Materena places the first tile and pats it good into the soil.

"You think the water is going to stay in?" Pito asks.

"Of course."

"You are sure about that?"

"*Oui*, I'm sure. I'm positive."

"You don't think the water is going to leak?"

Pito's questions are starting to get on Materena's nerves.

"*Non*," she says, "I don't think the water is going to leak, I think the water is going to fill my pond."

"The way you talk about that pond, it's like it's already a reality," Pito says. "Well, I'm telling you, woman, what you're doing now, it's a waste of time. You need concrete."

Materena shrugs. Pito's words — in one ear and out the other. "You can't build a pond with tiles, Papi?" Tamatoa just wants to confirm the situation.

"You need concrete," Pito says. Tamatoa looks at his mother and shakes his head.

Materena spends quite some time neatly laying the tiles into the dirt. And now it is time to get the hose. Moana rushes to the outside tap, turns it on, and runs back with the hose, grinning.

Materena fills the pond with water. The water escapes through the tiles, into the dirt. Pito and Tamatoa glance at each other and smirk. Materena readjusts the tiles but the water keeps escaping. Plus, it's mud in there.

She's getting very upset, but, looking at her face, you wouldn't know she feels like crying. Looking at her face, you would think she doesn't care if her pond is going to be a reality or not.

"Oh well," she says casually. "It's not for today."

"You need —," Tamatoa begins.

But with one look Pito commands his son to be quiet.

Materena wants to smash the tiles with the shovel, but there's no need to overreact. It's best to walk away and deal with the tiles later on. She's going to go and have a long, cool shower. She marches away with dignity as Pito and the kids look on.

Moana puts his clothes back on. "Poor Mamie."

Materena cries under the shower. She punches herself too — she's so angry about the situation. What got into me, wanting to build a pond? A pond, eh! Silly *andouille*. She grinds her teeth. You stupid woman. Why didn't you just get into the family-size washing tub, like you usually do? Why create complications? The washing tub is perfect!

Materena is not sure if she's crying because her pond didn't become a reality or because she thought about her wedding last night, the wedding that will never happen, meaning she will die without a ring on her finger and a framed certificate on the wall. Materena doesn't understand why the wedding came into her head last night. She really believed she was completely over all that — cured. Well, maybe she's not crying about that at all. Maybe she's crying now because she just feels like it. Because crying feels good sometimes.

A clap of thunder breaks, shortly followed by another. Fat drops of rain begin to splatter on the tin roof and within minutes it is pouring. There's excitement outside.

"Mamie!" Leilani calls out. "Come and see!"

Materena, thinking that Pito has done some magic with her pond, wraps a towel around herself and runs to the back door to investigate.

The rain has filled up the pond.

Leilani and Moana are squeezed into the pond, laughing and splashing each other with the muddy water and pushing Tamatoa out of the pond every time he tries to get in.

Materena stops feeling sorry for herself.

Who needs concrete when there's rain?

The Adoption

It is still raining, and just listening to the rain spattering on the tin roof is making Materena melancholic. And when Materena feels melancholic, she cries. This week she finds that tears are coming easily to her and sometimes there's no particular reason. She'll be sweeping, for instance, and then, just like that, she'll start feeling sad.

But today she's crying for her cousin Tepua.

Tepua's nickname is *po'o neva-neva,* head-in-the-clouds. Her cousin James said to her one day, "Tepua, the Pope is in Tahiti and he's celebrating Mass at the cathedral in Papeete this Sunday morning." Sunday came and Tepua scrubbed and dressed her kids all nice and they caught the truck to Papeete to see the Pope at the cathedral.

But since her tragedy, nobody calls Tepua head-in-the-clouds anymore. It happened almost a year ago to this day.

It was a Sunday after Mass when Tepua came in contact with the *popa'a* woman for the first time. The *popa'a* woman gave Tepua compliments about her kids looking adorable in their white Sunday clothes. Tepua didn't mind that woman saying nice things about her family, and they got talking more right next to the church about the weather, the priest's sermon, Tepua's sixth child, due in four months . . . the *popa'a* woman's inability to have children.

The *popa'a* woman, Jacqueline was her name, had known about her sad condition for years and said she'd accepted it until her man got transferred to Tahiti. But here, everywhere Jacqueline went she saw children. Children came into her dreams too.

Tepua felt sorry for Jacqueline and she invited her to visit her house for a little more talk sometime. She gave her all the necessary directions: behind the snack, fourth house, green and yellow, and there's a washing machine out the front. Tepua explained how it didn't work anymore.

Tepua cleaned her house from top to bottom, which was good, because Jacqueline came the next morning. They talked some more and when Jacqueline left, Tepua said to herself, "I like that woman — poor her, eh."

Jacqueline came back two days later, then two days later again, then it's a brand-new family-size washing machine that came. Tepua told the delivery people that they better check the address, because she sure didn't order a brand-new family-size washing machine. But her name was on the delivery docket, along with the name of her *popa'a* friend — Madame Jacqueline Pietre.

Tepua got a bit mad at Madame Jacqueline Pietre because not once had she complained to her about not having a washing machine, and you don't give people you don't know well a brand-new family-size washing machine. Tepua was going to give that washing machine back, but she was tired of washing by hand, and since her new friend (her sister, almost, now) had plenty of money in the bank . . .

Tepua asked her *popa'a* sister to be the godmother of the baby, and that lady, Jacqueline, accepted in a second. In fact, she fell to her knees and blessed Tepua.

It was after this that the weirdness began. Jacqueline, she started to talk strange — pain in her lower back, swollen breasts, nausea, cravings for strawberries and pumpkin. She started to act strange too, always wanting to caress Tepua's belly and reading poetry to the baby like it could hear. Tepua was concerned her *popa'a* sister was going mad on her.

Jacqueline dedicated a whole bedroom of her house to her godchild. She bought a brand-new cot with a mosquito net, mobiles to hang from the ceiling, toys, toys, and more toys. The layette too was under control, made of expensive embroidered fabric.

Two months before her baby was due, Tepua visited her *popa'a* sister's house for the very first time. Jacqueline showed Tepua around; then, speaking softly and holding Tepua's hands, she mentioned the word *adoption.*

Tepua snatched her hands away. "I'm not the kind of mother who gives her children away."

Jacqueline insisted that *adoption* didn't mean "give away." The child, she insisted, would be Tepua's still. But the food, the clothes, the education, she would pay. Jacqueline insisted that she was only trying to be a perfect godmother.

For nights, Tepua considered the proposal, wanting and not wanting — thinking about the washing machine, thinking about the bedroom, her life, her difficult life, all the other children coming her way, six, maybe seven. Tepua asked God for a little sign, and the next day she went to see the priest about getting an operation to stop children coming her way, but the priest wouldn't give Tepua the authorization because she was in good health.

So Tepua agreed that Jacqueline would get the baby and Tepua would get unlimited access to the baby — at Jacqueline's house, secured behind an electric gate.

"My house is your house," Jacqueline swore.

And to prove this, Jacqueline revealed to Tepua the code of her electric gate.

Some papers had to be signed — just a formality for the inheritance — and Monsieur Pietre took Tepua's husband to the bar and paid his fare home.

Madame Pietre's adoptive daughter was born on a Saturday morning. Madame Pietre felt the contractions and pushed her baby into the world. And when the doctor gave her the dark-haired and brown-skinned newborn, she cried out, "Oh, she looks just like me!"

It was two weeks after the birth that Tepua paid Madame Pietre a visit, her second. She entered the code and the electric gate opened. Then she heard her baby wail and ran to her rescue.

Jacqueline didn't kiss Tepua, she just looked at her up and down, all the while holding the baby tight. Jacqueline wouldn't let Tepua hold the baby. "It is for the best that you don't come to my house again," she said.

Tepua went home. She felt a bit lost. She didn't understand Jacqueline speaking to her like she was a stranger. They were friends. They were sisters. Maybe my sister is tired from lack of sleep, she thought. It can make you aggressive — not sleeping and a crying baby.

Tepua went back to Jacqueline's house two days later. She entered the code but the electric gate didn't open. Maybe it was broken. So Tepua climbed over the electric gate and called out, "Jacqueline! Jacqueline, girlfriend!"

Jacqueline immediately came out of the house. "Get off my property!" she shouted like a woman gone mad. She hurried back inside the house to telephone the gendarmerie and a gendarme came to throw Tepua off Madame Pietre's property.

"Do you know it is against the law to trespass on private property?" the gendarme said, violently grabbing Tepua by the arm.

"I've been robbed too many times, monsieur," Madame Pietre complained. "This must stop."

The gendarme agreed that stealing was a serious problem in Tahiti. He said, "The problem with those people is that they mistake the verb *stealing* for the verb *borrowing*."

Tepua smashed the brand-new washing machine with a hammer. Then she got an ax and destroyed the washing machine, all the while crying her heart out.

None of her relatives said to her: "You, head-in-the-clouds. Why did you sign the papers?"

Mori picked up the destroyed washing machine and took it to the dump. He also picked up the other broken washing machine, like he was supposed to do months before.

There was a prayer meeting the night before at Loana's house to beg the Virgin Mary, Understanding Woman, to help Tepua overcome her loss. Lily slapped Loma across the face because Loma said, "I can't believe Tepua gave her child away." And Materena cried out loud as if she were the mother who'd lost her child.

Materena is still sobbing, but the children are back from school; she can hear Tamatoa and Leilani arguing on the path. Materena gets to her feet and hurries to the bathroom to wash her face.

In the Trash

The sun is back!

After more than a week of rain, that sun is a relief for mothers all over Tahiti. It means clothes can be washed, leaves raked, and children sent outside to play while the house is getting cleaned from top to bottom.

Materena is cleaning the house and complaining.

She's complaining because she's picking things up off the floor. This is not her favorite part of the cleaning process, but, since she can't stand to look at things on the floor, she's always picking them up.

But mainly she's complaining because Pito is on the sofa resting his eyes, and just looking at him is irritating her. When she cleans the house, Materena likes everybody out of the house. Usually, Pito goes outside to practice on his ukulele as soon as Materena says, "I'm cleaning the house." But today Pito wants to stay on the sofa and rest his eyes. Materena tries to pretend that he's not on the sofa, but she can see him.

"Eh, Pito, you don't want to go outside?" Materena asks nicely. She doesn't want Pito to think that she's trying to boss him around.

Well, Pito, he just wants to stay right where he is.

Materena picks all the kids' things up off the floor and complains some more. First there's Tamatoa's beat-up robot that Mama Roti gave him for his tenth birthday, then Leilani's comb and hair bands, then Moana's pencil case.

And more things that shouldn't be scattered all over the living room.

Pito tells Materena that she should throw all the things that are on the floor in the trash, because when things aren't where they're supposed to be, it means nobody wants to keep them. He gets into his stride now: if the house management was up to him, he says, he would only have five forks, five plates, five glasses, five sets of sheets, five pillowcases, five everything.

"And when my mamie comes to visit, eh? What am I going to give her for a plate? A leaf?" Materena can't believe that Pito!

"One of the kids would just have to go without a plate and wait for a plate to be available," says Pito.

Pito continues that he would get the kids to shower with their clothes on, and they'd soon realize they best not muck around in the dirt if they want to avoid a long, hard scrubbing. He would also get the kids to fold the clothes as soon as they're taken from the washing line — that way no ironing would be required. And with the brooming, he would get it done once a day, not six, seven, times.

"You broom too much." Pito has said this to Materena many times before.

"I like to broom, and why are you talking about my broom? I never complain to you about my broom."

In Pito's opinion, Materena wastes a lot of time with that broom. If Pito were in charge, the whole cleaning would take *the kids* about half an hour, not hours.

"Pito, you just rest your eyes and don't open your mouth. I

never asked you for advice." Materena is looking under the sofa for more things to pick up.

"I just want to help you," Pito says.

Materena tells Pito to get off that sofa if he wants to help her.

"All right. Good night." Pito means, don't bother me, I'm not here.

Materena transfers all the things that were on the floor onto the kitchen table. Then, standing at the back door, she calls out to the kids, playing outside, to come and pick their things up immediately or they will go straight into the trash.

"I'm serious! This is not a joke!"

The kids come running to get their things, making sure to wipe their feet before walking into the house.

"And who owns this?" Materena is holding a dirty sock.

"It's not mine," the kids reply together.

"Okay. In the trash. And this?"

The kids look at the empty packet of Chinese lollies and chorus, "It's not mine."

"Okay," Materena says, at least twenty items later, "out, you lot. I'll call you when you can come back inside the house."

Pito's things are still on the table, and Materena knows that he's thinking, *Pah,* she's not going to throw out my things, she always picks up after me. Materena puts his thongs and two issues of his Akim comics into the trash. Later on, she retrieves the thongs. You can't throw away thongs. Pito needs his thongs. We all need our thongs. But, the Akim comics . . . well, they aren't as important.

Materena is feeling quite happy with herself. She's never thrown Pito's things in the trash before, but there's a beginning for everything. Not that she's going to be obsessed with it, like her cousin Rita. Rita, she throws Coco's things in the trash every time she's cross with him.

Materena gets into the brooming. She brooms under the sofa

and for one second she's tempted to hit Pito on the head with the straw broom. Then he opens his eyes.

In two hours, the cleaning of the whole house is finished, and Materena is satisfied. She calls out to the kids that they can come inside the house now if they want to. They come because they're hungry, and they make a mess in the kitchen.

It is night when Pito asks Materena if she saw his Akim comics — the latest two issues.

Materena turns her back to Pito. "Have you looked on top of the fridge?"

"I never leave my Akim on top of the fridge."

Pito goes and checks anyway, then comes back. His Akim comics — the last issues — aren't on top of the fridge.

"And under the sofa, you looked?" Materena is pretending to look for something in the pantry.

He goes and checks under the sofa.

"Under the bed, maybe? In the toilet? Behind the TV?" says Materena.

Pito looks annoyed. "The kids must have taken them," he says.

"Eh, don't accuse the kids, accuse your memory."

Pito scratches his head, he tries to remember the last time he was with Akim, but the past is a blur. "Are you sure you didn't see my Akim when you cleaned the house?"

Materena, her back turned to Pito still, insists that she's sure, she's 100 percent sure. If she had seen Akim, she would have put him in the cardboard box in the bedroom like she always does.

"Just open your eyes and you're going to find your Akim," she says.

"It's bizarre you don't know where Akim is. Usually you know where everything is."

"Eh, my friend — don't always rely on me. I'm not perfect," Materena says, smiling.

"A wife, she's supposed to know where all her husband's things are!" Pito is so cranky he can't find his Akim.

Materena turns around and faces Pito. "What are you going on about? You're not my husband. I don't see a wedding band on my finger."

Pito stomps out of the kitchen.

Words of Love

"Perfect day for sunbaking." Rita unfolds the mat and lays it on the grass. "Especially after all that rain."

Materena agrees that it is a perfect day for sunbaking. She makes herself comfortable on the mat with her pillows.

Rita is now busy spreading cooking oil mixed with soy sauce on her arms and legs.

"Lily gave me this tip," she explains to Materena. "It's supposed to make you go brown quicker."

"Cousin, you're already brown." Materena doesn't manage to sound too interested.

Rita is finished with the spreading. She lies next to Materena and immediately digs into the bowl of chips and avocado dip she's brought.

After several chips, Rita asks Materena if she is going to dig into the chips. She sure doesn't want to eat all those chips by herself. Materena informs Rita that she doesn't feel like eating chips.

"Well, how about the salted mangoes?" Rita asks. "Are you going to have some?"

"*Non,* it's okay."

Materena turns her head to Rita and attempts to smile. She's been acting very cheerful to Rita since Rita arrived, but Materena doesn't want to pretend that she's in a happy mood anymore.

Materena is feeling quite miserable.

She can't smile.

She's feeling so depressed. She'd like to tell Rita about her depression, she'd like to tell Rita about Pito's drunken marriage proposal, but Rita will be bored. Who wants to hear that Materena foolishly took Pito seriously and got carried away gathering quotes for the wedding cake, the music, and the drive to the church and around Papeete? It is not a long story — it is a very long story. A saga. Some pains are best suffered alone.

And, plus, Pito doesn't love Materena.

Yesterday afternoon Materena went through the family albums, and in all the family photos (well, not all of them, but most of them), Pito looks distant, bored, or annoyed. He looks like he doesn't want to be there, he doesn't want to have a woman and children, a family. But when he's with Ati, Pito is flashing a big smile. He's also smiling when he's had a few drinks, but Materena doesn't care about those photos, because when you drink, everything is happy.

Materena had a few drinks last night and listened to her new love-song tape. She went to bed feeling a bit happy, but when she woke up this morning, she felt depressed.

Leilani asked before going to school, "Mamie, are you all right?"

And Materena said, "Ah, girl, don't be concerned. It's only women's stuff."

Materena's lips quiver. Rita looks at Materena properly. "There's something wrong."

"Don't worry about it."

"Do I look like someone who doesn't want to worry about you?" Rita asks.

"You're going to laugh at me."

"Me!" Rita exclaims. "Me! Laugh at you! I laugh at you

when you're silly, but I don't laugh at you when you're not in a happy mood!"

Then, squinting, Rita adds, "Has it got to do with Pito?"

Materena remains silent.

"It is him, isn't it?" Rita asks. "What did he do? Did he look at another woman?"

"Cousin, it's not this."

"Well, what did he do?"

Materena sighs. "It's more like what he didn't do. It's more like what he's never done."

"Okay, Materena." Rita pushes the bowl of chips out of her way. "I'm not moving off this mat until you tell me the story. I'm serious. If I have to stay on this mat for days, I will."

"He's never said 'I love you' to me," Materena says.

Rita's eyes widen with stupefaction. "Never? Not even once, not even when you two started to go out together? When men say all sorts of nice words to get into a woman's pants?"

"Never." Materena remembers that it wasn't really Pito who wanted to get into her pants. It was more she who wanted to get into Pito's pants.

"Why are you feeling sad about this today? And not last month? Last year?" asks Rita.

Materena tells Rita the story.

Two nights ago, she was cleaning the oven and listening to the radio, and the love-songs dedication program came on. She always listens to the love-songs dedication program, as she likes to listen to love songs and she's never felt sad. But two nights ago, just listening to all those people, all those men professing their love for their woman on the radio for the whole island to know about . . . well, Materena felt sad.

"You must know," Rita says, "not all those love-song dedications are genuine. Some men call the radio to profess their love for their woman only because the woman is standing right next to the telephone making sure that he does. In fact, I know a woman, she dials the number of the radio herself to make sure her man isn't talking to the person who tells the time and pretending that he's talking to the person from the love-songs dedication program . . . And Giselle does this too."

Materena already knows that their cousin Giselle does this. Giselle also chooses the love song she wants her boyfriend to dedicate to her.

"How come you felt sad when you listened to the love-songs dedication program two nights ago?" asks Rita.

Materena tells Rita that it might have something to do with that song she heard in the truck on her way home from work. It was such a beautiful song. As a matter of fact, all the women in the truck started to cry, and one woman was about eighty years old.

"What was the song?" Rita seems interested, although she doesn't really like love songs.

" 'La vie en rose,' " says Materena.

Rita doesn't know that song and she would like Materena to sing it for her. But Materena can do better than that.

She bought the tape yesterday. She went to the music shop and just said to the salesperson, "I want to buy that song, 'La vie en rose.' " And the salesperson immediately knew which song Materena was talking about.

So Materena runs to the kitchen to get her radio. The "La vie en rose" tape is already in the radio. Materena listened to that song about twenty times last night. And it drove Pito crazy. He said, "I'm beginning to be *fiu* of listening to that woman's croaky voice."

Materena gets the batteries from her bedroom and puts them in the radio. She rewinds the tape yet again — "La vie en rose" is the first song.

"Here's the song, Rita." Materena presses the play button and closes her eyes. And Edith Piaf begins to sing about how when her lover takes her in his arms and speaks to her softly, she sees *la vie en rose.* There's a big lump in Materena's throat as Edith sings like a woman in love, a woman loved; sings with love and passion about her man — her man, who tells her words of love, everyday words. And it's he for her and she for him . . .

And this for life! Tears come pouring out of Materena's eyes.

"Well, okay, that's enough now." Rita presses the stop button.

"Didn't you like that song?" asks Materena incredulously, wiping her eyes.

Rita grimaces. "You know me. I prefer songs that make me want to dance. That song, it's making me want to sleep."

Rita has long since left and everyone's home now. Materena decides to climb for a breadfruit. Pito is outside practicing on his ukulele, and just the sound of it irritates Materena. She wants to tell Pito that he will never be able to play the ukulele right because he hasn't got a musical ear and you must have a musical ear to play music, like her cousin Mori has.

But Materena is not going to say anything. She's just going to climb up the tree higher and higher.

She did ask Pito to get her a breadfruit and he said, "Yes, in a minute." That was half an hour ago and Materena is not going to wait one more minute.

Materena is now about one yard and a half above the ground and she's thinking that she could fall off a speedboat and Pito wouldn't swim to her rescue. She could die tomorrow and Pito wouldn't even mourn her for more than a year.

She's thinking that Pito doesn't care about her and that she's just a habit. A tree, a table, a spoon.

She's thinking about packing his bags and sending him back to his mama.

Because, above all the things she'd like in life — more than a new bed, more than a new wardrobe, more than a wedding ring — she'd like to be loved.

A branch cracks. Materena falls and her arms stretch out to grab hold of another branch.

"Pito!" Materena calls out from the bottom of her heart.

She lands on her bottom and it hurts. And here is Pito, running toward her. Materena isn't sure if it is the pain that is making her see Pito run toward her in slow motion.

He's by her side now. "Are you all right? How's your legs, move your legs, can you move your legs, why did you have to go and climb up that tree? I told you I was going to get the breadfruit — in a minute. What are you trying to do to me?" Pito sounds worried and he looks worried too.

Then Pito looks deep into Materena's eyes.

Oh, she can see that the look Pito is giving her is . . . the look of love. Pito opens his mouth to say something but he seems stuck.

Finally, "You *stupid* bitch woman," he says tenderly.

Materena roars with laughter and punches Pito on the shoulder.

The Freezer

A week later Rita is paying Materena another visit. She toots the horn, and soon Materena and her kids are outside. The cousins embrace each other, and the kids eye the plastic bags that Rita is holding. Rita always brings something for Materena's kids.

Rita kisses the kids and messes up their hair.

"Here." She gives them a bag each. "Just a little something Auntie Rita got for you lot."

Then Rita goes on about how the kids have grown since she saw them last. She compliments Leilani on her shining black hair, Tamatoa on his strong muscles, and Moana on his beautiful green eyes. She teases Leilani for having a secret boyfriend and the boys for having a secret girlfriend.

And all the kids care about is what's inside their bag. Auntie Rita always brings them something to eat.

"All right, you lot." Rita dismisses the children with a wave. "Go and eat your ice cream before it melts. There's yogurt too, and Twisties."

The kids are gone in a flash.

Materena and Rita go into the kitchen. Rita plonks the bag of goodies for her and Materena to eat on the kitchen table, and she looks rather surprised to see a freezer in Materena's kitchen, squeezed between the kitchen table and the pantry.

"You bought a freezer?" she asks.

"Sit down, Cousin," Materena replies. "I'll tell you the story."

But first Rita has to lift the lid of the freezer to see what's inside. "There's nothing inside the freezer."

"Of course there's nothing inside," Materena says. "The freezer isn't plugged in. Did you feel the cold when you lifted the lid?"

Rita sees that the electrical cord isn't plugged in. "You don't want the freezer plugged in?"

"Just sit down, Cousin, and I'll tell you the story."

Rita sits down and takes a box of crackers and some cheese out of the plastic bag. She has also brought peanuts, chips, and a bottle of Coke. "I didn't have lunch," she explains. "Come on, sit down and let's get eating."

Materena digs into the expensive cheese and begins her story about the freezer. "Last week, Pito told me that he'd bought something for me. Something big, and he said that I was going to like it. Well, I thought he'd bought me a wardrobe . . ."

"Why did you think that?" Rita asks.

"Because the week before last week," Materena explains, "I told Pito that I wouldn't mind a new wardrobe . . . for the linen and the quilts. At the moment, they're packed in cardboard boxes and I'm a bit *fiu* of those boxes in the bedroom."

"*Oui,* okay, continue the story."

"*Oui,* so when Pito told me that he'd bought something for me and that it was big, I immediately thought he was talking about my wardrobe. I tried to get him to give me a hint, but Pito wanted me to be surprised. 'Your eyes are going to pop out' — that is what Pito said to me."

Rita looks at the freezer and raises her penciled eyebrows.

"I asked Pito how he paid for that big surprise," Materena goes on, "and he said, 'Don't worry about it. It's all been arranged.' I tell you, Cousin, my eyes did pop out of my head when the delivery people delivered me that freezer. I was so shocked."

"Why, because it was so big?" Rita asks.

"*Non,* Cousin, I wasn't shocked by the size of the freezer. I was shocked by the freezer, full stop. Think a bit. You get a freezer if you eat a lot of meat, but we don't eat a lot of meat here, we eat a lot of corned beef."

Rita nods. She knows all about Materena's financial situation. Corned beef is cheap.

"I was going to tell Pito to take that freezer back," Materena goes on. "But when he came home and said to me, 'So, Materena, you're happy with that freezer I bought for you?' I said yes. I couldn't say the truth. Then Pito told me that the freezer used to belong to a colleague and he got it for cheap. Ten thousand francs, to be paid little by little."

"*Ah oui,*" Rita says. "Ten thousand francs for a freezer is really cheap. Pito got a bargain."

"I don't think ten thousand francs for a freezer that doesn't work is cheap. I think it's a rip-off," says Materena, but she's smiling.

"Ah, it doesn't work?"

"*Non.* The freezer broke down after two days."

"Two days!" Rita almost chokes on her peanuts.

"*Oui,* Cousin. Two days."

"Well, can't you just get it repaired?" asks Rita.

"Eh, we got a freezer repairman to come and look at the freezer, and you know what he said?"

Before Rita has a chance to guess, Materena reveals that the freezer man said, "Take that heap of shit to the dump."

"*Non,* Cousin." Rita is sad for Materena.

"*Oui,* Cousin. That is what the freezer repairman said to us. 'Take that heap of shit to the dump.'" Materena gives the freezer a dirty look.

"And did Pito get his money back? Whatever he'd already paid to his colleague? How much did he pay?"

"Two thousand francs."

"And did Pito get the two thousand francs back?"

The conversation is interrupted.

Moana is in the kitchen. He jumps inside the freezer, and before he closes the lid, he says to Materena and Rita, "Don't tell Tamatoa I'm inside the freezer, okay? We're playing hide-and-seek."

"Moana," Materena says, "get out of the freezer. You can suffocate. Go and hide out the back."

"I like to hide in the freezer." Moana jumps out of the freezer and runs outside.

Two seconds later, Tamatoa is in the kitchen looking for Moana. He goes straight to the freezer. "I know you're in the freezer, Moana. You always hide in the freezer."

"He's not in the freezer," Materena says.

Tamatoa lifts the lid just to make sure.

"Didn't I just tell you that Moana wasn't in the freezer?" Materena says.

But Tamatoa is already outside, calling out, "I know where you are, Moana!"

"I told Pito to ask his colleague to pay him the two thousand francs back." Materena resumes her conversation with Rita. "But Pito refused. He said, 'When I bought the freezer it was working perfectly. I can't ask my colleague for my money back.' In fact, Cousin, Pito is going to pay that freezer off."

"Hmm," Rita says. "That's the problem when you buy something from someone you know instead of buying it directly from the shop. It's difficult to ask for your money back."

"That's the problem," Materena agrees.

"So, you're going to take the freezer to the dump?"

"Well *oui,* what do you want us to do with a freezer that doesn't work? Mori's got a friend who owns a truck and who owes Mori a few favors, and he's going to take the freezer to the dump for us."

Rita looks at the freezer. "It's a shame it isn't working."

"It's a shame and at the same time it's not a shame. What's the point of having a freezer if the only things you can afford to put in it are bread sticks? In a way, I'm glad the freezer broke down. I was a bit *fiu* of those bread sticks getting frozen."

The cousins laugh.

"Eh well," Materena continues. "I hope Mori's friend is coming soon, because I'm sick of that broken freezer in my kitchen. But Mori's friend's truck is at the garage getting fixed at the moment."

Rita looks at the freezer again and smiles. "I've got an idea. You want to hear about it?"

"It's got to do with the freezer?"

"*Oui,* Cousin."

"You know somebody who can take it to the dump for me tomorrow?"

"Eh, maybe you won't need to take the freezer to the dump at all."

Materena listens to Rita's idea and at first she laughs, but then slowly Rita's idea begins to make sense.

"Okay, let's go." Materena is already up and rubbing her hands with excitement.

So the cousins push the freezer into the bedroom. It's a bit heavy, so Materena calls out to the kids for help. They come, and before they have time to inquire about the situation, Materena tells them that they are to help push the freezer into her bedroom and they are to ask no questions about it.

The freezer is in Materena's bedroom now. Materena disinfects it and Rita wipes the inside of the freezer with a cloth sprinkled with eau de cologne.

Soon they are transferring the linen and the quilts from the boxes into the freezer. Then Materena covers the freezer with an old quilt and Rita goes outside to select a potted plant to put on top of the freezer.

There.

Rita and Materena, sitting on the bed, admire the new storage chest.

"You're a genius, Cousin." Materena is really impressed with Rita's idea now. She would have never come up with the idea herself.

"Ah, Cousin. All it takes is a bit of thinking," Rita says, then begins to cackle. "Pito's eyes, they're sure going to pop out when he sees your new wardrobe."

Materena cackles along with Rita. "Eh, he just wanted to please me. I gave him such a fright last week."

Rita swings her head toward Materena. "What did you do?" Before Materena has time to explain, Rita adds, "Did you pack his bags and throw them on the road?"

"But *non,* Rita. I just fell out of the breadfruit tree."

"You fell out of the breadfruit tree! How high did you fall from? Are you all right? Did you get some X-rays done?"

"Of course I'm all right, but, Pito, he got scared I wasn't all right. It happened so fast when I fell. He thought I was badly hurt."

Rita slowly nods. "Sometimes, a man needs to think that he's lost his woman to make him realize how precious she is."

"Maybe I should fall out of a tree more often, eh?" Materena jokes.

"Who knows what Pito might do next," Rita says. "Eh, he might propose marriage to you."

Materena laughs. "I'll have broken bones all over my body before that happens."

Not that she cares anymore about marriage.

Materena is feeling normal again — but she's getting that new bed anyway.

Pito notices the freezer isn't in the kitchen as soon as he comes home. "Ah, your cousin's friend who owns a truck came?" he says, opening the fridge for a beer.

"Go and see in our bedroom," Materena says softly.

She's speaking softly because she's apprehensive, and she's apprehensive because she's never heard of anyone turning a freezer into a storage chest, and Pito might not appreciate being reminded every single day of that heap-of-shit freezer he bought. So Materena follows Pito, all the while reminding him that the freezer is hers, so it means that she can do whatever she wants with it.

Pito is in the bedroom. He guesses that the big thing hidden underneath the old quilt and squeezed into the corner of the room is the freezer. He looks at Materena, then walks to the freezer. He takes the potted plant off the freezer and lifts the lid. He smells the eau de cologne and he sees the linen and the quilts neatly stacked in the freezer.

"So?" Materena is all sweetness.

Pito closes the lid and puts the potted plant back on it. He grunts, takes a pull on his Hinano, and admits that it isn't a bad idea.

But later, in bed, Pito tells Materena that he feels really bad that she has a freezer as a wardrobe.

"Don't worry about it," she says. "I like my new wardrobe."

Well, Pito still feels bad about it, and, actually, so he professes, he won't relax until Materena has a real wardrobe.

"Pito . . ." Materena hugs her man, thinking he's so sweet.

"I'm going to get myself a second job," Pito declares. "I'm not afraid of hard work. I will not rest until my woman has a real wardrobe."

"*Oui,* I know," Materena says, not believing a word of it. But she hugs her man like she believes in him. This is the most thoughtful thing Pito has said in a long while.

Employee of the Month

I'm not going to work today," Pito announces the next morning.

"And why not?" Materena already knows the reason, and the reason is that Pito doesn't want to go to work because he doesn't want to go to work.

"My stomach — it's playing up on me a bit," Pito says.

"What's wrong with your stomach?" Materena doesn't believe there's something wrong with Pito's stomach at all.

"I told you," Pito says. "My stomach's playing up on me a bit."

"I ate what you ate and my stomach is fine."

"Maybe it's something I ate at the snack yesterday afternoon."

"What did you eat at the snack yesterday afternoon?" Materena realizes that she's asking a bit too many questions here.

"*Ah hia hia!*" Now Pito is very annoyed. "Do you think you're a doctor or what? I'm going to see the doctor." Pito needs to see the doctor for the medical certificate.

"You're going to see your doctor or my doctor?" asks Materena.

Pito gives Materena the *you're asking me too many questions* look. "My doctor, of course. Why should I go and see your doctor? I'm happy with my doctor."

"Your doctor. He's only good at giving medical certificates."

"Well, that's why I'm happy with my doctor." Pito goes on

about how he only has to say to his doctor that he doesn't feel 100 percent today for his doctor to say, "How many days off do you want, Pito?" Whereas, Materena's doctor, he asks too many questions, like he doesn't believe that you're too sick to go to work. Not many sick people go to see him. They'd rather wait hours for the other doctor — the doctor who understands better.

"Call my work, okay?" Pito makes himself more comfortable in the bed. "Tell the secretary of the boss that I'm going to see the doctor."

"It's you who's going to call your work. I'm not calling anybody."

"You can't call on your way to work? What, it's difficult to dial the number of my work?"

"Why can't you call your work?"

"The sick don't call the office," Pito says. "Someone else has to call the office. Because if you call the office yourself, it means you're not really sick. The sick go to see the doctor."

"I don't like to talk to the secretary of the boss." Materena gets out of the bed. There's breakfast to prepare.

"You don't have to *talk* to the secretary of the boss," Pito says. "Just tell her, 'Pito, he's not coming to work today.'"

Materena lifts the quilt off the bed to fold it. "She asks too many questions. She likes to repeat, 'What's wrong with Pito?' like she doesn't believe me that you're too sick to go to work. And, that woman, she's got such an annoying nasal voice."

"You don't become the secretary of the boss because you've got a beautiful voice," says Pito. He pulls the quilt back his way, he's not getting out of bed yet. "You just tell that woman you don't know nothing. You just tell that woman that you're not the doctor. Yes, just say to the secretary of the boss, 'When Pito comes to work, you can look at the medical certificate.'"

"I can't leave the message with Josephine?"

"Josephine is not the secretary of the boss."

"And what are you going to do all day?" Materena asks. And before Pito has a chance to answer that he's going to do nothing but rest all day long, she adds, "Don't you go out fishing with Ati. You don't want to get a suntan."

And now, two days later, Pito, who just got home from work, tells Materena that he has an announcement to make.

Materena stops chopping the onions. "An announcement? A good announcement or a bad announcement?"

Pito gets a beer out of the fridge and sits at the kitchen table.

"What's the announcement?" Materena is a bit worried. Pito savors his Hinano. "Pito?"

"Can I tell my story when I'm ready?" Pito says.

"Ah, because there's a story to tell?" Now Materena is really worried. Usually when there's a story to tell with an announcement, it is a bad announcement. Usually.

"Just keep chopping your onions and listen," Pito says.

"There's a good ending to your story?" Materena wants to know now, but Pito wants to tell his story from the beginning, and when he gets to the end of it, Materena will know what the announcement is all about.

But first Materena has to promise Pito that she won't open her mouth during his storytelling, because every time she opens her mouth when he's telling a story, Pito loses the thread of the story.

Well, here is Pito's story about what happened to him today at work.

"The boss wants to see you," a colleague says to Pito.

"Why does he want to see me?" Pito asks.

The colleague shrugs, he doesn't know why the boss wants to see Pito. He tells Pito the boss just said, "Get me Pito — immediately."

That word, *immediately,* worries Pito. When the boss wants

to see you — immediately — it means you're in trouble, you've done something he doesn't appreciate. The last person the boss asked to see — immediately — got shoved through the door. Pito asks his colleague if he's certain the boss said "immediately."

"*Oui,* the boss said 'immediately.'"

The colleague advises Pito to report to the boss's office — immediately — and Pito walks to his boss's office — slowly. He thinks about all the extra hours he's worked for the company — at no extra charge. Ah yes, it happens that Pito is still at the cutting machine past four o'clock.

Pito thinks about the sick days too.

He reminds himself that he's entitled to sick days — you don't get a bonus check if you never get sick. Pito is not the only one who gets sick. Everyone gets sick — and Monday is a popular day to be too sick to work. Pito has never been sick on Mondays, though. The boss gets suspicious when you're sick that day — Pito is aware of that factor. Friday is not a good day to get sick either. Pito is never sick on Fridays.

The time before the last time that Pito took a day off, he went fishing with Ati and he got a bit sunburned. But he worked twice as hard the following three days. He didn't talk, he just concentrated on the machine.

Pito is about to knock on the door of his boss's office, but he's not ready to face the boss yet. Is he going to get shoved through the door?

The last person who got shoved through the door didn't really get shoved through the door. He got a serious warning and the employee shoved himself through the door.

But Pito likes his job. It pays reasonably good money. He's been working with the company for so many years he can't imagine himself doing anything else but cutting wood. He's used to cutting wood and he's used to the people with whom he works. His colleagues, his mates.

And his uncle got him the job, thanks to his connection with the boss. Not the boss now — the boss before. And if Uncle was alive today, he wouldn't be too happy about Pito getting shoved through the door, because when you use your connections to get a relative a job, that relative has to stay with the job until the retirement. That's the price to pay when you can't get a job without a relative having to use his connections.

Pito is nervous now, he wipes the sweat off his forehead. Another time he had a sickie, the one before when he went fishing with Ati, Pito went for a drink in town — with Ati.

Pito knocks. Two knocks.

"Come in!"

Pito opens the door and puts his head in the office. "Boss, you want to see me?"

"Sit down." The boss is signing some papers.

Pito walks into the office and sits in the chair facing the boss. Pito looks at his boss in the eyes. You should always look at your boss in the eyes. When you don't look at your boss in the eyes, it means you're hiding something.

"Do you like to work here?" The boss takes his glasses off.

"*Oui,* boss," Pito replies.

He wants to tell his boss that if he didn't like to work here, he would have got himself another job — he's got connections, he's got lots of cousins everywhere. But Pito says nothing, he just makes sure to look at his boss in the eyes.

The boss smiles, he says, "Ah, ha." He coughs, then he becomes silent and Pito expects to hear the words "It is with regret . . ."

But the boss begins, "It is with joy . . ."

The boss tells Pito that he's been nominated Employee of the Month, and Pito is so happy he shakes the hand of his boss. The boss goes on about how he's always watching his employees. Nothing — absolutely nothing — escapes his eyes and his ears.

He knows everything there is for him to know. He looks into Pito's eyes and repeats the word — *everything.* Pito nods and for a split second his eyes wander to the ceiling, the glasses, the thick eyebrows of the boss, then back to the eyes of his boss.

The sickie he took before he went with Ati to the pub, Pito went for a drink at the bar at the airport — with Ati.

Next time he's going to take a day off — he's going to stay inside the house, that's for certain. It's too risky being outside when you're supposed to be inside the house, in bed — resting. Did the boss see him at the bar at the airport?

Next time he takes a sickie, he's going to make sure that he *is* sick.

"Anyway," the boss says as he puts his glasses back on, "congratulations."

He hopes Pito won't make him regret his decision to have him nominated employee of this month.

"Okay, boss — thank you, boss."

Pito tells his colleagues about the Employee of the Month nomination and they say, "Good for you, Pito." It isn't a cause for a celebration at the bar. The nomination doesn't come with a bonus check, Pito isn't going to buy beers all round.

Pito goes back to the machine and works twice as fast.

And before leaving work, he goes to the front office to check his nomination form. The Employee of the Month nomination form is displayed in the front office on a notice board. The words EMPLOYEE OF THE MONTH are typed in capital letters. His name is handwritten underneath — *Pito Tehana.*

And Pito thinks about that nomination form in the truck on his way home. The Employee of the Month nomination system was introduced three months ago, soon after the boss came back from a seminar. The boss held a special meeting in the canteen. He talked about how they should all put their efforts together to ensure the company's growth, because if the company does well — so will they. The employees cheered, but when the boss announced that there would be no bonus check with the nomination, the employees stopped cheering and shut their ears. What's the use of an Employee of the Month nomination if there's no francs to shout your colleagues a few drinks at the bar?

Still, Pito is very happy about that nomination. It's better than getting shoved through the door.

It is the end of Pito's story and Pito looks at Materena, waiting for her reaction to the announcement.

"Employee of the Month!" Materena has been meaning to shout these words for the last five minutes. She gets Pito another beer.

"I tell you, Materena," Pito says, "when my colleague said to me, 'The boss wants to see you — immediately,' I thought the boss was going to tell me, 'It is with regret . . .'"

"So, when there's the word *immediately,* there's *it's with regret* after?"

"*Ah oui,*" Pito says. "But the boss said to me, 'It is with joy . . .'"

"That's very good your boss said to you, 'It is with joy,' and not, 'It is with regret.'" Materena resumes the chopping of the onions.

"Yes, that's good," Pito agrees.

"It's a good job you've got, Pito," Materena continues.

"I'm used to that job."

"It's like me with my job. The house of my boss is like my house. I'm used to cleaning her house. I know where everything is."

Materena lights the stove and puts the pot on the flame. She waits for the pot to get hot and she thinks about her man's Employee of the Month nomination. He's a good employee when he's at the machine — he must be. Yes, he's a good employee when he's in the mood to work. And when you get a nomination — usually you get a promotion later on, *non?* There's no reason why Pito can't get to be a boss one day. Not the big boss with the big office, but the boss beneath that boss. The second-in-charge boss. It's good to have a nomination like that for the future. If Pito ever gets shoved through the door, he can show the Employee of the Month nomination paper at his job interviews.

"And when the month is finished," Materena asks, "what happens to your Employee of the Month nomination form? You get it?"

"*Non,* it goes in the company files."

"You can't get a copy?"

"There's only one copy, and that copy goes in the company files."

Materena puts oil in the pot, then she throws the onions in the pot. It's silly Pito can't get a copy of his nomination. What if he wants to show it off to his family, what if he wants to put it in the family album?

An idea comes into Materena's mind.

She's going to photograph that nomination form.

It will be the proof.

The next day, on her way home, Materena stops by Pito's work. It's nice in the office, with the air-conditioning. The office girl, Josephine, who answers the telephone, smiles when she sees Materena. "Eh, hello, Materena."

"Eh, hello, Josephine."

"How's the kids?"

"Good. And, your Patrice, he's still running like the wind?"

Patrice is Josephine's son and Josephine mentioned to Materena two weeks ago that he had won the school running competition.

"That kid, he loves running, I tell you." Josephine is all smiles.

"There's other fast runners in your family?" asks Materena.

"Not in my family. But the father of my man, he was a bit of a runner in his days when he was a postman. In his days, postmen didn't ride Vespas, they ran."

"Eh, Patrice got his running gift from his grandfather."

"You think you can inherit things like this?"

"*Ah oui.*" Materena sounds very convincing. "It's got to do with the shape of the legs. My cousin Lily, she used to be a champion runner, and she got her speed from her father, who also used to be a champion runner."

Josephine widens her eyes. "Now, that you're talking. My man, he was a bit of a runner too."

"*Ah oui?*"

"*Oui,* he's got a few school medals."

"Eh, you see? And, Patrice, he wants to be a professional runner?"

"He never told me."

"You better ask him."

"*Oui,* I'm going to ask him. But, you know, last Saturday, there was a competition between the schools of Tahiti at the Stade Pater and Patrice won."

"*Ah non!*"

"*Ah oui,*" says Josephine.

"What race?"

"The eight hundred meters."

"What a champion!"

Josephine is smiling so much now that you can see all her teeth. And Materena knows that it is only a matter of seconds before Josephine shows her yet another photograph of Patrice.

"Eh, Materena," says Josephine, "I'm not the kind to show

off, but — you know, my son, he's in the paper. Did you see him? In *Les Nouvelles.*"

"I get *Le Journal.*"

"Well, wait a bit." Josephine hurries to grab her pandanus bag and gets *Les Nouvelles* out. She flicks the pages. "Here — look."

There's the head of Josephine's son — Materena recognizes him from the photos Josephine has shown her before. This photo in the paper must have been taken after the race — Patrice looks all puffed out. Materena looks for about half a minute. You can't just glance at a photograph a mother is showing you. You have to look for about half a minute, all the while smiling.

Well, now that's enough. Materena slowly shuts the newspaper, one more look at the photograph and one more smile — the newspaper is closed now.

Josephine puts the newspaper back in her bag. "And what are you doing here today?"

Usually, Materena only comes to Pito's work on Fridays, to pick up Pito's pay envelope.

"You know Pito got nominated Employee of the Month." Now it is Materena who is all smiles.

But Josephine is not sharing Materena's smile. "Yes . . . and?"

Materena looks into Josephine's eyes. "Josephine, do you know what I'm talking about? The Employee of the Month!"

"*Ah oui,* it's good, eh." Josephine forces a smile.

"Are you okay?" Materena asks, perplexed.

Josephine looks pale now. "I just don't feel well all of a sudden. I'll be all right soon. It's the air-conditioning. I'm fine now."

"Do you think I can take a photo of that nomination?" Materena asks.

Josephine quickly looks over her shoulder and nods to Materena.

"But don't tell Pito I was here today, okay?" Materena says. "I don't want him to think that I didn't believe him about his nomination and I had to come check it with my own eyes."

And, whispering, Materena adds, "It's good to have a photo . . . in case Pito gets shoved through the door one day."

"*Ah oui.*" Josephine is also whispering. "Well, you take the photo. I'll go back to my work."

Pito's nomination form is half-hidden behind a sale notice that says: *Suzuki motorbike for sale — good condition, price negotiable.* Materena rearranges the form so that you can see it better. She takes two steps back, gets her camera out of her pandanus bag, and immortalizes Pito's nomination form three times.

Materena thanks Josephine and leaves the office. But, once outside the office, Materena realizes that she can take two more photos and finish the roll of film. And so she's back in the office for more photographing, just in case the other photos don't turn out clear.

There's nobody in the front office, and Materena thinks Josephine is in the bathroom. Materena is about to shoot when she hears Josephine in conversation with somebody. And Materena is very interested in the conversation, since she hears her name.

". . . Pito's wife, Materena, she just came in the office to photograph his Employee of the Month nomination and I couldn't tell her no, because, Materena, she's really nice."

"Josephine!" Materena recognizes the annoying nasal voice of the secretary of the boss, who sounds like she can't believe Josephine let Materena take a photo of the Employee of the Month nomination.

The secretary of the boss goes on about how the Employee of the Month nomination means nothing. That the boss only started it because at the latest seminar he went to, they said not to give slack employees warnings, because that's a negative approach. Instead, they advised, give them an Employee of the Month nomination, because that's a positive approach. The secretary of the boss says that the Employee of the Month nomination is only supposed to make the slack employee feel special, so that they perform better. She says, the really exemplary employees, they get a pay raise.

"I know all this." Josephine sounds a bit annoyed. "But I couldn't tell Materena that the Employee of the Month nomination meant nothing."

The secretary of the boss says that in future the Employee of the Month nomination cannot be photographed. Also, that they have to be destroyed when the month is over because the boss doesn't want evidence that they've existed.

Materena hurries to take two more photographs of Pito's Employee of the Month nomination, then she's out the door in a flash.

The photographs all turn out clear, you can see the words EMPLOYEE OF THE MONTH, and Pito's name right underneath it.

Materena chooses the best one and files it in the latest family album.

The Radio

There is no *this is Materena's, this is Pito's* rule around their house.

Their things aren't divided into Pito's sofa, Pito's TV, Materena's land, Materena's house, Materena's fridge, and so on.

But the radio is special to Materena just as the ukulele is special to Pito.

Materena can practice on the ukulele anytime she feels like it. She doesn't have to ask Pito for his permission. But it's very rare she practices on the ukulele, she much prefers to listen to the music on the radio — love songs, in particular.

And, with Materena's radio, Pito can take it outside anytime he feels like listening to it, he doesn't need to ask Materena for her permission. Pito uses the radio a lot. He likes to listen to music when he's drinking by himself outside, next to the breadfruit tree. Sometimes Materena calls out to Pito to put the radio back on top of the fridge because she's in the mood to listen to music while she's cooking. But she's more likely just to ask Pito to turn up the volume and change the channel. When Pito has had enough of listening to the music on the radio (when there's no more beer to drink), he puts the radio back where it belongs, on top of the fridge.

Tonight, Pito wants to take Materena's radio to his meeting.

The radio of his mate who usually supplies the radio at the meetings is broken and Pito said to his mates that he'd bring the radio to the next meeting — which is tonight.

"Ah, we don't even ask for permission." Materena is a bit annoyed with Pito telling her that he's taking her radio without even consulting her first. She might have had plans to listen to the radio tonight.

"What, now we need to ask for permission? I never asked for permission to take the radio before."

"*Oui,* that's because you only took the radio outside, into the backyard, and not to your meeting place."

"So I can't take the radio, is that what you're telling me?"

Materena tells Pito that there is a special program on the radio tonight, and she promised Mamie to listen to that program. It's about religion.

"Ah, now that I need the radio, there's a program about religion on the radio you have to listen to." Pito gives Materena a suspicious look.

Materena repeats that she promised Mamie to listen to that religious program. But Materena is feeling bad and a bit sorry for Pito. He looks disappointed.

She feels compelled to give him permission to take the radio . . .

Loana bought Materena that radio for her eighteenth birthday. Loana said, "Every woman should have a radio. It's good to listen to music when you're cleaning. It's good to listen, to listen to music, full stop." Loana expects that radio to be in perfect condition for another thirty years, at least. Apparently it wasn't cheap. She bought it from the hi-fi store and not the secondhand store.

Materena is in a real dilemma.

But she knows well what happens at the "meetings." There's lots of wind talk, there's lots of drinking, and there's a high possibility of one of Pito's mates spilling beer on her radio, or smashing the radio on the concrete because he got contradicted once too often, or . . .

Anything could happen to her expensive radio.

"Come on, eh, Pito?" Materena pleads with Pito to understand her situation.

"You can keep your heap-of-rust, heap-of-shit radio," Pito says.

In fact, he continues, he'd be embarrassed to take that ancient thing to the meeting, his friends would laugh, for certain. In fact, as of now, Pito doesn't want anything to do with that heap-of-rust, heap-of-shit radio and he warns Materena if he ever gets his hi-fi system — when he gets his hi-fi system — she better never ever touch it.

"Fine with me, Pito," Materena says.

Pito stomps out of the kitchen.

He's gone.

And Materena thinks, Ah, he's got a nerve.

Materena goes to have a shower. She's a bit upset because she doesn't like to fight with Pito, but, still, he's got a nerve, calling her radio a heap of rust.

She hears Pito come back, he must have forgotten something. She calls out, "Pito! You forgot something?" There's no answer. "Pito!" Then, just like that, the suspicion that Pito came back to take her radio crosses her mind.

Materena rushes out of the bathroom hanging on to the towel and with soap foam in her hair. There's no radio on top of the fridge. She rushes outside in time to catch Pito running away with her radio on his shoulder.

"Pito, my radio!"

He laughs, and disappears around a corner.

Now Materena is in a bad mood. Pito is going to get it. Yes, she's going to blast his ears when he comes back. Her radio is not a heap of rust. He wants to show it off to his mates. And he's going to tell his mates that the radio is his. Materena goes back to her shower.

And now, sitting on the sofa, she's got Pito's ukulele and the scissors . . . but she can't bring herself to cut the strings. Materena puts the ukulele back in the bedroom and goes back into the kitchen for something to eat and do while she waits for Pito.

Pito comes home at about eleven o'clock, but there's no radio.

Materena springs to her feet. "Where's my radio!"

"Eh, calm yourself," Pito says, "I'm going to find the *titoi* who stole your radio."

"My radio got stolen!" Materena can't believe what she's hearing. Well, yes, and here's the story, which Pito swears to be true.

"Why do you need to swear your story is true?"

Because Pito knows Materena's not going to believe his story.

Pito went to his meeting, and his mates were really happy he brought Materena's radio along. One of the mates had brought his brand-new tape of Bob Marley — the best of the best. And, thanks to Materena's radio, the clan was able to listen to the best of the best of Bob Marley.

After his fourth beer, Pito decided to hit the road, he wanted to sleep. It'd been a hard day at work. The mates were a bit upset at Pito leaving early, as they were really enjoying the best of the best of Bob Marley, but when a man has to go home, a man has to go home. But halfway to the house, Pito stopped by a tree to have a little bit of a lie-down, his legs just couldn't keep on walking. He put the radio under his head to make it like a pillow and rested his eyes. But he fell into a very deep sleep, and while he was sleeping his very deep sleep, someone without a conscience took the radio from under his head and replaced it with a brick. Pito felt nothing.

It's only when he woke up that he found out about the replacement. At first, he thought his eyes were hallucinating. But then he realized it was truly a brick he was seeing and not the radio.

So here he is, without the radio.

Pito's story sounds like a whole lot of inventing to Materena. She shouts at Pito that if something else happened to her radio, he better confess, because she doesn't believe one word of that whole lot of inventing.

But Pito swears his story is nothing but the truth. He swears it on his grandmother's head. Materena has to believe Pito — you don't swear on your beloved grandmother's head if you're telling a whole lot of inventing.

"I told you not to take my radio," Materena says, "and now look. I told you."

Materena is devastated. And at the same time relieved.

That someone, he could have been worse than a someone without a conscience who robs the sleepers, he could have been an assassin. He could have smashed Pito's head with the brick. Just the thought of it makes Materena shiver.

"What's this sleeping by the side of the road like you've got no house?" she says.

Pito and Materena go to bed.

It takes a while for Materena to fall asleep. She thinks about her radio. She's had it for fourteen years. She's sure going to miss her radio.

My poor radio, eh.

It is now three days since Materena's radio was stolen, and here's one in front of the Chinese store, next to a pandanus bag and a rolled mat. Materena walks past, and into the store. She takes a shopping basket from the bench, but . . . she's going to check on that radio outside again.

That radio looked a bit too familiar.

Materena puts the basket back on the bench and goes outside. She stands about one yard away from the radio, she doesn't want people to think that she's plotting to steal it.

That radio sure looks familiar.

It's the same size as Materena's radio. Eh, it doesn't mean it's her radio. There are thousands of radios like hers floating around the island. But when you've been looking at something for fourteen years, you should be able to recognize it in a rapid second. And it seems to Materena that she's recognizing her radio.

Someone taps her on the shoulder, and Materena turns around. It's her cousin Giselle. The cousins kiss each other on the cheeks.

"What are you doing standing like a coconut tree?" asks Giselle.

"See that radio there?" Materena says. "Next to the pandanus bag and the rolled mat?"

Giselle glances at the radio and nods.

"I think it's my radio."

"Someone stole your radio?" Giselle is now looking at the radio with more interest.

"*Eh oui,*" Materena sighs.

"You're sure it's not a cousin who came into your house and borrowed it for a couple of days?"

Materena briefs Giselle on the story.

"Pito's story," Giselle says, "it's not a whole lot of inventing?" Pito's story sure sounds like a whole lot of inventing to Giselle.

Why is Pito's story so hard to believe? Materena asks herself. When Materena told Pito's story to her mother, Loana said,

"His story sounds like a whole lot of inventing to me." Even with the bit of Pito's swearing on his grandmother's head that his story is nothing but the truth, Loana still said, "His story sounds like a whole lot of inventing to me."

Loana and Pito had words and now they're not talking and Materena doesn't like when her mother and her man pretend they don't know each other. Pito said, "It's fine with me if Loana never speaks to me again." And Loana said, "It's fine with me if I never speak to Pito again."

Materena really wishes Pito never took her radio to his meeting. Now look at the complications. *Aue.*

"He swore on his grandmother's head that the story was nothing but the truth," Materena says to Giselle, thinking how much more suspicious other people are compared to her.

"Ah well, if he swore on his grandmother's head, his story must be true," says Giselle doubtfully.

"I'm just glad the person replaced my radio with the brick."

Giselle doesn't understand, so Materena explains that the person could have smashed Pito's head with the brick.

"*Ah oui,*" Giselle says. "That would be horrible. You think that radio there is your radio?"

"I think, but it's not for sure."

"You didn't write your name on your radio?"

"*Non.*" It had never entered Materena's mind to write her name on her radio. In fact, she doesn't write her name on anything, except her budget book, but that's a habit she got from school.

Giselle shakes her head. "You should always write your name on your things." Giselle confesses to Materena that she writes her name on every single thing she owns: her TV, her washing machine, her fridge, her thongs. Giselle even writes her name on her pareus.

Last week, she couldn't find her thongs — brand-new thongs

too. She looked everywhere outside, she thought the dog might have taken them, but then she remembered that her dog doesn't take thongs, she's trained that dog since he was a puppy not to take thongs.

She also remembered that dogs don't take *pairs* of thongs, they just take one thong at a time.

Giselle looked everywhere inside the house — no thongs. A few days later, she went to someone's house with her mama for a prayer meeting. She took her shoes off at the door and placed them next to the other shoes and thongs, and then what did she see? Thongs that looked just like hers. She checked underneath the thongs, and there was her name, carved into each one. So she put her thongs in her bag. Now, if she hadn't written her name, she'd still be wondering if those thongs really belonged to a person praying in the house.

"There's just too many cousins like James borrowing things without asking permission," says Giselle. "So write your name on all your things."

Materena wishes she had written her name on her radio.

Giselle asks Materena how long has she had that radio.

"Fourteen years."

In Giselle's opinion, when you have something for that long, you must be able to recognize it within a second.

"You recognize your radio?" she asks.

Materena looks at the radio. True, it looks really familiar, but she's not 100 percent sure.

"*Ah oui,* it's difficult to be sure when there's nothing to help you, like a missing button," Giselle says. "What about scratches? There's no scratches on your radio for you to check?"

There are no scratches on Materena's radio. She's looked after it real well. Her radio is in perfect condition. In fact, when you look at it, you'd think it was brand-new — just out of the radio store.

Ah, it's a nuisance.

But just a second, Materena is having an interesting thought. Her radio has been in the kitchen for years. Shouldn't it smell of onions and garlic? She asks Giselle for her opinion.

"*Ah oui,*" Giselle agrees. "I didn't think about the odor. Well, go smell that radio."

Materena goes and smells the radio. Ah yes, it smells of onions and garlic.

"So!" Giselle calls out. "It smells of onions and garlic!"

"Ah yes. The odor is very strong. So, I take it?"

"Well yes! What are you waiting for?"

But Materena hesitates. What if she takes that radio and it isn't actually her radio? That would be stealing. And what if the owner of that radio walks out of the shop just as Materena is picking up the radio? That would be embarrassing.

Materena goes back to stand next to Giselle and focuses on the radio. "I'm just going to look at that radio for a little bit longer."

"All right, Materena," Giselle says. "But I've got to go to the shop now. I've got a craving for gherkins. I think I'm pregnant again, but don't put the news on the coconut radio, okay?"

"Sure." Materena hopes for Giselle that she's not pregnant, it's a bit too soon. Isidore Louis junior is only four months old.

Materena is still staring at the radio when Giselle comes out of the shop with the biggest jar of gherkins.

"You're still here?" Giselle says.

"Well *oui.*"

"I've got to go home, Cousin. I'm busting to go to the toilet."

"Okay." Materena kisses Giselle. She could tell Giselle to go to the pharmacy for a pregnancy kit, but when someone tells you not to put the news on the coconut radio, you're supposed to forget the news as soon as that someone tells you about it.

And Materena keeps on focusing on her radio, wondering

when the person who owns the pandanus bag and the mat, but not necessarily the radio, is going to make an appearance.

"*Iaorana,* Cousin." It is Mori, with a case of empty beer bottles to be replaced with full ones at the shop. "What are you up to?"

Materena smells Mori as she greets him to check that he's not drunk. She doesn't really want to hold a conversation with a drunk. But Mori isn't drunk yet and so Materena informs Mori of the situation. Mori doesn't make any comments at all about Pito's story sounding like a whole lot of inventing. He just listens and nods.

And now Mori's got an idea. "I'm going to walk around the shop with the radio. If nobody says to me, 'What are you doing with my radio?' then you take it, Cousin."

Materena looks at Mori, with his Rastafarian hairstyle down his back and his homemade tattoos, especially that one of a green and red dragon spitting fire on his chest. Mori isn't wearing a shirt.

"Okay then, Mori. You go walk around the shop with that radio." She sure doesn't want to walk around the shop with that radio herself.

So Mori nonchalantly picks up the radio, turns it on, changes the channel for some more upbeat reggae music, and disappears into the shop, the radio perched on his shoulder.

And Materena waits. She can hear the blasting music.

A few minutes later, Mori comes out of the shop.

"Nobody asked you about that radio?" Materena asks.

"*Non.* Here's your radio, I've got to get my beer."

Materena is home now with her radio. She immediately writes her name on it and puts the radio where it belongs — on top of the fridge.

She tells Pito the story about how she got her radio back and he laughs his head off.

A Letter of Separation

It's many weeks since that time Materena nearly lost her radio forever. But on a sunny Saturday morning like now, when a beautiful love song comes on, she still gets a little feeling of relief that her radio came back to her.

The love song that's playing is one Materena hasn't heard before. It's about separation — how it's difficult, but we must move on with our life, we must go on our way. It talks about hoping to remain good friends, and good luck to you.

There is a paper on the kitchen table and a pen, so Materena writes down the lyrics because she likes that song a lot. And the chorus says,

I've got to find myself,
I can no longer live with you,
I've got to find my wings . . .
My wings of liberty.

Later that day Materena visits Loana.

In the meantime, Pito comes home. He sees the paper on the kitchen table. "What's this?" He's not really interested. He grabs himself a beer from the fridge and calls out to Materena, but she's not responding and he guesses that she's not home. He goes into the living room and makes himself comfortable on the sofa.

It's so quiet, he thinks. Just the way he likes it. The children are with Mama Roti for the day and for the night, and Pito is supposed to pick them up tomorrow morning, Sunday, before Sunday Mass. But where is Materena?

"Where's that Materena?" Pito asks out loud.

It's quarter past eleven and he's hungry. Pito looks at the ceiling, but he's too hungry to just lie down. He gets up and goes back into the kitchen. He opens the fridge and looks inside, but what he feels like right now is corned beef. He gets a can of corned beef from the pantry, opens it, and eats it straight out of the can. Pito looks at the paper on the table and thinks that perhaps Materena had to go somewhere and she's left him a note. He grabs the paper and he nonchalantly reads the words.

The room blackens and Pito feels like he's just been hit with a hammer.

What did I do? What did I do? What did I do?

In Pito's mind, this is a letter of separation. Materena wants her liberty, meaning she wants Pito out of the house, out of her life.

What did I do? Is this because of the radio? That colorful shirt?

Is this because I laughed at her when she tried to build that pond?

So many questions flash upon Pito's shocked mind, and he answers them one by one.

It's *true* that someone took the radio from underneath my head while I was sleeping. It's hard to believe it, but it is *true!*

I just couldn't wear that shirt she bought me for my birthday. It's just not my style.

I didn't help Materena build that pond, because you can't build a pond with tiles. You need concrete.

Pito reads the letter of separation again. There are always hints before a woman walks out on you, he thinks. Usually. One of his colleagues from work, he went home last month only to find an empty house. His woman was gone, just like that, no warning, no nothing. She took the children, she took the hi-fi system, and she took her bed too. One day Pito's colleague had his woman cooking and cleaning for him, and the next day his mama had to take over.

Pito buries his head in his hands, he wasn't prepared for this. There's a lump in his throat. It's the same lump he felt when his father died. The same deep sorrow. That unbearable feeling that as of today, his life will never be the same again.

The tears come and Pito lets them run on his face. He thinks of his colleague and how he tried to get his woman back. The colleague cried and begged, and his woman told him, "It's too late for the crying. I've got someone else. Someone who loves me."

Pito's tears are now choked sobs. But soon, anger replaces the sobbing. Pito is cranky now at Materena for wanting to separate from him. He thinks that she could have at least told him the news to his face. She tells him just about everything else to his face. And he thinks that he's a good man. He might be lazy every now and then — that's because his mama always did everything for him — but at least he's got a job.

"And I let her pick up my pay! What else does she want?" Pito bangs his fist on the table. "And when she gave my bed to her cousin Mori, eh? She didn't even ask for my opinion, and I didn't complain. Well, I yelled at her, but I'm not complaining now. That new bed she bought from Conforama is better than my old bed; still, she should have asked me."

Pito is so cranky at Materena.

"Plus, I gave her my bonus check! And what did she do with it? Eh, instead of buying me a little something, she gave the whole lot to her cousin Teva for him to tile the bathroom, and he did a shit job! You can see the concrete between the tiles. But I don't complain, I say, 'Eh, it's good that my bonus check paid Teva's fare back to Rangiroa!'"

Pito storms out of the house with Materena's letter of separation clutched in his hand.

Materena is chatting away with Loana on the terrace when Pito appears at the gate. He waves to Materena, she waves to him, and Loana says, "What does he want again?"

Well, Pito wants to talk to Materena, so Loana calls out to Pito, "Eh, come in, then, and don't act like you don't know how to open that gate."

But Pito wants to talk to Materena in private, so Materena goes to the gate. Loana gets to her feet for a better view of what is happening at the gate.

Pito, speaking in a low voice, asks Materena if there is anything she has to announce to him right at this moment.

Materena looks at his red face and the sweat on his forehead and wonders what the story is. She shrugs. *Non.*

"There's nothing you have to tell me right this moment?" Pito asks.

He then goes on and on about how he would appreciate it if Materena revealed her plans to him right at this moment and not at the last minute.

"What plans are you talking about, Pito?"

"You're sure there's nothing I need to know right at this moment?" Pito looks deep into Materena's eyes.

Materena is getting more confused by the second. "I don't understand."

Pito gives her one more chance to reveal the truth, the whole truth, the explanation.

"You smoke *paka* or what?" Materena says in desperation.

So Pito throws the letter in Materena's face. "What's this, eh? It's not a letter of separation?"

Materena reads the "letter" and bursts into laughter. Then she tells Pito the truth, the whole truth, the explanation.

Pito scratches his head. "It's just that when I read that letter . . ."

He doesn't finish the sentence, but Materena knows that the end of the sentence is "my heart broke into a thousand pieces."

Materena says good-bye to her mother and walks home with Pito.

As they are about to cross the road, a bridal car drives past, tooting its horn. Materena waves, and calls out, "Happiness to you two!"

Pito watches Materena and says nothing.

But he is now thinking about it, marriage. He remembers his marriage proposal to Materena — but that was months ago, and he was drunk. He didn't know what he was saying, and there was that silly love movie on the TV the night before.

Now it's very late and Pito wishes there was beer in the fridge to help him go back to sleep. He rolls to Materena's side and hugs her. She's fast asleep. He hugs her for a while and smells her perfume. It feels good, he thinks, to hug someone you care about. They had sexy loving this afternoon because there were no children at home and because they were in the mood. Pito hugs Materena tighter.

And he thinks that it is about time that he marries this good woman. He's sure that she'd be very interested. The way she looked at the married couple in the bridal car, the envy in her eyes, the secret desire to be a bride. Pito saw all that.

Pito remembers his parents' marriage. There was his father dying in the hospital room and there was his mother, and she kept saying, "Frank Tehana, don't you dare die before you slip that ring on my finger." And there was the priest hurrying the ceremony. Frank Tehana struggled with his marriage vows. He made Roti his wife and died soon after. Pito, then fourteen years old, couldn't believe that a woman would care more about a ring on the finger than losing her man. Pito had a big argument with his mother. He yelled, "You couldn't just let Papi die in peace, eh! You had to have that bloody ring. Well, he gave you that ring and then he died. You're happy now?"

Mama Roti yelled back, "Your father died a happy man! He died making me, the mother of his children, his wife. He didn't just give me a ring. He gave me his name! He gave me dignity."

Pito is thinking that it is about time that he gives Materena his name, and dignity.

Because he cares about her, she's a big part of his life. But there was a time when he wasn't interested in her. In fact, he wasn't interested in any serious relationship at all, but Materena fell pregnant . . .

He was so angry. His mother said, "Ah, that's the oldest trick in the book! What a rotten trick!" Then she said, "You don't owe that girl nothing, but I'm not having a grandchild with Father Unknown written on his birth certificate. Pito, you better do the right thing by your child or you are going to live to regret it."

And so Pito asked Materena to move in with him, but she wouldn't leave her mother. So Pito just paid her visits. Then he saw his son being born and that was a mind blast. He packed his bag, got a job, and moved in with Materena.

Then he got used to being with her.

But she's not just a habit.

Sunday morning, and Pito and Materena are having breakfast.

"Are you going to get the kids soon?" Materena asks. "Mass is in an hour."

Pito nods. "In a minute, but first I have to ask you something. It's important."

She looks at him and waits.

He takes a deep breath before committing himself. He knows that she'll say, *"Oui."* She'll probably shout that word. After all, she said yes to his marriage proposal before, but she mustn't have taken it seriously, since he was drunk.

But now he's sober, and very serious. If he asks, it'll be like being already married. Materena will tell her mother about it, then she'll tell her cousins about it, and before Pito knows it, everything will be organized, from his wedding suit to the bridal car.

"And so?" Materena asks. "Come on, give birth."

"Materena Mahi," Pito begins, "would you marry me?"

Materena widens her eyes. "Marry you?" She gets up and clears the table. "Marry you." She takes the cups to the sink.

"Non." She smirks. "There's too many complications when you separate, and I want to be able to just pack your bags and send you back to your mama if I get *fiu* of you." She turns the tap on and starts to wash the dishes.

Pito slowly rises. "I go and get the kids," he says.

How Materena Got Married

"Where's that Mama Teta?" The bride is getting anxious. "She's nearly half an hour late."

"Come on, Materena," Rita says. "Let's walk to the church, it's not far."

"We wait a bit longer." Materena really wants to arrive at the church in a bridal car.

"I'm not walking anywhere," Giselle says. "Look at me, Rita. You want me to start contracting on the road?" Giselle's second baby is due in two weeks.

Materena can't believe Mama Teta. She reminded her of the date and the time yesterday and Mama Teta said, "Girl, it's all recorded in my head. I'm going to pick up your godfather and then we'll see you at your house at about eleven."

"Maybe it's a sign for you not to get married," Giselle says as she munches a slice of bread.

"Giselle!" Rita gives Giselle an angry look. Then, to Materena, she says, "Cousin, don't you take Mama Teta's lateness as a sign. I'm sure Mama Teta just had a little trouble with a gendarme. You know how she is with gendarmes. She won't be long."

Meanwhile Pito is standing at the altar, waiting. He turns yet again to the entry of the church and there is still no Materena.

"She changed her mind," Ati jokes. But Pito isn't laughing. He's wondering what is taking Materena so long. Everyone else in the church is wondering too, and feeling sorry for Pito, who looks so worried.

"He looks worried," Loana says to Imelda, sitting beside her.

"It is God testing him," Imelda says.

Loana nods. She doesn't know how this marriage came to be. Materena just came to her house two months ago and said, "Pito and I, we're getting married, Mamie." Loana was going to ask Materena, how on earth did she manage to get Pito to commit? but now she can see that Pito might have committed himself. Loana gets up and goes to Pito. "You want me to go and see what's happening?" she asks.

Pito smiles. "*Non,* Loana, it's okay. You know women, they're always late." He is trying to see the positive side of the situation.

"She changed her mind," Ati says for the tenth time. Pito wants to grab Ati by the collar and shake him a little, but he just turns around to check the entry of the church.

He's thinking that it is possible that Materena has changed her mind. She has, after all, refused his marriage proposal many times.

"Marry me," he said over and over.

"*Non.*"

"Marry me."

"Don't worry about it."

"Marry me."

"I'm beginning to be *fiu* of you asking me!"

"Marry me."

"Why?"

"Because."

"*Non.*"

"Marry me."

Materena finally said, "Okay."

It took Pito about six months.

Back at the house behind the petrol station, Materena has given up waiting for her chauffeur. She's afraid that the priest will decide to go and change, and then what is going to happen to all the food that her godmother paid for?

"I'm walking to the church," she says, and calls out to her youngest bridesmaid, Leilani.

"What about Uncle Hotu?" asks Rita.

Materena has completely forgotten about Uncle Hotu. "Let's just hope that he's at the church."

"And what if he isn't?" Giselle just wants to know.

"Well, I'll take this as a sign," replies Materena.

And so the bride and her bridesmaids, all wearing identical missionary-white dresses with a breadfruit-leaf print, walk to the church. They're nearly at the church when a truck pulls to the side of the road, and out hops Hotu.

"Godfather!" Materena runs to him. She's so happy to see him.

Hotu gives Materena a big kiss on the forehead. "So, are we ready?" He's not even inquiring after Mama Teta's whereabouts.

And Materena takes her godfather's arm.

It is now eleven o'clock at night and the party behind the petrol station is going full blast. The dance floor is packed, as Georgette keeps on turning out great dance music. Tonight, her music is a wedding gift to the newly married couple. And so was the delicious chocolate wedding cake. And the bridal car, even though it never came.

In fact, when Materena's news of marriage hit the coconut radio, everybody came forward with something to give.

Rita put herself in charge of getting the dresses. Tapeta offered to sing for Materena when she walked into the church. Tepua, although still sad over the baby girl she lost to that *popa'a* couple, got busy all yesterday decorating Materena and Pito's house with plastic red roses. And Mori built the dance floor in the backyard.

Materena is so happy that everybody is having a good time tonight.

There's Mori now, trying to chat up one of Pito's cousins, who is as big as him. Rita and Coco are somewhere out the back. Loana and Mama Roti are talking and laughing! Leilani is dancing with her brother. Moana is dancing with Materena's godmother, Imelda.

And there's Pito. He's still wearing his wedding suit, and he looks so handsome. He's talking to Ati and that friend who's come home for the first time in more than seventeen years to be at Pito's wedding, Colonel Tihoti Ranuira himself. Lily and Loma certainly look very impressed with all Colonel Tihoti Ranuira's medals, pinned on to his military uniform.

Materena goes back into the kitchen to get some more food. She's in the kitchen cutting up more bread when she hears some moaning coming from her bedroom. It sounds like a moaning of pain but it could be a moaning of pleasure. Materena tiptoes to the bedroom to investigate the situation.

And here is Giselle, contracting on Materena and Pito's new bed. "Ah, it's you, Cousin," Giselle says, moaning. "My baby is coming."

"Can you feel the head?" asks Materena. She tries not to think about her new bed.

Giselle moans louder, and Materena rushes outside to get her auntie Stella, the best midwife on the island, but Auntie Stella has passed out. Materena needs someone who has a car and a driver's license, someone who is sober.

Right at that moment, Mama Teta arrives, tooting the horn. She turns the engine off, but she's not even out of the car when Materena opens the back door. Mama Teta immediately begins to apologize, but Materena interrupts her. "Giselle is having contractions. You have to drive her to the hospital."

"*Oui,* okay, okay, okay." Mama Teta is already turning the engine back on. Materena rushes to pluck Giselle's boyfriend, Ramona, away from the party, but he's too far gone. He would be of no use in the delivery room.

And so Materena hops into the car next to Giselle, who is now crying her eyes out, but Materena has got to tell someone what is happening in case people start looking for the bride. The bride just can't go disappearing like that.

"One second." Materena is out of the car and here's Rita, and her hair is all messed up.

"Ah, Rita!" Materena exclaims. "You save me! I'm off to the hospital with Giselle. She's having that baby tonight. Just pass the news."

But Rita also wants to go to the hospital, and so the message is passed on to one of the kids playing ticktack in the dark. Materena hops into the front with Mama Teta, and Rita takes Giselle's hand in the back and gives it a squeeze.

Mama Teta is now speeding away to town. Giselle has a big contraction and Rita whispers to her to hold on a bit or she'll have a daughter called Mama Teta junior. Giselle just has time to giggle before she has another huge contraction.

"What a day," Mama Teta says to Materena. "Nothing went according to my plan today. I'm so sorry, Materena."

Materena smiles. "Don't worry about it, Mama Teta."

"But I've got your good-luck gift," Mama Teta says. Materena had forgotten all about her good-luck gift. "Here." Mama Teta passes Rita a little box. "Pass it to Materena."

Materena slowly opens the box, wrapped in white paper, and there's a tape.

"Is this a love-song tape?" Materena asks. She was expecting something else.

"Well, give me that tape," Mama Teta says, chuckling. "You might as well listen to it now." She puts the tape in.

And there's Mama Teta's voice coming out of the car's speakers. "So, Pito," she's saying, "I hear you and Materena are getting married."

"That's right." Pito sounds a bit embarrassed.

"And why are you marrying Materena?"

There's a long silence and Materena can hear Pito breathing heavily. "Mama Teta," he finally says, "isn't this a bit —"

"Just answer the question," Mama Teta interrupts.

"Why am I marrying Materena?" asks Pito. "Eh, well, but, because . . . because she's a good woman."

"Did she force you to marry her?"

"*Ah non!*" Pito chuckles. "I forced her. I asked her to marry me until she accepted."

"*Ah oui?*" Mama Teta sounds surprised. "Why did you do that? You could have just taken her *non* for an answer."

"I really wanted to marry her," Pito replies.

"To regularize the situation?"

"*Oui,* a bit, but that's not the main reason why I wanted to marry Materena."

"What's the reason, then?"

Another long silence, and the three women riding with Mama Teta hold their breath — even Giselle.

"Were you scared Materena was going to go marrying someone else?"

Pito chuckles yet again. "*Oui,* maybe, but I wasn't thinking about that when I asked her."

"What were you thinking about?"

"I was thinking about . . ." Pito seems to hesitate. "I was thinking about . . . about how . . . how much I . . . how much I love Materena. I've never told her this, because . . ."

"Hey, you people!" Giselle yells suddenly. "I'm having a baby *right now!*"

Rita and Materena shriek, Mama Teta veers to the side of the road, and in the confusion the tape is completely forgotten.

Acknowledgments

I owe this novel to many good people . . .

My husband and most loyal friend — thanks, Michael, for putting your own dreams aside so that I could fulfill mine.

My little tribe, Genji, Turia, Heimanu, and Toriki — thanks for the cups of tea, doing the dishes, and understanding that mothers have dreams too. Thanks for the cuddles.

Thanks, Santi Mack, Tracy Marshall, Lisa McKeown, Terri Janke . . . friends and amazing women in many ways.

Laura Patterson — thanks for your encouraging words about my writing when I sent you my first three short stories. You greatly inspired me.

Louise Thurtell, editor with microscopic eyesight — thanks for such a great job.

Last, but not the least, thank you, Katie Stackhouse, for being such a perfectionist, counting glasses of wine, and wondering what happened to the heroine's shell necklace.

But this revised edition of *Breadfruit* is the brainstorm of another talented and dedicated editor, Amanda Brett. Mandy, you're the best, thank you so much for your vision.

To you all . . . *maururu.*

Reading Group Guide

Breadfruit

A novel by

Célestine Vaite

A conversation
with the author of *Breadfruit*

Célestine Vaite talks about love, life, and Tahiti

Although you grew up in Tahiti, you now live with your family in Australia. What is it like to write about a place from memory? Do you think the distance allows you to be more or less accurate in your portrayal of Tahitian life? Do you ever go back to Tahiti for inspiration and research?

I'm in Tahiti twice a year and speak regularly to my family on the phone so I know my place and my people inside out. But writing about them from Australia gives me the freedom to be bold. I'm not intimidated, for example, to have Materena speak up in court and tell the judge what she really thinks about his unfair court summons. And the electricity man is in for a real surprise as he tries to disconnect Materena's electricity when she didn't even receive her disconnection notice, which is, in her mind, so *absolutely* against the law!

Then there are the taboo issues that don't seem taboo to me at all writing on my kitchen table in Australia: teenage pregnancies, a woman having fun with another woman, transvestites, priests and confessions . . .

When *Breadfruit* was released in Tahiti, I was quite nervous. But a year later *L'arbre a Pain* won the *Prix littéraire des etudiants,* the first time such a prize was awarded to a native. So I guess I passed the test.

You have said in interviews that you began writing because you were homesick; this is how Materena came to be. What was the first story you wrote? With the various book contracts and deadlines you now juggle, is writing still as therapeutic for you as it was back then?

It's true. Pregnant with my third child and feeling very nostalgic, I began to write a short story — "The Electricity Man" — about a woman, Materena, telling off the electricity man for daring to disconnect her electricity when she didn't even receive a disconnection notice. I'd lived that scene so many times in my childhood that I knew it by heart. Writing it made me feel good, like I was back home.

The more I write about Tahiti, the more I love (and with passion!) my *fenua,* my birth land, our ways, our customs, the Polynesian sensibility, my people. Each trip home — for holidays, book fairs, or to visit schools — gives me new issues to explore and people to develop because I'm in a constant state of fascination. I take everything in: stories, people, colors, sounds — the whole lot!

Why did you decide to write in English, your second language? Do you think in English as you write, or do you think in your native language and translate your thoughts? Does writing in a second language affect the way you develop your characters or tell a story?

I always act out my dialogues (it helps me see my character as if she/he were standing right in front of me) and I talk in French as my character — professional cleaner, teenager, doctor, etc. — would. Then I write in English. As for the narrative voice, it comes out directly in English but with the French/Tahitian voice in my head, as if my mother or auntie were telling me the story. Very often I'm translating literally. So it's *Mind your onions* and not *Mind your business.*

Writing in English is a lot of fun! True, it is a lot of work, but it forces me to really think about what I'm writing, and gets me focused on the tempo, the rhythm of storytelling.

Throughout your novels, you allude to various political and economic problems in your native country. Do you, after living and writing in another country, want to see a change in Tahiti? Or does living else-where make you appreciate the way things are in Tahiti?

Becoming an avid reader at eleven years old profoundly changed the course of my life. Not only did books give me an insight into how people lived in other parts of the world (far from my fibro shack behind a petrol station in Faa'a, Tahiti) but they increased my vocabulary and turned me into a verbally confident young girl. And to be able to express yourself is, for me, power and freedom.

Going back to your question now, becoming a writer has given me access to places I otherwise wouldn't be allowed as an expatriate: meeting politicians at the National Assembly in Paris, for example, to discuss the low literacy rate in Tahiti. Personally, I want to see the literacy rate go through the roof!

How do cultural norms in Australia differ from those in Tahiti? Mar-riage, for example, is certainly treated differently in the two cultures. How would Materena and Pito's de facto situation be viewed in Australia as opposed to Tahiti? Which point of view do you identify with more?

Weddings are extremely rare in my family — the last wedding was twelve years ago and went on for days. The bride wore white and her children and grandchildren said she looked so beautiful. But we have a lot of baptisms. Priests might be telling us to get married before conceiving babies galore, but we know what works best for us.

In Australia, it's more, *Give me the ring and the honeymoon first, and then we'll talk babies.*

Each country their thing.

On relationships, I believe that they are tricky all over the world, ring or no ring. Two people, two hearts, two sets of desires, two ways of upbringing, children, encrusted habits, money matters, in-laws, phew! That is a lot to take on board . . .

Where do you tend to draw inspiration for your characters and stories? Are your characters based directly on certain people, or are they composites of many people and observations? What was your inspiration for Pito's character?

I have hundreds of relatives, which is very handy when you're a writer, bless my family, but I don't use them one hundred percent. I take one bit from this auntie and another bit from that cousin, and I might even throw a little bit of myself in the mix. A journalist in Finland asked me, "Don't you get confused?" No, I don't. By the time the camera is rolling, I know my characters down to their last pubic hair!

As for Pito, he's my brother and my husband, nice guys with strong ethics but oh la la, they really need their eyes opened up a little sometimes!

My married name is Pitt, so everyone from Ulladulla immediately thought, "Pitt — Pito, of course!" But I actually chose that name because Pito means belly button in Tahitian.

You are thirty-nine years old, with four children and three books — when do you find the time to write? Do you write at a scheduled time each day or whenever the mood may strike? How long does it take to write a book?

Although I'm now a full-time novelist (and I thank the universe for this every morning), I still write as I did ten years ago — at key points in my day, in between looking for socks, cutting onions, hanging clothes on the line, brooming, waiting for my youngest two children at the bus stop, sitting on the beach while they surf, organizing paperwork and other things for my older two children, etc. So at key points during the day I'm furiously writing down ideas (when I ask myself, what happens next?) and words for my dialogues (when I ask myself, what issues will my characters talk about here?), and then when the night comes and all is quiet, I jump on my laptop and furiously type away.

Breadfruit is a part of a trilogy, following the inimitable Materena and her life on a Tahitian island. When did you realize that you were writing a trilogy? Why did you decide to continue writing about Materena?

I wasn't expecting a trilogy out of Materena and her family with the aunties, the cousins, the extended family — *Breadfruit* was it. But Materena came back to haunt me (write about me again!) and *Frangipani* was born. Halfway through writing it, though, I knew there had to be a third book, one last one for the road.

People ask me if there's one more book about Materena on the horizon, one more, just one. There isn't. I love Materena to bits, she's a wonderful and fun woman to be with until the early hours of the morning, but she has fulfilled her purpose now. It is time for her to go. She can put her broom to rest.

Questions and topics for discussion

1. *Breadfruit* is, fundamentally, a story about love — above all, the love between Materena and Pito. How did you feel about Pito and Materena's relationship? How did their respective views of love differ? What do you think it was that made Materena want to get married after sixteen years of never thinking about it? Why was Pito so opposed to the idea at first?

2. When Materena begins covertly gathering information for her wedding, did you share in her excitement, or worry she was going to get hurt? Why do you think the author detailed Materena's secret wedding research? Did Materena learn anything (other than prices) when she inquired into Cousin Moeata's cakes, Mama Teta's car, and the seemingly excellent deal on the new bed?

3. In *Breadfruit*, Vaite set out to re-create the Tahiti she knew from her childhood — complete with an almost comically large extended family. What role did Materena's family, both immediate and extended, play in her everyday life? How would you characterize the women in her family? How would you characterize the men? Are their roles similar to or different from the gender roles in your family?

4. What did you make of the story of Loana and Materena's father? Why do you think Loana put "father unknown" on

the birth certificate, and why did she take so long to tell her daughter the truth? Did the story give you insight into Materena's relationship with her mother? Did it shine any light on Materena's relationship with Pito?

5. Materena lives in a small Tahitian town, with little access to the outside world and to the conveniences and luxuries we enjoy in many parts of America. And yet the characters in *Breadfruit* are acutely aware of the way the world is changing. In what instances do you see Materena and her family attempting to balance Tahitian tradition with modern beliefs? Would you identify any of the novel's characters as "traditional" or "modern"?

6. Vaite's characters face numerous difficulties in their lives, and yet no one in the novel is unhappy. Does this surprise you? Why do you think the author writes of hardship in such a jovial manner? With only a few overt political references, do you consider *Breadfruit* a political novel? Why or why not?

7. On one hand, Materena and her family are Roman Catholic. On the other hand, they find comfort in Tahitian beliefs that predate the arrival of Catholicism on the island. How do these two ways of thinking differ, and how are they similar? What role does spirituality play in the characters' lives?

8. Why do you think Célestine Vaite chose the title *Breadfruit* for this novel? Can you think of a particular passage or episode in the story that relates to the title? What does the title mean to you?

About the Author

CÉLESTINE VAITE grew up in a big extended family in Faa'a, Tahiti, where storytelling was part of her everyday life. She now lives with her family on the south coast of New South Wales.

... and her celebrated novels

Célestine Vaite is the first native Tahitian ever to receive the coveted *Prix littéraire des étudiants,* which she was awarded twice — in 2004 for *Breadfruit* and in 2006 for *Frangipani.* Both novels have been published in the United States, the United Kingdom, Canada, Italy, Spain, Norway, Sweden, Finland, the Netherlands, Brazil, France, Germany, and French Polynesia. *Frangipani* was also short-listed for the 2005 NSW Premier's Literary Awards and long-listed for the 2006 Orange Prize in the United Kingdom. Vaite's third novel about Materena Mahi and her family, *Tiare in Bloom,* will be published in 2007.

An excerpt from the opening pages of *Frangipani* follows.

The Day You Came to Me

When a woman doesn't collect her man's pay she gets zero francs because her man goes to the bar with his colleagues to celebrate the end of the week and you know how it is, eh? A drink for *les copains!* Then he comes home with empty pockets, but he's very happy. He tells his woman stories that don't stand straight to make her laugh, but she doesn't feel like laughing at all. She's cranky and she just wants her man to shut up.

Finally he falls asleep. He wakes up with a sore head and says that he'd like some slices of roast beef and lemonade.

Well, Materena is *fiu* of all this!

She's not asking Pito to give her all his pay down to the last franc. She just wants a few thousand francs, that's all. Just enough for food, gas, kerosene, washing powder, and bits and pieces for their son. That is why it is imperative that Materena collects Pito's pay, to which she believes she's absolutely entitled. She's Pito's cook, cleaner, listener, lover, and she's the mother of his son. It's not as if she does nothing all day.

Materena asks Pito if she could collect his pay, with sugar in her voice and tenderness in her smile.

"Don't even think about it, woman," Pito snaps, flicking a page of last week's newspaper. He tells Materena about his colleague whose woman collects his pay, and how all the others mock him. "Who's the man and who's the woman between you and your woman? Who's the noodle? Who wears the pants? Who wears the dress?" they taunt him. Pito doesn't want the same thing to happen to him. When you have no respect at work and the colleagues mock you from seven thirty in the morning to four in the afternoon, both behind your back and to your face, your life is hell. You don't get invited to the bar on Friday afternoon.

On Thursday night, Materena combs her hair wild-style, rubs coconut oil on her body, sprinkles perfume behind her ears, and attacks Pito with caresses just as he's about to drift off to sleep. Pito opens his eyes and chuckles. And while Pito is busy satisfying Materena, she's busy thinking about collecting Pito's pay, filling her *garde-manger,* painting the house, buying a new oven. The future and not just tomorrow.

Materena often imagines herself old, with her gray hair tied up in a thin and tidy bun. She's sitting in a colonial chair and Pito, old too but still handsome, is standing behind with one hand on Materena's shoulder and the other leaning on a walking stick. They are in a photo studio.

Materena moans with pleasure because Pito sure knows what he's doing. She loves him so much right now. She adores him. He's the king of the sexy loving.

"Pito, I love you!"

With a grunt, his nipples harden, Pito sows his seeds.

After the romance, Materena tenderly and lovingly strokes Pito's hair as he falls asleep with a smile, his head nested on Materena's chest. Materena hurries to ask Pito about his pay before he falls unconscious. "Pito, *chéri* . . . You're so wonderful . . . your muscles are so big . . . Can I collect your pay?"

Pito's answer is a tired whisper. *"Non."*

That *con,* that jerk! Materena yells in her head. He only says *oui* when it suits him! Well, sweet water is over. Materena lifts Pito's head off her chest and plonks it onto his pillow.

The following Thursday Materena (one hand around nine-month-old baby Tamatoa sitting on her hip and the other stirring the breadfruit stew) asks Pito, who's just walked into the house, about his pay.

"Are you going to leave off about that pay?" Pito growls.

"*Non!*" Materena's answer is loud and clear.

"You want the colleagues to laugh at me?" Pito professes again how he sure doesn't want the colleagues to laugh at him. He doesn't want the colleagues to say behind his back: "Between Pito and his woman, who's the noodle? Who's the boss? His woman, she wears the pants? Who slaves by the machine five days a week? Pito or his half?"

Materena, who didn't even have enough money to buy a can of tomatoes for the stew, explodes, "Ah! It's your mates who decide these days? It's not you? It's your mates who wash your clothes, who cook your food? It's your mates who open their legs when you need?"

Pito gives Materena a cranky look and stomps out of the house.

"Pito?" Materena calls out, rushing to him. "You're not eating?"

But he's gone.

Materena and Pito have a miserable week. There's no yelling — no drama. Pito doesn't talk to Materena, and he sleeps on the sofa.

A few times Materena tries to lighten up the atmosphere, but Pito refuses to cooperate. When Materena tells Pito, "It's hot, eh?" he doesn't reply. When she irons his clothes in front of

him, Pito looks at the ceiling. When she asks him if he'd like to
eat corned beef with peas and tomato sauce or corned beef with
breadfruit and tomato sauce, he shrugs. But he eats everything.
He even has second servings.

Four times Materena says, "Pito . . . ," and waits for him to
say a word, but he's lost his tongue.

Days pass.

A week . . .

Gradually things get back to normal. Pito sleeps in the bed
again. He agrees with Materena that it's hot. He smiles. He rakes
the leaves. Materena forgets about his pay. Materena smiles.

Then Materena finds out she's pregnant. She cries her eyes
out because she's happy but at the same time she's devastated.
Another child, with the pay situation still the same! Materena
can't believe what's happening. *Aue eh . . .* eh well, the baby is
conceived, she tells herself. Welcome into my womb and into
my life. Now, Materena decides, she will simply have to collect
Pito's pay.

Materena is very nervous as she opens the office door. She's
wearing her old faded brown dress. She wants to make the right
impression.

"*Iaorana.*" Materena does her *air de pitié* to the young woman
at the reception.

"*Iaorana.*" The woman's greeting is polite and professional.
A bit abrupt too because, so Materena understands, the woman
doesn't know who she is and maybe she's mistaking Materena
for someone who's here to sell something to eat. So Materena reveals her identity (I'm with Pito Tehana, he works here, we live
in Faa'a behind the petrol station, we have a ten-month-old son,

he's with my mother today for a few hours, etc., etc., etc., and how are you today?).

Minutes later Materena knows that Josephine has a *tane* and a fifteen-month-old son. She lives with her *tane's* parents but that's only temporary, she's looking for a house to rent. Josephine's mother-in-law is a bitch woman. Josephine's father is a postman. Josephine's mother died a long time ago, she fell out of a tree. Josephine was in labor for forty-eight hours with her son, Patrick. Josephine's *tane* just stopped smoking . . .

Finally there is a silence and Materena can explain her delicate situation.

Josephine immediately understands. "*Aue oui,* of course," she says. "There's food to put on the table . . . There's bills to pay . . . No problems."

She gives Materena the envelope with Pito's name written on it and Pito's pay in it and asks Materena to sign her name in full in a black book — the picking-up-pay procedure. After the procedure, Materena opens the envelope and takes Pito's pay out. Then she puts back one thousand francs. There, that should be enough for Pito to buy himself three beers at the bar tonight.

Less than two hours later Materena is in her house feeling very happy as she puts away the cans of corned beef, the packets of rice, the washing powder, and the chocolate biscuits for Pito. The family-size can of Milo that was on special and . . . what else did Materena get? Ah, mosquito coils, two cans of salmon for Pito, a bottle of Faragui red wine for Pito, soap, aluminum foil, shaving cream for Pito. Materena's arms are sore from carrying the shopping bags, but she's not complaining. It hurts more walking home from the Chinese store carrying just one can.

After putting away all the goodies, Materena steps back to admire her pantry stacked to the maximum. Nothing compares to a pantry that is stacked to the maximum; an empty pantry is so sad to look at. Materena hopes Pito is not going to be too cranky with her. She hopes he's going to be very happy about the salmon, the chocolate biscuits . . . and the baby inside her belly.

At quarter past midnight, the baked chicken is still on the table, but it is now cold and stiff, and Materena is still waiting for Pito to come home.

He's absent the whole weekend and by Wednesday he's still missing. To explain things to the relatives who ask where Pito is hiding, Materena invents a story about Pito looking after his sick mother. Six relatives, including Materena's mother, say, "Ah, that's nice of Pito to be with his mama when she's sick. I didn't know he was like that. We learn things every day."

Pito makes a brief appearance one Friday morning very early to inform Materena he's leaving her, and she can keep his sofa, but he's taking his shorts, his shirts, and his thongs. Materena, half awake and standing still like a coconut tree in the living room, wants to shout, "Stay! I'm pregnant and I love you! I'm never going to pick up your pay again! I swear it on top of my grandmother's grave!" But she just looks at Pito from under her eyelashes as he turns around and leaves.

She remembers herself with him in the shower and they're embracing like they're under the rain. She pushes the soap away with her foot. The last thing she needs right now is to slip on the soap and crack her head open.

She's with Pito under the frangipani tree behind the bank and he rips her sexy black underpants with his teeth before she has the chance to tell him that they're not her underpants, they're her mother's from a long time ago when she wasn't religious.

Pito busts a wall to install a shutter so that more light

and fresh air come into the bedroom. Materena passes him the nails. He doesn't know what he's doing and she tells him what she thinks. He gets cranky and yells at her. She yells back at him.

Pito is gone now, and Materena walks to the kitchen to get her broom. She starts sweeping long, sad strokes.

She doesn't know what else to do.